EX LIBRIS

Romance Treasury

Romance Treasury

THE ROMANCE TREASURY ASSOCIATION

NEW YORK · TORONTO · LONDON

These stories were originally published as follows:

WAYAWAY
Copyright © 1972 by Dorothy Cork
First published by Mills & Boon Limited in 1972

THE WAY THROUGH THE VALLEY
Copyright © 1971 by Jean S. MacLeod
First published by Mills & Boon Limited in 1971

NOT WANTED ON VOYAGE
Copyright © 1972 by Kay Thorpe
First published by Mills & Boon Limited in 1972

ROMANCE TREASURY is published by:
The Romance Treasury Association, Stratford, Ontario, Canada

Editorial Board: A. W. Boon, Judith Burgess, Ruth Palmour and Janet Humphreys.

Dust Jacket Art by William Biddle
Story Illustrations by William Biddle
Book Design by Charles Kadin
Printed by Kingsport Press Limited, Kingsport, Tennessee

ISBN 0-919860-21-4

Printed in U.S.A.   A022

CONTENTS

Wayaway
Dorothy Cork

Keitha was going to the lonely outpost of an Australian cattle spread to act as companion to a woman. She needed both a rest and chance to sort out her feelings about her undecided love affair in England.

But the woman resented her presence, seeing Keitha as a threat to her daughter's chances of marrying the extremely eligible Dane Langley— owner of Wayaway.

As usual, in her determination to obtain it, Keitha had miscalculated the value of what she had wanted so desperately.

Even so, she was determined to stick it out— though she found she'd only exchanged the problems of one romance for the confusions of another!

CHAPTER ONE

Keitha Godwin and her brother Martin had been holidaying in Cairns for almost a week. Today they had taken the launch out to one of the coral islands to spend the morning drifting over the reef channels in a glass-bottomed boat.

The beautiful flower-like coral with its delicate tints, the gorgeously colored tropical fish, and the hypnotically waving tentacles of the sea anemones had fascinated Keitha. Her thoughts had gone to Donn, back in London, wishing that he were there beside her under the palm-thatched awning of the long flat boat. It was dreadful being away from Donn—far worse than she had imagined it would be when she had decided to fly to Australia to stay with Martin for a while in Queensland. But if she wanted Donn to realize just how much they meant to each other, this, she was sure, was the best way to do it. Absence was supposed to make the heart grow fonder.

Now, hundreds and hundreds of miles from London, she and Martin were lunching at the Coral Reef Hotel Restaurant. While she enjoyed her meal of reef fish and salad and talked to Martin of the pleasures of the morning, her eyes were continually—almost compulsively—drawn to a party of four at a nearby table. Everyone in the restaurant was in holiday dress and these were no exception; only their clothes had a subtle air of being exclusive—of being resort wear rather than simply summer clothes. There were two pretty blonde girls, obviously sisters, and a fair-haired young man who must surely be their brother. The fourth member of the party was entirely different. He was older, somewhere about Martin's age, definitely over 30, with a strong jaw and brown hair very much bleached by the sun. He had a rangy, rather ruthless look about him, and his fashionable shirt with its pink and mauve design on an ivory ground, unbuttoned almost to the waist, was in contrast to his masculinity.

He looked a tough type of man. Leaning back in his chair smoking, eyes narrowed, a half smile hovering over his mouth, he sometimes talked, sometimes listened to his companions. But at all times he had a curious air of command. It was while she was speculating about him; wondering what niche he would fit into in life, rejecting the city as his milieu, rejecting after no more than a moment's hesitation the sugar cane fields of the north, that she missed what Martin was saying to her.

The waitress had brought their coffee, and Martin, pouring cream, had a slight frown on his pleasant face. He was a good looking man, his eyes, very dark like her own, framed by square dark-rimmed glasses.

"Come on now, Keitha," he adjured. "Smarten yourself up. Where were you? Back in London with that television producer who's doing his best to ruin your life?"

Keitha blinked with annoyance. This was the first time Martin had shown any sign of interfering in her affairs. Up till now, all he had cared about was that she should eat, sleep and soak up some sunshine; lose the dark shadows that were around her eyes and get a little more flesh on her bones. It was a pretty serious thing, in his eyes, to be suffering from overwork at the age of 22!

Of course she had known that fussy little Aunt Jane would tell tales and write Martin all about her. But she had taken it for granted that her brother would concede that she knew what she wanted. He had always been kind, tolerant, and uninterfering. She remembered that well, although he had left England eight years ago when she was still a schoolgirl.

Now she sent him a warning look that said—she hoped—"Don't interfere" and told him lightly,

"Actually, I was trying to work out how those people over by the window fit into the social pattern here."

Martin turned his head, and Keitha caught the eye of the older man for the first time. Sardonic, aware, he tilted an eyebrow at her. She noticed as she looked away hastily that his eyes were of a peculiar fiery blue.

"I've met those two girls in Townsville. Good to look at, aren't they?" said Martin approvingly, turning back to her with a smile. "They're from Brisbane—name of Warner—their father's an architect. I made up some opal jewelry for them last year—haven't seen them since. I might see what I can do about that."

Keitha allowed herself a little smile. Martin saw only the girls, whereas it was the man who intrigued her.

"To return to our conversation," said Martin. "Tell me one thing, if you can, Keitha. Why are you so set on getting yourself tied up with Donn Gorsky? Aunt says he's too sophisticated for you by half, and even I can see that working for him is too demanding for a girl of your constitution. You don't really want to marry him, do you?"

"Yes, I do," said Keitha. "I want it more than anything else in life."

Martin drummed on the table with his fingers. "I take it then he hasn't asked you to marry him yet."

"Not yet," said Keitha. She gave him a straight look. "Donn belongs to a crowd that doesn't believe in marriage. He wants me to—to shack up with him." She looked at her brother warily, watching for his reaction, but he was not shocked, merely annoyed.

"You turned *that* offer down, of course?"

"Yes, of course. But only because I do believe in marriage."

"Well, that's something," said Martin dryly. He signaled to the waitress to bring them more coffee, and Keitha was suddenly conscious that the man at the table by the window was studying her. A slight turn of her head and she met his gaze—speculative, intense. For some reason the color rose in her cheeks, and she thought with annoyance, "What is he staring for? How rude can you get?"—forgetting that a few minutes before she had done her share of staring. She turned deliberately away from him and back to Martin, who said thoughtfully, "You were always a determined little puss. Has it ever struck you that you quite frequently miscalculate the value of what you want in your determination to get it?" He paused while the coffee was poured, then continued. "You were a pretty child, with those great dark eyes and your fair delicate complexion—you still are. In my opinion, Aunt was too soft with you—sorry for you, I suppose, because you were an orphan. I remember one school holiday when I was 16 or so. Aunt took us to lunch in London. You couldn't have been more than four years old. You refused milk and demanded water—but you wanted sugar in it. You got it finally." He smiled wryly at Keitha across the table. "You didn't like it—I can still see the face you made!—but you drank it. Every bit of it."

"I don't remember," said Keitha, smiling faintly. "But what's the moral?"

"Simply that there are girls who will hold out for what they *think* they want, and when they get it, it often doesn't suit their taste at all. You're one of those girls."

"If you're trying to prove something about Donn," said Keitha, annoyed, "then none of this is relevant. We're in love. I'm not making a mistake there, Martin. And all that was a long time ago. I'm not like that any more."

"No? Let's refresh your mind with something more recent, then—your job as assistant to a television producer. You went all out for that when even I—who hadn't seen you for quite a while—could have told you it would be too much for you. It's a job that needs a thick skin, a logical mind, and the constitution of an ox. You possess none of those attributes, and it's not surprising you eventually broke down under the strain."

Keitha shrugged. "You're exaggerating. I enjoyed the work. It was a challenge. I'd return to it—and I probably shall." She looked at him coolly. It *had* been exhausting work. The hours were irregular, and there were so many things for which she had been responsible—studio bookings, instructions regarding sets and costumes, notifications of rehearsal times, the shooting script to be retyped overnight if changes had been made during the day. She had stuck to it mostly because of her boss, Donn Gorsky. When she had been a secretary, he had noticed her and arranged for her to be his assistant. Of course she had fallen all over herself to make a success of the job. She might not have the constitution of an ox, but she had ambition, determination and tenacity. She wouldn't have tossed in the job even temporarily if the doctor hadn't been so adamant that she needed a long spell off. She had turned it to her own advantage by coming to Queensland right away. It was a move designed to force Donn to a reassessment of their future relationship, and she fully believed it would bring a different proposal from him—one of marriage. Particularly if she showed signs of falling so in love with Martin's tropics that there was some doubt as to whether she would return to England at all. . . .

Martin said, "Well, that brings us back to what I was talking about when you fell into your daydream. I was proposing that instead of going back to your old job, you stay here and work for me. One of the girls in the workroom is leaving to be married in a couple of weeks. With those long sensitive fingers of yours and your artistic flair—I remember that from when you were a kid—you might like to try your hand at jewelry fashioning and designing. As you know, opals are my speciality, and if you like a challenge, you have it there." He smiled at her in his open friendly way. "So how about it?"

"No, thank you," said Keitha blithely. "I really don't need to be cajoled and wheedled onto the path of morality and righteousness, Martin. I have a very level head. I know exactly what I want and what I'm doing."

He looked exasperated. "That's your opinion of yourself. Aunt appears to think it's open to conjecture. And though I haven't met Donn Gorsky this I know—you're becoming rather a handful, and Aunt isn't getting any younger. I wish you'd think about it."

Dear Martin! He pictured himself taking her off Aunt Jane's hands. She gave him a sympathetic smile. "All right. I'll think it over this very afternoon."

"Good girl! Finished your coffee?" He pushed back his chair. "I suggest we go down to the Underwater Observatory now. I can guarantee you'll be more than fascinated."

Keitha followed him out into sunshine that was slashed with shadow from the tall palm trees. "I think I've seen enough underwater life for one day, Martin. You go if you want to, and I'll lie on the beach to sunbathe and think upon my sins."

He sent her a reproving look. "Think about my suggestion instead," he amended. "All right, I'll pick you up later on."

Twenty minutes later Keitha had changed into her brilliant orange ribbed cotton swimsuit and was lying on glistening white sand in the shade of a huge green and white umbrella. Back from the beach, coconut palms rustled softly and soporifically in the warm wind. In the water vacationers cruised lazily in boats, waded in the clear green shallows searching for shells, or exploring the coral reef.

Keitha lay there for a long time. Mostly she thought about Donn, but some of the time she thought about

Martin's proposition. She thought of the opals she had seen in his jeweler's shop in Townsville. Black opals, water opals, milky opals—beautiful and fascinating, all of them. Some were from Lightning Ridge in New South Wales, some from the Coober Peedy fields in South Australia. Others were from the lesser-known fields of outback Queensland—Martin had fossicked for those himself. But while she thought it might be fun designing settings, the idea didn't really excite her. Now if Martin had suggested a week or two in the opal fields that would have been different altogether.

At all events, she had an uneasy feeling that Martin was now all to ready to play the big brother and deafen her with advice. For all she knew, he might even have some young man lined up in Townsville as opposition to Donn. But it was no go. She was mad about Donn—but she had no intention of shacking up with him. It was marriage or nothing. She was going all out to get that proposal from him—and she rarely failed to get what she wanted. In her letters to Donn, she wrote gaily of the wonderful time she was having in Queensland, of how she was reveling in the sunshine. She didn't mention the future, and she didn't mention marriage. That was going to irk Donn, sooner or later. His own letters were full of longing for her; she really mattered to Donn—it was plain in every line he wrote. If it was a battle to see who could hang on the longest for their principles, she knew who would win. Donn would finally have to realize that some things hadn't changed so drastically since "that funny little maiden aunt of yours" was a girl.

The thought made her smile to herself; his face floated tantalizingly before her closed eyes—lean, intelligent, his hair thick, wavy and dark, his eyes—

She gave a start and opened her own eyes guiltily. Donn's eyes were smoky gray—they weren't that light and penetrating blue. Where had she seen eyes like that recently? Of course—that man in the hotel restaurant who had stared at her so rudely!

She put her head down on her arms again, noting that she was acquiring a faint tan. She could feel the sea breeze gently lifting the silky dark brown hair from her bare shoulders. She slept lightly. . . .

She woke to hear the soft sound of footsteps crunching on the sand close by. "Martin," she thought and turned her head lazily without bothering to open her eyes. She said dreamily, "I've thought about what you offered, Martin, and it's very attractive, but the answer's definitely no. I shan't pretend—I haven't the slightest intention of spending the rest of my life in sunny Queensland."

No reply. She opened her eyes and sat up slowly. The man who stood looking down at her quizzically was not her brother at all. He wore blue swim shorts, his torso was deeply tanned, and his eyes, narrowed against the glare from the white sand, were a vivid electric blue.

He was the man who had occupied her attention at lunch time. For a full five seconds she stared at him and he stared back. His brows, heavy, straight, and sunbleached, were lowered. She was uncertain whether or not he was smiling, but the mouth above the jutting, aggressive chin had an upward tilt at the corners. There was a distinctly sensual look about it that unnerved her.

He shifted his weight and looked her over—the full slender length of her in the high-necked orange swimsuit. Instinctively she groped for her sunglasses and curled her legs beneath her. With the merest quirk of a smile that was wholly and stunningly masculine, he drawled out, "What sort of way is that to talk to a stranger? Especially to one who's not used to taking no for an answer. I'll guarantee I'd soon make you say yes, so for your own sake I hope Martin is easier to reckon with."

She felt her cheeks stain with color that rapidly ebbed away. Of course he was joking. She should laugh and pass it off lightly, but her heart was hammering. There had been something oddly and reasonlessly shocking in the way he had said "*I'd* soon make you say yes". She decided she didn't like it. She had, as well, as Donn would have put it, lost her cool. So she turned her back on him and pulled her white beach coat over her shoulders. "I'm not in the least interested in what you hope," she told him coolly.

His low laughter was genuinely amused and irritated her more than it should have done. If he had any sense, he'd realize she wasn't the sort of girl who took to being picked up by a stranger—even anywhere as informal as on a coral island. But he didn't go away. He said, "Given just a little time, we could surely change that too."

Keitha's annoyance was increased. She didn't like people who were so confident of changing the opinions of others. She began to collect her belongings and to wish that Martin would arrive. After a minute she turned cautiously around. That maddening man was halfway down the beach. She leaned forward, elbows on her knees, chin in hands, watching until he plunged into the water and swam out with powerful strokes.

Well, that was that. She gave a rueful laugh. Maybe she was losing her sense of humor! She wondered exactly what sort of an "offer" he thought she had refused. All the same, to say *he* would make her say yes—change her views—that was going too far. Obviously he liked to be the boss and was both arrogant and conceited. . . .

Martin was a long while about coming to find her. Finally Keitha grew tired of waiting on the sand and wandered up into the shade of the palm trees. They met up again there. Martin was looking very pleased with himself and admitted that in the Underwater Observatory he had renewed his acquaintance with the two Warner girls and met their brother, whom they had seen in the restaurant.

"And the other man?" Keitha queried.

Martin shrugged, not interested. "They'd parted

company with him, whoever he was. We've an invitation to visit them in their bungalow up the coast on the mainland tomorrow," he added. "You'll come, won't you?"

Keitha said she would. She decided not to mention her own little adventure on the beach. After all, there was really nothing to tell.

But as they drove up the coast the next afternoon, she couldn't help wondering if she would encounter the "boss man", at the bungalow, as she called him in her mind. It was possible. And she would snub him if she did. . . . She was wearing an attractive cotton dress in bright blues and greens—jewel colors were her favorites—and Martin complimented her on her appearance.

"You're beginning to look really fit again already. Shouldn't be too much to take on a job again in a couple of weeks' time."

"I quite agree," said Keitha. "But don't you make plans for me, Martin. You may think of me as your kid sister, but I've been a working girl for quite a while now and can look after myself."

"Well, the job's there if you should change your mind," he said lightly. During the drive, to Keitha's relief, he left the subject strictly alone. He was most probably thinking of the Warner girls.

The road up the coast wound through fields of sugar cane and through tropical rain forest. Staghorns and orchids grew in the treetops. The sent of frangipani was heavy in the air, and hosts of brilliantly colored birds chattered incessantly. Beyond a high headland, Martin turned down to a beach where the sun struck glitter off a sea whose sapphire waters surged gently against dazzling sand and the salmon-pink of granite rocks. It was here that the Warners were holidaying in a charming white bungalow with cool tiled floors and airy bamboo furniture. The girls were Angela and Julie. Keitha met them and their mother. The brother, Tony, was not there and neither was the "boss man". Keitha was surprised and annoyed at her feeling of letdown.

After lunch they went down to the beach to swim, but presently Keitha left the others and came to sit on the sand with Mrs. Warner, who sat back in a canvas chair leafing through a magazine. Lying in the sun, Keitha lapsed into one of her favorite daydreams about Donn, imagining he was here beside her on the hot white sand, listening to the palm trees whispering, watching the yellow banana birds with their red eyes, and the bright parakeets that flew among the trees. She thought of dancing with Donn in the warm moonless tropical night—of walking by the sea with him, washed by the soft languorous air. . . . She moved restlessly and sat up hugging her knees, her eyes dark and wide.

Mrs. Warner closed her magazine and smiled down at her. "I hope you're not bored, my dear." Her voice was gentle and attractive. She was a pretty woman, small and fine-boned, her hair a soft silvery blonde that looked—and probably was—natural.

Keitha smiled back. "No, I'm not in the least bored, Mrs. Warner. I don't think I've ever been bored in my life! I hope you don't think me rude—I was almost asleep. I've been sleeping a lot out here—I'm sort of convalescing, though I'm strong as a horse now."

"I'm glad of that. I gather from your accent that you haven't been here as long as your brother. I hope he's showing you more of Queensland than the coast. Have you been up on the tableland?"

"Yes. We drove up to Lake Barrine and Malanda for a couple of days. We did quite a tour, and I loved it."

Mrs. Warner nodded approvingly. "Such lovely rain forest. I used to adore to go there when I was a girl. I was brought up outback in the Gulf Country on a cattle station called Wayaway. My father named it—you can guess why! My nephew Dane Langley owns it now. I haven't been back since I was married, which is a long while ago. You're a city girl, I suppose?"

"Very much so. My only experience of country life has been school holidays on my uncle's farm in Devon. I loved riding there. But I lived mostly in London and worked for a television producer there. I've had to take a break for health reasons and have been reveling in the life out here. My brother's trying to persuade me to stay and work in his jewelry business in Townsville."

"If that doesn't appeal and you want a job you should have no worries. There should be plenty of positions open to an attractive, intelligent girl like you—temporary or otherwise." She frowned faintly. "I have a rather difficult position to fill. I've been commissioned to find someone to give a hand to a girlhood friend of mine at the outstation of Wayaway. It's something of a worry to find someone whom Patty will like, and who will at the same time not be averse to life on a remote cattle station. I'm afraid I shall have it hovering around me like a black cloud till we go back to Brisbane, and then my life will be plagued by interviews. Quite frankly, I don't believe it's worth a great deal of my time, either. Patty complains of loneliness and will finish by coming over to the coast to live, I'm sure."

The others came out of the water then, and no more was said on the subject, but it was one that captured Keitha's imagination. A remote cattle station. It sounded romantic—exciting—different. Like nothing she had ever known before. Much more enticing than a jeweler's shop!

The moment she woke the next morning in the hotel at Cairns, there was the idea fully formed—opening like a flower in her mind. She would offer herself for that job on the cattle stations. Why not? She was sure she could get it if she set her mind to it. She could stay until Donn had decided he couldn't do without her and wrote asking her to marry him. How long would that take? A month? She didn't think that was being too optimistic. And while she was waiting, she would be seeing another side of Queensland.

She had a letter from Donn in the morning mail. "All I

can think of is when you'll be back," he wrote. "Life without you is sheer hell, and I mean that, darling. My new assistant is horribly organized and efficient, and as insensitive as a lump of wood. She's a machine rather than a person. She smiles and smiles and wins every battle with anybody. So swallow your vitamin pills or iron tablets or whatever they're feeding you and come back. I promise I'll shield you from all nerve-shattering encounters in the future. . . ."

No talk of marriage yet. Still, it was in many ways a comforting letter. The thought of that new assistant had worried her a little and given her the occasional nightmare.

"What's the news from London?" asked Martin, joining her by the hotel pool where she sat reading her letter.

Keitha shrugged. "Nothing much."

He took one of the gay fiberglass chairs nearby and lit a cigarette. "I wish you'd change your mind about working for me. You needn't start work right away, you know—though you're looking considerably better than you did when you arrived."

"I'm feeling wonderful." She gave him a direct look. "But don't keep on at me, Martin, I'm definitely not going to work for you. I know very well that you're trying to get me into what Aunt Jane calls a more wholesome world to make me forget Donn. That's what this is all about, isn't it? But it will all come right, you'll see. It's only a matter of time."

"Then you're just going to give yourself a big, long holiday in the sun, are you?"

"That was the idea—the doctor's idea," she added wryly. "But I think I shall take on a job."

"But not with my outfit? I thought, being your brother— Oh well, when we go back to Townsville I'll see what else I can dig up for you."

Keitha shook her head. "No—I think I may have

found something for myself." She smiled at his look of surprise. "A job on a cattle station."

Martin stared. "How on earth did you get on to something like that?"

"Oh, I put in some good work with Mrs. Warner while you were frolicking in the sea with those two pretty daughters of hers," she said lightly. As she spoke she recalled for no apparent reason her disappointment at not meeting the man from the coral island again and wondered fleetingly who he had been. "An old friend of Mrs. Warner's needs a sort of companion or helper at the homestead. Of course I haven't presented myself as a candidate yet, but I'm pretty sure I shall be able to have the job for the asking."

"Sugar and water," said Martin cynically. "It's a perfectly idiotic idea. I'm certain Mrs. Warner will set you straight very smartly."

"Want to bet?" Keitha's dark eyes challenged him. She was quite determined to get that job.

"Helping on a cattle run probably means cooking for a dozen hungry stockmen—and waiting on all the idle women at the homestead. Supervising the children's correspondence lessons—being at everyone's beck and call. Where is this cattle station, by the way?"

"In the Gulf Country," said Keitha. "Wherever that may be."

"Hmm. South of the Gulf of Carpentaria. Flat unending plains, sizzling heat, not enough water till the Wet comes, and then too much of it."

"Have you been there?" she asked aggressively.

"No, but I've heard about it. I have no desire to live there. Like you, I'm pretty well geared to city life."

"It wouldn't be a case of *living* there," argued Keitha. "I'm sure I should enjoy the experience anyhow, and I needn't stay long."

"I'd give you a week." His eyes ran over her delicate

features and slender shoulders. He laughed suddenly. "You're a mad sort of a girl. You turn down a job in a jewelry business because you think I'm trying to woo you away from your sophisticated London life, yet the next moment you go all out for becoming some sort of drudge in the tough world of the Gulf Country. You won't like it, you know. However, I'm certain you won't even have a chance to try it. . . ."

As it turned out, her brother was quite wrong.

The next day she took the bus up the coast—for Martin refused flatly to aid and abet—and went to see Mrs. Warner. The older woman was very much surprised at the purpose of her visit and at first inclined to take her interest lightly.

"You're a charming girl, but I don't think—I really don't think—you are the right sort of person for the job."

"Why not?" asked Keitha frankly. They were on the balcony of the bungalow, sipping long iced drinks in the shade of huge mango trees and watching the hypnotic surge of the brilliant sea on the sheltered beach below.

"Why not? Oh well—because you're a London girl—you wear up-to-the-minute clothes, you're obviously used to living at high speed." She stopped and made a wry face. "You're just not right for a cattle run, that's all. Too young. You'd be cut off from all the diversions you're used to—you'd be bored."

"I told you the other day I was never bored. I meant that. I'm sure I should enjoy the life. That is—" she hesitated and went on with a smile, "my brother is convinced I'd be expected to cook for a dozen brawny stockmen. I don't know how well I'd cope with *that*."

Mrs. Warner laughed. "Oh dear me, no! You wouldn't have to do anything like that. The fact is that Patty Drummond's husband died last year, and she's finding life a little difficult without him. She's lonely. Her daughter Melanie has finished school now, but she's out on the run all day—she's one of those girls who's happiest in the saddle. I imagine that Patty needs companionship more than help. No, as far as I know there'd be no really hard work entailed. All the same—" She stopped and looked at the girl beside her speculatively.

"All the same—?" Keitha prompted. "Please, Mrs. Warner—I've set my heart on going to Wayaway. Couldn't I at least be given a trial? I'd pay my own fare—and it would interest me so much to see an Outback cattle station."

To her amazement and delight, Mrs. Warner gave in suddenly and charmingly. "Well, if you're really eager to try your hand—it would save me a great deal of trouble. All right. I don't really see why not. Let me see—the mail plane goes out to Wayaway in two days' time. You could fly out and see how you fit in. If it isn't a success, you can simply fly back the following week. I'll see the employment agency when I return to Brisbane as originally planned. Will that suit you?"

"Wonderfully! I just knew you'd give me a chance."

"I hope we shan't either of us regret it," the older woman said a trifle dryly.

Before she left, Mrs. Warner wrote Keitha a letter of introduction, while the girl waited on the balcony with its polished quarry tiles and bamboo furniture. The bungalow belonged to her nephew, Mrs. Warner had said when Keitha remarked how attractive she found it; the one who owned the Wayaway cattle run. Keitha wondered what kind of a man he was and whether she would see much of him, since she was to be at the outstation; whatever—and wherever—that was! Presently the older woman rejoined her and presented her with an envelope, addressed not to Mrs. Drummond but to Dane Langley.

"Never mind that they're not expecting you," Mrs. Warner said. "That doesn't matter in the Outback.

They're used to unexpected arrivals. Lots of pretty girls go there on all sorts of excuses. If I send a telegram it will be read over the radio. Everyone in the Gulf Country will be gossiping and wondering about you. And that's not what we want at all, is it? Especially as you're going more or less on trial—"

Keitha agreed that it was not what they wanted, though she rather wondered who was being referred to. Did Mrs. Warner mean herself and Keitha? Or did she mean herself and Patty Drummond and this nephew, Dane Langley?

She wondered too why it was that lots of pretty girls went out to Wayaway—on all sorts of excuses.

CHAPTER TWO

Martin was still very sceptical about the whole business when he saw her off on the plane two days later. He was convinced she would be back the next week, and Keitha was equally convinced that she would not be.

The DC3 carried freight and mail across the tableland to several remote cattle stations, stayed overnight at a town on the Gulf, then returned to the east coast. The front of the aircraft was filled with crates and packages, and behind was a variety of passengers, among them five American tourists, all women, and all intent on seeing something of the Outback. Keitha was seated next to one of them.

She watched with interest the country over which they flew and listened carefully when the freight officer answered questions put by the tourists, thinking of the letter she would be able to write to Donn, telling him of her experiences in the fabled Outback.

Once they had left the coastal plain with its lush green fields of sugar cane and belts of darker tropical rain forest, it was not long before the whole aspect of the land changed. Finally the brilliant greens gave way entirely to dull greens and browns. About an hour after take-off the first homestead showed up on the slopes below. Keitha knew a sense of excitement as the plane landed on the station airstrip. One of the passengers—a well-dressed elderly woman who was on a visit to relatives—was ready to leave the plane as it taxied to a stop in a whirl of dust. The traffic officer opened the rear door and soon had a set of folding steps in place. A Land Rover arrived, freight was carried down the passage-way of the aircraft and unloaded. A mail bag was handed over, and another one taken on board. The pilot and co-pilot exchanged a few words with the man in the Land Rover, and in ten minutes the plane was on its way again.

Another hour of flying, a ten-minute put-down at a tiny town that sweltered in the sun, and they were flying over the great flat plains of the Outback. For the first time Keitha felt a faint tremor of doubt at the wisdom of what she was doing. Glittering white salt pans showed up on the red-brown earth; the vegetation became tough and stunted. The rivers were no more than chains of water-holes strung out like necklaces across the bosom of the land. In the Wet, the traffic officer told them, those watercourses would be covered with rich and beautiful green pastures, and the cattle would grow sleek and fat and shining. . . .

There was another small town, more cattle stations, and then Tyrone Park, which Keitha knew was the last set down before Wayaway, some 20 minutes farther on. The Americans were fanning themselves. "My, it's hot," remarked the woman next to Keitha. "I wish I had your figure, and then I wouldn't feel it so. You look as cool as a lettuce leaf!"

At the Tyrone Park airstrip, a pretty girl in a pink silk shirt and white jeans sprang out of the station car and came to talk to the pilot while the freight was unloaded. She was slim and had long light brown hair that had an unusual silvery gleam in it. Keitha could hear her voice quite clearly.

"Tell Dane Langley I'm coming over to Wayaway after the border muster if not before, and Mellie had better watch out!" There was laughter and determination in her voice. "One of our little band of adoring females is going to break down those impenetrable defenses of his one of these days. Who knows, it might be me!"

"Oh, come off it, Dusty," the pilot said good-humoredly. "It's not to every man's taste to take a wife.

Dane Langley's a hard nut to crack. Why don't you forget about him and go back to the coast? You're not all that hooked on the cattle country, are you?"

"I could be—under the right circumstances. Beside, nothing ventured, nothing gained." She laughed again, but her laughter had a brittle note in it.

"There's a lovely feeling of camaraderie here in the Outback," remarked Keitha's companion. "I must note it in my journal. . . . "

Keitha missed whatever else the girl called Dusty said, and now she was walking back to the car. Keitha could see she had a full soft mouth that looked a little wilful, and that her skin was golden rather than brown. She wondered if they would meet when she came to Wayaway. She thought of what had been said about Dane Langley and found that for some reason she was prejudiced against him. Which would not do.

Twenty minutes later she looked down on the Wayaway homestead and outbuildings arranged by a huge lagoon on the empty plain below. Wayaway was certainly remote! The homestead was set among dark trees in a long rectangle of garden. She didn't know what the other buildings were and wondered if one of them might be the outstation.

The airstrip was some three miles from the homestead. A cloud of red dust raced along the track as the aircraft came down. By the time they landed, it had resolved itself into a Land Rover and had pulled up alongside the plane.

At the sight of the man who climbed out—tall and tough-looking in narrow-legged cord trousers and checked shirt, a broad-brimmed hat tilted back on his head, Keitha's heart gave a jolt.

"So I was right," she thought, unable to take her eyes off that strong-jawed face with its startling blue eyes. She had not once *consciously* thought that Dane Langley, Mrs. Warner's nephew, might be the man she had encountered on the coral island, yet somewhere inside she had known it. She thought of the letter of introduction in her handbag and wondered what sort of reception she would receive from him. Excitement and a readiness to assert herself rose in her strongly. Not that his reaction mattered very much. She was here to work for Mrs. Drummond—at the outstation. She moved to the top of the steps at the rear door, knowing that he had not yet seen her.

"Hi, Dane," said the officer with a grin, confirming her belief.

"Hi, Jim," he drawled. At that instant his eyes rose and met Keitha's. She smiled faintly at his little shock of surprise.

"We have the art materials Miss Langley ordered and—" The traffic officer broke off, because Dane Langley stood, thumbs hooked through his narrow leather belt, staring at Keitha with a half-humorous, half-disbelieving expression on his tanned face. "Oh, and here's a passenger for you—Miss Godwin."

Keitha came down the steps. She thought Dane Langley might have smiled at her, but he didn't. He screwed up those disconcerting eyes and stepped forward. His fingers closed lightly on her slim upper arm.

"Well, Miss Godwin! You've surprised me. Come along and sit in the Land Rover while I get this business completed. I'll be with you as soon as I can." No smile, no questions, just a searching acute look from his fire blue eyes.

"Thank you." Keitha spoke coolly, pleasantly, and walked the few dusty yards with him, aware of an odd shiver of excitement. He saw her into the front seat of the Rover, and she put on her sunglasses as he strode back to the plane. She wondered if he was the reason why so many pretty girls came out to Wayaway, and hoped he did not think she was another of them.

She watched the freight being unloaded—not much of it, the mail bag seemed to be the main item. Dane Langley had strolled up to have a word with the pilot, and Keitha wondered if the message from the girl called Dusty would be faithfully relayed to him. The freight officer brought the mail bag and two cartons over to the car, and heaved out the station mail bag.

"Have a good time," he said to Keitha. He was a nice young man with a friendly grin. Keitha knew from his speculative look that he was curious about her. She smiled at him and said, "Thank you for the flight. I enjoyed it."

"How long are you staying on Wayaway, Miss Godwin?"

Her smile deepened. "I don't really know."

Dane Langley came back, receipts were signed, and then they were off along a bumpy track that led to a gate. Behind them, the small aircraft taxied down the dusty runway and was airborne.

"Well, Miss Godwin, so you decided to put me to the test, did you? I'm amazed at your ingenuity. You must tell me how you worked it." He drove fast and expertly, and considering the condition of the track managed to look at Keitha fairly frequently.

"How I worked what? What test?" she asked, confused.

"Come now, we haven't had so many conversations that you don't recall the challenge I threw out—and that you so solemnly refused to take up? How did it go, now? Didn't I threaten that in no time at all I could have you caring pretty keenly about my opinions?"

"Did you?" said Keitha haughtily. "I'm afraid I *don't* remember. I'm sorry to disappoint you." How conceited can you be? she wondered and felt furious that he should connect her coming here with himself and what he must consider his irresistible appeal. "I'm right in supposing that you are Mr. Dane Langley?"

"Sure I'm Dane Langley," he said easily. "And you know it."

"I didn't know it until today. I have a letter of introduction to you from Mrs. Warner. I've come to help Mrs. Drummond."

"Good God!" Now she really *had* surprised him. "Aunt Grace sent you along!" A look of intense amusement fleetingly crossed his face. "How on earth did you manage that? You certainly are quite a girl, Miss Godwin. I'll admit your tactics have knocked me out."

"I don't know what you mean by tactics," said Keitha with annoyance and exasperation.

"No? Well, all things considered, if you were so keen to come to Wayaway it would have been a lot simpler to have Aunt Grace send you out as a guest. Plenty of the girls do it that way. We all have a lot of fun."

"I'm sure you do." Her voice was icy. "But I'm not interested in fun. I'm here to take up a position."

He laughed softly. "Can you possibly be serious? It's incredible!"

Suddenly, Keitha was intensely aware of his nearness. At the same time her mind began to whirl, and she couldn't think clearly. Disconcerted, she gazed out at the country they were passing through. There was an immense impression of vastness; the plains seemed to go on forever, painted in dull olive, brown, and straw colors. The grasses were tall and paper dry; the trees stunted and ancient-looking, and over all was the huge almost colorless sky. She had the weird sensation that she and this Dane Langley who was somehow not quite a stranger were alone in a no-man's-land, driving to nowhere.

They bumped along over a yellow grassy plain that was

broken by patches of eucalypts and acacias. Ahead, a heavier line of trees marked the wide, dried up course of a river with spreading sandy banks. Red-brown mounds taller than a man appeared frequently among the trees. She realized presently that they were termite mounds—anthills. A flock of rose-crested white cockatoos flew screeching into the air as the car passed by, and she watched them swarm across the sky, then settle again.

In control of herself once more, she turned to the man beside her and asked politely, "Will you please take me straight to Mrs. Drummond? After all, my business is with her, not with you."

He gave her a sardonic look. "Honey, anyone who comes to Wayaway has business with me some way or another."

"Not me," said Keitha obstinately. "I shan't be working for you."

"Well, that too's a debatable point." There was an edge of laughter in his voice that irritated Keitha, who was determined to make him take her seriously. They had emerged from the belt of trees. Some way ahead she could see the string of long, low, white buildings and the fenced yards that she had glimpsed from the air.

"Is the outstation here?"

"Honey, you haven't done your homework. The outstation's 50 miles away."

"Oh!" Keitha knew a sense of shock. Fifty miles away! How was she to get there?

"But don't let that set you back," the man beside her continued laconically. "Patty Drummond's away just now—staying with friends over at Mary Creek."

Keitha sank back against the leather seat with a sudden feeling of despair and exasperation. What a mix-up! It looked as though her job was for the time being non-existent. Under the circumstances, she could hardly go back to the coast and come out again in a few days' time.

"Now keep calm. You'll be taken care of and we'll all enjoy ourselves. We like company now and again, Kate and I—if it's the right sort." Kate? Who was Kate? Keitha wondered. But at least it was another woman—she would not be here alone with Dane Langley.

"You can hardly blame me for being a little sceptical about this job business, you know. I had the impression the other day that you were pretty keen to get away from—sunny Queensland, didn't you call it? And by the way, did you persuade Martin to take no for an answer?"

"Martin is my brother," said Keitha coldly. She turned her head away, indicating that personal questions were not going to be encouraged.

"You must tell me about it some time. I like to know all I can about the people who come to Wayaway. By the way, I'll have that letter when you're ready."

"Certainly." Keitha took it from her handbag.

They were approaching the outhouses now and past them, almost hidden behind tall dark-leafed trees that Keitha recognized as mangoes, was the homestead, tucked away in its garden and surrounded by a white railed fence. The Land Rover spun along a well-defined track and pulled up on a graveled square near a long, white building that had a loading ramp in front of its veranda. As she climbed out of the car, Keitha felt distinctly helpless. She had come all this way to a job she knew virtually nothing about, to work for a woman who wasn't even here, and when she was, it would be 50 miles distant. Moreover, this man Dane Langley was not taking her seriously and even assumed she had come here because of him. Her mind groped toward the thoughts of Donn. Just now that was no comfort at all.

Dane Langley held out his hand for Mrs. Warner's letter and said, "Now stop looking so completely lost, Miss Godwin. Those great dark eyes are going to swallow me up in a minute. I promise that Kate and I shall take good care of you."

Keitha blinked, making a desperate effort to release herself from the magnetism of his gaze. She heard a screen door swing open and slam shut in the building behind her, and turning saw a young man come onto the veranda and stand there, a cigarette in his mouth. Thick, wavy, brown hair falling across his forehead reminded her vaguely of Donn.

"Unload the stuff, will you, Bill?" Dane Langley called. "I'll be with you later." He took Keitha's arm, and they headed for the homestead garden.

Wayaway homestead was white-walled and red-roofed, and looked cool in its setting of green trees and garden. Bougainvillea, its oddly angled papery flowers a deep and vibrant crimson, cascaded from a trellis at one side; pink and white oleander blossoms breathed their musky perfume along the path. Beyond the garden, a windmill rose against the cloudless sky. Keitha climbed three steps to a wide shadowy veranda, and Dane showed her into a big comfortable room with a polished floor and hand-loomed scatter rugs of thick soft cream and tobacco brown wool.

She was reassured by the woman who came forward to meet her—a gray-haired woman of statuesque build, with a slow calm way of speaking; a mouth and eyes that were used to laughter, and a very obvious respect and admiration for the owner of the Wayaway cattle run. Dane introduced her as "Miss Kate Langley—my house-keeper, backstop and comforter. Kate and my father were cousins, and she has been at Wayaway ever since I can remember. . . . Kate, Miss Godwin appears to be Aunt Grace's answer to my request for someone for Patty." The irony in his voice underlined the unlikeliness of the situation. "Will you look to her comfort while I read Grace's letter?"

"Of course, Dane. Sit down, Miss Godwin, and I'll see if Lena has the tea ready and have her set out an extra cup. Dane, did my art materials arrive?"

"They did, darling. Bill's unloading the freight now. In one moment I'll fetch them for you."

Keitha sat down, Kate excused herself and went off to the kitchen, and Dane stood reading the letter. When he had finished, he folded the pages carefully and made a wry face. His eyes flicked over Keitha—her dark hair, her delicate face, her long slender legs. Kate came back into the room and Lena—a slim aborigine girl in a neat blue overall—followed with a loaded tray that she placed on a table near the wall.

Dane Langley waited till she had gone, then said, "Well, knowing how Grace hates putting herself out for anyone, I suppose I might have expected this. But was it so much to ask? I set out my requirements most meticulously in legible handwriting. All she had to do was put the thing in the hands of an agency in Brisbane and sit back. Then—a couple of surely quite painless interviews, the final choice made—after all she knows Patty inside out—and the thing would be over." He moved across to Kate who was pouring the tea, handed a cup to Keitha, took one himself and drank down at least half of it scalding hot. Kate Langley looked at him in silent sympathy, and Keitha thought fractiously, "What's so wrong with me? And who does he think he is to decide offhand that I will not do?" For that, very plainly, was the tenor of his song.

He gave another sardonic look in her direction and continued, "So she had the bright idea of being rid of the whole box of dice in double quick time by sending along a sexy, trendily dressed girl who looks as though she'll blow away in the first puff of wind—and probably will!—whose only probable interest in the job is that it will give her a good look at the inside of a cattle run. . . ."

"Now, Dane," said Kate, gently, cajolingly.

Keitha, her cheeks scarlet, looked for words that would put him in his place. His reference to her as a sexy, trendily dressed girl was rude in the extreme and totally unfair. Before she could think of a thing to say, he had finished his tea, put his cup on the table, and told her uncompromisingly, "Of course you must stay for now, and we'll entertain you. But I'm afraid you'll be back on that mail plane next week. You're not what I ordered at all."

This utterance delivered, he strode from the room. Keitha heard the wire door bang as he went outside.

Kate said mildly, "What a pity, dear. Never mind, you will enjoy your week with us. Dane knows it's Grace's mistake and doesn't blame you."

"Isn't it up to Mrs. Drummond to decide whether I'll do or not?" asked Keitha, holding onto her temper. "I'm quite sure I'll be able to please her."

"Well, Dane knows best in these things. We must leave it to him."

Leave it to Dane Langley! That was something Keitha had no intention of doing. She wasn't going back on the plane next week, with Martin waiting at the other end to say "I told you so." She was going to work for Patty Drummond if it killed her. And she would wait for her return if it took 100 years.

Presently Kate showed her to a bedroom that opened onto the veranda and left her there to unpack and freshen up. Her luggage reposed just inside the door of the room.

"Please excuse me—I must open my parcel," said Kate Langley, and with a smile she hurried away.

Keitha stood at the door of her room and looked across the wide shady veranda to the garden. Through the trees, a long way off, she could see the sails of a windmill and the silver gleam of water, that must be the long lagoon she had seen from the air. The bedroom itself was wide and airy with slightly old-fashioned furniture and fresh flimsy curtains. There was a modern bathroom along the hallway. She bathed her face and changed into a sleeveless yellow blouse and matching skirt. Kate would presumably be busy with her art materials, Dane Langley with the mail, so she decided to take a walk around on her own. She might as well make the most of her freedom until Mrs. Drummond returned. She would have plenty to tell Donn, and if Martin was imagining her toiling away in an immense kitchen, then he couldn't be more wrong!

She slipped her bare feet into the red linen shoes she had bought for the beach, tied back her hair with a red ribbon, and walked around the veranda. She encountered Dane Langley at the screen door near the front steps.

"You've forgotten your hat, honey," he drawled.

She looked at him warily and he laughed.

"Weren't you going to have a look around? Fetch your hat and I'll come with you. That way you'll see a lot more."

That was true enough, so she did as he said and reappeared in a flimsy red straw hat with a wide dipping brim and ties to keep it in place. He screwed up his eyes appreciatively.

"Straight from the fashion magazines! You must tell me some time what made you want to come to an isolated part of the world like this." He took her arm as they went outside into hot clear sunshine. "We'll have a look around the homestead area, Keitha. Unusual name, that. I hope I have it right, Aunt Grace's writing's not the best. Ask any questions you want—I'm at your disposal."

"Thank you," said Keitha stiffly. She was not sure that

she wanted him to call her by her first name, but to protest would be too stuffy. She wished though that he would let go of her arm, for she found his touch unnerving. There was something so personal about it. He took her down a covered way that led to a huge kitchen, the domain of Mrs. Dimmick, absent for the moment. The old-fashioned scrubbed deal table was spotlessly clean, as were the shining laminex counters. There was an immense fuel stove, a freezer and a refrigerator. On the veranda Lena and another girl were peeling vegetables.

"The stockmen are away at mustering camp," Dane told Keitha. "They have a camp cook with them, and every few days the bookkeeper or I take out fresh supplies to them. Mrs. Dimmick's husband looks after the vegetable garden, milks the cows, and does odd jobs about the place. A very handy man is Harry.... Now out here we have the holding yards and the outbuildings." He held a gate open, and Keitha walked through and looked about her curiously, wishing that she had brought her sunglasses. She began to see why Dane Langley's eyes always seemed to be narrowed. He had let go of her arm now and walked a little way ahead of her, pointing out the various buildings and so on in a businesslike way.

"Poultry down there—can you hear a cackle? Means fresh eggs and chicken as a change from beef. Here's the stockmen's mess, next the meat house, and then we have the garage, work shop, store sheds. . . . Stockmen's quarters—wonderful riders and good with the cattle. Down by those trees is Len Hooper's bungalow where he lives with his wife. He's my head stockman and my right arm." He waited for a moment while she caught up to him. The sun was hot on her arms, and she was glad of her hat.

"Here we have the saddle shed and hay store. Feel like a walk over to the drafting yards and the dip? No?" His mocking look suddenly softened, and Keitha lowered her head so that the brim of her hat shielded her eyes from him.

Strong brown fingers reached down and encircled her wrist. "You're drooping like a hothouse flower. Don't fret, pet, I'll lay off and we'll save the drafting yards for when there's some action there. . . . Better meet the book-keeper and get that over." He let go her wrist as abruptly as he had taken hold of it. She found him rough, tough, unpredictable. He called her pet and honey, touched her bare arm, stared at her for minutes with those screwed up blue eyes. She had never met anyone like him, and she knew she ought to be able to tell him without a single spoken word that she didn't like his careless intimacy. But she couldn't.

She hastened along at his side in the direction of the homestead. His arm reached out casually, and his hand rested lightly on her shoulder, bare in the sleeveless shirt. She drew away from him deliberately.

"I don't like to be touched, Mr. Langley."

"Dane," he said. "Christian names in the Gulf Country." His arm dropped to his side. "Have a complex, do you? All right, I'll try to keep my hands off you. Though it's bound to happen again. I'm used to warm-blooded easygoing girls—not city girls with their obsessions and maladjustments. . . . What kind of work did you do in England, honey?"

Honey. There it was again. You simply couldn't win.

"I was assistant to a television producer."

He laughed briefly. "Great heavens! You've certainly changed your stamping grounds. How the other half lives, eh? Well don't be disappointed if you don't fit in—or if we're not as amusing as you hoped. We're just ordinary normal human beings, you know."

"And so am I," retorted Keitha. "Even if I do work in television."

He grinned slightly at that. "Fair enough. But by the

way, don't expect to impress the bookkeeper. He's something of a misogynist—probably left a disastrous love affair behind him when he came Outback. Right now, he just isn't kindly inclined toward even the nicest of girls. In fact he's a bit of a hermit altogether."

They had reached the bookkeeper's office by now. It occupied one end of the building that held the stores, and Bill Sutton came toward the door to meet them. His eyes appraised Keitha with a hardness and coldness she found disconcerting as Dane made the introductions—very briefly and with no reference to the reason for Keitha's being on Wayaway. "He's going to have me off the place in a week," thought Keitha and was more determined than ever that she would not leave.

The bookkeeper was around 30, but his smoky gray eyes were a lot older, the whites slightly reddened. He wore an open-necked shirt and shorts, and while they talked his glance went now and again to Keitha with a detachment she found chilling. She wondered if it was true he had left a disastrous love affair behind him and felt a little sorry for him.

"Well," said Dane after a minute or two, "Keitha and I are doing a tour of the homestead area, so we'd better get on with it. The next few days she'll be coming around the run with me."

Keitha looked at him in surprise, but he was shepherding her toward the door. She gave the bookkeeper a quick and friendly smile. "See you later."

He made no response, and she felt dampened. She wondered if Dane had noticed and almost expected him to say, "I told you not to hope to make an impression." Instead, he asked, "I suppose you don't ride?"

"I do a little," said Keitha cautiously. She had loved riding on her uncle's farm in Devon, but she was not going to make a fool of herself by pretending to be any sort of an expert.

"That's something—puts us one step ahead," said Dane.

They continued on past the homestead garden and through a thick belt of trees to the flat that sloped gently down to the lagoon.

It was an immense sheet of water, bluer than the clear sky above. Tall gum trees and smaller eucalypts, white tea trees and a variety of acacias were grouped along the banks. Patches of lotus lilies spread across the water here and there; their pink and white flowers very beautiful against the bright broad leaves. With a whirr of wings, a swarm of brightly colored little birds flew up from the tall grass to settle farther along the flat.

"Painted finches," said Dane, his eyes following their flight. "Pretty things, aren't they? Come down here at sundown if you're interested in bird life, Keitha—you'll see plenty of it. Kate observes patiently and eternally, and is for ever doing sketches that she develops into line and wash drawings. You might like them. Kate is very creative and has a great reverence for nature. Get her to show you some of her work—she takes it so much for granted she's not likely to think it could be of much interest to anyone. It will show you another aspect of the Outback people," he added dryly, leaning back against the smooth white trunk of a tree. "We still make our own amusements here to a large extent. . . . Well, you've been very quiet. Any questions?"

"Yes. I'd like to know why you're so sure I'm not the right person to work for Mrs. Drummond?"

He quirked an eyebrow at her. "You don't answer the requirements I laid out in writing for my aunt."

"Mrs. Warner must have thought I did," she persisted—though she knew that was not true. "Besides, it's not a job that requires any special training, is it?"

"That's true enough. But some strength of will—some force of personality—are necessary. Do you think you can put your 20 or so years against a woman roughly twice your age? I doubt it, determined though you might be. Patty's been coming over to Wayaway far too often—encroaching on our lives, on Kate's preserves. Kate is a highly organized person and likes to run things her own way, and to be free to use the leisure she creates for her painting."

"Then that's why I must go around the run with you," said Keitha thoughtfully.

"A nice piece of deduction, honey, but wrong. You'll come around the run with me because as your host it's up to me to see you get something worthwhile out of your visit to Wayaway."

"I don't care for your use of the word visit. And if all I must do is see that Mrs. Drummond is happy and occupied at the outstation, I don't think it will be so difficult. I get on with *most* people," she added, giving him a dark look. "Rather than waste your time, wouldn't it be a good idea if I were to go straight to the outstation and settle in there?"

"Honey," he drawled, "I can't let you go over there and shack up with the overseer. That's not to be considered at all." Keitha flushed at the phrase and bit her lip. "No, you'll do as I say and come around with me. That way you'll get a good look at this particular part of sunny Queensland before you take off."

So he remembered what she had said on the island—and he was holding it against her, imagining, no doubt, that she had no intention of staying here any more than a week or two in any case. Well, she would stay six months if it suited her. Meanwhile—right! She would go out on the run with the boss. That would suit her very well. She glanced up and met his eyes.

"You're altogether too kind, Mr. Langley."

"I'm your host," he said blandly. "And I wish you'd try and call me Dane."

CHAPTER THREE

Keitha slept soundly that night. She had no dreams at all. When she woke it was well and truly daylight. She padded out onto the veranda in her bare feet to look at the morning. There was little of the vast plain visible through the thick sheltering screen of mango trees and oleanders that crowded around the house, keeping it cool and protecting it from the glare. Down toward the lagoon lay the vegetable garden. She could see the dark shining leaves and bright globes of fruit in the citrus trees.

She dressed quickly in shirt and jeans and tied her bronze-brown hair back securely. She used only the most basic make-up—cream, and powder to protect her skin from the sun and the dust. No eye make-up at all. It didn't look right in this stark, primitive setting. Even at the coast she had used it sparingly, for the bright sunshine emphasized anything that smacked of the artificial. Her lashes were naturally thick and dark; her eyes this morning looked bright, sparkling and full of health.

Early though it was, she found when she went out to breakfast on the side veranda that Dane had gone out to the mustering camp long ago. She felt a pang of disappointment. She refused steak and eggs, but ate the grapefruit and toast that Lena brought her and drank two cups of coffee. Kate was busy issuing the orders for the day and seeing that the housegirls got on with their work. The bookkeeper, who ate with the family, was nowhere to be seen, so Keitha breakfasted alone.

Afterward, she tidied her room and fetched her hat, for she had decided to go down to the store and talk to Bill Sutton. She was not going to let his attitude frighten her away. Perhaps if she asked him, he might take her out riding. But as she walked around the veranda she came face to face with Dane Langley.

His eyes checked her over efficiently.

"Very nice! I guess a girl like you has something for every occasion in her wardrobe. What are we going to do with you today?"

"You don't need to do anything with me," said Keitha with a bright smile. "I can ride, you know, and I don't want to put you out. If I have your permission to saddle up one of the horses, then I can go around the run myself."

"You'd be lost inside of five minutes," he said dryly.

"I don't think so. But if you're worried, then I shall ask Bill Sutton to take me out."

His eyes glinted dangerously. "I've warned you about that. You'll find yourself out of luck. Apart from the fact that the bookkeeper has plenty to keep him busy, he's just not interested in girls like you, honey—over-civilized, over-dressed, and intent on nothing but fun. He'd have stuck to the city if that was what he wanted."

Keitha felt her temper rise. "Is that how you sum me up?" she demanded.

"Now calm down!" He actually sounded surprised. "Don't take it so hard. I didn't mean to hurt your feelings. What's wrong with being over-civilized and up to the minute in your dress? Isn't it a condition of smart city living? And you're young and on holiday, so of course you're bent on having fun."

"I am not on holiday," Keitha snapped. "I came here to work."

"Well, we've gone into that," he said affably. "All the same, give Bill a miss. I have yet to see a girl he'll be bothered with. And if you will go chasing after him, then you mustn't blame me if your feelings get hurt; you do seem to me to be on the touchy side." He paused and studied her intently. "On second thoughts, I'll make that an order. Stay away from the bookkeeper. A lot of damage can be done in a week, and Bill's not madly happy here as it is. Our community is too small and enclosed to risk dangerous involvements. It's part of my job to keep things running smoothly. In the Outback, you learn to think long and hard before you get too personally mixed up with your daily companions."

Keitha eyed him but said nothing. She didn't know who he was trying to protect—her or the bookkeeper. But she had no intention of taking orders from him. He was not her employer. She would make her own friends and her own decisions. No matter what he advised, or what he ordered, if she wanted she would ask Bill Sutton to take her out riding.

"You'll come out with me, Keitha," he said into her thoughts.

She hesitated only a moment. She did want to see the cattle run, so why not make use of the boss? Besides, Bill Sutton might not be free just now.

She went out to the yards with Dane.

He didn't take her out to the mustering camp that day, but she saw something of the run and learned at least a little about it. She suspected that Dane was assessing her ability to ride, and she was on her mettle. The horse he had chosen for her—a little chestnut called Summer—was reliable and quiet, but not too quiet, and Keitha could manage her easily.

They rode out to one of the waterholes at a leisurely pace, talking very little. There, red and white Hereford cattle grazed beneath the trees or lay in the shade. Dane dismounted and inspected the rails of a holding yard near by.

"Routine check," he said when he returned. "A rotten set of rails can lose a valuable mob of cattle and cost a lot of time."

They didn't see a single solitary person in all the miles

they rode. Once they had left the homestead area, they didn't go through another gate. Dane explained that there were holding yards at various strategic points all over the run—never far from a waterhole. These were used to hold the cattle temporarily before they were drafted for branding or for market, during mustering.

"What size is your property, Mr. Langley?" Keitha asked, as they rode on through the shade of a belt of bloodwoods that grew on a small rise.

"Come now, can't you manage Dane?" He screwed up his eyes in the way that had become familiar to her. "The Wayaway run's roughtly 4000 square miles."

Keitha stifled a gasp. Her gaze took in the yellow plain, a low gravel ridge, a thick line of trees that marked a waterhole or the river bed, the great flat endless horizon. "Four thousand square miles! And all that land belongs to you?"

"No, honey. We lease it from the government. Most of the grazing lands in the north are government-owned. My grandfather took out the first lease here some 70 years ago, and the Langleys have carried on ever since. Most of the neighboring runs are owned by companies, who put in managers. They're nearly all run on the open range system. That's to say, we have few fences if any. The waterholes keep the cattle from straying too far—they're all we need in the way of restraint, except in the Wet."

"I would like to see the stockmen mustering," said Keitha after a few moments.

"So you shall. I'll take you out to the camp in a day or two."

"What is this muster for?" she asked curiously, and he sent her an amused look.

"Want to make notes? Is it to go in a letter home? What family have you left behind in England, Keitha? Or are they all out here?"

What a barrage of questions! She answered the last couple. "Only my brother is here. Back home I lived with the aunt who brought me up."

"Isn't there a lover somewhere in the background?" he asked shrewdly.

The abrupt question took her by surprise, and she colored furiously. He was certainly determined to find out all he could about her. "That's my own business."

"So it is. But I calculated that it couldn't be solely on your aunt's account that you were so dead against settling in Queensland."

"I have a job to return to," she said, riding a little ahead of him.

"Oh yes—the television thing. Are you in love with your boss? Or is that too much of a cliché?"

Keitha didn't answer. She touched Summer's flanks with her heels and raced ahead, reveling in the sensation of flying over the ground. He joined her again in a patch of open forest where she rode more sedately and took up their conversation at the point before which it had become personal.

"Ready to have your question about the muster answered?"

"It doesn't matter. I can find out anything I want to know later, if it's too much bother," she said coolly.

"Honey, it's no bother. A cattleman is always ready to talk about his run. The problem is to stop us. . . . The men are mustering to brand and earmark the calves and clean-skins, to desex where it's necessary, and to cull inferior cows. We're interested in improving herd quality on Wayaway, hence we muster most of the year except during the Wet. We have a big area to cover. Every two years I buy bulls from a stud property on the east coast—that was one of the objects of my recent visit, by the way. Those are my herd bulls—the ones we use as breeders. To make it work, we have to stop the station bulls from breeding—hence the constant need to brand and castrate."

Keitha had been listening intently and with interest.

"A scrub bull, then, is one that has escaped muster?"

"Yes. I believe you're really interested. A scrub bull is usually a wild one too, because he hasn't become inured to the routine of yarding and drafting. In rough country such as we have on the eastern half of this run, over at the outstation, there are always a few scrubbers however scrupulously we muster the timber. . . . Well, that's about enough instruction for today." He gave her a slant-eyed smile. "I guess you didn't come all this way just to hear a lot of dry facts."

"No," Keitha reminded him smartly. "I came all this way to work." She smiled slightly and refrained from admitting that she found his "dry facts" endlessly fascinating.

That evening he took her down to the lagoon again. It was just sundown as they walked through the garden with its warm, sense-stirring fragrances, through the beautifully laid out vegetable garden and the grove of lemon, orange, and grapefruit trees, and on to the lagoon flat. As they came through the trees, Keitha saw a flood of pure vibrating color washed over the entire sky—flame red and dazzling low on the horizon, then softening through coral and rose to delicate lavender; high above, a limpid watery green. There was not even the vestige of a cloud to be seen.

The colors were reflected in the long still lagoon; already the birds were flying in, floating down to the water like leaves, their reflections coming to meet them. Heavy-billed pelicans waded off shore, then came the long-legged, long-billed ibises, a pair of brolgas, and flocks of finches, white cockatoos, and pearly grey galahs with rose-colored breasts. The air was noisy with cries as the birds flew down to drink.

Keitha had never seen such a sight. She could have stood and watched for ever. The man beside her was silent. Once she was aware that his hand was reaching out to her, but it stopped in mid-air and fell back at his side. She knew a fleeting regret.

They stayed there until the sky began to pale; the richness of color to disperse. Then for some reason they both looked up and saw the first trembling white star prick like a crystal through the colorless gauze of the sky above. Dane said softly, "If anyone insists on compensations for living in the Outback, sundown's one of them."

They both turned and walked slowly through the trees toward the gate that led into the garden.

"Do civilized girls demand compensations, honey?—even for a short stay on a cattle run? Or is the thought of returning to London enough to sustain you?" He drawled out his questions as he stood aside for her to go through the gate ahead of him. She felt deep in her being that he was determined to have her talk to him about herself. Why? Was it because he was so used to being the boss—the man to whom everyone looked, with 4000 square miles of cattle country under his command? Well, he had forgone the right to question her when he had said he would put her on the mail plane next week. So she merely gave him an enigmatic smile and hoped she found her as maddening as she found him.

There was no doubt that he had immense personal magnetism. At the homestead at night, she found that simply to be sitting in one of the cane chairs on the veranda so near him was infinitely disturbing. She was acutely conscious of his presence all the time. He had a passion for Beethoven symphonies. After dinner he would select one or two to play on the record player, then sit out on the veranda to listen. It was a routine; this sitting on the veranda at night—smoking, listening to music, staring out over the garden at the immense star-studded sky and the limitless plains glimpsed through trees that were heavy with perfume. Sometimes Kate sat there too, though more often than not she was painting. Bill Sutton usually returned to his own quarters after dinner, so Keitha and Dane sat alone, while from the darkness of the homestead behind them music swelled, filling the great empty silence of the Outback night. It was infinitely more moving than music heard in a London apartment. The lovely sound seemed to invade Keitha's innermost being, and there it wrought an almost chemical change that was awesome and frightening. . . .

She went out on the run with Dane every day. He was always up before dawn to drive out to the mustering camp, but he came back to the homestead for her later on. She felt she must be an imposition, but Kate told her calmly that Dane would have done the same for any guest. He had a head stockman upon whom he could depend absolutely and had he wished could have spent much of the year at the bungalow on the coast, or in his harborside apartment in Sydney. Yet he kept his hands on the reins at Wayaway. As a result it was one of the best cattle stations in the Gulf Country. So Kate said.

Keitha liked Kate—even if she was entirely devoted to the boss of Wayaway and completely blind to the fact that he just might have the odd flaw in his make-up. In Kate's eyes he could do no wrong, and there was no problem that he could not solve.

Kate initiated Keitha into the mysteries of the station radio transceiver, located in the office in the homestead. Station routine demanded that someone—usually Kate—tune in three times a day, to the early morning, the midday, and the afternoon schedules. Keitha had the opportunity to listen only once, and then only to the first part of the broadcast, that included weather checks from various cattle stations, calls to the doctor, and incoming and outgoing telegrams. She knew that this was followed by the galah session, when all the news of the district was passed around.

One morning while she and Kate were having a cup of coffee on the veranda and she was waiting for Dane to take her out on the run, she asked idly, "Does everyone know that I am at Wayaway, Kate?"

Kate gave her an odd look. "Nobody seems to know. I sometimes wonder how you managed it on the plane."

"I think I was identified with some American tourists," said Keitha, and Kate's slight frown disappeared.

"That would explain it. No one's breathed a word about you on any of the scheds, and I did wonder."

"Does Mary Creek come on the air?" Keitha wanted to know.

"Yes, of course. I was talking to Patty yesterday afternoon. Melanie is having a wonderful time with the boys over there."

"Haven't you told *her* that I'm here?"

Kate looked at her almost apologetically. "No, dear. Dane doesn't want that. He wants Patty and Melanie to stay at Mary Creek a little longer. And after all, you're not to stay, are you?"

"So Dane says. But even if Mrs. Drummond knew I was here, she would hardly cut short her holiday on that account, would she?"

Kate smiled faintly. "Dane thinks she would. And I think so too."

It didn't make sense to Keitha, but she said no more.

By now she had seen some of Kate's paintings that she did solely to amuse herself. They were all bird or plant studies—meticulous, detailed, delicate, true in color, and altogether delightful. Aunt Jane would love them, and Donn would find them so wildly old-fashioned he would long to have one to hang in his apartment. Keitha determined to sound Kate out about a sale one day.

She encountered the bookkeeper at dinner, but rarely otherwise. One morning she rose earlier than usual and having breakfasted, made her way to the store on the excuse of needing an extra pair of jeans and a more serviceable hat than her red straw. Bill Sutton's uncompromising, "What do you want?" when she knocked on his office door was disconcerting, but she smiled determinedly and told him without fuss. He didn't smile back—he had not smiled at her even once—but he unlocked the store and let her in ahead of him.

It was a long room with a wooden floor and a counter at one side. On the rows of shelves that reached from floor to ceiling was ranged an enormous variety of commodities—soap, toothpaste, sugar, flour, salt, canned foods of all descriptions, clothing of a utilitarian type, some bolts of pretty cotton materials, boots, hats, belts. Hanging from the ceiling there were even saddles and bridles. Keitha began trying on hats at once, and the bookkeeper put a pile of jeans on the counter.

"All this stuff!" she marveled. "It's incredible. Do you need all this at Wayaway?"

"What do you think? Our main order goes out only once a year. The big trucks have to go over to town and bring the stuff back before we're cut off by the Wet."

Keitha laid aside the hat she had decided on and reached for the jeans, looking at the sizes. "How long have you been here, Bill?" she asked casually.

"Going on for a year," he said not very graciously. "Like you, I came from the city—Brisbane, in my case. Think you'll be here that long?"

She raised her eyes and found his, hard and cynical, on her face. "Why not? If I like it here—and I do."

"Now I wonder why that is?" He removed the cigarette that hung from one corner of his mouth and tapped ash off it. "Could it have something to do with the boss?" The gray eyes flicked her way for an instant. "He'll play you along, if that's what you want. Pretty soon you'll be well and truly hooked. It happens to them all. But make a note of this, sweetheart—there'll be nothing in it for you. Have anyone waiting for you at the coast—or back in England?" He paused, but Keitha didn't answer. She didn't much like the way he was talking to her, but she couldn't help listening. She had a very, very definite idea that he didn't like Dane Langley much. She wondered why not.

He drew on his cigarette again and shoved some of the jeans aside. "You stay here long," he told Keitha, "and you'll have eyes for no one but Dane Langley. Eventually he's going to marry that red-headed piece from over at the outstation. That's my bet. She was born out here, and she belongs here." He stared at her hard. "Take a look in the mirror when you go inside—look at that frail pale face of yours, those great dark dreamy eyes. You just don't belong. But like some others I could name, you won't see it; you'll think you're going to be the one." He tossed his cigarette butt on the floor and ground it out with his heel.

Keitha was thinking of what he had said about the "red-headed piece from the outstation." Was that Melanie Drummond? And was it true that Dane would marry her? And who were these "others", who thought they were going to be the one? She remembered suddenly the girl called Dusty.

"If you want to try those on," the bookkeeper said, "better take them over to the homestead. You can settle up later. . . . Meanwhile, take it from me, the smart thing for you to do would be to get out before you've ruined your life."

Keitha gathered up the jeans and gave him a level look. "I don't need your advice, Bill. I'm in no danger of falling for your boss. I'll let you into a secret, for I can see no one's enlightened you. I'm here to work for Mrs. Drummond when she returns, not to swoon over Dane Langley." Outside she heard the Land Rover come in and pull up on the gravel. She was aware of a feeling of guilt—though she was not sure if it was over what she had told the bookkeeper, or what he had told her. He followed her out onto the veranda, slammed the door shut and disappeared into his office. Dane waited on the gravel for Keitha. He gave one look at the hat perched on her head and the garmests draped over her arm, and drawled, "What's the point in getting new gear, honey? You'll be back in the bright lights soon. . . . Or was it just an excuse for disobeying orders?"

She gave him an enigmatic look, and he put his hand on her arm. "How did you get along with the book-keeper?"

"I learned a thing or two," said Keitha carelessly. "But not about myself." She left him to make what he could of that.

That was the day Dane took her out to the mustering camp. They drove out, taking with them supplies to replenish the camp stock. Keitha found the day an absorbing experience. The activity at the camp excited her. Sitting in the shade of a tree, she watched the growing mob of cattle that the ringers were bringing in. There was dust everywhere, the ringers shouted to each other and to the cattle. Every one of them was an expert rider. They looked as if they were part of the horses that they rode. Most of them seemed to walk awkwardly when they dismounted for a smoke or for lunch.

She met Len Hooper, the head stockman, stringy and straight, with a face tanned to leather, and bright blue eyes that saw everything though they were even more screwed up than the boss's own. He asked no questions about Keitha, but he was not shy with her as the Aborigine stockmen were, barely able to bring themselves to look at her from under the wide brims of their dust-stained hats.

Driving back to the homestead with Dane, Keitha expressed her pleasure in the day, but she did not admit that the horseman she had enjoyed watching most of all had been the boss himself.

Dane said laconically, "Oh, everyone likes to watch a muster—other people doing all the work. It's fine to sit in the shade of a tree and think what a picture it makes, what you'll write home about it all. But you'd really have something to enthuse about, honey, if you'd done some of the riding yourself."

For a moment Keitha was at a loss for words. Was he throwing her a challenge? If so, then she was going to take it up. She remembered that other challenge of his—that he would in no time have her caring very much about his opinions. She didn't think he had won that yet! She said carelessly, "I'd have liked to ride at the muster, but I didn't like to push myself forward, especially as this is the first time I've seen the procedure. But if I'd had a horse—"

He took her up mockingly. "We'll go out again tomorrow, and you can have a go at it."

She blinked, but she didn't turn her head, knowing that he was watching for her reaction.

"Marvelous," she said calmly. She hoped she had disconcerted him.

Later, when she thought of what she had let herself in for, she felt more than a little apprehensive. She avoided Dane that night and went into the garden to walk restlessly by herself. She never had time these days to think about Donn. At night she was always so physically tired she fell asleep almost as soon as she hit the pillow.

Now, deliberately, she let her mind dwell on Donn and wandered toward the lagoon. The sweet scent of the orange blossom that bloomed on the trees among the fruit, made her long for Donn and his kisses and loving words.

She was taken by surprise when she saw Bill Sutton strolling toward her from the trees on the lagoon flat. In the eeried brightness of starlight, he looked for a moment very much like Donn. Her heart began to hammer when he passed her with nothing but a curt, "Good evening."

Now her reverie was broken. Her thoughts, almost against her will, drifted from Donn back to Wayaway and the immediate present. She went over that conversation she had had with Bill Sutton in the store and wondered at the vehemence with which he had warned her against Dane Langley. Had the girl *he* was in love with fallen under the boss's spell? And if so, who was she? Keitha wondered if she would ever find out. His insistence that all the girls had eyes for no one but Dane had certainly had more than a touch of bitterness in it. . . .

As soon as she woke the following morning, she remembered that today she was to ride at the mustering camp. What would she have to do? She had a pretty fair idea that, rather than being expected to bring cattle into the camp, she would be waiting on the edge of the mob that was ringing on camp and going after any breakaways. She suspected, too, that Dane Langley would admit he had only been teasing her, and that of course she was not going to work at the muster.

When he came into the homestead and found her ready to accompany him out to the camp, he gave her a rakish look from his narrowed eyes.

"Ready? Or are you going to chicken out of our little scheme for today?"

Keitha might have conceded if he had made the first

move, but—chicken out. She had never in her life chickened out of anything—unless you could count not staying in England while Donn Gorsky changed his mind about the sort of arrangement he wanted with her in the future. At any rate, she was not chickening out now and she told Dane with a smile, "Of course I'm not. Only I can't promise that my performance will even slightly resemble that of one of your ringers."

"You'll be all right," he said negligently. "I have a little black colt reserved for you—a great little camp horse. All you'll have to do is keep your wits about you, and you won't take a fall."

Those blue eyes were narrowed mockingly, and Keitha's heart began to pound. If he wanted to frighten her with his talk of falls, then he was not going to succeed. She had watched the camp horses—watched them race after a beast that had broken away from the mob, shoulder it around, swerving at full gallop so that one of the rider's stirrups all but brushed the ground. She had marveled at the way the stockmen kept their seat. Would this little black colt go through the same motions? And if it did—would she be able to hang on? She would just have to. Because she was sure Dane Langley was laughing at her. She was going to call his bluff. She could do it if she put her mind to it. She was going to demonstrate that clearly.

He talked to her easily on the drive out to the camp. It took longer to cover the miles in country where there was no track to follow. They had to go over stony ridges, across sandy creek beds, through trees and long grasses that might conceal a crippling stump. But the boss of Wayaway knew all the hazards; he was a more than competent driver and never let his attention stray unless he knew he could afford it.

He talked, it seemed to Keitha, about anything other than the test ahead of her—because by now she regarded it as a test. If she passed, perhaps she would be allowed to stay. Whereas if she failed, would she then meekly pack her bags and go tomorrow? She was not at all sure. She only knew that to fail was unthinkable.

When they reached the muster, there was a sizeable mob already ringing on camp, and two or three stockmen riding around the outskirts to keep them under control. In the center of the mob, in among the tossing horns that rose from a sea of swirling red dust, rode Len Hooper, drafting out the calves and the cleanskins. They would be yarded and branded; the rest of the cattle would be let go.

Dane had arranged for the black colt and his own big bay to be saddled ready. Today Keitha wore a hat with a chin strap—the one she had bought at the station store—and she tilted it over her eyes as she stepped from the Land Rover and looked at the mob of cattle. In a few more minutes, her heart in her mouth, she rode over to the surging cloud of dust to take up her position with the other ringers. She sat easily, listening to the bellowing of the bulls, the men's voices as they called out, the occasional crack of a stockwhip, and the thundering of hooves as a few more beasts hunted from the scrub came to join the mob. She was so fascinated that for a little while she forgot that she was now meant to be part and parcel of it all until suddenly, close at hand, a bullock broke away and headed for the timber.

Her start of awareness was enough for the black colt which turned and galloped across the flat. Keitha's heart was pounding as she clung to the pommel and put her trust in her mount. Dust was flying all around her and her eyes were smarting, but the next thing she knew, the bullock had surrendered and was lumbering back to the mob. It had been easy! She hadn't had to ride in close at all, and she was exultant.

She was breathing quickly, and the perspiration was

coursing down her back. On the outskirts of the mob, she waited again. The black colt fidgeted nervously, and she knew it was on the alert. She glanced around quickly, wondering if Dane had seen her little escapade and wondering if it would have impressed him at all. She had been lucky the bullock had been so easily dealt with. Some of the wild scrub bullocks would have been very different. Once they reached the timber, they were the very devil to bring back again.

All too soon, another opportunity came for the camp horse to go into action. Keitha nearly lost her seat as it swung around and went flying across the ground after a great wild-looking beast. Surely a scrub bull, this! Keitha knew she was scared. They were getting close to the timber; still the bull refused to turn. The pony was closing in, soon it would be on the bull's flank and shouldering it around and then—

What would have happened then she was never to know. Suddenly Dane on his big bay cut in ahead of her, her own mount slowed and dropped back, and she watched, her heart thumping, as Dane swung the animal and brought him back.

Why had Dane let things go so far? She could have had a bad accident. He must be even harder and more ruthless than she imagined. He could even want to frighten her away from Wayaway. But she felt excited and oddly exhilarated, and pleased that she had stuck it out until he had forced her to give way. She knew that she would never have given in otherwise—no matter what had happened. She hoped he knew that now and would apply it to other things. . . .

She knew a feeling of regret when the cutting out was over, and the stockmen slid from their saddles and went over to the camp for lunch. Two of them remained to watch the calves and the cleanskins, and Keitha turned her horse and made for the camp. In a moment Dane was beside her, and they ambled side by side in the direction of the camp fire. She was thirsty! Hungry too, and she looked eagerly at the hunks of meat and damper that the men were tucking into.

"For a city girl," said Dane, riding close to her, "you put on a pretty good show. You're no shirker. Tell me, honey—do you do all this for the sake of experience. What is it that drives you?"

She wanted to say "You, Dane Langley—you drive me." Instead, she simply smiled at him before she slid from her horse. Before she could take one step toward the camp, his hand was locked on her wrist. "Better go down to the waterhole for a wash. You've a very dirty face."

Did he think that would take the city girl down a peg? Keitha simply laughed and took his advice.

She tucked into the rough fare with great gusto later on, and afterward rode on the flank of the mob that was being walked to the holding yard a mile or two away.

"I love it here," she thought, taking herself by surprise. Donn would think she was off her head. As for Aunt Jane—she wouldn't be able to sleep at night if she knew what her niece had been up to today.

Dane spoilt the pleasant dream that she had fallen into by saying when they were back at the homestead yards, "Well, you've one more morning left to you, honey. How do you want to put it in?"

She was somehow shocked. It seemed so callous. In her own mind she had won a battle, she had proved herself more than an over-dressed, over-civilized guest, and she was going to stay.

"One morning?" she repeated. Her winged eyebrows went up. "I think I have more than that. When are you going to play fair and let Mrs. Drummond know that I'm here?"

"I have no intention of giving Patty the good news," he said dryly. "You don't belong here." His voice sharpened. "Come on now, admit it. Your heart's back in London, isn't it?"

"I'm surprised to hear you talking of such elusive things as hearts," she answered evasively.

"I'm as much concerned with hearts as most men. But I've been conditioned—by a number of things—to think of you as a tourist, someone passing through. I like to face facts as they are; in spite of your tricky persuasive way of doing whatever you set out to do and looking picturesque as you do it. . . . No, tomorrow we reach the end of a chapter."

"Indeed we don't," thought Keitha stubbornly. She waited while he called to one of the men to take care of the horses—he had left Len Hooper to bring the Land Rover back. Then as they walked across the dusty yard toward the homestead she told him, "I'm no tourist, and I'm afraid you'll have to re-do your thinking, Mr. Langley." That, of course, was no way to speak to the boss, and she saw him frown. Yet there was amusement in his eyes as he looked down at her.

"Is that meant to be an answer to my question? Are you telling me your heart's not back in London?" he asked insistently.

Was her heart back in London? Somehow she couldn't answer that question even to herself. Last night, strolling through the orange trees, she had thought of Donn with such longing. And then, distracted by the bookkeeper and her thoughts of the people she had met here in the Gulf Country, she had forgotten him again.

Suddenly she felt utterly confused. She simply didn't know where her heart was. She didn't even know what her heart was. A while back, riding at the muster, it had been very much here—right here, beating so hard in her body, harder than it had ever beaten before. That was the heart she thought of now. . . . She was at a loss and looked up at Dane without speaking.

He gave a sudden brief laugh. "You don't know what you're asking for, Keitha. Patty Drummond will want to be rid of you even faster than I do."

CHAPTER FOUR

She thought about that afterward. So he wanted to be rid of her. But why? More definitely than ever she made up her mind that she was not going. But it was not because of Dane Langley—no matter what the book-keeper might imagine.

That night Len Hooper drove in from the camp, and after dinner he, Dane and Bill Sutton retired to the office. Keitha and Kate sat on the veranda engaged in the silent thought that seemed to come comfortably and without self-consciousness to the people of the Outback. Presently Keitha asked, "What is Mrs. Drummond, like, Kate? Do you think she and I would get on together?"

"Dane says not," said Kate, unhesitatingly. Her utter and absolute faith in the boss of Wayaway was maddening to Keitha.

"I would like to find out for myself. Is that so unreasonable? I've come a long way."

"It's for Dane to say," Kate said simply. "On a big cattle station someone has to be in command and make the decisions. I'm afraid I don't think you have any option, Keitha." She looked at Keitha sorrowfully, and in sudden impatience the girl jumped to her feet.

"I think I'll take a walk in the garden and then turn in," she told Kate.

She was returning from her walk when Dane was beside her. "Your last night," he said laconically, looking down at her in the starlight. "Pity, isn't it? I'm used to seeing you around the place. I've asked myself more than once what keeps you going. You're such a fragile thing, like a bush orchid. And yet out at the mustering camp today you rode like a good 'un. . . . Well, no more to be said."

She watched him warily. No more to be said. Perhaps not. But surely something to be done. If Kate had not been so rock-hard and inflexible in her support of the boss, Keitha would have got on the transceiver before this and told Patty Drummond that here she was and here she would stay until she and Melanie came back from Mary Creek. But now another plan was forming in her mind. She was not going to be put on that plane tomorrow. She was going to disappear. Dane would have to go out to the airstrip without her, because she simply would not be available.

And there was not a thing he would be able to do about it.

She disappeared most effectively the following morning, well before it was time for Dane to come in from the camp. She persuaded Mrs. Dimmick to give her a lunch basket and a thermos and told Kate she was taking Summer out along the lagoon bank.

"Don't go far," Kate warned unsuspectingly. "Dane will want you back in good time for the plane."

"Don't worry," said Keitha ironically. "Everything will be all right."

They were going to be angry with her, she knew, but she didn't care. Of course she didn't go along the lagoon bank, but chose her way carefully so that she would not be lost. She rode a few miles out in the direction of the camp, then crossed the plain to a waterhole where there were trees and shade. She had brought writing materials. She would write letters to Aunt Jane and to Martin. Somehow she didn't feel like beginning another letter to Donn yet. She had written him one already—long and rather disjointed—and it must now be reposing in the mail bag in the office. She was sure she would not be found. They would be expecting her at the homestead all the time, and in any case they wouldn't know where to look. She had made certain of that by telling Kate she would be by the lagoon. . . .

The time passed very slowly. It was hot and utterly silent except for the occasional screeching of cockatoos or the sounds of the cattle moving. Keitha didn't really enjoy herself at all. Ordinarily she would have been happy with her thoughts, but today she could not even concentrate on Donn. Simply because of a slight resemblance, Bill Sutton's face with its moody eyes kept getting in the way. And then she was continually coming back to the question of Dane's possible reaction to her tactics. They were pretty impertinent tactics in one way, for after all, she had been a guest at Wayaway. But Dane was not giving her a fair deal. She wondered if there would be letters for her in the mailbag, or if Martin would assume that she would be back at the coast this week.

She wandered down by the waterhole and saw two kangaroos bounding through the trees. Otherwise there were only the birds, the cattle, and Summer cropping the grass. She didn't dare ride around in case she was seen. She ate her lunch slowly at noon and drank her thermos of tea. Not until at long, long last she heard the mail plane droning across the sky did she feel safe. By then it was too late for Dane Langley to do anything about her presence on Wayaway. With a sigh of relief she packed up her few things and prepared to ride back to the homestead. As Summer ambled along she thought with some trepidation of what lay ahead of her.

Well, she would have to face up to it; the boss would have to make the best of it. He would see that in this battle of wills she had won. And after all, she had right on her side.

She did not feel nearly so sure of this when the station buildings came into sight.

She rode into the horse yard and left one of the men to take care of Summer, then slowly made her way to the homestead. The Land Rover was pulled up outside the station store. Bill and Dane were unloading the freight. Neither one of them took any notice of her as she slipped by, and she wondered if they had seen her.

Kate was on the veranda looking consideringly at an unfinished drawing and glanced up as Keitha came through the screen door, hot and perspiring and feeling very much in need of a cool refreshing shower.

"Did you get lost?" She asked the question dryly, and Keitha started. She didn't want to answer that question.

"I hope no one was worried—and that Dane wasn't late going for the mail."

"Dane is never late for the mail." Kate sounded mildly reproving.

"I hope he didn't waste too much time looking for me."

"No. He said if you were lost then you could stay lost a little longer."

"Did he indeed?" thought Keitha with indignation. So the mail—the freight—were more important than she was, were they? Another thought struck her: Had he devised some other way of removing her from the station? She was going to meet that one head on.

"I suppose he'll see that I pick up the plane at a neighboring station later on."

She stood there, her hat swinging from her hand, watching Kate aggrievedly. And Kate held her drawing this way and that, put on her glasses, inspected it critically, and finally said, with her serene but enigmatic smile—only there was something disapproving in it now—"You'll be pleased to know you're to stay. If you'd waited this morning you'd have heard the news. Patty and Melanie are on their way home—they'll be here tonight. So Dane said that in the circumstances you may as well stay another week."

"Oh." Keitha felt deflated. Those long, hot, dreary

hours by herself had been unnecessary. And Dane had let her sweat it out. Probably he had known very well that she wasn't lost—that she was simply making herself scarce. Somehow, she had to know exactly what he had done. She asked haltingly, "Did anyone go along the lagoon looking for me?"

Kate looked at her in surprise. "No. Why? Weren't you there?"

Keitha flushed. "I changed my mind."

"Well, don't be upset about it. You can count upon it—if Dane had wanted to find you he'd have done so."

Keitha stood for a second and then went around by the veranda to her bedroom. She was fuming. The wonderful, all-knowing, all-powerful Dane Langley. Everything went his way. If he had wanted to, he'd have found her! *How?* She just didn't see how. And yet somewhere inside her, she had a suspicion that Kate was right. She had thought it was all too easy. . . .

By the time she had showered and changed, Lena had brought afternoon tea. Dane, Kate and the bookkeeper were sitting on the side veranda. No one commented on Keitha's failure to be at the homestead when it was time to leave for the airstrip. Dane smiled at her pleasantly. His remark that she had a good color in her cheeks made her flush deeply.

It was all anticlimax.

Kate went to the office for the afternoon schedule, Bill returned to the store, and Keitha was left alone with Dane.

"Well, you'll have your wish tonight, Keitha. You'll be able to present yourself to Patty as her prospective helpmate." There was laughter in his eyes and a tilt to the corners of his mouth.

"And you hope she'll turn me down," Keitha flared.

His eyebrows rose, and he gave her a long hard look, then stood and strolled across to look out into the garden.

"Well, you don't care what I hope, do you, honey? I'll tell you what will happen, though. Patty will find you too young and pretty by far to want you anywhere around this cattle run."

"If she really needs some company, she may be prepared to put up with that," Keitha said to his back. Her cheeks were bright with anger. Maybe she was spoiling for a fight.

He turned to face her again, leaning one hand nonchalantly on the rail. "Patty thinks there's better company to be had here at the homestead."

"But that interferes with Kate."

"I didn't know you had Kate's interests so much at heart. It didn't seem so today when you did your little disappearing act. She was very upset."

"Why? Because she though you would fly into a rage when your wishes were thwarted?"

He looked at her in silence, but he was unperturbed, even faintly amused. "I'd not have blamed Kate. Besides, when have you ever seen me fly into a rage?"

She shrugged and said stubbornly, "Then why was Kate upset?"

"She thought you'd lost yourself."

"And you didn't think so?"

He allowed himself a deeper smile. "I had an idea what you were up to, honey." He came across to her and his hand rested for a moment on the silkiness of her hair. "You like to win your battles, don't you?. . . . By the way, no mail for you today. That brother of yours must have been expecting you back. We must talk about it some day."

And then he was gone.

The Drummonds arrived an hour or so after dinner. Bill had disappeared as usual, and Keitha, Dane and Kate were in their chairs at the end of the veranda when car lights swept through the darkness of the plain beyond the homestead garden. Kate rose at once.

"I'll make some tea. They'll need it after that long drive." She went unhurriedly toward the kitchen. The kitchen girls were off duty at night, and Mrs. Dimmick, who with her husband had quarters near the kitchen, was never disturbed after dinner. Dane stood too, and going inside switched off the record player.

By that time the car lights had come in close. Now they swung around in an arc over the gravel beyond the garden. Dane reappeared and without a word or a look in Keitha's direction, went down the steps. Keitha thought she had better keep out of the way until the greetings were over and the news of her presence had been broken. She listened to the voices outside in the warm night and strained her ears as if by catching the timbre of a voice she could prepare herself for what sort of a woman she had to impress. She knew practically nothing about Patty Drummond, beyond the fact that she had been widowed not so very long ago, and that her husband Bruce had been a distant relative of the Langleys. This much she had learned from Kate, who was loath to talk about anyone—except of course, Dane, the apple of her eye.

As for Melanie—she was 18 and red-haired.

The two voices that Keitha could hear were very different from each other. The young voice, Melanie's, was drawling like Dane's and came in excited bursts. The other voice was pretty and soft and reminded Keitha of Mrs. Warner.

In a few moments the three figures appeared in the light that fell from the veranda. Dane had switched on the center light to illuminate the steps, but Keitha still sat in semi-darkness. She saw a slight, pretty woman with a brown face and black hair that looked untouched by gray, and a big well-built girl whose straight reddish hair was tied in a bunch on each side of her face. The girl had good eyes, a straight narrow nose, and full lips. She was a beautiful, big, country girl, and looked overflowing with health and vigor. No one could have called *her* a bush orchid.

Mrs. Drummond was quite different.

"I have such a headache, Dane. Does Kate have my room ready? I must go to bed straight away. Mellie can tell you all about the exciting time we had. Those Palmer boys made such a fuss of her I thought it was high time I brought her home before her head was completely turned. . . . Oh, it's really wonderful to be home again!"

The voice babbled on prettily as they went inside, Dane's arm affectionately around the shoulders of the big beautiful Mellie. Keitha thought, "Home again". Did Patty Drummond mean Wayaway homestead or simply the Wayaway cattle run? Wasn't her home 50 miles away? And Dane, with his arm around Melanie—Keitha was irritated by the sense of hostility that gave her. But Bill had said that eventually Dane would marry Mellie. Yet how could he know?

She sat alone on the veranda feeling very much an outsider and a little forlorn. Inside, Kate's voice had joined those of the others, and she knew that tea had been brought in. She began to wonder if she should go and present herself when Dane appeared and glanced along toward her.

"Come along in, Keitha. All the welcoming's over, and it's time for you to be introduced."

She was aware that her heart was beating too fast. She had to make a good impression on Patty Drummond. Yet now that the moment had come, she was smitten with doubts about herself. Suddenly she knew that she should be a stout, dowdy, middle-aged woman if she was to inspire Patty Drummond with confidence. She was quite wrong. Dane had come along the veranda and now stood looking down at her, an amused expression in his eyes, his lips curving in a half-smile.

"Are you having doubts, honey, now that you have what you wanted? Or is it the thought of those 50 miles?" His fingers had closed compellingly around her wrist, and she shook them off, tossing her head, and stalked ahead of him to the door.

When she stepped into the sitting room, Kate was pouring tea at the side table, Melanie was sprawling in a chair, her legs in their denim pants stretched out in front of her, and Patty Drummond leaned back exhaustedly in an armchair. Her blink of surprise when Keitha appeared was impossible to miss. The girl made an immense effort to give her an easy, reassuring smile. Dane was close behind her and his hand rested lightly on her shoulder as he said drawlingly, "Patty—Melanie—this is Keitha Godwin. Keitha—Mrs. Drummond and Melanie, from the outstation."

Patty's eyes hardened, and red color stained Melanie's cheeks. They had both straightened up somewhat. Her own friendly smile was met by blank surprise and even hositility, that unnerved her. Kate turned from the tea tray.

"Will you have some tea, Keitha?"

"Yes, please, Kate."

"Sit down, honey," said Dane, guiding her to the sofa. He then proceeded to elucidate the situation.

"Patty, while I was over at the coast, I went to the bungalow for a couple of days. Grace was there, as no doubt you know, so I asked her to find a nice reliable woman who would be prepared to live at the outstation to keep you company and cheer you up when things became too much for you." He crossed over to Kate and helped hand out the cups of tea. "Grace came up with an answer that was rather unexpected."

The expression on Patty Drummond's face might have amused Keitha had the circumstances been otherwise. She looked positively stunned. She stared at Keitha as if she were a woman from outer space and seemed totally incapable of speech. Keitha's spirits plummeted, and she caught herself looking to Dane as if for help. He waited until Kate was seated, then took a chair himself and screwing up his eyes looked around at the company.

Mellie spilled her tea in her saucer and colored again; Mrs. Drummond at last managed a little laugh. "Grace is a dear, but she's hopeless! I wish you'd told me what you had in mind, Dane, because I wouldn't have allowed it for a moment—things are not as bad as that. How long has Miss—Godwin—been here? You should have let me know."

"Keitha's been with us a week, and I left you in happy ignorance so that you could finish your holiday and reap the full benefit of the change."

"And so I have, Dane," Patty Drummond said. "I feel wonderful—except for this headache." Her brown eyes looked at him reproachfully. "You shouldn't have done this, Dane—it's totally unnecessary. I'm not a bit pleased."

"What a welcome," thought Keitha wryly, sipping her tea. She had not realized that she was going to be such a complete surprise to her employer. Apparently Dane had acted without consulting her at all. She stole a glance at Kate. Just at that moment, Kate said firmly,

"Speaking as an interested observer, Patty, I'd say it was not unnecessary at all. You've been so restless lately you've had me worried. Another woman at the outstation will make all the difference to you."

Patty ignored her and spoke to Dane. "If you'd told me, I'd have come back at once."

"And I could have left today," thought Keitha.

"That's just what I didn't want. Besides, it's given

Keitha an opportunity to look around the run and get the feel of the place. As it happens, we're in luck, for she's taken to it like a duck to water." His eyes met Keitha's mockingly. "For all I knew, Patty, the girl might have hated it here and decided to take off today."

Now for the first time Patty Drummond gave Keitha a full and prolonged scrutiny from her beautiful moody eyes. "I'm quite sure she wouldn't have done that," she said dryly. "Though as far as I'm concerned she might as well have done. . . . I'd like another cup of tea, Kate, and then I'm going to bed. My head aches so."

That was all. Keitha was dismissed. Patty Drummond quite plainly was not going to discuss the situation further tonight. "Well," thought Keitha, trying to be fair, "I expect she is tired, and Dane has not been very considerate in springing a surprise on her like this." But why was she so decided about not wanting another woman at the outstation? What had Dane said?— "Patty's been coming over to Wayaway far too often— encroaching on our lives, on Kate's preserves." Why did he want to put a stop to that? Was it simply on Kate's account? Was that the whole story? Keitha didn't think so.

Patty was saying a general good night. Keitha thought, "I've really had it this time. She's going to refuse point blank to have me." Would it be any use putting up a fight to stay? And did she really want to stay? Apart from the fact that it would be annoying to have to see Martin and admit defeat—why did it matter to her so much that she should stay here? Perhaps she wanted to prove something to Wayaway's boss. Though it might be better sense to take herself off to Brisbane and find work there. She remembered the bookkeeper's warning about the apparently fatal charm of Dane Langley, but told herself that had no significance for her.

She became aware that Melanie and Dane were talking. Mellie was asking about the bulls he had bought at the coast and was now saying, "Where are they mustering at the outstation? I hope Col hasn't done the Big Scrub Waterhole yet—it's the most exciting of all."

"Tomboy," teased Dane. "I'll have to tell Col to put one of the men off if you go at it as hard as you have been doing."

"I love it," said Mellie. "And Col lets me do absolutely anything. It's terrific fun hunting the cattle out of the scrub and teaching them it's no use trying to go wild again. At Mary Creek I wasn't even allowed to ride any of the camp horse. Most of the time I had to sit around with Jen and Mrs. Palmer while the boys had all the fun. It was rotten." To Keitha, listening, she sounded as ingenuous as a schoolgirl. But after all, she was only 18. Was she the girl Dane would eventually marry?

She rose quietly and took her cup over to the tea tray. "I'll wash the cups, Kate. And then I think I'll go to bed."

Dane sent her a mocking smile and wished her sweet dreams. Mellie looked at her as vaguely and impersonally as if she had been a stranger passing by in the street and then returned to her conversation.

Keitha didn't have sweet drems. She dreamed of Dane instead of Donn, and her sleep was restless and troubled. She woke in the morning with the depressed feeling that she had made a mistake in insisting on staying on Wayaway. Dane knew that and was going to have the last laugh.

She jumped out of bed and began to dress quickly.

"Not if I can help it," she thought with sudden determination. "I'm not going to be beaten so easily."

Dane had gone out on the run, and Mrs. Drummond was having breakfast in bed. Mellie, in riding pants, a green shirt, and a man's wide-brimmed hat, was wandering off to the horse yards.

Keitha said to Kate matter-of-factly, "I don't think Mrs. Drummond is prepared to like me."

"Then you must make her do so," said Kate surprisingly. She was sharing a second cup of coffee with Keitha on the side veranda before going to the kitchen to get the day's business organized. "Dane wants you to go over to the outstation with Patty and Mellie."

Keitha blinked. So Dane wanted her to go to the outstation, did he? Was that because otherwise she would have to stay at the homestead for another week?

Kate had gone to the office to listen to the morning schedule when Patty Drummond finally came out onto the veranda. Mellie had long ago ridden off looking very much at home on a big chestnut horse. By now Keitha's nerves were taut.

Without preliminaries, Patty Drummond sat down beside her, proceeded to file her long pretty nails and to tell Keitha where she stood.

"I'm sorry about this, Miss Godwin, but you'll have to make up your mind you're out of a job. Dane had misunderstood my needs. I suppose you know I lost my husband last year—he was related to the Langleys and manager at the outstation. Of course it's left a big gap in my life. But there's nothing at all a young girl like you can do about that. I'm far happier coming over here occasionally to the people I know and love. You're obviously quite out of your element here, aren't you?" She smiled brightly and glanced over Keitha's fine cotton dress of vibrant orange, her pretty white Italian sandals. Then, with a steady and penetrating glance from eyes that were the opposite of friendly, she asked deliberately, "How on earth did you ever manage to insinuate yourself into this household?"

Keitha felt herself slowly crimsoning. The question was pretty close to insulting. But to admit it, was no way to hang onto a job that was going to slip out of her fingers unless she was careful. She managed a smile. "Please don't put it like that. I was looking for work, and my brother is a friend of the Warner girls. Mrs. Warner thought it might be worth my while to try the position here, as I was interested."

"I'm sure you were interested—and I'm sure you thought it would be worth your while. I suppose you met Dane at the coast." She didn't wait for an admission or a denial—and Keitha didn't know if she could have given the latter without looking guilty—but continued rapidly, "Well, I don't quite know what we're going to do with you. It's very vexing. Dane obviously feels obligated to give you a trial out of politeness to Grace. But poor Kate must be thoroughly tired of you."

"I haven't bothered Kate," said Keitha quickly. "I've been out on the run with Dane most of the time."

That was a mistake. The fine nostrils dilated and there was a furious expression on Patty Drummond's face as she filed away at a fingernail. It became clear that she did not welcome any competition for Dane's attention. And of course—of course, thought Keitha, as it all fell into place: she wanted the picked position, here at Wayaway homestead, for Mellie! That was certainly why she came to stay so often. Keitha made an effort to allay her fears.

"I'd really appreciate it if you would give me a trial, Mrs. Drummond. I've been so looking forward to seeing the outstation."

"I don't intend going back to the outstation yet," said the older woman petulantly. "You can surely not expect me to change my plans to suit your convenience. No, Mellie and I shall stay here for a while. I'll see what else can be arranged about you. Someone may be going over to the coast in which case we could arrange for you to be picked up somewhere. The bookkeeper could drive you. . . ."

But when Dane came in to lunch, he swiftly put an end

to these projected maneuvers. "No, Patty," he told her. "My mind's made up. You need company on the spot. I've promised that the outstation will continue to be your home as long as you need it, and you have a right to be happy there. You shouldn't be continually uprooting yourself and Mellie and coming all the way over here to us." He smiled kindly as he spoke, and he looked so genuinely and warmly concerned about Patty Drummond's happiness that Keitha had to remind herself that somehow or other he was working things to suit himself. For she was quite certain that the boss of Wayaway always pleased himself—and usually managed to persuade others that he had their interests at heart.

Patty Drummond sighed and looked out into the garden wistfully. "I appreciate your concern, of course. But someone's made a mistake this time." Her glance wandered to Keitha who was eating her lunch and keeping quiet, while Mellie, who didn't seem very interested at all in what was going on, did the same. "How can a girl like Miss Godwin—charming though I have no doubt she is—be of any help to an experienced countrywoman who takes her way of life for granted and is used to wheels turning smoothly?"

Dane reached for a mango and proceeded to deal with it expertly, slitting the flesh from the stone with a curved knife, then eating it from the skin with a spoon, having first, however, passed half of it across to Keitha with an oddly intimate lift of one eyebrow that did not go unnoticed.

"I've brushed Keitha up a little on Outback life, Patty," he said consolingly. "But if you'd rather, then she can stay on with us some more and get further training from Kate, till you feel she's ready to face life with you."

Keitha thought she would choke on her first mouthful of the delicious juicy fruit. What on earth had got into Dane Langley, sponsoring her cause like this? It seemed he was always intent on forcing his will on someone or other. This time it was Patty's turn. He was certainly winning hands down. Patty looked exasperated and helpless, and Keitha felt a vague sympathy for her. She knew that she would have to give in.

She said irritably, "Kate has quite enough to do already. No, Dane, if you insist, then of course I shall try to train Miss Godwin myself." She looked at Keitha with dislike. "I'm sure at least that I shall be able to find plenty to keep her occupied."

"Then we shall all be pleased," said Dane, sending Keitha a wicked look. "Because Keitha is dead keen on getting involved in some work." He seemed to be amused at the whole business and at everyone's discomfiture.

Patty Drummond's idea of staying on at Wayaway evidently did not meet with his approval, for a short while after lunch he told Keitha that she and the Drummonds were to leave for the outstation as soon as they were ready. Keitha packed her belongings and reflected that now the time had come for her to go, she was filled with regret. Mrs. Drummond was not at all kindly disposed toward her, and she had really been happy at the homestead. She liked Kate, and Dane was, all other things aside, at the very least stimulating.

She took her luggage out onto the veranda when she was ready. Surprisingly, Kate came and kissed her goodby. "You're always welcome to come and visit us when you have some free time," she assured Keitha.

"Thank you, Kate, I shall certainly come." If I can arrange transport, she added to herself. She had not yet asked Kate about the possibility of buying one or two of her paintings, and that would surely make a reasonable excuse for a visit—if Dane Langley should demand an excuse. He had told her, when he broke the news that she was to leave that afternoon, "Remember—one of your main duties is to keep Patty happy at the outstation and stop her from racing over here at the drop of a hat. I know you have a strong will—you've proved that to me without a doubt—so I'll expect results!"

She slipped down to say goodbye to Bill Sutton, mostly out of politeness, and found him checking the water and the batteries in the Drummond's station wagon.

"I'm off to the outstation," she told him when he looked up at her with that chilling expression she had learned to expect from him.

"You'll be back." He slammed down the hood. "Fifty miles is nothing. Girls come from a lot farther than that to get a chance to captivate the boss of Wayaway."

"I discovered that on my way out here," said Keitha. "But I haven't joined the line-up yet."

"No?" He was looking at her thoughtfully. "Who was it you met up with on your way out here?"

"We didn't actually meet up. It was a girl called Dusty, I think, at Tyrone Park."

"Justine O'Boyle," he said, a watchfulness in his gray eyes. "What'd she say?"

"Oh, that she'd be over after the border muster. Something like that."

"Very interesting. Well, you hang on till the border muster, Keitha, and then you come along too. Will you do that for me?"

Keitha looked at him curiously. "Why should I do anything for you, Bill?"

He shrugged. "Please yourself."

Keitha relented. "I'll come if I'm still on the property. Will that do?"

As she turned away, she almost collided with Dane, who took her arm and drew her into the shade of some mango trees. "You're a trier, aren't you?" he remarked. "I just wanted to remind you to leave me a forwarding address—in case you forget on your way out next week. Meanwhile, enjoy yourself if you're able. You have what you wanted, don't you?"

Keitha returned his stare unblinkingly. "Yes, I do, thank you."

"Well, chew hard on it. It's all part of sunny Queensland."

On that inconclusive note they parted.

CHAPTER FIVE

It was sundown when they reached the outstation, bumping over the track across the yellow plain. Keitha felt some slight misgiving during the long journey. What on earth had she let herself in for this time? Martin would be sure his judgment of her was correct. And that judgment seemed to be shared by Dane Langley. She could feel Patty Drummond's antagonism toward her in her very silence, but nevertheless she was prepared to make the best of what she had opted for. She had no idea of Melanie's feelings. Mellie just didn't seem particularly interested in her, which was a pity, because she thought Melanie would be a nice girl if one got to know her.

She sat alone in the back seat and neither of the others addressed her at all, though now and again Patty made some remark to her daughter in a low tone. Now they were almost 50 miles from Wayaway. Fifty miles from Kate and Dane Langley. Keitha had no idea what to expect of the next week, but she hoped that, at the end of it, she would still be there. Dane had been right when he said she liked to win her battles.

When they arrived at the homestead all thoughts were driven out of her head. It was sundown and the sky was full of birds. They swarmed like leaves driven by the wind, filling the sky as they wheeled and screeched and settled; in the trees, in the long spiky straw-colored grasses, in the shallow waters of the lagoon above which, on a long low ridge, the homestead was perched.

Climbing from the car, Keitha forgot everything else in her pleasure in the scene. She was eager to see the house, which was obviously different from Wayaway, for it was built up on high piles, so that its upper veranda looked out over treetops to the lagoon that provided the house and garden with water. Keitha took her own luggage and moved with the others toward the garden gate where they encountered a broad-shouldered, suntanned man of average height, wearing the narrow gabardine slacks and checked shirt that were so familiar in the Outback.

"Hi, Col!" cried Melanie cheerily, and Patty Drummond said, "I'm glad you're in, Colin. Were you expecting us?"

"Sure. I listened in on the transceiver yesterday and heard the news. Hoped you'd come home today."

He smiled at Keitha in an inquiring way, and Patty said shortly, "This is Miss Godwin, Colin. Miss Godwin, this is our overseer, Mr. Andrews. Miss Godwin has come to help in the house," she added.

Keitha noted that. She had suspected it would come to "helping in the house." She liked the look of the overseer at once. He had a good-humored face and an easygoing manner; his eyes were blue and honest and friendly.

"How're things at Wayaway? I must have a talk with Dane about what size mob he wants for the sales."

"I can tell you about that, Col," babbled Melanie as they all went inside.

The homestead was old, but it was comfortable, pleasant, and airy. Upstairs the bedrooms and two bathrooms opened off a wide veranda that overlooked the lagoon. Downstairs were the office and a big living room with a cool green cement floor and cotton floor rugs. Green ferns in huge pots added a soft note. Mango, papaw trees, and leafy vines clustered closely around the veranda so that the light was cool, green, and subdued. The kitchen was in a separate building connected to the house by a covered passage, as at Wayaway, but here there was no Mrs. Dimmick. Mrs. Drummond cooked for the homestead, and the workers had their own quarters with their own cook.

Col Andrews undertook to show Keitha the ropes while

Patty and Melanie went upstairs to unpack and to change. Patty had said casually, "You might as well start straight in, Miss Godwin, and show us what sort of a job you can make of getting dinner."

Though Keitha knew very well this was not what she had been engaged to do, she fell in with Mrs. Drummond's wishes agreeably.

Col gave her some welcome help and advice, but it was not a chore. There was plenty of steak in the refrigerator and plenty of fresh vegetables and fruit from the homestead garden that Col told her was looked after by an old man called Tucker.

Col was inclined to be apologetic about her having to get dinner her first night, but Keitha told him cheerfully that it was the way she liked it. She didn't want to sit around and be waited on.

"I had no idea you were coming," he admitted. "You'll be able to cope all right, though. Some of the girls help in the house doing cleaning, laundry, and kitchen work. They don't do any of the cooking; you'll have to manage that yourself. You'll soon get your bearings." He looked as though he would like to ask her a few questions about herself but was too polite.

Keitha decided that the status quo suited her admirably. With definite work to be done, she had more of a chance of making a success of her job and pleasing Patty Drummond.

That night Patty went to bed early, and Melanie messed around downstairs, playing snatches of melodies on the piano, or spinning around on the stool to listen to what Col was saying to Keitha as he answered her questions about the outstation. She did not join in the conversation, but there was a curious listening look on her face. Keitha couldn't really make Melanie out. She decided she would have to reserve judgment until she knew her better. Perhaps Mellie was doing that too.

Outside in the warm dark of the night, the stockmen were in from camp and could be heard singing and laughing along at their quarters. Fires burned against the blackness of the plains, and tiny bright sparks floated upward. Keitha stood for a while on the downstairs veranda before she finally went up to her room. Mrs. Drummond had told her she must get the overseer's breakfast for him in the morning, and that he started work soon after daybreak. Mrs. Drummond, of course, didn't want breakfast till much later.

Keitha made her early start the next day. It wasn't so long after Col had gone that Mellie came downstairs. She was dressed in black jeans and high-heeled boots, and wore a man's broad-brimmed hat on her head. She told Keitha after she had eaten, "I'm going out on the run. I'll have lunch with the men."

Keitha felt a spasm of envy. But there was plenty for her to do, she discovered. Patty Drummond issued orders all day. It looked as though she expected Keitha to take over the entire running of the household. Well, it would be good training for—something, Keitha supposed, and she was not going to complain. She might be a city girl, but she could pull her weight anywhere.

"Don't let the servants put anything over on you—watch everything they do and let them know you're watching. They'd far sooner play than work," Patty said. She lounged about on the shady veranda and later went outside to water her garden plants.

The days were all much the same—and very different from the days at the Wayaway homestead. Keitha liked the Aborigine girls who were full of a sense of fun and liable to go into fits of giggles for no reason that she could see. She found time to go over to their quarters once or twice to see the babies and play for a while with the older ones. Those of school age were sent to live on the mission station during term time.

Keitha would have liked to saddle up one of the many horses and ride out to the waterhole that was being mustered, but she was given no time for that. About the only task that she was not expected to take over was that of listening in to the daily radio schedules. The transceiver was in the office downstairs, and while Col or Mellie took the early morning schedule, Patty dealt with the others. One afternoon she came out of the office just as Keitha, who had been down to the vegetable garden to see why Tucker had not sent any beans to the kitchen, came into the living room.

"Sit down, Miss Godwin," Patty said. "I want to talk to you." She was wearing a finely striped red and white dress that emphasized her youthful figure. She looked very attractive as she arranged herself gracefully in a cane lounger. Not for the first time, Keitha thought it was a pity she should be living such an isolated and lonely life. She should marry again. But who would she meet out here?

"Shall I make the tea first?" she asked.

"Tea can wait a few minutes." Patty waited till Keitha was seated, then told her, "I've been talking to Wayaway. They want to know how you are getting on here."

"Dane wanted to know?"

"Dane deputised Kate to inquire," said Patty chillingly.

"Of course. I understand." Keitha flushed faintly. She had sounded so eager. "What did you tell them?"

"What could I tell them? That you are being kept busy. But I shall be quite frank with you, Miss Godwin. I can very well do without you. Of course while you are here you must earn the wages that Wayaway is paying you, but I want to remind you that the week is nearly over." She paused as if expecting Keitha to say something.

"What do you mean?" Keitha asked at last.

"This is not your kind of work, is it? And it's not your kind of life."

"I like the life very much," said Keitha firmly. "And I can manage the work."

"In your fashion," was the chilling response. "But you're far too lax with the house girls. They're laughing and chattering all day long these days."

"I'm sorry," said Keitha thinking the criticism was not altogether just.

"You see, you were not born to this life. Now Mellie. Mellie was born on Wayaway and couldn't live anywhere else. She will make an ideal cattleman's wife."

"And now we come to the point of this conversation," thought Keitha. Patty Drummoned still seemed to have the idea that Dane was the great attraction and wanted to get rid of her on that account.

"Of course, it's a foregone conclusion that Dane and Mellie will marry. It's only because Mellie is so young that nothing has yet been said. She is only 18, you know, and Dane wants to give her time to settle down after her years away at boarding school in Brisbane. She misses her father terribly. When he died she was so afraid that we would have to live on the coast. Dane wouldn't hear of it. Luckily we had a wonderfully competent head stockman in Colin Andrews. He was promoted to overseer. It's made it a very happy situation for all of us. I want to keep it that way." She looked across at Keitha from under heavy lids.

"Of course you do," said Keitha mildly. She stood up. "I'll get the tea now."

She went out to the kitchen. Tucker had brought in some beans and the kitchen girls, Mary and Pearlie, were already stringing them. Even if they were giggling together they were hard at it. Keitha didn't really see that there was any cause to complain. As she made the tea, she thought of all that Patty Drummond had said to her, and of those final words—"I want to keep it that way." Meaning the happy situation. Why did she need to worry if Dane was going to marry Mellie—if he was just waiting for her to grow up? Big, beautiful, bouncing Mellie, who still had so much of the gaucheness and uncertainty of a schoolgirl about her.

That night after dinner, Keitha walked through the garden beyond the papaw trees and sat looking dreamily over the still waters of the lagoon. There was an awesomeness in the hugeness of the night out here. Behind her the lights from the homestead shone softly. Mellie was playing the piano rather badly, and Patty Drummond was looking through a fashion book because she was planning a new dress for Mellie. One of the bedrooms upstairs was fitted out as a sewing room. In the camphor-wood box there were several dress lengths of beautiful expensive materials.

As Keitha sat there wrapped up in her thoughts, Colin Andrews came through the garden and stopped a few feet away from her. He was smoking a cigarette, and the tip glowed red in the warm darkness.

"Hi, Keitha. Not asleep, are you?"

"Daydreaming," she said with a laugh, pleased at the thought of company. She had felt comfortable right from the start with this honest straightforward Australian. "That is, if one can daydream at night."

"You can daydream any time you like. I do it when I'm rounding up cattle. Leads me into a bit of strife at times, I can tell you. Feel like a walk, or are you too lazy?"

She rose with alacrity. "I'd love a walk. To tell the truth, I'm a bit afraid to walk too far by myself at night."

"Then let me escort you." As they left the garden and walked down from the ridge to the lagoon, she asked him lightly, "What do you daydream about when you're rounding up the cattle, Colin?"

"The usual thing," he said. "Girls."

She didn't know if he was teasing or not. He had a very Australian sense of humor and was a great one at leg-pulling.

"Any girl in particular?"

"You're not fishing for a compliment, are you?"

"I could be," she joked.

"I'll make a deal with you. You tell me your day-dreams, and I'll tell you mine. Just now, for instance—" His arm went lightly around her waist as he spoke and drew her gently toward him. They had stopped on the grassy margin of the lagoon in the deeper darkness of a river gum. Keitha, looking up, could see the pale blur of his face above her, the lips curved in a smile, the white teeth glinting.

"You'll think you've made a poor bargain," she said. "My mind was occupied with the various people who live on this cattle run—I was turning over the pages and looking at them all as if they were picture portraits."

"And where did you linger the longest? I'll make a guess—"

"Now who's fishing for compliments?"

She saw the surprise plain on his face, then he laughed. "I may be a conceited sort of bloke, but I'm up against some pretty stiff competition in this outfit. I have yet to meet the girl who'll drool over me when she can drool over the boss."

"The boss?" Now they were both leaning against the broad trunk of the tree, his arm was still around her waist; her face still turned up to his. "Why would I be drooling over the boss? From what I hear, there are too many girls at it already."

"True. Oh, very true."

"And who's going to win him?" She didn't know what made her ask, but now they had started talking about Dane she felt a compulsion to go on.

"It's not a case of who's going to win him, my good

girl—it's a case of who he is going to choose. . . . And my money's on Mellie."

"Really?" Mellie certainly seemed to be first favorite hereabouts. She was going to ask him to elucidate, but there was no need. He was well away.

"The boss could have sent the Drummonds off the place after Bruce died, but he didn't. Guess why not?. . . . Mellie's just the girl for a cattleman; she loves riding and working the cattle, she can talk sense about the whole show, and she takes an intelligent interest in the business side of it. She has the constitution of an ox, and as well she's beautiful, wholesome, and enduring."

Keitha listened to him in surprise. Did he really sound as if he were more than a little in love with Mellie himself, or was she imagining it? She hazarded a guess. "Is it Mellie you daydream about, Col?"

He laughed ruefully. "I guess so. But believe me, they're only daydreams. I haven't a chance. There's a pecking order out here and the boss has first peck. And rightly so. Besides that, he's top of the popularity poll. There's a lot of girls going to stay single until he's married and then—wham! There'll be weddings all over the Gulf Country."

"You mean," said Keitha, not believing it, "that other men will be content to be second best?"

He looked thoughtful. "It's not exactly like that. Dane represents a sort of ideal, I guess. It's the thing for the girls to set their sights on him. But once a girl knows for sure she's out of the running, she accepts what's in her reach and is perfectly happy I reckon."

"How do you know all this, Col?"

"Because I'm the brotherly type—girls confide in me. And I kiss 'em and comfort 'em—like this."

His arms went around her, and he had kissed her gently on the lips when there was a sound beyond the trees and Mellie was there.

"What on earth are you two doing?" She sounded cross. "I've made a jug of fruit punch—from a recipe I got from Jen Palmer at Mary Creek. Are you coming in to sample it, or aren't you?" She was down beside them now. Col put out his free arm and gathered her in beside him.

"Sure we're coming to sample it. Aren't we, Keitha? Just so long as it's not a love potion you're offering us—"

"You don't need a love potion, by the look of you," said Mellie, pulling away from him.

"Cut that out now, young Mellie. And don't go spreading rumors that aren't true. Keitha and I have been exchanging life stories and offering each other a consolation kiss."

"Why does Keitha need a consolation kiss?" asked Mellie suspiciously.

"Maybe because she thinks she's failed to fascinate the boss."

"Not true, Mellie," said Keitha lightly. "I'm one girl who hasn't even tried."

The boss let it be known through Kate over the transceiver the following morning that he would be at the outstation for dinner and would stay the night.

"Get Dolly to make up the bed and prepare the room for him," Patty told Keitha. "And I hope you've planned a suitable dinner for tonight."

Keitha felt tense and excited. She had planned a special fried chicken dish; one that Donn particularly liked. As an accompaniment there were to be baked potatoes with sour cream and a simple side salad of lettuce and tomato with an Italian dressing. Now when she thought of it, it seemed a little pretentious. Would Dane Langley think she was trying to impress him—and in a way that did not only concern her work? Tommorrow was mail day, and that of course was why he was coming. He had told

Keitha that she would not suit Patty Drummond, and he was right, though efficiency had nothing to do with it. As sure as could be, she was going to be packed off on that plane tomorrow. This time it seemed there was nothing she could do about it. . . .

When everything for dinner was under control, she went down to the lagoon to watch the birds coming in for their evening drink. This would probably be her very last chance to do that, and she found the thought unexpectedly depressing. She wanted to stay on the Wayaway cattle run more than she had ever wanted anything in her life. That was surprising. Did she want it more than she wanted Donn to ask her to marry him? Or did it seem like that simply because England was so far away?

It was a beautiful sky tonight, the colors so pure and limpid that they seemed to flood her innermost being. There was a very deep spiritual value in watching the Outback sunset. It gave one a sense of awe, wonder, and uplift.

Among the birds that came in were four brolgas. They flew down to the lagoon clumsily, necks outstretched, long legs trailing as they landed. They were big birds, four or five feet tall with an amusingly grave air about them as they paraded together, long necks arched, small gray wings folded neatly. Keitha hoped they might dance, but she had heard that mainly happened after rain, so she was not very hopeful. She stood watching them with deep interest, forgetting the galahs, cockatoos, parrots, and the myriad small birds, until their screeching and the beating of their wings as they rose into the air once more in hundreds startled her anew.

When the sky had paled, she went back to the homestead, thinking once more of Dane. She was in the kitchen putting the finishing touches to the dinner with the help of Mary and Pearlie, whose admiring glances at the pretty salad and the brown potatoes split ready to receive their dollop of cream made her want to laugh, when she heard the Land Rover. Immediately her heart began to pound.

She heard his voice a few minutes later as she walked down the covered way to the living room. That voice—after less than a week—did very strange things to her. One hand went up to smooth the dark hair from her forehead. She hoped the heat of the kitchen hadn't put too much of a flush in her normally pale cheeks. She could feel the brightness of her eyes. What on earth was wrong with her? She was ready for battle, of course!—ready to assert herself, to get her own way. But she was afraid it was going to be a losing battle this time.

A pink-shaded lamp shone from the table, and another soft lamp by the sofa cast its light on Patty Drummond, half lying there and looking very attractive in an off-white pants suit. Mellie sprawled in a chair as usual, one hand idly pulling a fern to pieces. She was still in her jeans and a crumpled shirt. And Dane—

They all looked up as Keitha came in, a graceful slim girl with shining dark hair. She was bare-legged, her narrow feet encased in blue sandals. She wore her favorite jewel colors—peacock blue and emerald green in a soft cotton print that had an exotic eastern look about it.

"Well, hello! You look thriving for a girl who's being bugged by her responsibilities." It was Dane's drawling half amused voice. "I hear you've been having some trouble managing the girls."

Keitha blinked, met his eyes, and wished she hadn't. She had best stay away from those electric blue eyes that were always enigmatically screwed up, sunlight or not. If a man like that had asked her to be his mistress, she might have been helpless to refuse. With an effort she pulled herself together and took in what had been said. She didn't want to make a liar of Patty Drummond, so she said with a careless smile, "It hasn't worried me really. . . . Shall I serve dinner, Mrs. Drummond?"

"It might be an idea. We're all waiting." Patty sounded petulantly reproachful—as if, thought Keitha, dinner was late, which it was not at all.

"Very well." As she went, she heard the reprimand in Patty Drummond's voice as she said irritably, "I wish you'd change when you come in, Mellie. You don't do yourself justice. Go and get into something pretty and fresh—it's not as if you had no clothes—"

Mellie was in a yellow concoction that was very flattering to her figure when they sat down to dinner. Colin, unfolding his starched white table napkin, remarked, "Mellie's looking particularly glamorous tonight."

"She is indeed," agreed Dane. The two men eyed Mellie, who widened her eyes and looked almost schoolgirlishly from one to the other.

Keitha took her seat and the girls brought in the dishes.

"Mmm—the cooking's good," Dane remarked presently. "I must congratulate you, Patty. You've trained those girls to within an inch of their lives. Keitha can't have done much harm so far."

"I never let the girls do the cooking," said Patty. And failed to add that it was Keitha who had cooked the dinner.

"Terrific," pronounced Colin. "Must be a special occasion to warrant fare like this." He looked at Keitha, and she shrugged slightly. Patty had silently accepted credit for the dinner, so it was for her to explain the occasion. She helped herself to salad, and Patty changed the subject. She wondered what the Warner girls were up to over at the coast.

"Grace spoils those girls of hers. I often wish she'd married a cattleman instead of an architect. It's a much more wholesome life out here than the one they lead."

"Oh, they're nice girls," said Dane offhandedly. "What did you think, Keitha?"

She blushed as he turned his gaze on her and drew her deliberately into the conversation. "Yes," she agreed awkwardly. "I liked them very much."

"So you're a friend of the family, are you?" This was Colin, and Keitha could not help thinking how much easier he was in his manner when the boss was there. Patty was inclined to treat him with a trace of patronage, but Dane treated him exactly as an equal.

"I thought you'd have discovered that before, Col," said Dane sardonically. "I've been hearing about the long hours you and Keitha spend together down by the lagoon."

Mellie flushed and reached for the salad bowl. Dane added, exonerating her, "I can always depend on Patty to pass on all the news."

Keitha was furious. The long hours she spent with Col! That was more than mere exaggeration. She wondered what else Patty had told Dane to her disadvantage.

Zabaglione followed the chicken and was praised by the men. Keitha went to the kitchen to make the coffee. The others had installed themselves outside under the starry sky when she brought the tray.

Tonight there was a moon, a small slip of a moon that slid into the vastness of the sky like a golden arc. Col wandered off when he had finished his coffee, and Dane called after him, "I'll be with you later, Col." He turned to Keitha. "Now this bit of business that's brought me over here— What do I do about you, Keitha Godwin?"

Keitha felt Patty looking at her hard and saw her pretty mouth curve unkindly. She almost expected to hear her demand that Dane send her back to the coast, but that was not the way things were done in the boss's kingdom. And after all, she had paved the way very nicely. She had told Dane that Keitha couldn't contend with the kitchen girls, insinuated that she was playing around with the overseer, and who knew what else? The result was pretty well a foregone conclusion.

Unconsciously she sighed. "Well, what do you do about me, Mr. Langley?"

Suddenly she thought she saw the glint of laughter in his eyes. He put his cap aside, stood up and said gravely, "I think we'd better go into the office. Will you excuse us, Patty?"

CHAPTER SIX

"So you think too much is expected of you, do you?" he asked two minutes later when she was sitting opposite him in the office.

"Not at all," contradicted Keitha with spirit. "I don't mind the work at all—I certainly didn't expect to be paid for sitting around doing nothing."

He was watching her steadily, his eyes crinkled, that mobile mouth curved in an enigmatic smile. Keitha could not keep her eyes off him—the lines beside his eyes, the sunbleached hair that was a little too long and a little untidy, the jutting chin; and that mouth— She lowered her lashes defensively to give herself a chance to regain her senses.

"The dinner tonight was superb," he said after a moment. "Who prepared it, Miss Godwin? For I'll swear it wasn't Patty Drummond."

Miss Godwin! What had become of "honey"? Or was this the boss's way of intimating that this was strictly a business interview?—though it was an odd one at that.

"I prepared it, Mr. Langley."

"You did, Mr. Langley," he mocked. "Well, there's a point in your favour. You can cook. I wouldn't mind a taste of your cooking over at Wayaway. Mrs. Dimmick is a fine plain cook, and Kate, when she puts her mind to it, can turn out a hearty banquet. But you're in a class of your own. . . . What did you say you did in television?"

"I was a producer's assistant," said Keitha. His praise was sweet, yet she felt uneasily that it was not altogether deserved. She too was a fairly plain cook, but it happened that there were one or two dishes that she had worked on to please Donn on the occasions when he had asked her to play hostess at his dinner parties.

"What do you do in your free time?—here, I mean."

She nearly asked, "What free time?" but said instead, "I go down by the lagoon and watch the birds—talk to the women over at the stockmen's quarters—"

"And at night you seek out the overseer. Is that it?"

Her brows lifted. "I haven't made a habit of it. Why? Is there any law against it?"

"No law. I just like to check up on what's going on." He glanced at his hands, clasped before him on the desk. Tonight he wore a white shirt and a tie with his dark slacks, and his rakish good looks were very much underlined. She was watching him again, her eyes moving over his face slowly, when he looked up, disconcerting her.

"Are you ready to leave us yet?"

She flushed at the unexpected question. "No. I'm quite happy."

"For how long? When do you mean to go back to whatever—or whoever—you left behind in London?"

"I have no immediate plans," said Keitha. And she reflected that this was very true.

He laughed mockingly. "You aren't very forthcoming. Too evasive by far. . . . I have a notion I'm asking for trouble if I don't chuck you out right away." He pushed back his chair abruptly. "All the same, we'll have another round. . . . By the way, have you reached any agreement with Patty about taking time off?"

She shook her head. "There didn't seem any need," she said frankly.

"Then I suggest a free day tomorrow." He got up, signifying that the interview was at an end, and waited at the door for her to pass through. She felt dazed—incredulous. Her confusion was the only excuse she could find later for what she said then.

"Thank you, Donn."

His eyebrows tilted, and he looked displeased. "The name's Dane, honey."

She was scarlet and could have bitten her tongue.

She didn't see him again till the following morning, for he left her then to find Colin. In the living room Mellie was messing about disconsolately with the piano and Patty was reading—or pretending to. She looked up frowning, when Keitha came in.

Keitha said cheerfully, "Dane says I'm to stay."

There was a second's silence—except that Mellie went on picking out a melancholy little tune in the treble.

"Oh? Then if that's what you want, I suppose you must think yourself very lucky," said Patty. "How do you manage to persuade people to let you have your own way, Miss Godwin?"

"I really wouldn't know," said Keitha with truth.

In the morning at breakfast, Dane told Patty he thought Keitha had earned a day off. "You've certainly been seeing to it that she earns her wages," he added.

Patty frowned. "I think Miss Godwin's been misleading you. I've been doing as much as she does and a lot more besides for many years now." She went on quickly, "I thought Mellie might go over to Wayaway with you today, Dane, and possibly stay a night or two."

"I want Keitha to come with me," he said implacably, and Keitha gave a little start of surprise and knew a feeling of pleasure. "Besides, Mellie won't want to miss her day at the muster. How's it going, Mellie? Is Col teaching you to be a good stockman?"

"I *am* a good stockman, Dane," protested Mellie. "I'm just as good as some of your ringers, I can tell you."

"I'll check up on that some time. Meanwhile, no showing off or taking idiotic chances. You hear me?"

"I hear you, Dane," agreed Mellie. "But I've been riding all my life and—"

"Maybe you have, but you don't know everything, and don't you forget it."

Patty came out to the Land Rover when Dane and Keitha were leaving.

"I hope Miss Godwin will be home this evening, Dane. I shall need her in the morning."

Dane gave a grin. "Is she becoming so indispensable already? I'll send her back, Patty, never fear." There was irony in his tone. Of course he knew that it was not because she was indispensable that Patty wanted her back. She simply couldn't bear the idea of her being over at the Wayaway homestead when Mellie wasn't there.

As they drove along the track out on the plain, Dane said, "Kate's looking forward to a visit from you, honey. She's rather taken to the little English girl."

"Has she? I'm flattered. I like Kate very much—even if she is rather too devoted to the boss," she couldn't stop herself from adding.

He tossed her a glance. "No doubt you're devoted to someone too. Tell me, honey—who do you put on a pedestal? I would really like to know."

"Not you," she said instantly, and he laughed heartily.

"I didn't think you did. You parried that question very nicely, Miss Godwin." He didn't press it, but changed the subject. "Here's a direction: don't spend so much of your time with Col Andrews when you're back at the outstation."

"The rules are certainly very strict in the Gulf Country," remarked Keitha. "I suppose it's no use assuring you I haven't spent much time at all with Colin. Where, by the way, do I go for masculine company if I want it?"

He gave her a sharp look. "Do you want it? If so—to me," he said with a glint in his eye.

Keitha managed a faint laugh and retorted acidly, "Not for me! From what I hear, all the girls for miles around go to you if they have the chance, Dane. I don't intend to stand in a line-up and wait my turn anywhere."

"Well, it's up to you," he agreed laconically. "But there are times when it may be worthwhile to wait in a line-up."

"Perhaps. Still, I'm a very long way from the line, aren't I?"

"Fifty miles?" He looked at her with amused surprise. "Fifty miles is nothing, honey. A little matter of distance isn't going to put anyone off—though there are those who think it an advantage to shorten it, and forget that sometimes distance lends enchantment. What do you think? Or do you incline to the view that distance puts things in their right perspective?"

It was odd that he should say just that. She thought of Donn and wondered whether for him distance had lent enchantment, as she had hoped it would. She was beginning to suspect that for her it had not. She didn't think of him nearly so much these days as she had when she first left England. She said briefly, "I haven't given it much thought."

They drove on in silence for some distance. Keitha did not find the landscape monotonous, though there was certainly a sameness about it. Around the waterholes, cattle were always gathered or lying in the shade of trees. There was something mesmeric about it all—the stillness, the heat, the brilliant sunshine, and the huge all-embracing sky that grew almost colorless as the day wore on. She watched for birds, cattle, and the occasional kangaroo that came loping through the trees or across the plain. She forgot the man beside her in her intense scrutiny of the Wayaway lands.

There was a rhythm here, a rhythm of distance and line; a feeling of harmony and meaningfulness. They moved slowly along the track. No racing along at 50 or 60 miles an hour here. It would take them two hours at the very least to reach Wayaway homestead. Two hours alone with Dane Langley. Keitha though of the letter she had written to Donn—"My boss here is immensely attractive physically—one of those overwhelmingly magnetic personalities. You know? But as an individual he doesn't attract me at all. He's so assured, so wrapped up in his own world, so certain about the way life should proceed. And so very, very arrogant." She and Donn had always talked to each other frankly about the people they met, but Keitha had never met anyone in the least like Dane Langley before. She could not come to grips with her feelings for him at all. She wondered if what she had written to Donn was altogether true. As an individual, didn't Dane attract her at all? Weren't his self-assurance, his devotion to the world of Wayaway, even, perhaps his arrogance, very necessary to a man in his position? Perhaps too his world was not so strictly limited as she was inclined to think. He had a bungalow north of Cairns and an apartment in Sydney. Then again, she had known him for only a couple of weeks—excluding, of course, their first brief encounter on the coral island.

Two weeks! It seemed impossible. Perhaps that week she had spent going around the run with him had counted for far more than a week. Yes, she was sure that it had. They might not have exchanged so much in the way of personal confidences, but something had definitely developed between them. There was some sort of a rapport. A crystal had been formed. She thought of that star that had pierced the sky one evening after sundown at Wayaway. And she remembered how Kate had said last mail day, "If he had wanted you, he'd have found you." Hadn't he then, really wanted to send her away?

She stole a glance at him, trusting that her sunglasses would shield her.

He acknowledged her glance at once. "By the way, honey, I meant to remind you to bring along any mail you wanted sent. Or have you put it all in the outstation mail-bag?"

"I have another letter in my purse," she admitted—it was the one to Donn. "I put a couple in the mailbag as well."

"You've been busy communicating, have you? Who do you write to? That aunt of yours in England? Your brother at the coast?"

"That's right," said Keitha. "You have a good memory."

There was a pause. "Another little matter I meant to bring up—that slip of the tongue last night. I object to being called by another man's name, and I had the distinct impression you called me Don. Am I right? Do you know someone called Don?"

"Donn Gorsky is my boss in London," said Keitha, conscious that she had flushed. There was, after all, that letter in her purse. She didn't imagine for a moment that he wouldn't look to see who it was addressed to if he wanted to. He would be quite open about it.

"Is? Or was?"

"If I go back, the job will be there."

"If you go back? Is there some doubt about it, then? I thought it was quite decided. Or have you changed your mind somewhat since that day on the island?"

"Heavens!" said Keitha, her color deepening. "You're as bad as a four-year-old child with all your questions.

"Some people have to be questioned before they'll give of themselves. In the Outback we share freely—we don't have to tear the truth and the humanity out of each other with a barrage of questions. "We're honest with each other. We know where we stand."

"It sounds wonderful," said Keitha sceptically. "But I'm afraid I'm far from convinced. I haven't been here long, but I know already that everyone's wondering what you are up to. There seem to be a good many girls in your life—or on the fringe of it. But perhaps that's your way of sharing."

He gave an amused grin. "I didn't know you were so involved with local gossip. Do you listen in to the galah sessions?"

"No. I haven't been included in those."

"We'll have to remedy that. Unless you're set on heading back to England. I don't think you really answered my question about that. Are you by any chance in love with your boss?"

For a second she imagined he was referring to himself and her thoughts whirled. Then she got her bearings again and parried the question lightly.

"Falling in love with the boss is a cliché. You told me that once yourself, and you should know."

There was something exasperated in the short silence that followed. "You're too elusive by half," he said at last. He sounded displeased. "Then will you at least tell me why you came so far from home?"

That was easy enough. "I was suffering slightly from overwork," she told him cheerfully, minimizing the situation. "I needed a break, and Martin—my brother—asked me to come and stay here for a while. He seemed to think my aunt needed the break as badly as I did," she finished wryly.

"I see. And that's all you're going to tell me, is it?"

"What more do you want?"

"Oh, I want a great deal more. However, I see that I'm not going to get it just now. But I'll persevere. I generally succeed in finding out anything I really want to know."

Keitha could believe that. But she was far from ready to tell her life story to anybody. She was certainly not going to confess that the main reason for coming so far from home was to force Donn Gorsky either to forget her, or to forget his unconventional ideals about relationships between men and women! So far, he had shown no signs of forgetting her, yet she, distracted by a new and totally unfamiliar way of living, seemed at times in danger of forgetting him almost completely.

"On consideration," said Dane, interrupting her thoughts, "I think it might be a good idea if mail day brought you and me together each week. You can't have anything special to do on your day off, Kate will be pleased to see you, and you and I can get to know each other better. Does that appeal to you at all? Or would you rather we forgot it?"

He looked at her with that fiery intense glance, slowing the car almost to a halt, and waited for her answer. Truth to tell, the idea appealed to her very much and her heart was beating fast. But she forced herself to say coolly, "You're the boss, Mr. Langley!" and left him to make what he could of that.

Kate seemed genuinely pleased to see her when they reached the homestead. Over lunch Keitha mentioned that she would like to buy one or two of her paintings if they were for sale. Kate protested that they would be a gift and promised to pick out some bird and plant studies very soon. Keitha felt she was pleased at her enthusiasm and found it a little sad that she should be so pleased. Had she no idea just how attractive her studies were?

It was a question she put to Dane when she went out to the airstrip with him to meet the mail plane.

"Doesn't Kate place any value on the work she does?"

He gave her an astonished look. "That question strikes me as being singularly naïve. Painting is like breathing to Kate. It's as important as that—and as natural. I thought I told you long ago that she's a creative person."

Long ago. Less than two weeks. Yet it was long ago. It was in another life time.

"You did," said Keitha. "But—other people—do they appreciate her work? Do they tell her how much they like it; how talented she is?"

"You want to be special, do you, honey?" he asked ironically. "Don't fool yourself. Kate's pictures hang in living rooms, hallways, and bedrooms all over the Gulf Country. Everyone wants to own a painting Kate has done. Christmas time she gives with abandon."

Keitha felt chastened. Still, Kate had been pleased at her praise.

"Maybe we're not what you'd call a cultured lot," said Dane. "But we do appreciate what's our own. You'll find stockmen, fencers, and drovers—yes, and cattlemen like me—quoting Henry Lawson and Banjo Paterson all over the place. Same way, we like what Kate does. But we don't protest too much about it. Kate knows what we think. And she's humble and unassuming, which is a good way to be when you've been given a talent and you're using it."

They were almost at the airstrip now. It was a thrill for Keitha to watch the plane coming down and to be actually in the station car as it raced in its cloud of dust over the track and pulled up alongside. The freight officer recognized her and greeted her cheerfully. She peered into the aircraft to see who was aboard. It was as if she belonged, as if she were really part of the great Outback. The freight was collected, and the little ceremony of the mailbags gone through. Later, as they drove back to the homestead, she asked Dane, "By the way, did you get the message the day I arrived from a girl called Dusty?"

"Dusty?" He looked puzzled, then his brow cleared and he gave her a quizzical smile. "I like that—Dusty. You must mean Justine O'Boyle. Yes, I believe I did receive some sort of a message from her. Why? What do you know about it?"

"Nothing. I heard her talking to the pilot," Keitha admitted. She remembered quite well what Dusty—*Justine* —had said about breaking through Dane Langley's impenetrable defenses. "Will she be coming to visit Wayaway?"

"Some time for sure; she's a regular visitor," he said with a casualness that would surely not have pleased Justine had she heard it.

"What's the attraction?"

"What would you think?"

Keitha pretended to consider. "The boss, I suppose," she said finally. "You tell me Bill Sutton gives no encouragement to anyone, so I imagine it must be you."

"There's a trace of censure in your tone, Miss Godwin. Do you think I encourage her?"

"I wouldn't know really. I haven't seen you in action."

"You know," he said speculatively after the briefest of pauses, "there is something amazingly ingenuous about you after all. To make a remark like that—"

She didn't know what he was talking about.

"Well, there's Mellie," she said after a moment.

"You think I encourage Mellie?"

"Does she need your encouragement? You've known each other for a long long time—"

"So we have. I understand Mellie very well. She's a sweet girl."

Keitha would have liked to ask, "Is that all?" but could not go so far. Besides, they were back at the homestead now; the frieght had to be unloaded, and the mail sorted. She left him at the ramp in front of the store and went inside to find Kate and see what she could do to make herself useful.

They were talking together when Dane came in again. He had letters for Kate and some for Keitha.

"I'll have someone drive you back to the outstation when you've had a cup of tea," he told Keitha abruptly. He stood looking down at her as she glanced eagerly at her letters. There was one from Aunt Jane, one from Martin and four from Donn—mailed on by Martin from the coast. "You'd better get home before dark."

She didn't know if she was imagining it, but there

seemed a coolness, a remoteness in his voice. She looked up and found his eyes watching her thoughtfully. "Do you want to read all your letters now, or are you going to save some for later? You certainly have more than your share. Still, you're a long way from home."

She smiled uneasily. Somehow his words sounded strange in her ears. She didn't really feel a long way from home. . . .

Dane disappeared after saying he'd be in for tea shortly. Kate went to the office for the afternoon schedule, so Keitha read her letters. She read Donn's first. They were so distinctly love letters that they brought color to her cheeks, and for some reason exasperated her more than a little.

"I miss you with every breath I take," she read. "It's as if my life has disintegrated. When are you coming back to London?"

One thing, however, he did not say in any of the four letters, and that was, "Let's get married." Yet he knew how she felt about the other thing. She sat still and thought about him. Sometimes Bill Sutton's image got in the way, and sometimes Dane Langley's did. She concentrated hard on Donn's idiosyncrasies—the things she had loved about him. The way he chewed his lower lip when he was thinking, the way he ran his fingers through his hair so that it stood on end; the way he gnawed his knuckles, and looked at her with his eyes fixed as though he didn't see her—that was when he was working madly on some new idea. Dane never looked at you as though he didn't see you, even if his eyes were narrowed to mere slits. Those eyes saw every bit of you. They burned into you like a tongue of flame. . . . Keitha folded the pages and put them back into the envelopes and opened her other letters. Martin was seeing a lot of Julie Warner. The others were going back to Brisbane, but Julie was coming to Townsville. She was going to take the job that

Keitha had turned down. She was mad about opals, and it was apparent that Martin was mad about her.

"I hope your job's working out all right—Julie says it's sure to with her cousin Dane Langley there. She says quite likely nothing on earth will pry you away from the Gulf now."

Keitha made a face. Did absolutely everyone have to fall in love with Dane Langley? It certainly looked like it. Thank goodness she hadn't slipped yet herself, but he was getting some sort of a hold on her mind. She would have to watch it. Well, at least Martin seemed happy about her being at Wayaway now.

Aunt Jane's letter was brisk but affectionate. This silly rushing off to work in the Outback would surely cure Keitha once and for all of rushing into situations with her eyes shut. "Cooking for a lot of hungry stockmen will be very hard work, I am sure. You will be only too glad to come back to civilization. It would be sheer foolishness for you to return to your old job. In any case I hardly think it will be available. When you come back I shall help you to the best of my ability to find something that will not overtax you, you know that, dear. On the other hand if you would like to stay on with your brother I shall be very happy about that. . . ." And so on. Aunt Jane had always been fussy and over-voluble, but Keitha was fond of her just the same.

Presently Kate came back from the office, and afternoon tea was served. Though Dane joined them, Keitha had no further conversation alone with him. In no time at all she was on her way back to the outstation with one of the stockmen, a very shy man who scarcely said a word to her all the way.

She felt oddly disappointed over her visit. Yet what had she expected of it? And was it Dane's habit to—chat a girl up, as he had surely done with her, and then simply drop her? Or hadn't he dropped her? Had he been caught up mentally in station affairs? She didn't know what had happened, or if anything had happened at all.

Patty Drummond seemed pleased to have her back. She was resting in the living room. The heat had given her a sick headache, she said, and she would be relieved to have Keitha take over again. It seemed an odd attitude to adopt when she had obviously done her best to see that her helper was sent off on today's mail plane. Keitha had to delve into the work as though she had never been away.

When Mellie came home, she seemed innocently pleased to see her and inquired about Wayaway and Kate as if they were an intimate part of her family.

That night, quite by chance, she found herself sitting alone in the dark with Col. Mellie, tired out from a day in the sun, had gone to bed, and Patty, still headachy, had retired even earlier.

"Enjoy your day?" asked Col.

"Not all that much," admitted Keitha. "It was good to see Kate again—"

"How about the boss?"

She shrugged. "I don't know where I stand with him."

"Nowhere," said Col promptly. "So don't go getting any ideas."

"I'm not likely to do that," said Keitha, nettled. "Why is everyone so convinced I'm going to get what you call 'ideas'? It may amaze you to learn that I'm not so bereft of admirers that I've had to come to the Gulf Country to find one. I'm far from having taken root out here. Anyone who can manage it may have Dane Langley and welcome as far as I'm concerned. The general opinion seems to be that it will be poor Mellie—"

Col grunted. "I've lived here for over five years now. I've seen Mellie growing up, and I've seen Dane bringing her along. I know for a fact that he's never come near marrying any other girl. It's true he's a man who plays his cards pretty close to his chest, but he has his eye on Mellie all right. Now she's home from school is the crucial time. He's waiting to see how she shapes up."

"It sounds pretty cold-blooded to me," said Keitha. "I wouldn't like to be in Mellie's position if what you say is true. Tell me, Col—how do you think Mellie shapes up? You see a lot of her out on the run, don't you?"

"She shapes up pretty well," Col said.

After that they were both silent.

CHAPTER SEVEN

If Keitha had thought she would now get a bad time from Patty Drummond she was wrong. Patty was agreeable, businesslike, and appreciative of the fact that Keitha took many chores off her hands, leaving her free for her gardening. Also, she was busy now making clothes for Mellie who hadn't had much new since she left school and was ready to blossom out.

The days passed quickly enough. Mellie and Col went out on the run; Keitha and Patty were busy around the homestead most of the day. Sometimes Keitha went over to the workers' quarters to talk to the women and admire their babies; even to give advice on little ailments or matters of hygiene. Once or twice she looked thoughtfully at the two motorbikes in the garage, wishing that she could ride. They were used, as at Wayaway too, for speedy checking of waterholes and holding yards, but most days at least one of them was there in the garage.

Every evening when the stockmen came in from mustering, there was the smell of cooking. Lights gleamed in the darkness, and there were sounds of laughter and singing. At the homestead, the Drummonds, Col and Keitha got on very well together. It often struck Keitha as odd that Col should be happy with the status quo, seeing that he was in love with Mellie. She wondered if he knew many other girls in the district and wished that she could listen to the voices on the galah session. But for some reason, Patty never invited her. It seemed a silent underlining of the fact that Keitha was an outsider—didn't really belong and never would. Even though Wayaway frequently talked with the outstation, Patty rarely passed on any news.

All through the week, Keitha was looking forward to

mail day when she would see Dane. He had practically promised her that. The thought stimulated her and made her restless too, for she could not make up her mind what her feelings toward the boss were. She certainly didn't intend to join his band of admirers. She had learned a chastening lesson from him last time they met when she had more or less glowed under his attention and then, for no apparent reason, been pushed aside and treated with extreme casualness. This time she might give him a little of his own treatment—turn on the charm and when he had warmed to it, turn it off again. Yes, she thought that would give her quite a deal of satisfaction. She was sure it was not the sort of thing the boss of Wayaway was used to.

Late in the week, Patty asked her into the sewing room upstairs to consult her about a dress she was planning for Mellie. She showed her the design she had roughed out and asked how Keitha thought it compared with London fashions.

"I suppose we are behind the times here," said Patty, "though not so much as we used to be. I have fashion magazines sent out in the mail. I order dress materials from Brisbane, or buy them in Sydney if we go there with Dane during the Wet. Parties do crop up occasionally even Outback, and I like Mellie to have something unusual and attractive. Now what do you think of this style—with Mellie in mind?"

They discussed the style at some length, and Keitha suggested a minor alteration that seemed to please the older woman. Patty then produced two dress lengths from the camphor-wood chest and asked Keitha's opinion as to which would suit Mellie best.

"Dane would probably prefer the blue," Patty said. "It's a color men are inclined to favor, don't you think? I suppose the muted pink and mauve is more fashionable, but I think I shall have to make that up for myself. It wouldn't really do anything for Mellie's healthy beauty." She smiled at Keitha. "This must all be a little boring for you. You worked in the television world; didn't you? I expect there's a fair bit of interest in dress there."

"A fair bit," Keitha agreed.

"And in men too? I mean, it must be a competitive field where men are concerned?"

Keitha, not sure what she was talking about, agreed vaguely that it was.

"You didn't come to Queensland because of an unhappy love affair?" The brown eyes watched her shrewdly while the slender hands were busy folding the dress fabrics.

"No," said Keitha with a smile.

"I hardly thought so. You don't look like a girl with a broken heart, in spite of those soulful dark eyes. But I'll admit I can't fathom you. To exchange that world for this. . . . Though of course it's only temporary, isn't it?"

"Of course," agreed Keitha smoothly. "I'm sure you won't need me here once your nerves have settled down."

Mrs. Drummond grimaced. "You think I'm neurotic, which I'm not. But there's a lot of adjusting needed when one is widowed. Dane has made too much fuss, though. But we were talking about you. Do tell me about your work in London and the people you mixed with." Skilfully, she led the conversation so that before she knew it, Keitha was talking about Donn. It was natural enough as Donn had been the man she worked for.

"He sounds fascinating. And of course you fell in love with him?" Patty suggested with a vague smile. She had begun to draft out her pattern as she listened to Keitha. Her attention to what she was doing gave the impression that she was not listening very closely. Keitha admitted cautiously that quite a few of the girls had been in love with Donn, who was so clever and good-looking. She herself had been extremely lucky to be chosen to work for him.

"Lucky? A charming girl like you?" Patty frowned over a measurement. "I'm quite sure he must have fallen completely in love with you. Isn't that so?" She looked up and smiled in a friendly way.

"Oh, of course," Keitha said laughingly. "He was mad about me." Somewhere inside her a voice asked how she could talk so superficially about her love affair. Yet she could, and did, and it amazed her.

"And what happened?"

"Nothing happened—except that I was ordered off work for a while by the doctor."

"And when you go back you'll have your old job again? Or has someone else taken your place?"

"Only temporarily. Donn assures me he much prefers me to work for him. But of course I may not want the job."

"I see. Well, it all sounds wonderfully interesting." Patty changed the subject then, but she was extremely affable for the rest of the day.

Looking back later, Keitha was to see that conversation in a different light. At the time, it had seemed lighthearted and harmless. Patty had been politely interested, and she herself had enjoyed talking about Donn for a change. It had seemed to bring her old life back into focus again for a while. . . .

When mail day came, Keitha asked Patty casually at breakfast, "Any news from Wayaway over the early morning schedule?"

Patty looked at her in surprise. "No. What were you expecting?"

Keitha shrugged and tried to hide her disappointment. Patty watched her with a faint smile.

"You're anxious about your mail. Don't worry. One of

the stockmen has taken our mailbag over. You'll get your letters. Dane always sees that our mail is sent over, and I'm sure they all know over there that you must be longing for news."

All day Keitha felt edgy and restless, wondering if Dane would come. It seemed pointless to have a day off under the circumstances. She planned pepper steak for dinner. It was one of her best dishes, and it was possible that Dane would be at the outstation for dinner. He would enjoy her pepper steak; he was differnet from the stockmen who couldn't have cared less about fancy ways of serving up steak.

But Dane didn't come to dinner. He didn't come at all.

"You're restless, Keitha," said Patty. She had taken lately to calling the girl by her first name in a more friendly way. Keitha had wandered out onto the veranda after dinner and then come back inside again. "Don't worry, your letters will come."

Keitha was not thinking of her letters. It was Dane she wanted to see, and she was annoyed with herself because of it. Yet she couldn't seem to help herself. What had she planned for this meeting that had made it so important? To smile into his eyes through her lashes—to fascinate him absolutely—and then to walk off and show him that he didn't matter one bit to her. Was that what she wanted? She didn't know. She only knew she longed to see him. Maybe this was what happened to you in the Outback. You became obsessed with whoever was available.

When she heard the sound of a motorbike, her heart began to beat fast. She could have wept when one of the stockmen clumped heavily up onto the veranda.

"The boss said he was too busy to come over today," she heard him telling Mrs. Drummond. By that time Keitha was going blindly out into the darkness of the garden, where she could get over her disappointment, wipe away her tears of vexation, and come back able to pretend that nothing had happened to her heart.

Another ten minutes and Col came out to find her.

"Hey, Keitha—Patty says to come in for your mail. What's up? Afraid you'll be disappointed? I promise you won't. There are two letters from your boyfriend."

She gave him a sharp look. "What on earth are you talking about, Col?"

"Oh, come on, Keitha, don't get on your high horse. Everyone's private life soon becomes public property in the Outback."

"Is that a fact? It seems to me you're a very nosey lot. At all events you don't know a thing about my private life. I just wish you'd mind your own business."

"Heck, I sure have touched you off! Sorry, I didn't mean to tread on your toes. Not another word will I utter."

Keitha stalked past him. She felt a little ashamed of her outburst. Col had meant no harm. Of course he had seen that it was Donn's name on the back of her letter. He was only pulling her leg about it. She was just too touchy for words, that was all.

She took her letters upstairs, and in her room read through them impatiently. It looked as though Donn were implacable. He was going to hold out forever—so sure that asking a girl to shack up with him was just as good as asking her to marry him. Well, she could hold out forever too. And she was beginning to think that she didn't really care what Donn did any more, or who he shacked up with, so long as it wasn't her. Certainly he wasn't proving to be very considerate; especially for a man who claimed to be so very much in love with her!

A few days later, Colin came in from the muster camp in time for the midmorning radio broadcast. The little daughter of one of the stockmen, a girl of ten who was at the mission school, had been operated on for appendicitis. Albert was anxious for news of her. Patty had been in the office for a few minutes, and Keitha had just entered from the garden. She had been idly picking up some of the frangipani blooms that had fallen and wishing aggrievedly that she had been asked in to the galah session. She would have liked to talk to Kate and perhaps arrange to go over and see her one day. It was only an excuse, of course. She was aware of that.

She saw Col go to the office door and stop frustrated when it would not open.

"Mrs. Drummond, open the door, please!" he called. In a second Patty did so, offering the excuse that the door must have stuck.

The little incident worried Keitha. Had the catch stuck, or had Patty locked the office door? And if she had, was it to keep Keitha out of the galah session? It seemed mean and petty to Keitha.

When Col came out again he told her cheerfully, flicking her cheek as he came up to her on the veranda, "Peggy's doing fine. Albert will be a happy man. Hey, Keitha—" He turned back as he had been about to go down the steps, the wide-brimmed hat already back on his head, "You don't look all that busy. Like to come out to the camp with me?"

Her pulses leaped. "I'd love to!" She was feeling singularly stale and in need of diversion. "But I don't know if Mrs. Drummond will agree."

"Sure she'll agree. She'll have finished her gossip session in a minute, and we'll ask her."

To Keitha's surprise, Patty seemed to think it a good idea.

"Yes, go along. I've been wondering what we could do with you to give you some time off. It's an excellent idea, Colin. I shall get on with my sewing and won't be in the least lonely. Will you have some lunch before you go?"

"No, thanks. Albert will be waiting for news of Peggy. We'll have something out there. Run along and hop into your jeans, Keitha. Get yourself a hat. I'll saddle up a horse for you."

Feeling elated, Keitha hurried off to do as he told her. In no time she was riding with him out of the dusty yard and through the tall straw-colored spear grass. They went through a grove of bloodwoods and ironbarks, and across a dry creek that had steep red banks. They rode around the highest rise she had seen on the property, though it was probably no more than 50 feet. She remarked to Col that this was certainly rougher and wilder country than that in the vicinity of the home station.

"You're right. What's more, you have to know it thoroughly if you're going to run the place properly. I reckon I know every waterhole and every patch of scrub where the cattle hide out. I learned the place from Bruce Drummond—he started here as a jackeroo when he was 19, and he knew it backward. Mellie's going to be the same. It would take a pitch dark night, or a blinding thunderstorm to bush Mellie. She's a girl in a million."

Keitha wondered if Dane thought so too, or if he were still waiting in a cold-blooded calculating way to see how she "shaped up".

They rode into some thick scrub not far from the muster camp where Col had caught sight of a few cattle. He spurred his horse and was off at a gallop, standing in the stirrups. Keitha was having a little trouble holding her mount back. She thought, "Why should I?" She dug in her heels and rose in the saddle, emulating Col. The excitement of that wild ride did a lot to release some of her pent-up emotions. She was hot on Col's heels when the two of them finally emerged from the scrub with three cows and a couple of calves lumbering ahead of them.

Col turned back to Keitha with a grin. "Those beasts are well trained. They're not bush cattle. We'd never have got scrubbers out into the open as easily—they're as cunning as they come."

She laughed, for she had been thinking that if this was all the trouble scrub cattle gave, there was nothing to it.

Now the camp was in sight. A sizeable mob was being held by a couple of easy-riding stockmen, one of whom was apparently Albert, for Col rode toward him waving cheerfully. Keitha, occupied in watching him receive the good news, started with surprise when a voice that was unmistakably Dane Langley's said from a few yards away, "Hold it, Miss Godwin!"

Her heart began to thud as she saw him coming toward her on his big bay. She put up a hand to straighten her hat that had fallen askew in that race through the bush. Her cheeks were flushed. She was still panting a little and knew a wild thrill of elation.

Over in the shade of some white-boled river gums, the camp cook was busy with dinner. A slow stream of cattle was coming in from various directions to join the mob. Smoke was rising beyond the dust they made. There was a smell of burning gum leaves. It was a picture that stayed clear and bright in Keitha's mind.

"Who brought you out here?" Dane asked a moment later. The question came abruptly, and something in the tone of voice had the instant effect of damping her elation.

Her voice was very cool as she repled, "Colin Andrews. Who else?"

"I thought as much. Didn't I tell you to lay off the overseer? Can't you do what you're told and stop trying to make mischief?"

"I'm not trying to make mischief," she flared. "That's an absurd thing to say."

Instead of answering, he suddenly swung his mount around and careered off past the ringing mob of cattle in a cloud of dust.

Keitha watched in amazement, for a moment almost stunned. Away over there she could see Mellie riding very fast and very cleverly. She was standing in the stirrups; superb control in every line of her strong beautiful body, her hat hanging down her back. Yes, Mellie on a galloping horse was certainly a sight to see! She was chasing a calf, and Keitha watched it run, astonishingly fast for such a stocky little bundle of beef. In fact, she calculated it ran as fast as any bullock. Mellie was trying to bring it around, but the calf was heading for the scrub and refused to turn. Mellie's horse drew closer. In a moment, she would be right on top of it—

Keitha heard Dane shouting something unintelligible, Mellie's concentration relaxed, her horse faltered. In a final dash, the calf reached the safety of the scrub and disappeared.

Now why on earth had Dane done that? Why hadn't he let Mellie bring that little calf back to the mob?

All the ringers were converging on the camp now. Horses were hobbled and the stockmen, with the peculiar almost pigeontoed gait that came from spending long hours in the saddle, drifted over for their dinner. Col looked around for Keitha and rode toward her. Mellie and Dane were approaching the camp too, talking to each other furiously and heatedly across the few feet that divided them. Mellie's color was high and she was scowling; Dane had lost his customary air of good-humored confidence.

"What was that all about?" Keitha asked Col.

"What? I didn't see it. Mellie's getting a slating, is she?" No criticism of the boss, nothing but an acutely intelligent look. Col was like Kate Langley in that he appeared to think Dane could do no wrong.

"Why did he interfere with what Mellie was doing?" Keitha wondered; and she wondered it rather loudly. So loudly in fact that it was obvious Dane heard her, for he sent her a sharp frowning look.

A bough shelter had been erected under the trees, possibly for Mellie's comfort. She and Mellie sat in its shade and enjoyed the same fare as the men. Mellie, her eyes still dark and angry, occasionally raised her voice to join in the general conversation of the men who were some yards away.

"Did Colin ask you to come out? Or did you ask him to bring you?" she asked Keitha after a while. She had not taken a great deal of notice of the English girl, but then she never did.

Keitha, who was feeling stimulated and very much alive, said, "Colin asked me. Aren't I lucky?"

Mellie stared at her over the large steak she was eating. "D'you mean coming out to the camp, or coming with him?"

Keitha thought about it. "A little of each," she decided. "I like Col very much."

Silence. Then Mellie burst out, "Well, I tell you what. I hate Dane Langley—making a fool of me, bawling me out in front of everyone just because I was chasing a calf!" She looked up as a shadow fell on the ground. Keitha looked up too and saw Dane towering over them. He dropped down on his heels and occupied himself for a minute or two with his steak and damper sandwich, during which time Col Andrews came to make it a foursome. He too settled on his heels, his back against the white bole of the tree. Keitha had noticed that the men out here had a habit of squatting on their heels and somehow always looked very comfortable in that position. These two were no exception. Col's hat was on the back of his head and his blue eyes smiled over at Keitha.

"I'll fetch you two girls a mug of tea in a minute. How's the food?"

"Marvelous," said Keitha, smiling back at him brightly. There was tension in the air, and she was acutely aware of Dane. For some reason she wanted to impress on him that she was utterly carefree and happy. But Dane was not paying her much attention.

"Having a moan about me, were you, Melanie?" he drawled. "Think you can chase calves as well as any stockman, do you? Well, let me tell you there's more than one stockman in this outfit has wished he hadn't tried to get the better of a calf. Another few seconds and that little fellow'd have dived under your horse's neck. The three of you wouldn've been tangled up in a nasty heap on the ground."

"We wouldn't," retorted Mellie, her face reddening with fresh anger. "I'd have turned that calf back—or if he wouldn't turn, Skip would have pulled up."

"You've ridden Skip before, have you?"

"Yes."

"Chased calves?"

Mellie shrugged. "I can't remember."

"You'd remember it you had. . . . Next time you come to a muster—and that'll be tomorrow—confer long and carefully with your elders and betters upon your choice of a horse. But in any case, the unalterable rule for you is—just don't ever chase a calf." Mellie glared at him and he added, "One more thing. Don't try to persuade yourself that you know better than I do."

"Oh, sometimes I hate you, Dane Langley!"

His eyes narrowed. "That's fine as far as I'm concerned." A little smile, not altogether pleasant, was on his lips as he stood up and strolled nonchalantly toward the camp fire and the tea. Col, looking serious and thoughtful, and not saying a word, followed him.

"Pig," mutter Mellie, referring apparently to Dane. "He said I was showing off; that I was a stupid irresponsible exhibitionist." Her eyes burned.

Keitha, who knew nothing about chasing calves, thought there was a lot to be said for Mellie's fury. Maybe Dane was concerned for her well-being; maybe he did know a lot more than an 18-year-old girl could know about working cattle. But he didn't know how to handle women. No, thought Keitha to herself, that was one field where the wonderful Dane Langley definitely fell down. He was so arrogant, so sure he knew best, that he didn't stop to think that Mellie was just an excitable overgrown schoolgirl, who still had her pride and needed treating with tact. Keitha thought he could have handled Mellie very differently and made a lot better job of it.

Then another thought struck her. Was this, after all, some kind of a lovers' tiff? Was Mellie underneath reveling in Dane's brutal, masterful treatment of her, in his careless trampling on her pride? Was the hatred Mellie expressed just another side of love? She glanced cautiously at the other girl from the shelter of her lashes and saw her sitting there still scowling.

Poor Mellie, she thought suddenly. She looked so young, so bewildered, so unsure of herself.

The men came back with mugs of tea, and Mellie took hers ungraciously. Keitha noticed that she drank it down scalding hot as the stockmen did. She herself had to wait for hers to cool.

Mellie refused to look at Dane, or to speak to him. When he strolled off to talk to some of the men, Col said to her quietly, "Now calm down, Mellie. You know Dane's only concerned about your safety. He doesn't want you killing yourself in his service."

"His service!" scoffed Mellie. "Why am I always supposed to do everything he says and never speak up for myself?"

"You're not," said Col. "Don't exaggerate."

"I'm not exaggerating! You know I wouldn't have come to harm Col. Why didn't you speak up for me?"

"Dane is the boss," the overseer said shortly.

"He's not my boss." Mellie sounded stubborn. "Not yet—and not ever."

"Now hold on," Col interrupted, but Mellie had turned away. Keitha knew she was hiding tears. The big, beautiful, bouncing Mellie, who had the constitution of an ox, hiding tears. In a moment she rose to her feet and wandered off to Skip.

The stockmen were dispersing once more. This afternoon the beasts to be sold were to be cut from the mob and finally taken to the holding yard.

Col asked, "What would you like to do, Keitha?"

"Don't worry about me. I'll be quite happy sitting here or riding around. I won't try to round up anything even as small as a calf."

Col's smile was very restrained. He didn't approve of even so slight a criticism of the boss.

"A fall over a calf is usually serious—for both horse and rider," he said. "Though the calf usually comes out of it all right. By the way, if you decide to go home, be sure to tell someone."

"I shall," promised Keitha. She was pretty sure she would not want to go "home". She would enjoy herself much more watching the cutting out procedure. She wondered if Dane had come over to select the beasts he wanted for sale, or if he would leave it to Col. She would soon find out.

He left it to Col, and she respected him for that. She spent most of her time watching him from the trees, but he never even glanced her way. Well, he was watching the cutting out pretty closely. Perhaps he had come to check up on the overseer. Or was it to keep that promise he had made to Mellie to see how she was progressing as a stockman? He had done that, all right!

She sat under the bough shelter and watched the

stockmen through a haze of red dust that was thickening by the minute. Lazy in the heat, her eyes screwed up against the glare, she was lulled by the shouts of the stockmen and the bellowing of the bullocks. She started when Dane appeared and flung himself down beside her.

"Well, how are things at the outstation?"

"Fine, thank you." She looked at him and in spite of herself, knew there was reproach in her eyes. He saw it, of course.

"Those great dark eyes of yours have an accusing look," he said with casual mockery. "What have I been doing wrong now?"

She chose deliberately to misunderstand. She knew well enough he was thinking of last mail day, but raising her fine eyebrows, she said, "Surely you must know! You upset Mellie. She was almost in tears."

"Mellie? Are we to talk about Mellie? Very well then. But I can't take all the credit for Mellie's tears. You had a share in provoking them too, I think."

"*I* did?" Keitha was incredulous. "I certainly did not!"

"You did indeed. But I wouldn't worry too much. All that's wrong with Mellie in the long run is that she's growing up. And about time too. Maybe your coming to Wayaway will serve some purpose after all, as far as Mellie's concerned."

"I can't think what you're talking about. I hardly see anything of Mellie—"

"Exactly. But you fraternize with Col, don't you? I did tell you to leave him alone. I'll repeat that. You're supposed to be at the outstation to run around for Patty, not to be coming out to the muster with Col Andrews. Is it a usual occurrence?"

"Of course it's not," said Keitha with annoyance. "This is the first time. And Mrs. Drummond was pleased for me to come. She said it was time I had a day away from work."

"I don't doubt she was pleased. But couldn't you think up some other way of spending your free time?"

She stared at him, feeling the hot color coming into her face. He could say that to her after so calmly forgetting what he had half promised. She said coldly, "This way of relaxing appeals to me. Besides, I'm always being warned not to go off alone and get lost, thereby causing a lot of trouble to people who have better things to do—"

He looked amused. "Come now, it's not only the trouble we're thinking of. You're something very special out here even if you're like a hibiscus flower in that we don't expect to enjoy you for long." There was a pause. "Well, I missed out on checking up on you the other day. Can I put it down in the books, figuratively speaking, that you're relatively happy at the outstation? And if I look you up now and again will you leave Colin alone? I'm afraid I'm not able to provide much personally in the way of excitement for you—"

Keitha looked at him squarely. His attitude hurt. She said deliberately, "I agree. You're far from able to do that." It was a rude thing to say, and she said it rudely and felt she had scored a point. It had given her quite a kick to look straight and hard into those mocking blue eyes.

She was not surprised that in another minute he left her.

When the cutting out was over, Keitha and Mellie rode at the back of the mob that was being driven to the yards. Now and again Col or Dane, or both, came to join them. Now Dane's very presence did something to Keitha. There was something heady in his nearness so that she was acutely aware of her physical being, of the feel of the reins in her hands, the sun striking on her face, dazzling her eyes. He had nothing at all to say to her, and even that seemed to stimulate rather than aggravate her.

Well within Mellie's hearing, she heard him tell Col

conversationally, "If that girl's to be any use on the run then she'll have to be taught to be more levelheaded and less of an exhibitionist. What's more, she must obey orders otherwise she'll finish up braking her pretty little neck and that will be that. If she won't take any notice of you, then leave her at home."

Col whitened, and Keitha knew he took the implied criticism hard. She was sure he would never allow Mellie to come to any harm.

"I haven't the time to be tutoring you, Mellie," Dane concluded.

"That suits me," mutter Mellie rebelliously, though she blinked hard as if tears were close again.

Keitha listened and thought Dane too bossy altogether. She couldn't let it pass and exclaimed in exasperation, "What on earth is there such a fuss about? What did Mellie do? Why shouldn't she go after a little calf?"

Dane looked at her impatiently. "Oh, you city girls! Haven't you been paying attention? Do I have to spell it out? I thought you were a reasonably intelligent girl. Don't tell me after what you've heard that you'd go chasing after a calf."

"You let me chase a bullock the other day," said Keitha. The altercation aroused her. "I don't know what grounds you had for thinking I wouldn't come to any harm, seeing I know nothing about working animals."

"You'd watched. You had a picked horse, and what's more, your pride wouldn't have let you fall," said Dane and capped that off with a final, "And I was there."

"Wonderful you," muttered Mellie and suddenly dug her heels into her horse's side and raced up at the side of the mob.

Dane gave Col no more than a look and the overseer followed her.

"Wonderful you," thought Keitha, and looked at Dane maliciously.

"Why don't you keep out of our domestic squabbles?" he asked curtly. "Stick to what concerns you—your continental cookery, and your long letters to England. You're certainly having some fun, but just don't start making too big a nuisance of yourself before you go running back home."

Keitha was furious. She had been rude, but he was ruder. Yet he was supposed to be such a polite and considerate host. Well, he was host no more, it was true. She didn't know what he was. Reluctant employer perhaps. Her cheeks were flushed; she knew she must look a sight, her face stained with dust and perspiration. But at least her shirt, unlike Mellie's, was well and truly tucked in. She didn't know why Dane was being so hard to get along with. For good measure, he added just then, "Don't forget to let me know, will you, just as soon as you've had your fill of this part of sunny Queensland. I'll put you on the plane personally."

"Will you!" thought Keitha angrily. Mellie's words came into her mind. She echoed them to herself with feeling. "Sometimes I hate you, Dane Langley." That "sometimes" was the trouble. What had got into him this evening? She told herself it would be a long time before she gave him the opportunity of seeing her off from the Gulf Country. When she did go, she would go without his even knowing it—if she could find a way. . . .

CHAPTER EIGHT

Over two weeks went by when she saw nothing at all of Dane. However, she knew Mellie had been to the home station once or twice. It was obvious now that he was deliberately avoiding her, and she felt unutterably frustrated and restless.

She wrote a letter to Donn that had been in her mind for some time. She knew now that she had never really loved him, otherwise she could not have willingly gone so far away from him as she had chosen to do. When you really loved, you wanted to be near the one you loved, no matter what the circumstances. She was sure of that.

She wrote, "You say you love me, Donn. You say it over and over, so easily, so lightly. Yet you can't bring yourself to say 'Marry me'. I've put my own interpretation on that. You said once that living together would be the same as being married—that for you and me it would be forever. It's not very flattering really, you know. Because I believe in marriage. In fact, I believe in a lot of the things that you've discarded. I just don't belong in your world, so I think we'd better say goodbye to each other. I loved knowing you, Donn, but I've somehow changed since I've been out here. I could never go back—in any sense of the word. . . . Don't hold that job for me. I know you'll find someone else to love. I hope it will be someone whose ideas are not as old-fashioned as mine. . . ."

Her letter would have to wait for next mail day to go, but she wouldn't change her mind about sending it. She didn't think she would ever return to London, and if she did, it would certainly not be to Donn. She was under some sort of a spell out here. There was something mesmeric in the long sunny days. The heat from the sky, and the shimmer of the sun-drenched plains danced like a haunting melody through her mind—a melody that burst into a crescendo of sound and color at sundown, when the birds filled the sky as they came down to the lagoon for water.

"If you demand compensation for living in the Outback"—Dane's words came back into her mind every evening—"then sundown's one of them."

Perhaps her life would regain some sort of perspective when she returned to the coast, but just now she couldn't even contemplate a time when she would fly east.

Sometimes as she lay sleepless in her bedroom, listening to the thud of mangoes on the roof and the screeching of the fruit bats breaking the deep throbbing silence of the outback night, she wondered what she wanted from life. If perhaps in her heart she knew the answer to that question, she refused to acknowledge it.

Col taught her to ride the motorcycle one Sunday, and she found it not difficult to master. Patty approved of the lessons, though Keitha knew Dane would not have done so, suspicious that she was trying to enmesh the overseer in some fleeting affair that would disturb the peace of the cattle station—if peace existed. Keitha saw undercurrents of unrest everywhere: in Patty, in Mellie, in Col and certainly in herself.

Col didn't take her out on the run again, though Patty vaguely suggested more than once that he might do so. Keitha wondered if he were acting on the boss's orders and thought it extremely likely.

One night after dinner, she took a stroll in the garden. As she came back through the soft, warm darkness that lay like silk against her bare arms and legs she could hear Mellie playing the piano. It was a Beethoven sonata she was playing. She had been over to the Wayaway homestead that day. Keitha paused to listen. Mellie didn't play well—there was not a single piece that she had perfected. And this sonata—she was having a terrible struggle with it. Was it for Dane, whom she had said she hated, that she was trying to master it? That seemed utterly ludicrous and unrealistic. By no stretch of the imagination could one imagine Dane choosing to listen to Mellie's efforts when he had some beautiful recordings. Unless, of course, Dane were madly in love with Mellie. But he was not madly in love with Mellie. On the other hand, he was possibly calmly and coolly waiting to see how she "shaped up".

A voice broke into her reflections.

"A penny for your thoughts," It was Col, lounging in a garden chair near the papaw trees.

"Oh, you startled me. I was just listening to Mellie." She took a chair near him. "She'd never take a prize, would she?"

"Maybe not. But I like to listen to her. There's something very nostalgic in the sound of a piano being played in a house at night. Imperfection has more appeal for me than technical brilliance—there's something of Mellie's heart coming from that music."

Quite obviously Col thought more of the person who was playing than he did of the music. The things Mellie was doing to that sonata were pretty well unforgivable, if you liked Beethoven. Col was protected because he was thinking of Mellie and her heart.

"I wonder how she got on with Dane over at the home station today," she mused aloud. "Does she still hate him?" She hardly knew why she asked it except that it gave her pleasure to talk about Dane even indirectly.

Col laughed. "Never in a million years. Mellie says things like that. She doesn't mean them. Dane hurt her pride a bit, that was all. But the reprimand was necessary," he added quickly. "She takes a lot of chances she shouldn't."

"Why don't you stop her?"

There was a slight pause. "I watch her," said Col quietly. "I wouldn't let anything happen to Mellie. . . . By the way, did you know there's to be a picnic at the Tyrone Park border muster tomorrow?"

"No." Keitha's heart began to beat fast. "Who's going?"

"About everyone, I guess. Dane and Kate—Bill—the O'Boyles—us—"

"Me?" interrupted Keitha quickly.

"Well, of course."

Keitha was suddenly filled with a wild excitement. She would see Dane again. The thought was there in her mind before she could censure it. All right, so she wanted to see Dane. That didn't mean she was falling in love with him. He was just part of the general spell of the Outback. He dominated life out here whether he was present or not. She asked Col eagerly, "What is a border muster, Col? Tell me about it so I won't look a fool."

"You're no fool, Keitha," Col assured her. "You could work it out for yourself if you did a bit of thinking." But he explained obligingly, "As you know, fences are practically non-existent hereabouts, which means that cattle from one station are bound to stray onto the neighboring runs. It's only in comparitively small numbers. Except during the Wet, they stick within a comfortable distance of the waterhole they habitually use. Tyrone Park is mustering at the Blue Waterhole near Wayaway's boundary—up this end of the run, that is—so they've let us know and Dane will send along a few stockmen. Any cattle with the Wayaway brand, and any calves with cows that carry our brand, will be cut out of the mob they muster. We'll bring them home and brand them next day. Do you get it?"

"Yes," Keitha was listening intently. "Go on."

"Well, that's about it. Cleanskins, unbranded cattle, stay on Tyrone Park and will be marked with their brand.

If the muster were on our side of the border, it would be the other way around, of course. The cleanskins would stay with us and henceforth belong with our herds."

"I see. Yes, I expect I could have worked that out. . . . Whose idea was the picnic, Col?"

"Justine O'Boyle's. Should be a good day. You'll enjoy it, Keitha. It'll be something else to add to your little store of Queensland experiences." And though Col didn't mean it that way, his words had the effect of instantly, and rather dampeningly, making Keitha realize anew that they all considered her an outsider.

And she wanted rather badly to belong.

It was Keitha who prepared the picnic basket the following morning. Patty Drummond came out to the kitchen just as she finished packing away the last piece of fruit.

"I'll take that out to the car, Keitha, if you want to go upstairs and fetch your things. Then we must be on our way. We're already later than I promised Dane we'd be," she added, glancing at her watch.

Keitha hoped that she wasn't going to be blamed for not having the picnic basket packed earlier and quickly took off the apron she had tied on over her clean jeans. Col had left the homestead early as usual and was going to meet them at the Blue Waterhole. Keitha was all but out the kitchen door when a distraught girl appeared, a yelling child of about a year clutched in her arms. She was a shy girl called Oobi with whom Keitha had made friends at the Aborigine quarters. Blood from her baby's leg had stained her skirt and was still flowing.

Keitha reached for the child and asked quickly, "What happened, Oobi? Let's have a look at that leg. . . ." In a moment she was able to say reassuringly, "It's not such a deep cut. But there's some glass in it. We'll have to get that out." She turned inquiringly to Patty, to make sure she wanted to leave it to Keitha. To her surprise she found the other woman sitting in a chair, her face, deathly white, lowered into her hands.

"It's not serious, Mrs. Drummond."

"I know—I know. But I could never stand the sight of blood. I'll be all right in a minute."

Keitha thought it an unfortunate weakness in one whose proud boast was that she was born and bred a countrywoman. By the time she had fetched a bowl and the first aid kit from the locked cupboard upstairs, Patty was more or less in control of herself again. Johnnie was still howling, and Oobi was weeping in sympathy.

"I want to leave in five minutes, Keitha," Patty said. "So be quick, won't you? Pick the glass out and let Oobi do the dressing herself. She has been told about antiseptics and so on often enough."

"I'll be as quick as I can, Mrs. Drummond," said Keitha. It was going to take her a lot longer than five minutes to deal with this cut. What was more, she was going to find out how dirty the glass had been and was going to clean and dress it herself.

Mrs. Drummond left the kitchen, taking the picnic basket with her. Keitha worked quickly and gently on the baby's leg, removing glass and trying to soothe the young mother at the same time. She talked cheerfully until her weeping had stopped. Johnnie had quietened too and removed his fat brown fists from huge dark eyes to peep at what was happening to his knee.

"Now tell me how it happened, Oobi, and where the glass came from."

"Him clean fella bottle, missus—get broken up longa the floor and Johnnie he crawl that way."

"We'll go and have a look presently."

In another minute Mellie came into the kitchen. "We can't wait all day, Keitha. If you want to come to the picnic you'd better come now. Oobi will be all right. It's only a little cut, isn't it? Mother says you'll have the girls spoiled if you do everything for them."

Keitha looked up. "There's still a bit of glass here. I'll have to get it out—it's a bit tricky. Can't you hang on for a bit?"

Mellie looked helpless. "Mother says not. She told Dane what time we'd be there, and we're late already. He likes people to stick to what they say."

"Regardless? Well then, you'd better go without me," said Keitha. Of course she didn't want to miss the picnic, but Johnnie was 12 months old and was an important little fellow. He took priority over any picnic. She looked up at Mellie, who stood biting her lip nervously. Poor Mellie! She was still little more than a schoolgirl in many ways. Keitha thought with a trace of pity, "You'll never grow up till you get away from that quietly domineering mother of yours."

She said brightly, "Cheer up, Mellie. If I feel like it I'll come over to the picnic on one of the motorbikes. Someone will tell me the way. I can't leave this job half done."

"I'll tell Mother," said Mellie. "I'll persuade her to wait."

But her persuasive powers were not great enough, for only five minutes later Keitha heard the station wagon leave the yard. She really had hoped they would wait for her, and her heart sank. But she pushed her disappointment aside and gave her mind entirely to the task in hand.

Now that there was no hurry, she took her time. It was half an hour before she was ready to go. At the Aborigine quarters, the other women had come clustering around shyly, giggling and talking. Keitha checked up on Oobi's story of clean glass and then told them that she wanted to go to the Blue Waterhole on Tyrone Park. They all knew where it was, but none of them could tell her how to get there. Dolly, one of the housegirls, said, "You ask Tucker, missus. That old fella he knows everything. He tell you real good how to get there."

Tucker was in the vegetable garden. He thought long and deeply and then took Keitha out to the yard in front of the homestead garden. With much pointing and with references to landmarks as "yella stump like big fella dingo", "trees like old men talkum", and "plenty big anthills walkum through scrub", described how to reach the Blue Waterhole.

Keitha listened attentively and having thanked him, fetched the motorcycle from the garage. Her need to get to the picnic—to see Dane Langley again—was so urgent that she persuaded herself that she would find the way from Tucker's somewhat picturesque directions.

The first part of the track was not hard to follow, for the station wagon had been over it a short time ago and flattened the long grasses. But where there was no spear grass there was no track, for the ground was as hard as iron. Then she spied that stump like a big yellow dingo and headed toward it elatedly. Beyond that was a sandy stretch. She once again picked up the station wagon's tracks.

She was doing fine! It was certainly an uncomfortably hot and bumpy ride and she was a tiny bit afraid of the motorcycle, but she would get there. She was absolutely determined.

At last away across the plain she could see a group of trees hunched and bent—"like old men talkum". That exactly described them. Tucker certainly had an apt and memorable way of describing landmarks that made them unmistakable.

By the time she had reached the distant trees, she was dusty, parched, and quite sure that she must look a sight. At her approach a few cattle that had been standing in the shade began to disperse to more trees that grew around a small waterhole. She pulled up at a safe distance and watched them. The sight of the water with its muddy banks and reflections of tree and sky made her long for a drink. She knew that she should have brought a flask of water with her, but in her eagerness to be on her way she had not given it a thought.

Well, she had better look for those anthills. But first she decided to tidy herself a little. Using the mirror from the small tote she had brought with her, she wiped some of the dust from her face with a tissue, combed her hair, and applied a little fresh lipstick. Then from the shelter of the "old men" trees she began to scan the plain for anthills walking through the scrub. There was scrub all right; a great wide belt of it at the far end of a long stretch of open plain, but she had no idea whether the anthills were left, right or center.

The best thing to do seemed to be to study the ground for wheel marks, and this she began to do. She hunted for what seemed a very long time and was beginning to despair when something made her look up. Out toward the far end of that belt of scrub was a cloud of red dust whirling along in her direction. It was surely not a willy-willy, and it was moving too fast to be cattle. Soon she heard the hum of a motor. The dust revealed itself as a Land Rover.

Keitha felt as excited as a shipwrecked sailor who has sighted a sail. Her first thought was that she would get a drink—she was as parched as that—her second was to wonder who it could be. Whoever it was, surely they would be able to put her on the right track for Tyrone Park and the Blue Waterhole.

Another three minutes, and her heart began to pound. She knew who it was. It was Dane Langley.

He pulled up two yards from where she stood, climbed

out of the Rover and came to stand and stare at her, hands on his hips, broad-brimmed hat slanted rakishly over his eyes.

"So it's the bush orchid rearing its pretty head."

She flushed. "What brings you here, Dane Langley?"

"Why, you do, Keitha Godwin. What else? I missed you at the muster, and Patty said you wouldn't be along. I was going to the outstation to fetch you. It wouldn't do for you to miss the picnic." His mouth quirked. "However, I'd forgotten about your determined spirit. Of course you had to try to make it on your own, and here you are—lost."

"I'm not lost at all," said Keitha. "So you needn't have bothered about me."

His blue eyes looked her over quizzically. "I can't seem to help bothering about you, honey. And if you're not lost, it's amazing. You really should have come with the others, you know. Why didn't you?"

"One of the babies had had an accident—"

Understanding showed on his face. "And accidents make Patty squeamish, I know. But they'd have waited for you, surely."

"I told them not to," she said quickly. "I told Mellie I'd get there if I wanted to."

"And you did want to?"

A slow flush suffused her cheeks. "Yes, of course. . . . If you have any water, I'd like a drink. I forgot to bring a flask."

"You were in a hurry." He offered no further criticism, but fetched his waterbag and poured her a mug of cool water. She drank it down thirstily so that her eyes watered and thought it was the most delicious drink she had ever tasted.

"Shall we be on our way now?" he asked conversationally when she had finished.

"Yes."

He waited, but she did not move. In her heart, she had been very relieved to see him come. She didn't really know the way. Even if she found those anthills she didn't know what came after that. She could follow him now, at all events, and he need never know.

"After you, Miss Godwin," he said softly, his eyes mocking.

After her! She felt furiously angry with him. Was he determined on proving her a liar if he could? Couldn't he—just this once—be a gentleman and go ahead?

As if he had read her thoughs he said, with a tilt of his brows, "Or would you rather follow in my dust?"

She bit her lip. She had misjudged him.

Suddenly he relented.

"Look, honey, we'll leave the motorcycle here. Somebody can pick it up on the way home. You hop in the car with me. That way, you won't arrive at the picnic shaken to pieces." Now the screwed-up blue eyes had softened, and like Mellie she found herself turning away to hide sudden tears. Because after all, she was hot, tired, just a little bit frightened, and now it was going to be all right.

He didn't speak again until they were traveling across the plain toward the scrub. Then he said musingly, "Come to think of it, you've quite a bit of initiative and courage for a city girl. One can't help admiring you for it."

"Thank you, Mr. Langley." Her voice was husky though she had herself under control again. "It's nice of you to praise me. Because sometimes I get the distinct feeling that you'd as soon I left Wayaway."

"Hmm. Scratch the formality bit anyhow, honey. Trouble is, I get the feeling that you're definitely going to quit Wayaway."

How did she take that? Did he mean she was going to leave of her own volition? Or did he mean that he would see to it that she did leave? She was floundering, uncertain, and felt completely at his mercy. She longed to lean against him and to say, "I surrender. I don't want to fight you any longer, I just want to rest here, near you, and not think at all."

That proved of course that she was crazy. Maybe it was what happened to all the girls. They just gave up trying to work out where they stood with him; as long as they could be there it was enough. Except for Mellie, who had said, "I hate you." Mellie had spirit. Did he like spirit? Well, even if he did, he couldn't care less about Keitha Godwin. She was someone passing through. When she had gone he would forget her. And just how soon would that be?

Soon they had reached the Blue Waterhole. She hadn't even looked out for those anthills. There was a great mob of lowing cattle and dust everywhere. There were stockmen from Tyrone Park and a few from Wayaway, shouts of laughter, the cracking of stockwhips. Away under some trees was the picnic camp. Kate was sitting there placidly drawing, an outsize sketch pad on her knees. Keitha smiled at the sight of Kate. There was someone who would be glad to see her!

Patty Drummond was there too, and another woman—Mrs. O'Boyle, probably.

As Dane drove slowly past the mob, giving it a wide berth, a girl came riding out of the dust. She pulled on her horse's reins and laughed as she cantered up and bent down toward the Rover. It was Dusty—Justine; the girl Keitha had seen at the airstrip, and she looked just as attractive now as she had then. There was scarcely a dust-streak on her face. Her sleek, silver-brown hair was flipped neatly back from under a black ranch hat that had a silver chin strap. Her eyes were a clean gray-green, and she wore a pink shirt and smart black jeans.

"Hi, Dane! So you got the reluctant girl." She walked her horse alongside the car until it came to a halt, then swung herself lightly down from the saddle, and tossed her reins over a bough. Almost the moment Dane put his feet to the ground her hand was through his arm.

"So you're the girl who has us all curious," she exclaimed as Keitha stepped from the car. Her eyes flicked over Keitha quickly and efficiently. Keitha was glad she had made time for that little bit of sprucing up on the plain. "I was beginning to wonder if any of us would meet you at all before you left the place. And you know, you really mustn't go home without saying hello to us all over the radio schedule. Must she, Dane?"

"That's up to Keitha," said Dane. "This is Justine O'Boyle, honey, as no doubt you already know. You'll have gathered Justine knows all about you—probably more than you know yourself, if I know anything about the galah sessions."

The three of them strolled together toward the picnic camp. Keitha wondered why Justine took it so much for granted that she would be leaving Wayaway cattle run soon. They were well out of range of the stirring dust now. Keitha greeted Kate and was introduced to Mrs. O'Boyle. She received a not overenthusiastic welcome from Patty Drummond, who nevertheless lost no time in suggesting that now she was here, she might help to serve out the picnic lunch.

"I'll leave you to it, girls," said Dane. "See you at lunch."

Mellie had ridden up, leading Dane's horse. Keitha spent a moment watching the two of them ride off together. She wondered if Mellie had quite forgotten her avowal of hatred and if she was after all in love with the boss of Wayaway. Beyond the dust that hovered over the mob of cattle, she thought she could see Col and Bill. Justine had decided not to rejoin the muster, but to stay and help with the lunch.

A trestle table, brought from Tyrone Park, had been put up and spread with a red and white check cloth. The picnic baskets were opened, and Keitha discovered they were to picnic in style. There were china plates and cups; silver knives and forks. No beef and damper today, though the stockmen would have their usual hearty fare, for at the other end of the waterhole Keitha could see that the camp cook had lit a fire.

Justine said casually, "You must have made quite a hit with Dane to have him go to the outstation to pick you up. Patty Drummond was livid."

"Was she? I don't think she need have been."

"One wouldn't think so, seeing that you'll be gone before we know where we are," agreed Justine, who was making no more than a show of helping with the picnic. "Were you really not going to bother coming? Or did you hope that Dane would go and fetch you?"

Keitha, who hadn't cared much for the suggestion that she would so soon be gone, flushed with annoyance. "If you really must know, I was well on the way here on a motorcycle."

Justine looked at her disbelievingly. "A London girl looking for the Blue Waterhole on a motorcycle! You'd have been lost for sure. . . . Well, wasn't it nice for you that Dane came to the rescue? He's quite a pearl, isn't he?"

Keitha thought it a strange way to describe the attractions of the boss of Wayaway, but lightly agreed that Dane was a pearl. Which didn't seem to please Justine as much as it should have.

"I suppose you have at least a passing interest in him."

Keitha smiled brightly across the table that was beginning to look very attractive with its bowls of salads and platters of cold meats. "I understand he more or less belongs to Mellie."

Justine fished a stack of good-looking glasses from a deep basket and began to set them out on the table. "Oh, that's a load of rubbish. It's only what Patty would like. Dane couldn't possibly marry Mellie; she's far too simple and countrified for a man of his discrimination. Of course Mellie tries. She's trying now because Patty's brought her up to think it's expected of her. Patty's father was head stockman on Wayaway once upon a time. Did you know that? Poor Patty has some sort of inferiority complex. She's quite sure that if Mellie married Dane it would prove that she was better than anyone in the whole of the Gulf Country. And wouldn't that be lovely?"

Their conversation ended there, for all the musterers were now converging on the camp or on the picnic site. To Keitha's surprise, Bill Sutton made straight for her and greeted her as keenly as if they had a date. "So you made it, Keitha! That's terrific. Anything I can do?"

"Not a thing, thanks, Bill. We have everything under control."

He moved away momentarily. Soon the picnic was in full swing. Justine stuck determinedly to Dane, openly wooing him, and Bill Sutton stuck just about as closely to Keitha, having somewhat strangely deputized himself to make a fuss of her. He assured her that if she wanted to do some riding during the afternoon he would see she had a safe horse.

"You can come with me if you want to ride around and kid yourself you're taking part in the muster."

"Thank you very much," she said ironically. But she reflected that quite possibly she would take up his offer, for it looked as though Dane was going to be fully occupied with Justine. Mellie too was hovering indecisively and worriedly on the sidelines.

"I'm a little surprised you came to the picnic, Bill," Keitha said a little later.

He shrugged. "Maybe you came to the picnic, *I* came to the muster. But don't forget what you promised me, will you, about coming over to Wayaway later on. I notice Justine's brought all her gear. She'll be riding back with our outfit after the day's work is finished."

"I'll see what I can do since I promised," agreed Keitha. "But it may not work out."

When lunch was over, Keitha set to work clearing away the debris and repacking the crockery and cutlery. Kate returned to her drawing, Patty considered it her right to relax, and Mrs. O'Boyle looked so hot and tired that Keitha could not imagine letting her do anything but sit down and rest.

"Don't you want to join the others?" she asked Justine who had stayed to help her.

"Oh, I'll get hold of Dane in a minute or two. There's no sense in overdoing it. I like to stay cool and calm and feminine at least some of the time. Look at poor old Mellie! She's having marvelous fun, but doesn't she look a mess? How on earth can she hope to fascinate Dane that way? It's a wonder Patty doesn't stop her."

Keitha watched Mellie racing past hot on the trail of a wayward bullock. Not far behind was Col with his eyes on Mellie rather than on the bullock. Mellie did look a mess, but she was happy and obviously didn't give a thought to her appearance. Keitha reflected, to Col's eyes at least she probably looked radiantly beautiful.

"Someone will come back for us now we've cleared all this up," said Justine. "Or would you rather sit around in the shade with the oldies and save your lovely complexion?"

"If you can take it, so can I," said Keitha cheerfully.

"Who do you expect to come back for you?" Justine wanted to know. She was arranging her pretty hair under the smart black hat, and her gray-green eyes were not entirely friendly.

"Bill said I could stick with him."

"Really? You're doing very nicely with Bill, aren't you? I'm beginning to suspect you're quite a collector of scalps."

"Are you? Then you're wrong."

"Oh, I don't know. First Dane Langley, then Bill Sutton. And then of course there's always what's-his-name—" She paused and leaned down to remove a spike of spear grass from her boot. At that moment Dane arrived leading two horses, so Keitha didn't have the opportunity to ask who what's-his-name might be. Just as well perhaps, as there was something rather disagreeable about the trend the conversation was taking.

"Do you girls want to ride?"

"Keitha's waiting for Bill," said Justine instantly. "But I'm coming with you, Dane."

He tilted a quizzical look down at Keitha. "I just can't keep up with you, Miss Godwin—"

"Don't try," she said coolly, but as she watched him ride off with Justine, her heart contracted and she was aware of a spasm of acute jealousy.

Nevertheless, she enjoyed the afternoon once Bill came to collect her. She loved the horses, the riding, and the sight of the cattle. She even loved the dust. And the excitement of riding around the outskirts of the mob and watching Michael O'Boyle's skill as he cut out the animals he wanted: the cleanskins that were to stay on Tyrone Park, the bullocks and cows, some of them with unbranded calves, that belonged on the Wayaway run and would be taken back there later on. She was glad she had Col to explain to her what it was all about, so that she was able to watch intelligently. She loved the heat pouring down from the sky and the shining waters of the Blue Waterhole where reflections of gray green trees and blue sky alternated with patches of beautiful lotus lilies. . . . She loved the break when the billy was boiled, and the men filled their quartpots; the picnickers drank mugs of steaming hot tea and ate the cakes, scones, and biscuits brought from the homesteads.

She had no further talk with Dane, though she watched him whenever she could. Bill stuck to her pretty closely; Justine stuck to Dane, and Mellie seemed pretty well unaware of anyone. It occurred to Keitha that she was possibly more in love with the run than with anyone on it, and in that perhaps she was like Dane. . . .

It was nearly sundown when the work was finished. The stockmen from Wayaway began to drive their mob slowly toward the nearest waterhole on the station run. Dane and Bill, Mellie and Col stayed with the mob. Justine got into the Land Rover with Kate.

They all met up later at the outstation where Bill and Dane left their horses. They came inside briefly for a drink. Dane said, "Seeing we're to have a houseguest for a few days, I think we'll have to arrange a party. What do you say, Kate? You must all come over and stay a night or two with us."

Keitha thought she must be imagining it, but it seemed that Dane looked especially long at her across the lamplit room. Then the bookkeeper said unexpectedly, "Terrific! What sort of a dancer are you, Keitha?"

She felt herself coloring and barely heard Kate remark to Patty, "We'll arrange it between us over the transceiver. But we'll make it soon."

"Before Keitha goes," said Justine with a tinge of malice, and Patty added sweetly, "I expect Justine will only stay a day or two."

"You hope," thought Keitha aware of the meaning behind the sweetness. Yet she, crazily, hoped so too.

CHAPTER NINE

From that night on, Keitha could think of nothing but the coming visit to Wayaway. Dane was there in her mind whether she like it or not, and she couldn't seem to get him out of it. Nor could she stop herself from thinking about Justine O'Boyle—riding with the boss, dining with him at night, listening with him to music on the dark veranda. Maybe walking down by the lagoon with him at sundown. What would she accomplish? She was a very attractive girl. The first time Keitha had seen her, that day at the Tyrone Park airstrip, she had more or less openly avowed her intention of breaking through his defenses. Having seen her in action at the picnic, Keitha suspected that she would stop at nothing. And at present, she had the field to herself.

Still, the pilot had been right when he said Dane Langley was a hard nut to crack. Besides he was no fool. No girl was going to win him by tricks or flattery. Whether Mellie Drummond would win him because she had "shaped up" well was quite another matter. Or did he have a vulnerable heart beneath that arrogant, self-confident exterior after all?

Keitha simply didn't know and was more and more inclined to wish she had left Wayaway long ago. In which case, would it still be Donn she dreamed about at night? She didn't think so. No—somehow she was sure that the end result of her coming to Queensland would have been to get Donn out of her system. Perhaps it had been her subconscious reason for leaving England in the first place. Because what Donn had offered her was not good enough. It had been altogether a shoddy deal to hand out to the girl he professed to love. She was glad she had sent him that letter—that it was all over. And while he might be hurt at first, she was pretty certain he would get over it quickly.

She didn't know quite what she expected of the visit to Wayaway, yet as soon as the date was set, she began feverishly planning what clothes she would take; dreamed of dancing with Dane, of going riding with him the way she had in her first week on the run. All as if neither Mellie nor Justine existed. She hoped that Bill Sutton would not try to monopolize her. Why did he want her to come to the home station while Justine was there? She was very much inclined to believe that it was Justine who was the cause of his embittered outlook on life and on women in particular.

When at last the day came for them to leave the outstation, her nerves were taut. They set out in the station wagon in the late afternoon, with Col driving. He would stay away only one night, returning to the outstation the next day. Patty, who did not want Keitha along but couldn't do a thing about it, had given her a little talk during the afternoon; a talk that made the girl feel rather like Cinderella.

"Now you do understand, Keitha, that though you have been invited as a guest to come with us, you will still be working for me. You won't be able to go gallivanting about just as you please. Three of us will give Kate extra work, and you will have to do your share of it."

"Yes, of course, Mrs. Drummond," agreed Keitha readily. She would in any case have offered to help Kate. It constantly surprised her that Mrs. Drummond didn't fire her, for though she worked hard enough at the homestead, she was aware that her presence was not necessary as far as the older woman was concerned. Perhaps while they were under Dane's roof she would manage to convince him that Keitha's services were no longer required. And then what? Would Dane be more inclined to agree about that now?

Keitha had an intuitive feeling that matters were coming to a head at last, but she could not bear to contemplate the thought of leaving Wayaway—of never seeing Dane Langley again. In fact, she refused to look farther ahead than the next day. . . .

Darkness fell as they drove across the plains. The sky was as clear and starry as ever, but lightning danced away on the rim of the horizon. Now and again a long, low growl of thunder could be heard.

"Not long now till the Wet," said Col. Keitha sat in the front beside him. In the back of the station wagon, behind the other passengers, was such a mountain of luggage that one had the impression Patty Drummond meant to stay with the Langleys almost indefinitely. "We'll have to get our mob on the road soon for the sales and send out the trucks for next year's supplies. Before we know it the rivers will be flooding."

The Wet, Keitha knew, lasted for about three months of the year. During that time about 40 inches of rain would fall in torrents, filling the rivers and creeks; making the land break out in a cover of unbelievable green.

"What a pity you will never see the green grasses on our pastures, Keitha," Patty remarked from the back seat. She didn't sound as though she thought it was a pity at all. "You'll be back in England long before that, though."

Keitha's heart sank. Her conjectures had been right. Patty was going to put her case to Dane, and she would have to go. But it would not be back to England.

She said restrainedly, "It would be wonderful to see the Gulf Country after the Wet. And who knows—maybe I shall."

Patty Drummond sniffed. "I very much doubt it. Very much. . . ."

When they reached the homestead, it was Justine who came forward across the veranda at Dane's side to greet the guests—like a hostess—while Kate stood to one side, though her smile for Keitha was full of welcome and friendliness.

The mere sight of Dane; the brief touch of his fingers on her hand, the oddly wary smile in his eyes, made Keitha's nerves jangle.

She was given her old room. After a quick refreshing shower, she changed with trembling hands into one of her London dresses, a bright orange affair, and made up her face with rather more care than usual, adding eye-shadow and mascara. She had not missed the fact that Justine was looking particularly glamorous in a long gown of a clinging, filmy material in one of the newest designs. Mellie too would be at her best in one of the new dresses Patty had made so professionally for her.

When Keitha went into the dining room, she found the dinner table formally set with a starched white cloth and candles in silver candlesticks. There were crystal goblets, and wine was to be served with the meal. Some of this was Justine's doing, she was sure; though not, as it happened, the cooking.

When they were seated she was sure, too, that Justine had planned the seating arrangements. Dane sat at one end of the long table, Kate at the other. One one side were Patty, Col and Mellie, with Patty next to Dane. Opposite them were Justine, Bill and Keitha, Justine, of course, being beside Dane. This arrangement made Keitha do a little thinking. Justine had put herself between Dane and Bill. And she had put Mellie next to Col. Keitha suspected that Justine didn't very much like the attention Bill had paid her at the border muster—she had even made a crack about collecting scalps. But she was more interested in underlining an association between Mellie and Col than she was in keeping Keitha away from Bill. Keitha didn't really count for much in the order of things as far as Justine was concerned, because she would soon be gone. Keitha had no idea what made Justine so sure of this, but sure of it she was, judging from various remarks she had made the other day.

After the wine was poured and dinner had begun, Dane commented with a touch of irony, "We certainly are festive tonight! Do I detect your hand here, Justine? Or is it Kate who has suddenly become romantic?"

Justine smiled at him in the candlelight, which put lovely lights in her eyes and hair—and in Mellie's too, Keitha noticed.

"A little bit of gracious living, Dane, so we can make believe we're in Brisbane or Sydney instead of in the Outback."

"The Outback will do me every time, Justine," said Dane. He indicated the dinner plates. "The fare's Outback at all events. But definitely! There's no mistaking good Wayaway beef and Mrs. Dimmick knows how to cook it. Eh, Col? Or have you developed a taste for fancy cooking, lately?"

Col grinned. "I just like good food well cooked, Dane. And we're lucky our womenfolk know how to deal with it."

Justine looked slightly displeased that the talk had switched from atmosphere, created by her, to food, cooked to perfection by somebody else. She said maliciously, "Our womenfolk, Col? That phrase has a proprietorial ring about it." She smiled innocently at Mellie. "I didn't know you found time to cook the meals at the outstation, Mellie."

Mellie went scarlet, and Patty looked infuriated by Justine's insinuation. Mellie Drummond was earmarked for Dane, not for Col. But before she could speak, Kate put in smoothly, "Keitha does the cooking at the outstation these days, Justine. And Dane tells me she does it very well indeed."

"But not for much longer," said Patty, smiling sweetly

now, while it was Justine who looked put out. Keitha would have liked to ask Patty exactly what she meant, but a dinner party was hardly the time to do so. Dane at all events created a diversion by getting up to refill the wine glasses. And Bill, who was the only one who had offered nothing so far in the way of conversation, asked, "Is it true? Are you really leaving us soon, Keitha?"

Keitha looked at Patty. "I don't know," she said cautiously. Dane was filling her glass and said, in her ear, so softly that only Kate could have heard it apart from Keitha, "Don't you know, Keitha Godwin? We shall have to talk about that."

Keitha's heart thudded. Such a talk could lead in only one direction. She was going to be finally and permanently excluded from Wayaway. As far as she was concerned, the rest of the dinner was spoiled.

Later, they went onto the veranda to dance. Justine had unearthed a few dance records, and having put one on the record player made no bones about asking Dane if they could start the ball rolling. Bill claimed Keitha, and Col, satisfied that the boss had had first choice, danced with Mellie.

In no time at all, Justine and Dane disappeared into the garden. If Patty Drummond appeared agitated about this, it was nothing to the way Keitha was feeling. She was furious with herself. When would she ever learn sense? She forced her attention back to Bill, who had been making no effort at conversation, and remarked lightly, "You're a good dancer, Bill. You must have done a fair bit of it in your time. What happened to make you go sour on the fair sex?" She would never had asked such a personal question if she hadn't been talking for the sole purpose of keeping her mind occupied and was quite astounded at his instant and savage reply.

"Haven't you guessed yet? You must be as blind as the boss . . . Justine O'Boyle happened to me."

She looked up at him thoughtfully. "I thought it might

be that. I didn't think you were paying me so much attention for my own sake. But what went wrong, Bill? Is it the pecking order I hear about that holds you back?"

"I don't give a damn for the pecking order," he said, his eyes hard. "Miss Justine O'Boyle simply hasn't looked my way since I came here. And I'm not going to crawl for any woman. When I fell for her in Brisbane, I was fool enough to think it was the great Outback that was calling her when she wouldn't commit herself and insisted on coming home to Tyrone Park. To please her, I found myself a job out here. What did I find?" He stopped dancing and looked down at Keitha. "She's just one more of several stupid females busting themselves to get the boss to fall in love with them. Can you wonder that my opinion of women has reached an all-time low? I'm quitting this outfit. I'll be back in Brisbane before the Wet."

"Maybe you're wise," said Keitha. She wondered if he included her among those stupid females and reflected that if she had any sense she would follow his example; though of course she knew she might have no choice. There was no doubt that the boss of Wayaway was a powerfully attractive male.

When the record ended, Mellie and Col went happily inside to put on another one. They at least appeared to be enjoying themselves. Bill and Keitha started dancing again, Dane strolled around from the side veranda, and presently there were two other couples on the floor. This time Justine, her cheeks flushed, danced with Col, and Mellie was where they all longed to be—in the boss's arms. But Mellie looked faintly bored.

Suddenly Keitha almost wanted to laugh. What a funny lot they were—herself very much included! She wanted to dance with Dane—yet wouldn't that only serve to bring her dismissal nearer? If he danced with her, he would want to talk about her going.

Yet, when he did dance with her, such depressing

thoughts went clean out of her head. Because dancing with Dane was something she had dreamed about. He was more magnetically and sexually attractive than any man she had ever met. To be in his arms, to be so close to hm, threw her mind into utter confusion. He was not a wonderfully proficient dancer. He interpreted the rhythm in his own way, lazily, almost mindlessly, so that it seemed to pulse through their two bodies.

After a long, long time, Keitha managed to say, glancing up at him through dark lashes, "I thought I was on your black list tonight, that you weren't going to dance with me."

"Now why would you think that? It would have been inexcusable in a host, wouldn't it?" He looked down mockingly into her face. "No, honey, there was a little matter I wanted to clear up with Justine first of all. And then you were rather occupied with the bookkeeper, weren't you?. . . . But you're far from being on my black list. Remember I once called you a hibiscus flower? Well, a hibiscus bloom needs a light touch. And I've been far from sure I could use a light touch when it comes to Keitha Godwin."

She didn't know what he was talking about. It was like a riddle, but she couldn't drag her eyes from his. Her heart was hammering. Somehow they had drifted to the far end of the veranda where there was scarcely any light. They were barely moving, but stood close, locked together, his two arms holding her to him.

He asked softly, his sensuous mouth curving in a half-smile that might not be a smile at all, "Are we going to talk about your love life in London?"

"I thought we were going to talk about my leaving Wayaway." She felt herself trembling.

"Isn't it the same thing?"

There was a pause. She tried to sort herself out, but with his arms about her she could not think clearly at all.

She wanted to say, "My love life in London has ended," but she could only shake her head.

"All right." He sounded suddenly positive, even brisk. "We'll forget London if that's how you want it. But watch out, honey—for in future there's going to be no more light handling."

Suddenly they were dancing properly again, down toward the others at the lighted end of the veranda, and nothing had been resolved at all. In next to no time, Kate came to tell them that supper was ready and to remind them that it was a working day tomorrow.

Keitha finally went to bed feeling thoroughly restless and on edge. She tried to tell herself, "I hate Dane Langley," but she knew that she didn't and never would....

In the morning when she got up, Mellie, Col and Dane had already left the house, and Patty Drummond wore an air of smug satisfaction. Although she had insisted that Keitha would have to help with the household chores, Kate would not hear of it, saying that the housegirls were perfectly capable of coping and that Keitha must treat herself to a holiday. So she tidied her room after breakfast and finally made her way to the veranda. Justine was sitting there smoking and staring moodily out over the garden. Keitha asked her, "Aren't you going out to find the others?"

Justine's eyes narrowed. "That's just what I'm not going to do. No, Keitha, as from now, I leave Dane strictly to Mellie. It appears that's what he wants."

Keitha blinked. It seemed an extraordinary change of attitude. She asked curiously, "What's happened?"

The clear gray-green eyes were turned toward her. "Seeing you're only a visitor and don't belong here, I'll tell you something, Keitha. It's not all signed and settled yet, but Dane let me know pretty definitely last night that he's made up his mind who he's going to marry. It's

Mellie, of course. No more playing around, was the way he put it. You might have noticed I was looking a bit dashed when we came in from the garden while you were dancing. . . . But shut up about it, won't you? We don't want to precipitate matters with a lot of talk."

Keitha was staring at her. She felt all the color drain from her face. So Mellie was to be the girl after all! Mellie had somehow made the grade. Lucky, lucky Mellie. All the life and energy seemed to drain out of her; she wanted to close her eyes and weep. Which was utterly ridiculous, because everyone had told her the boss had his eye on Mellie.

Justine was saying, "This is why he's asked the Drummonds to stay, of course. . . . So you see now why I'm not running after them this morning. A girl has *some* pride. And strictly between us, Keitha, if I can manage it I intend to be nicely tied up myself before Dane drops his bombshell on the rest of the community. He's a heartless brute, when you come to think of it. Oh well—" She grimaced tiredly and reached for the cigarettes on a nearby table, lit one and squinted through smoke into brilliant sunlight. "I'm not all that keen on the Gulf Country. How does it appeal to you?"

"I love it," said Keitha without even having to think. Her heart ached. Soon—very soon—she would have to leave it.

"It's easy enough to love when you're just passing through," commented Justine. "For my part, I prefer the city. But for Dane, I'd never have come back to Tyrone Park. Even so, there are times when I look at those endless, endless plains, at that distant, distant horizon; or lie in bed listening to the empty, empty silence. I don't think I can stand it another day." She flicked Keitha a half rueful look. "Well, I won't have to now, shall I? Funny, isn't it? Col loves it, Mellie loves it—she couldn't wait to get back here after boarding school, not like me. To Dane, it's more than life. But I wish my father had done anything else in the world other than run a cattle station out here. If I'd never lived on Tyrone Park, never met Dane Langley, I'd have been perfectly happy in the city. Instead, it worked on me like a sickness. I forgot the everlasting plains, the dust, and the heat; because I was haunted by a certain face—a certain man, who seemed like a god or something." She laughed briefly. "I guess I'm cured this time. You're lucky; safely in love with someone else, not likely to be caught that way."

Keitha listened confusedly. She was lucky—not caught. How wrong Justine was! Wherever she went in the future she knew that a certain face would haunt her; the face of a man who called her honey, and was rough, tough, casual, cruel, certain that he was always right. A man who was heartless and was going to settle for a marriage that would be sensible for a cattleman— She was by no means safely in love with someone else and wondered why Justine would think she was. And who did she mean?

Someone stepped onto the veranda, and the screen door shut with a bang that made Keitha jump.

"What's got into you two?" It was Bill Sutton. "I've been expecting all morning to see you come pelting across the yard to saddle up your horses and chase after the great white boss."

"Well, that's just what we're not going to do this morning, Bill," said Justine with a provocative smile.

Bill stared. "I don't get it." He looked at Keitha. "How about coming out riding with me?"

"I'd like to," said Keitha, who was hardly responsible at the moment for what she said.

Justine butted her cigarette and stood up. "I'm coming too," she announced.

Bill gave her a long, hard, unrelenting look. Then, with

a shrug—"All right. I'll see you both over in the saddling yard as soon as you're ready."

The girls went off to change into jeans and shirts. Keitha was ready first and went to find Kate to tell her they were going riding with Bill.

"See you all stick together, then," said Kate, who was busy sorting fresh vegetables on the kitchen table. "And make sure you have a reliable mount. Dane wouldn't like you to take risks."

"I'll take Summer," said Keitha. She felt numb, as if her very heart had stopped beating. She knew she meant to get away from the others somehow, for like Justine she had some thinking to do.

When they reached the saddling yards, Summer and a little black colt named Joe had been saddled as well as the horse Bill usually rode.

Justine took one look at the black colt and headed for Summer.

"I don't trust that little devil," she told Bill.

"There's nothing wrong with Joe. Summer's Keitha's mount. Come on now, Justine, you're so wild about the Outback. Keitha's a London girl."

"I'm not the pioneering type," Justine said with a smile. "Maybe Keitha is." As she spoke she swung herself gracefully and agilely into the saddle. "Keitha loves the Gulf Country. She'll try anything—more tales to take home to her boyfriend when she leaves us."

Her boyfriend. There it was again. Where did Justine get her information? Well, it didn't matter. None of it mattered now. Keitha looked at the little black horse. He was standing quietly and didn't look a devil to her. She would sooner have had Summer, of course, but there was no question of that now. She put a hand gently on his neck and he eyed her mildly. Bill crossed over and gave her a leg up into the saddle.

"Joe's all right. He doesn't like the spur, that's all, so

just use your heels with caution, and you'll be all right."

A moment later they all trotted out of the yard, and Justine in the lead flung back over her shoulder, "How much longer do you intend working out here, Bill?"

"I wouldn't have a notion," said Bill, though it was not what he had told Keitha the night before. "Why? Are you interested?"

"Not particularly. But I'm going back to Brisbane." Justine touched her horse's flank, and Summer broke into a gallop and was away across the plain. Bill followed, but Keitha's horse was suddenly fractious, pulling on the bit and tossing his head back, and prancing sideways. It was a minute or two before she had him under control and set off after the others who were by now some way ahead.

She didn't try to catch up with them and looked for an excuse to leave them. She had the distinct impression that Justine would prefer it that way.

She allowed them to get a long way ahead of her, and presently they showed down to a walk and moved along side by side. Obviously they were talking to each other. Keitha had no intention of intruding and making a third. After a few minutes she galloped closer and called out, "I think I'll go back. This horse and I don't agree terribly well."

They both drew rein and turned around to wait for her.

"Yes, go and talk to Kate," suggested Justine, obviously far from displeased at the idea of Keitha's leaving them.

But Bill said, "Want me to come with you?"

"No, of course not. I'm all right. It's just I'm not really enjoying riding Joe."

"Bill should have made a better choice," said Justine. "We'll see you at lunch, Keitha."

"Right."

She started back the way they had come, but she didn't

intend returning to the homestead. She wanted to be by herself. She knew the track to the airstrip and thought she would go that way. Then no one could accuse her of trying to get lost, or to create trouble making adventures for herself.

She let her horse amble along as slowly as it pleased, and she thought hard about what Justine had told her. So Dane Langley had made up his mind, had he? And he had kindly told Justine, and Justine—exactly as Col had said, though he had not been speaking of any specific girl—was not prepared to think again about Bill. Somehow Keitha did not think that Bill would make it easy for her. He was not the type to come meekly running when he was whistled.

And what about Mellie? Keitha wondered if Mellie had been told the verdict yet—if Patty was rejoicing. Wasn't Mellie supposed to have a mind of her own? Wasn't it even conceivable that given the chance she just might prefer Col? But then Mellie would be given no choice. "That's not the way we do things out here."

Keitha was working herself up to feel good and angry about the boss of Wayaway, who was so arrogant and domineering he could throw everyone around him into a turmoil. She found anger more bearable than heartbreak.

She had bypassed the homestead now and ridden almost to the airstrip. Before they reached the gate, she turned her horse's head and rode out toward a line of trees. Her mind went back to the conversation she had had with Dane the night before. What had he meant by saying that there was going to be no more light handling? Did he mean that her days at Wayaway were over, that he was going to pack her off at last? Well, she would get in first. She would ask to be taken to the outstation for the rest of her things, and she would take the next mail plane. That would show him how little she cared. It was a great pity she hadn't paid more attention to what Bill Sutton had told her weeks ago. She had thought then that she was impregnable. And she hadn't been, after all.

She was so deep in her thoughts that she had been paying almost no attention to where she was going. Dimly she was aware that there were trees, giant anthills, and now she had to lower her head, or sway to one side every so often as they passed among the trees. Then suddenly a small branch crashed down nearby, her heart leaped and her muscles tensed. She must have dug her heels into the black colt's sides. Either that or the falling branch startled him, for suddenly he seemed to go crazy and raced hell-bent through the trees in a mad gallop.

Keitha was terrified. Sooner or later she was going to fall or to be swept from the saddle by one of those overhanging branches. All too soon she realized she simply hadn't the strength to control the horse in his present mood.

Then before the disaster she feared could happen, they were clear of the trees and pounding toward a steep creek bank. The perspiration was pouring down her back, and her face felt cold and clammy. She tried desperately to check the maddened horse and then, exhausted, gave in. All she could do was to hang on and pray.

Seconds later, she heard the thundering of hooves behind. A horseman overtook her; riding in so close that before she knew what had happened he had shouldered her runaway mount around. In no time at all he brought him to a halt. Keitha sat trembling and exhausted in the saddle.

Dane's voice—for of course it had to be Dane—exclaimed angrily, "My God, you're a fool of a girl! Were you trying to kill yourself, galloping at the bank in such a murderous way?" He had swung out of the saddle and reached up to lift her to the ground. Her legs seemed to give way beneath her and she relaxed against him.

CHAPTER TEN

She must have lapsed into momentary unconscious-
ness. For the next thing she knew, his voice came to her
swimmingly through a ripple of yellow grass and dazzling sunlight.

"Here—drink this."

She sipped, swallowed, as the fiery taste of brandy
made her cough. She was half lying, half sitting against a
tree trunk, and Dane's arm was about her shoulders. The
two horses stood nearby, their reins thrown over a
branch.

"Honey," Dane said, "why do you do these things?"
His face was very close to hers, and those strange blue
eyes seemed to look right into the depth of her being.
There was neither anger nor laughter in them now. For a
long moment she felt she was confronted by the very
essence of the man: deeply serious, vital, intense. She was
like a needle being drawn to a magnet, slowly, inexorably.

She shuddered and pushed the flask away.

"I don't like anyone to be killed on my cattle run," said
Dane. "Not anyone at all." Still his eyes burned into hers,
and she leaned back weakly against the strength of his
arm. It was not until he moved to screw the cap onto the
flask that she roused herself enough to say shakily, "I
would never let myself be killed on your cattle run, Dane
Langley. I intend to walk off it under my own steam."

"Do you indeed? And just when are you planning to do
that?"

"When the Drummonds go back to the outstation."

"Well, that won't be for quite a while yet," he said
humoringly. That of course was because he wanted Mellie

around, to complete his wooing. The memory made her rally.

"Then I'll go sooner. Just as soon as you like."

"As soon as I like? Have I something to do with it, then?" That was unanswerable, and she remained silent. "In my opinion, it would be a pity for you to pull out. You've acclimatized so well, when I think back to that first day." He smiled into her eyes, and she had to close them. It was like a knife in her heart. "You stepped off that plane looking so much like the trendily dressed tourist come to take a look at the unthinkable Outback. Since then—" He broke off and took a packet of cigarettes from his pocket, lit two, and gave her one. Though she seldom smoked, she took it. She needed something to steady her nerves just now; as he lounged beside her in the shade of the trees, his eyes narrowed against the glare from the plains.

Watching him through her lashes, she found herself thinking, "I'll have this to remember. It will be something and yet nothing." It was both pain and pleasure simply to look at him: his jutting chin, his sunbleached hair, his deeply tanned face. . . .

He turned his head suddenly and caught her staring. She felt the color rush into her pale cheeks. His lips curved in that enigmatic suggestion of a smile.

"I've never yet persuaded you to talk about London, have I? Well, I warned you last night that I was finished with using a light touch. And now I have you lying here, full of brandy, and scared stiff, all the fight gone out of you, I'm going to really outdo myself and twist your arm until you give."

She stared at him fascinated, put the cigarette to her lips and drew on it; saw the trembling of her hand.

"My private life is my own concern," she said shakily.

"Is it?" His eyes were quizzical. "Isn't this a sort of private life, though; you and me lying here together in the midday heat, alone in the world? Doesn't it seem fateful, too, that I called in at the homestead to pick you up and thereby arrived here just at the right moment to save your life?"

Was there a tinge of irony in his voice? Was he playing her along? She said defensively, "I'm sorry, but I don't really think you saved my life. I got through that belt of trees without an accident. I might have taken a tumble in the creek, but I don't think I'd have been killed."

"No one ever thinks they're going to be killed, honey. But I tell you I was really afraid of what was going to happen to you."

"And you weren't ready for it because you hadn't heard the story of my life?" She was trying hard to be flippant because she was somehow frightened of him in his present mood.

"Something like that," he agreed nonchalantly. His face came closer. One hand took hold of hers that was holding the cigarette and pressed it hard against the ground. The other pulled her to him—even harder—and his lips were against hers. . . .

Despite herself, despite what Justine had told her about Mellie, she felt herself surrendering, going limp. With a sudden effort, she pushed him away and drew back breathing quickly.

"How can you do that when—"

"When you're all but passing out? When you haven't recovered from the fright you gave yourself just now? Frankly, honey, I think there couldn't be a better time. I told you I was going to twist your arm. I have you at my mercy now. I can find out things I wouldn't find out if you had all your wits about you and all your usual defenses in position."

"What kind of things?" She hadn't even meant to ask the question.

He gave a deep-throated laugh. "Come on,

honey—admit that you're more than attracted to me. You did give yourself away pretty thoroughly just now, you know."

She refused to answer his eyes, half-closed her own and stared at the ground. She saw an ant move, this way, then turn back; hesitate, move on again. Then back once more. "That's like me," she thought miserably. And she thought of Mellie and wished she could hate him too.

He said gently, "All right, I'll make the first move. I'm very much—maybe too much—attracted to you, Keitha. It happened right at the beginning, over at the coast."

Her eyes flicked up warily and looked straight into blue fire. The bookkeeper had said, "He'll play you along—if that's what you want. But there'll be nothing in it for you." She bit her lip hard and looked away from him.

He drew a sharp impatient breath. "You tantalizing, maddening, tormenting girl! Let's get to the bottom of all this. Are you, or are you not, going back to England?"

"I—I don't know," she said desperately.

"Then listen to me, honey. You'd better damn well make up your mind. What's the strength of all this talk about you over the galah sessions?"

That drew her glance again. "What talk?" she asked sharply. She thought suddenly of the locked office door at the outstation; of Patty Drummond's refusal to let her join in the talk with the women from other cattle runs. She thought of the one day when she had chattered freely to Patty about Donn Gorsky. . . . "*What* talk?" she repeated.

"Don't you know? Honey, it's all over the Gulf that you've a man waiting for you in London—that you'll be married as soon as you get back. Well, I calculate you don't act like a girl in love, but there are all those letters to think about. And remember the night you called me Donn?"

Color flooded her face, then drained away again. She

felt furious with Patty Drummond for talking about her, for being so indiscreet. But of course it had been done deliberately. It explained why Justine O'Boyle had said, "You're safely in love with someone else." Well, it was not true. She was not going back to London to be married. Yet why tell Dane that? He was going to marry Mellie Drummond; he had no right to be kissing Keitha Godwin out here under the trees.

Troubled, she stared out at the line of trees that marked the steep river bank, at the shadows that fell across the long grasses, at the distant line where sky met land, and a heat haze shimmered and danced.

His voice cut through her thoughts with whip-like cruelty. "Come on now, let's have it. Are you going to marry him?"

For the life of her, she couldn't tell the direct lie. There was a long pause. He waited relentlessly.

She said at last, her voice low, "There's never been anything definite. I—"

His eyes narrowed, the pupils were pinpoints of blackness. "Well, that's an admission of some sort. But what a time it's taken to get it out of you! That kiss we shared just now—that wasn't merely a friendly kiss on either side, was it?—Right, we'll take it from there. The inquisition's over." He gave her a dark look, and there was a glint away back in his eyes that she couldn't fathom.

Her head was spinning, and it was not the brandy. What did he mean when he said, "We'll take it from there?" When he commented on that more than passionate kiss? Hadn't he told Justine only last night, "No more playing around?"

She said, groping for caution, for sense, for escape from the utter madness that was ready to swallow her up, "Correction, Dane. The inquisition's not quite over. I have a question. What about Mellie?"

"Mellie?" The sunbleached eyebrows went up. "My God, must we always come back to Mellie? What about her?"

"You're—you're going to marry her, aren't you?"

"Have you been listening to Patty Drummond? No, I am not going to marry Mellie."

Keitha blinked. "But Justine said—" She stopped. Justine had said to "shut up" about that. She said instead, "Does Mellie know? Have you told her?"

The brows came down darkly now. "What do you take me for? Mellie's been brought up from childhood with the idea that if she plays her cards right she'll finish by being Mrs. Dane Langley. She isn't beyond that yet—not quite. But she will. One day she'll find out for herself what love is all about, and that day she'll have grown up. But she has to do it on her own. I'm not going to push her. I can only continue to treat her gently." He stopped. Keitha's mouth had opened in protest, and his lips quirked. "All right. Except on the odd occasion when I find her chasing calves and dicing with death." He stood up and reached a hand to her. "And now I think we'd better get you home. How do you feel about getting back onto that black colt?"

Keitha looked at Joe. "I can manage," she said firmly.

"That's my girl!" Her hand was still in his hand. He pulled her against him, and his lips came down on hers in a kiss that was all fierceness and passion.

At last, weakly, she broke free. "Please, Dane—"

He grinned down at her. "Hardly the time or the place, is it? I agree. Come on, let's get going."

They rode back to the homestead together and Keitha felt oddly happy. But it was a shaky, precarious kind of happiness, a happiness that she could not trust.

The following days reminded her of her first week on Wayaway, when Dane had taken her out on the run with him every day. But this time Mellie was always there too. Dane was so soft with Mellie, so gentle and affectionate that Keitha could feel the poison of jealousy eating into her in spite of what he had told her. She could not help seeing herself as an intruder who had pushed her way into the life on the Wayaway cattle run and was trying to disrupt the ordered pattern of events.

Her new relationship with Dane had not crystallized. She still had no real idea where she stood with him except that he found her perhaps disturbingly physically attractive. Hadn't he at the very beginning called her a "sexy, trendily dressed girl"? Perhaps he was looking for no more than a light affair—like the one he had had with Justine.

Justine, despite Dane's rejection of her, was in no hurry to return to Tyrone Park. Pretty, poised, and unruffled as ever, she still teased and provoked the boss of Wayaway, though Keitha often thought she could detect a touch of barely concealed malice in her banter. She never came out riding with them, and Keitha knew she was concentrating all her attention on the bookkeeper. What progress she was making was uncertain. Keitha had an idea that Bill would make it hard for her, if he played along with her at all. He was not a soft or forgiving sort of man by any account. If Justine had decided she would be happy with him, she would have to fight for him and to forget her pride pretty thoroughly. Otherwise she would have little hope of getting herself "well and truly tied up" before Dane dropped the bombshell she at least expected him to drop.

One thing was for sure: those who loved Dane Langley and lost had it hard—

As in Keitha's first week on Wayaway, Dane went out early, then came back for her later on. Sometimes Mellie went with him at sunup, sometimes she waited with Keitha. But always Patty Drummond was hovering in the background, cold, disapproving, hostile toward Keitha, full of orders and instructions for her daughter.

There was something a little sad and desperate about Mellie these days. Much of her bounce and vitality had gone and she had a vaguely lost air. Even when there was work to be done with the cattle, and she was in the thick of it, she seemed always conscious of Dane's critical eye upon her and fearful that she would invoke his displeasure. It was hard to remember that she had ever defied him—said she hated him.

All during that week the mobs that had been mustered on various parts of the run for the sales were being brought into the holding paddock near the homestead. The size of the mob there was growing and growing. One evening as they rode home behind the cattle, and Mellie was somewhere ahead hidden in the sunstruck haze of red dust, Dane remarked, "Mellie's like a bee in a bottle just now. I'd like to know how much longer it's going to take her to wake up to herself and discover what it is that ails her. Right now, she thinks her world's in pieces because it looks very much like the boss of Wayaway isn't going to marry her. Yet that's not really Mellie's trouble at all." He glanced over at Keitha who rode beside him and his eyes had a thoughtful look.

Keitha wanted to ask, "What is Mellie's trouble?" but she was terribly afraid that Dane was wrong and that Mellie was in love with him and eating her heart out. Mellie tried so hard to please him these days. It could not be doubted that she would make a wonderful wife for a cattleman, even if Justine thought her too unsophisticated.

This evening the sky on the far horizon was covering over with cloud, and there were rumblings of distant thunder. Vivid streaks of lightning spilt dramatically through dark purple clouds, and Keitha felt restlessly that these threatening storms seemed to heighten the general tension. The Wet was still weeks away, but soon there would be stars in the evenings. Dane had said that morning that Justine must go back to Tyrone Park before one or two heavy falls made the rivers impassable. There was always the chance of that happening, and then they would be isolated at Wayaway in their little closed community.

When they reached the homestead that evening, Justine had gone. The bookkeeper had taken her, Kate said, and he would stay away overnight and return the following day.

"That girl should go back to city life," Patty Drummond remarked complacently at dinner. "She doesn't really belong out here."

Keitha caught Dane's satirical glance across the dining room table. Someone—Kate or Patty—had put candles on the table. The women were dressed up. Patty always dressed for dinner, because she had good clothes, designed and made by herself, and she liked to wear them; Kate dressed because she always had and it was habit; Mellie dressed up because her mother nagged and nagged at her until she had to change for sheer peace of mind. And Keitha—Keitha changed into her pretty, dressy clothes simply because she wanted Dane to like the look of her.

Now he said laconically, "What Justine does is up to her. You're too fond of ordering people's lives for them, Patty."

Patty looked down at her plate to hide her expression, and Keitha wanted to laugh. She thought she knew what Patty would have liked to say! Dane was something of an expert at ordering people's lives for them too. Instead, Patty said coldly, "Not at all, Dane. You know perfectly well that all of us do just as you decree."

"Well, that's how it should be," he said equably. "Another glass of wine, Kate?" He reached for the bottle and poured it. "Ask Kate. She's submitted to my father—and to me—for a good part of her life and never regretted it. As for you, Patty, d'you think I made a mistake—insisting you stay on at the outstation?"

"Sometimes I do think that, Dane," said Patty a little bitterly. "Sometimes I wonder why you asked us to stay on."

"One of these days," said Dane, "when Mellie's a little bit older and wiser, you'll know why, Patty. Meanwhile, if you don't want to stay, you're free to go to the coast. You've always been free."

Mellie, who was staring down at her lap, suddenly raised her head and burst out into the momentary silence, "I'd die at the coast! I'd hate it!"

"That's what I thought," said Dane. "What are we going to do with you, Mellie? We'll have to marry you off to someone who's as much in love with the Gulf Country as you are yourself. That reminds me—I was going to suggest you go back to the outstation tomorrow, after the mail's come. It's pretty lonely there for Col, and he'll be here in the afternoon."

Patty tossed her head. "It's lonelier for me, Dane."

"I thought you'd changed your mind about that," he mocked. "And you can take Keitha with you, you know."

Patty fingered her wine glass and looked coldly across the table at the pale-faced slender girl whose eyes were deeply shadowed in the candlelight. Her dislike was plain. "Keitha will be leaving us soon. She has ties, commitments, in England."

"She has an aunt," said Dane mildly.

"And a man friend," flashed Patty. "Perhaps she hasn't told you that." She turned to Keitha, her look intense. "Didn't you tell me that the man you worked for at the television studio is in love with you; that you were in love with him?"

"I suppose I did," said Keitha slowly. She had flushed

crimson and would have given anything on earth to be able to have that conversation unsaid.

There was a hard light in Dane's eyes. "Keitha's not in a hurry to go."

"Oh, really, Dane," Patty snapped. "You can't possibly think she would change the excitement of her life in London for our little backwater, that would be too much to believe."

If only Dane would ask her that question, Keitha thought. She knew very well what her answer would be. But Dane didn't ask her.

Later that night, while they were all sitting on the veranda, she went out to the kitchen to make coffee. Before taking it out to the others, she slipped into her room for the magazine she had been reading. It had an article in it that Kate wanted. She didn't bother putting the light on, and as she moved across the room she heard Patty's voice saying her name.

"I don't need her any longer, Dane, and if you must know, we don't get along. You'd be doing me a favor if you put her on the plane tomorrow. After all, she'll want to see something of her brother before she goes back to England to be married."

Keitha was about to switch on the light to warn them that she was there, but now she paused. What did Dane believe? She had told him she had no such plans. Did he believe her or Patty?

In a moment his voice came drawlingly. "Now, Patty, you've built on to what the girl told you to suit yourself."

"Indeed I've done no such thing! If you knew how many letters she writes, how many she gets from that man— You're blind, Dane, if you think there's nothing in it. Of course she wants to have a good time while she's out here, and an engaged girl isn't likely to get that. She's enjoyed herself flirting with Colin—with Bill—and of course she'd like to flirt with you."

Keitha's blood boiled. She had listened too long. She flicked on the light, and the voices receded.

When she woke the next morning she heard the bellowing of cattle in the holding yards. Soon the mob of 900 beasts would be on the road, soon the Wet would come, soon the Drummonds would depart for the outstation. Everything is going to happen at once, yet nothing—nothing—happened to her, Keitha Godwin. It was as if Dane were playing a cruel game with her that had no ending. It was mail day, and she tried to distract herself wondering if and what she would hear from Martin. She was half expecting that he and Julie Warner were announcing their engagement. That would mean a link between the Godwins and, indirectly, the Langleys. Which brought her, maddeningly, back to Dane.

She jumped out of bed and went to the doors that opened onto the veranda. The day looked exactly the same as any other. Bright sunlight filtered through the crimson flowers of the bougainvillea, the mango trees were motionless, their leaves unmoved by even the slightest breeze, and the faint nostalgic scent of the oleanders drifted about the veranda.

Justine had gone. That was the only difference in the day. And that meant exactly nothing, because it was some days since she had been vitally concerned with Dane Langley. He had told her he had made up his mind who he would marry. And he had told Keitha it was not Mellie. Then who was it? Keitha decided she would be a fool if she took anything for granted.

Her nerves were stretched taut. She was edgy, distracted, uncertain, and beginning to feel that she had been mad to allow herself to fall in love with Dane. The whole situation was becoming subtly intolerable. Something was going to have to happen to break the tension.

And yet today was exactly like any other day.

She showered, got into her jeans, and went out to breakfast. Dane and Mellie had gone already, Patty was still in bed, and there was only herself and Kate at the end of the veranda.

Keitha said, pouring black coffee, "I never did settle with you about those paintings, Kate. I'd like to send one to England in time for Christmas. And of course I would like one for myself."

"Why the hurry?" asked Kate, with her friendly smile. "But if you like, we'll get something sorted out this morning after I have things organized in the kitchen."

Dane arrived before she had come back from the kitchen. He found Keitha waiting on the veranda, her hat under her chair.

"Do you want to come out today, or have you had enough? I'll be back in time to meet the mail plane, if you prefer to have a lazy morning. You look tired."

She didn't want a lazy morning. If she looked tired it was because her thoughts of him had kept her awake. Didn't he know yet how she loved the run; the dust and the cattle and, more than anything else, riding at his side? She stood up unhurriedly. "I must have my exercise."

He gave her an odd look. "Exercise! Is that all it is?" She flushed deeply and refused to look at him. "Well, hang on for a minute. I want to remind Kate that Col will be here later on. We've plans to check over to get the mob on the road."

"All this will be over soon, won't it? Once you have your cattle moving—"

"Yes. Then in no time we'll have the Wet, and we can all take it easy." He disappeared in the direction of the kichen, and she stood waiting, looking pensively out into the sunlit garden. When he came back she asked, as they headed for the addling yard, "What will you do during the Wet, Dane?"

"Well, that rather depends," he said guardedly. "I usually go over to the coast."

"And the Drummonds?"

He shrugged. "They come along too."

"So there'll be no job for me at the outstation."

"That's right." He smiled at her in an intimate way that made her heart thud. They both knew that there was no job for her at the outstation already.

He saw her mounted, swung himself into the saddle, and they were off.

She came back with him after lunch. Mellie was somewhere behind with the stockmen. Keitha wondered vaguely if she would hear Donn's reaction to her letter when the mail came in. She didn't particularly care one way or the other. Donn had faded very much into a background figure. She hoped she had done the same as far as he was concerned. He was always involved with a number of people. One thing was certain. He would never lack for admirers, and being Donn, even if he thought Keitha had broken his heart, he would soon be circulating freely again.

They left their horses in the yard, and Dane looked back frowningly. "Mellie's taking her time."

His arm was across Keitha's shoulders as they went toward the garden, and she remembered how once she had told him she didn't like to be touched. Now—his arm laid across her shoulders was like the kiss of life.

In the garden Patty, wearing a wide-brimmed cotton hat and green gardening gloves, was watering some small plants.

"Wait till I tell you the news," she said as they drew near. She turned the stream of water aside, and they both stopped. "It came over the radio transceiver on the morning schedule." Her eyes were bright and malicious. For some reason Keitha's heart began to pound.

"Yes?" said Dane. His arm was now around Keitha's

waist, and the girl saw Patty's glance flick there and back.

"Justine O'Boyle and Bill Sutton have decided to get married."

Dane looked really surprised. He obviously hadn't a notion that this was an old affair come back to life, or that he had ever been the cause of obstructing it.

"Well, what do you know! I thought Justine came to see me. Is Bill going to work on Tyrone Park?"

"Dear me, no. They're moving to Brisbane. They mean to get away before the Wet, and they'll be married at the coast."

"Well, that's fine. I knew we were going to have to find a new bookkeeper. Bill misses the life of the city."

They started to move on. Patty said, her voice cracking. "Oh, Keitha, there's a message for you in your room. Something you've been waiting for, I think."

Keitha's nerves jumped. Was it to do with leaving the outstation? Surely Patty was not giving her formal notice.

They had reached the veranda steps when Patty called Dane back. "There's something I wanted to tell you, Dane."

He went back, and Keitha continued still wondering about that message.

When she reached her room, she threw her hat on the bed and crossed to the dressing table where she saw a folded sheet of paper. She opened it out.

Carefully written out in Kate's handwriting was a telegram that had been relayed over the morning schedule. It said simply, "You win. Come home and we'll be married with all the trimmings. Love, Donn."

CHAPTER ELEVEN

She read it twice, feeling somehow shocked, aware that it was public property. It was what she had wanted. Long, long ago, it seemed. Now it meant nothing at all. She stood at the dressing table, the message in her hands, and looked up to meet her own eyes, dark and troubled, in the mirror. For the first time, she felt for Donn, really felt for him. Yet hadn't he taken her letter rather lightly? He had thought he had only to use the magic word "married", and she would come running back to him.

"No, Donn," she thought. "You're much too late. I could never marry you now, no matter what happens." It amazed her that he did not know it; that he didn't sense that this ephemeral thing between them had dissolved, vanished. It had never been based on a real understanding. Otherwise, he would never have even suggested that she should shack up with him.

She heard footsteps coming around the veranda, and then Dane stood at the door, hands low on his hips, bleached hair ruffled, brows down, eyes flashing fire. On his mouth that half smile that was not a smile at all.

"So you have what you were waiting for, have you? It's all definite enough now, I take it, Keitha Godwin. You'd better pack your things, and I'll put you on the plane. One thing I'd like to say—I don't appreciate being used in a battle of tactics."

Keitha stared at him appalled. She understood perfectly that Patty Drummond had told him what was in that telegram and had given her own interpretation of it.

"You don't understand," she said confusedly, hardly knowing where to begin. "I wrote to Donn—I told him—"

And at that fateful moment there was an interruption. It was Kate, too urgent for ceremony.

"Dane, Mellie's been thrown from her horse. One of the stockmen's come in. He didn't like to move her. You'll have to drive out at once—"

He swung around, eyes alert, watchful. "Where is she?"

"Mick will show you. He's waiting outside."

He paused for a second at the door to say, his voice hard and impersonal, "Kate, see that Keitha gets packed up. She's going on the plane this afternoon."

Then he was gone.

Keitha looked at Kate. She felt dizzy, stricken, her face was white. "Mellie—is it bad?"

"I hope not. Dane will take Patty along. We'll soon know." She looked at Keitha, her eyes puzzled. "You're going? You mean to marry this man in England? I never believed it was true—"

Keitha, who had felt numb, now wanted to weep. She sat down abruptly on the side of the bed. The sheet of paper was still in her hands, and she stared at it blankly. "No. Of course I'm not going to marry him." She looked up at Kate. "Dane doesn't understand. Perhaps he doesn't want to understand," she went on hopelessly. "Perhaps none of it matters." She stood up and went mechanically to the closet. Her eyes were blinded by tears, but she began to take down the desses she had chosen with such care. She put her suitcase on the bed and began to fold her clothes carefully. It was all too much: the telegram, the misunderstanding, Mellie.

Behind her, Kate, who could not see the tears running down her cheeks, said gently, "Tell me about it, Keitha."

The girl wiped her eyes quickly and turned with a bright smile. "Donn never wanted me to marry him before. We were in love—in a way—but he was in favor of one of those casual arrangements. It didn't suit me.

And I didn't care any more after a while. I knew I would never go back, and I wrote and told him. So then after all that, he changed his mind about us."

"Men!" said Kate. "They think they can mend things in a minute—be forgiven anything." She put a hand on Keitha's arm. "Don't pack your clothes. You must tell Dane."

"What's the use? I'd have to leave sooner or later."

Kate looked at her and shook her head. "Do you want to go? Do you want to leave Wayaway—and Dane?"

Keitha bit her lip. The tears were coming again. "I love it here," she said shakily. "More than anywhere on earth. But I was a fool ever to imagine— And now this accident's happened, Dane will see it's Mellie he cares for."

"Rubbish," said Kate briskly. "Mellie's never been more to Dane than a little sister, though Patty is too stubborn to accept it. I've never known him really in love until he met you." Keitha gasped. What was Kate saying? Kate smiled a little. "Then that silly woman spread those stories over the radio transmitter, and of course everyone heard them, Dane heard them. That's why he tried to keep away from you, I could see that. No, you mustn't go. You put your clothes away again, Keitha, and in a minute I'll have a pot ot tea made. Patty will need a cup when she comes home. You need one now."

"But Dane said—" began Keitha weakly.

"Never mind what Dane said." It was the first time Keitha had ever heard Kate defy the boss, and now she was quite determined about it. "You do as *I* say this time."

Keitha abandoned her packing. Her thoughts were whirling. How would Kate know what went on in Dane Langley's mind? Yet Kate would know—he was the sun in her sky and she would make it her business to know and to understand. She dried her tears, and her thoughts returned to Mellie—big, beautiful, healthy Mellie, who wasn't yet really grown up. It was inconceivable that anything should have happened to Mellie.

Twenty minutes later the Land Rover was back. By that time Keitha and Kate were drinking tea on the veranda, saying little, waiting, and thinking of Mellie. Dane came up the steps carrying the girl who was limp in his arms, her red hair hanging down. Patty, close behind them, looked sick. She was only too glad for Kate to take control, help her to a chair, and hand her a cup of strong black tea. Dane had gone through into the sitting room and deposited Mellie on one of the couches. Keitha, without thinking, followed him, and waited mutely. When he spoke, Kate was behind her listening too.

"No bones broken. I've already made sure of that. She's knocked herself out, probably has a bit of concussion. We'll have a word with the doc this afternoon over the transceiver. But I don't think there's anything to worry about." He smiled grimly. "She was after a calf, of course. But even when it comes to being thrown by a horse in dangerous circumstances, it seems Mellie knows how to fall. Though she mightn't be so lucky next time."

Kate looked tenderly at the girl who lay unconscious in the room. "I'm glad she's all right. I'll slip back to Patty now."

Someone else came into the room then, tiptoeing clumsily in his stockmen's boots. It was Col, and he went straight to the couch where Mellie lay.

"Is she all right? I just arrived. Patty says she's had a fall."

"She's right as rain," said Dane. His smile was gentle and reassuring. Col looked almost as green as Patty.

At that moment Mellie moaned, moved, opened her eyes. The two men stood looking down at her. Her eyes went to them both; dazedly at first, and then with dawning recognition. But it was on Col's face that her glance stayed, and suddenly she began to cry.

"Oh, Col, Col." She put her fists to her face in a childish gesture.

Keitha saw Col and the boss exchange one brief telling look. There were tears in her own eyes, and she didn't really know what passed between them. But something had. Some minute but subtle signal had been given and received. In an instant Col was on his knees beside Mellie, soothing her, murmuring to her, her hand in his.

Dane turned away and went silently out to the veranda, and Keitha followed.

Once they had left the cool shadowy room behind them, his manner changed abruptly.

"Ready?" His voice was curt.

Keitha shook her head helplessly. Along the veranda there was now only Kate. Patty must have gone to her room, leaving her daughter to the care of those who could stand the sight of pain and hurt. Kate came toward them.

"I'll look after Mellie now, Dane. Is she conscious?"

"Just about. Better get her into bed presently. But leave her with Col for a minute or two. There's nothing much wrong with her. She's knocked herself out and probably given herself a bit of a fright. Col too." His mouth twisted in a faintly sardonic grin.

"Thank God it's no worse," said Kate. "You have a cup of tea, Dane. Then you've the plane to meet. Keitha might like to go out with you for the run."

He stared at her. "I told you to see she was packed," he blazed.

"I know you did, Dane. But she's not leaving."

"She damn well is. I'm the one who gives the orders here—"

"Dane," Kate broke in, "I must go and see to Mellie. I'm not going to argue with you. Keitha will explain."

Keitha didn't know that she wanted to explain. The boss of Wayaway was white around the nostrils. She had never before seen him in such a fury, and it was all waiting to descend on her head; even though she had done absolutely nothing to deserve it. When those blue eyes were turned on her behind Kate's departing back, she said with dignity, "I'll pack, if that's what you want, Dane."

"Surely it's what you must want too," he retorted coldly.

"Is it? Then if you say so, it must be right." She went quickly, head up, in the direction of her bedroom, and he followed her.

He lounged against the bedroom door while she bundled her clothes unceremoniously and rather angrily into the suitcase. He was puzzled, watchful; silent now. "I still have some things at the outstation, Dane."

"They'll be sent on."

Silence again until she had snapped shut the lid of her suitcase. Then she raised her head and looked at him. She was debating with herself whether or not she should say anything about that telegram. If only she knew whether Kate was right! She said, with a cool smile, "Mellie's sorted herself out, hasn't she? I'm glad about that. Col is very much in love with Mellie. Do you suppose Patty will mind? And Justine. I hope she'll be happy with Bill."

He was tapping impatiently against the door frame with the knuckles of one hand. Then he said with a savage movement, "Mellie—Justine—all this evasion. What about you, Keitha Godwin? Kate said you'd explain. Have you sorted yourself out?"

"I sorted myself out long ago." She turned away and began opening and closing drawers to make sure she had missed nothing. But the fact was, she couldn't go on looking at him without giving herself away.

But it was no use. A quick movement and he was

behind her—had seized her shoulders in a painful grip, twisted her around so that she faced him helplessly. His eyes blazed down at her.

"It's time you gave me a full and proper explanation of a lot of things," he said from between clenched teeth. His fingers bit into her flesh cruelly. "I've asked you already God knows how many times—"

"You'll be late for the mail plane," she breathed.

"So I'll be late for the mail plane. So it can wait for once, or take off, or do what it damn well pleases. But we're neither of us budging from this room until you've told me exactly what you mean by that statement."

"That I've sorted myself out?" Despite herself she was bristling with antagonism. How dared he ask her to state her position first! She looked him straight in the eye, and thought she would die for the pain and pleasure of it. She said distinctly, "It's hardly your business. I'm not aware that it ever was. The position seems to be that you're throwing me out—which you've wanted to do since my very first week here. Well, now you're to have your wish. I'm going."

"You implied that you didn't want to pack—"

"You're the boss, aren't you?" she said with irony.

He made an infuriated exclamation. "This news you were waiting for, this proposal from that fellow in England."

"That comes under the heading of private business too," she said stubbornly. Why should she explain? She didn't have any sort of a proposal from him!

There was a long silence. Her heart had begun to beat fast. He was staring at her, waiting. It was a battle of wills; his attitude was an uncompromising and dogmatic "Please explain"; hers was a stubborn, "Tell me what you want first and risk a rebuff."

Then suddenly she knew she was going to give in. He

was the stronger, and she liked it that way. It had been different with Donn.

She sighed, and her lashes fell.

"Of course I'm not going to marry Donn."

"Why not?" He was relentless.

"Because I don't love him."

"Do you love—me? Come on now, this isn't the time to be putting on your bush orchid act. Put your head up and look at me. And for God's sake don't tell me it's none of my business."

She looked up and he was laughing at her, but away back in his eyes was that dark intensity she had seen once before; the day her horse was out of control. She opened her mouth to say "Yes—yes—of course I love you", but before she could say it, his lips were on hers.

A breathless moment went by, and then he let her go and said with satisfaction, "Of course you love me. Now come on, or we'll miss that plane."

She heard herself gasp, and he laughed again. "Little idiot! What do you think I mean?—Leave your stuff alone. But I have to meet that plane, and there are things you and I have to say to each other, honey, that can't possibly wait till I get back." He had her fast by the hand, and she almost ran out of the room with him, along the veranda and down the three shallow steps, the screen door banging behind them.

She was breathing fast when they reached the Land Rover, and in five seconds they were off.

"Are you sure Mellie will be all right, Dane?"

"Of course I'm sure. Besides, Col's there to look after her. Kate's there—Patty's there—though she won't be much use, as both you and I know." He sent her a quick laughing look. "Col's in heaven, Patty will be like a bear with a sore head on two counts. Now you and I can forget the lot of them and think about ourselves. When are you going to marry me?"

She blinked and caught her breath. He was a fast worker!

He said musingly, "Once the Wet's here, there's nothing much that can be done on Wayaway. We'll go over to the coast and make our plans from there. You'll want to tell your brother, of course. What do you say to Townsville for the wedding? Or would you prefer Brisbane? And a honeymoon in New Zealand? Or do you prefer Fiji?"

"Anywhere at all," said Keitha blithely. "Just whatever you say, Dane."

He laughed softly and reached out to take her hand for a second. "It's taken me longer than I've liked, Keitha Godwin, to make you say yes—to make you decide you care about my opinions after all."

They could see the plane coming down now, and the Rover roared along the track in a cloud of dust and finally pulled up on the airstrip with perfect timing.

"We'll start spreading the news right away," decided Dane, as they walked the few feet to the aircraft, his arm about her waist. The rear door opened, the pleasant young freight officer appeared, the steps were down.

"Hi, Dane. How're things?" He looked at Keitha with friendly curiosity. "I reckon you must be enjoying yourself on Wayaway, Miss Godwin. You've been here quite a few weeks now."

"She's enjoying herself so well I've persuaded her to stay on for good," said Dane with a grin. "And you have my permission to pass on that news to anyone and everyone. In fact," he added, pulling Keitha possessivly close, "we shall be very disappointed if it doesn't come back to us over the galah session this afternoon. Won't we, honey?"

Keitha, aware that they were being watched from the plane by several pairs of interested eyes, felt suddenly shy and could only nod. Truth to tell, she was just a little bit afraid of her happiness yet. She waited while the freight and the mail were dealt with and was not satisfied until Dane's arm was about her again.

Then, looking up into the strength of his face, she wondered how she could possibly be scared of anything ever again if she was loved by the boss of Wayaway.

He was grinning down at her. "Honey, don't look at me like that in a public place! Wait till that mail plane's gone. Then I'll be ready for anything!"

THE WAY
THROUGH THE VALLEY

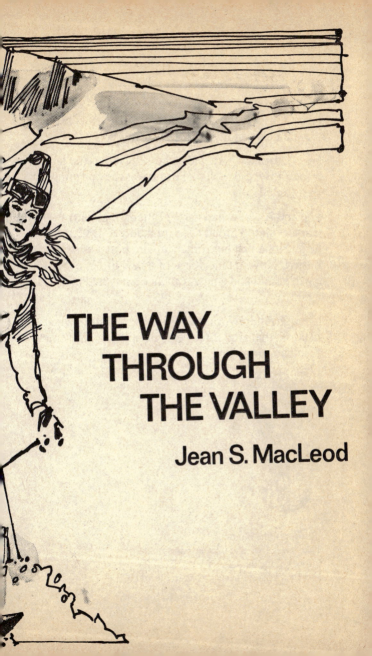

THE WAY
THROUGH
THE VALLEY

Jean S. MacLeod

·"What do you expect of me?" Andrew asked, his voice firmly controlled. "A broken heart worn dramatically on my sleeve?"

No, Catriona whispered to herself, it was the last thing she would look for. But it was the one thing she wanted.

She and Andrew had parted bitterly and with tears, both too proud for explanations. It seemed to Catriona that her romance with him was safely buried. Now, on the verge of a new life in Switzerland and a new romance, they had met again.

Though Andrew was as cold as ever, Catriona had to admit that after three years he still held the same fascination for her!

'Flower o' the bloom;
Take away love and our earth is a tomb.
Flower o' the quince;
I let Lisa go, and what's good in life since?'

ROBERT BROWNING

CHAPTER ONE

Edinburgh, gray with rain, suddenly came to life as a shaft of sunlight pierced the clouds above the Calton Hill and slanted down the glittering length of the Royal Mile. Castle, monument and rock were brilliantly looped in gold, while far across the Firth, the Ochils gradually took shape, clearing to reveal the dark ramparts of the Grampians guarding the gateway to the North.

It was early and the traffic had not built up along Princes Street, although a thin stream of it trickled toward the city along the Queensferry Road. From her bedroom window in a second floor apartment in Eton Terrace, Catriona Sutherland looked down at the bridge, guessing the time with amazing accuracy. In half an hour she would be ready to go. Half an hour to eat breakfast, polish her shoes, and make sure that everything was neatly packed into her bag before she started on her daily round. Her uniform coat lay on the bed behind her; the cap that went with it was hanging in the hall. At 24 she was a fully qualified State Registered Nurse completing her midwifery course in the most romantic city in the world, with a rewarding career before her and no regrets.

No regrets? Momentarily her gray eyes clouded as she looked beyond the bridge to the Water of Leith flowing in its deep canyon toward the sea. Still and dark and hidden, it seemed to reflect something of the past for her; the hopes and promises and joy which had died so painfully three years ago when young, brilliant and ambitious Andrew Bishop had walked out of her life. The future had stretched ahead for him straight and clear, the only way for him to go. Because she would not—or could not—go with him they had parted in bitterness and tears. The bitterness had been Andrew's; the tears she had shed secretly in the quiet watches of the night, wetting her pillow with them when no one could see.

"Kate, I've made the coffee. Do you want fruit or toast—or both?"

Nan McCarthy approached the bedroom door swathed in a blue dressing gown which had seen better days.

"Yes—fruit, thanks, Nan." Catriona turned from the window, her gaze still distant although her thoughts were now in the present. "You should be in bed," she added, "after such an early call."

"I can stay in bed all day if I like, and the call was worth it." Nan was looking at her critically. "It's not every day we get twins twice in one night. Or is that too Irish for you to understand?"

Catriona laughed.

"You have all the luck," she said. "Two babies for the price of one."

"They seem to come in twos in Calder Crescent," Nan reflected. "Perhaps it's something in the air." She moved back into the living room, which she had tidied before she had started to prepare their breakfast. "Madge was late last night. I wonder if I ought to act the heavy parent and reprimand her, or just turn a blind eye and hope for the best."

"You could never be a 'heavy parent'," Catriona declared, following her in. "It's tough, though, trying to strike a happy medium when you feel responsible for someone younger than yourself who has a lot of spirit and has just come to the Big City for the first time."

"Is that what it is" Nan asked ruefully. "I thought my young sister was just being plain awkward, but, since she *is* my sister, I have to do what I can to keep her on the Right Path."

Catriona stood beside the table, buttering a piece of

toast. "Your parents will be grateful," she said, "knowing you're here to keep an eye on her."

Nan sighed. "I suppose so, but it can be wearing, you have to admit. Apart from the undoubted spirit, Madge is about the most untidy person I've ever met. The apartment is like Paddy's Market as soon as she comes in. I wonder how you can stand us, you're so methodical."

Catriona gave her an affectionate smile. "It takes all sorts!" she conceded. "Madge is young and new to everything. She'll change."

"Like we all do, you mean?" Once again Nan's glance was probing. "Kate, do you plan to stay in Edinburgh?"

The gray eyes met the questioning blue gaze across the table.

"I don't know." Catriona lifted the apple from her plate. "I had thought of taking a job in London eventually," she confessed.

"You said so at the beginning of the summer." Nan glanced toward the second bedroom which she shared with her sister. "But I thought—well, what about Robin Pettigrew? Hasn't he made a difference?"

Catriona took a full, reflective minute to reply.

"In some ways, I suppose he has," she answered slowly. "I like Robin very much, but I haven't known him very long."

"Since the beginning of August," Nan pointed out. "Four months, and he's obviously keen."

"Nan, you're the Matchmaker of the Year." Catriona protested. "I met him during Festival week. He's taken me out fairly regularly since then, but that doesn't mean he wants to marry me."

"I know the signs," Nan persisted, unperturbed by such reasoning. "He's ready to propose."

"Who's ready to propose?" Madge, her hair wild, her eyes still heavy with sleep, put in an appearance at the bedroom door. "I wouldn't get married, if I were you, Kate," she added sagely. "There's very little future in it. Have fun while you're still young! Can I have my breakfast now, or must I wash and brush up first?" She glanced at her sister.

"Wash first," Nan decided emphatically. "And don't drop your pajamas in a heap in the bathroom floor for me to pick up. I'm going to bed."

"Been out delivering babies again?" Madge inquired distastefully. "The hours would slay me, for a start. I can earn far more money in an office."

"Everyone to his trade." Nan agreed, standing between her and the table. "Off you go, and don't be too long or you'll not be in an office by the end of the week."

Catriona poured herself a cup of coffee, drinking it with one eye on the clock. The room they shared was ample for their needs, warm and charming, with the sun flooding into it now through the big oriel window overlooking the bridge. These old Edinburgh houses, with their spacious rooms and deep hallways, made excellent apartments. They had been lucky to get this one; so near to the heart of the city and in such congenial surroundings. They could walk to work without incurring the extra expense of bus fares, and coming home in the evenings after a hard day climbing the endless staircases of the "lands" was less fatiguing than if they had been forced to line up for a bus or wait for a taxi. Nan and Catriona, at the end of their midwifery course, were eternally grateful for the comforts of Eton Terrace. Madge took them in her stride, confident that her older sister would always provide for her so long as she did what she was told—within reason. Gay, carefree and altogether likeable, Madge had brought a new element into their life. She was never at a loss for words and was immensely popular with everybody she met, encouraging her many escorts to call for her and introducing Catriona as well as

Nan as "my family". Her laughing Irish eyes and gay, lilting voice seemed to match the sunshine, and her wit was captivating. "Straight out of the bogs of Ireland" she described herself, and a waft of bog-myrtle seemed to pervade the room when she entered it. Catriona had been quite prepared for Robin Pettigrew to fall in love with Madge when they had first met because they were so alike, but Robin had continued to invite her out, and Madge was soon in the throes of a new romance with a student from the University.

These students came and went, nice young men generally answering to a nickname, who became scarce only when examinations were looming or when they took holiday jobs in the long vacation. Robin Pettigrew was different.

Catriona thought about him as she slipped into her coat and adjusted her cap at the mirror in the hall. He was an apparently well-heeled young man who had dabbled in art for some time, making a living out of buying and selling pictures, but now he was about to purchase a half share in an antique business in a side street off the Mound. The idea interested her in the same way that Robin interested her. It was new and exciting, something with which she had not come into contact before. She was well aware how deeply he felt about it. He had talked, nonstop, for a whole evening about his chance to broaden his horizons, and she had felt the excitement of the venture running along her veins, although she knew nothing of the world of art.

"When will you be in?" Nan called. "Accidents excepted?"

"About five." Catriona picked up her bag. "Don't cook for me. I'll be going out again."

"With Robin Pettigrew?" Nan did not wait for an answer. "See you around five."

She watched as Catriona left. They had known each

other since their student days at the Infirmary and had shared the apartment for over a year before Madge had come to join them. They got on well together and had very few secrets from one another. Sometimes Nan wondered if Catriona had ever really forgotten Andrew Bishop; the clever young pediatrician who had been her first love. They had seemed so ideally suited to one another, yet, suddenly, it had all been over. Andrew Bishop had disappeared from the hospital scene—gone abroad somewhere to another job—and Catriona had tried to hide her hurt as best she could. Nan had not known her so well in those days, although even then she had been aware of a sensitive nature deeply scarred by an unhappy experience. After they had taken the apartment together Andrew Bishop's name was never mentioned. Nan thought of it as a sort of "genteman's agreement" which she honored without question. Gradually Catriona had picked up the threads of her living again and was once more the bright, cheerful companion of their student days.

Almost! It was an irritating word to intrude upon her thoughts, Nan decided, as she went into the kitchen to make fresh toast for Madge's breakfast. Surely Catriona had forgotten about that old love affair now that Robin Pettigrew had come upon the scene. Nan liked Robin. Everybody did. He was bright, charming and kind, and there was never a dull moment when he was around.

Catriona was thinking much the same thing as she went her rounds of the "lands", climbing endless stone staircases in endless tenement buildings in the Auld Toon, where most of her patients lived. This was the work she loved, the profession for which she had been trained, and her day sped past quickly. Toward four o'clock she had an emergency to deal with, riding in the ambulance to the Infirmary with her patient because this had been her last call of the day. The woman clung to her in a pathetic bid for reassurance.

"You'll bide wi' me," she implored. "It's nice to hae a kent face beside you when you're whisked awa' at a moment's notice."

The busy Infirmary was much the same as it had always been. Catriona walked away from it remembering the years she had spent there as a student nurse and all the fun and the companionship and the heartache which had gone to make up life on the wards. She remembered Andrew Bishop, but turned resolutely away from the memory of him, pretending that she had cured herself. Yet before she reached the foot of the brae she thought that she saw him—a vague glimpse of a man in a car with the same turn of the head, the same broad-shouldered height and the same level, penetrating gaze.

Of course, it wasn't Andrew, and why, in one day, should she have remembered him so often? He was out of her life now, gone away, out of her reach forever and ever. If his image was still in her heart she must tear it out ruthlessly so that she could really forget.

How long did it take to do that? Her lips trembled a little as she stood waiting on the sidewalk for a gap in the traffic so that she could cross the road. It was over three years now, and she ought to have made some sort of adjustment. She had put her disappointment behind her—she was quite firm about that. Only occasionally, very occasionally, did she look back. "What can't be helped has to be tholed," her mother used to say, and she believed it to be true, but deep in her secret heart she new only too well about enduring.

Robin was waiting for her when she reached the apartment.

"I mean to lodge a complaint," he greeted her with mock chagrin. "Your patients will have to learn that you have a private life to lead as well as administering to their needs until after six o'clock."

Catriona smiled at him.

"It was an emergency," she explained. "I suppose I needn't have gone to the Infirmary with Mrs. Currie, but she looked so lost and she had nobody else."

"So Florence Nightingale stepped into the breach!" he suggested. "Okay, Nurse, you win, but I've got a table booked at Danielle's for seven-thirty, and you know how popular the place is. They won't hold it for us if we're more than ten minutes late."

Catriona glanced at her watch.

"Give me quarter of an hour," she suggested. "We can still make it."

He sat down on the sofa to wait; a tall young man with fair, fly-away hair brushed to one side of a high forehead and smiling, wide-spaced eyes that gave his face an open, friendly expression and made her think of all the happy times they had already spent together. Robin had been so easy to know. He had streaked across her horizon like a bright meteor trailing a certain amount of stardust in his wake, taking her to unexpected places, opening up what was a new world for her.

Nan came in to talk to him while she changed into the yellow two-piece she had bought only the week before. It was a color Robin liked, and she noticed the admiration in his eyes when she rejoined them ten minutes later. Nan had poured him a drink.

"Sherry?" she asked as Catriona came in.

"No, thanks. We're late." Catriona picked up her purse. "I don't suppose there was any mail for me?"

She asked the question regularly, as a matter of course.

"Only a postcard." Nan handed it down from the mantelpiece where she had propped it behind the clock. "It's from Switzerland."

Robin looked alert.

"Who do you know in Switzerland?" he wanted to know.

"One of the girls who trained with me." Catriona was reading the message on the back of the card. "Jenny Murdoch," she turned to Nan to explain. "She's there on holiday, having a wonderful time."

"Everybody has a wonderful time on a postcard," Robin said, laying down his glass. "Ready?"

His battered sports car was standing at the curb. It had seen better days, but the engine was still good, and they roared off across the bridge. He had chosen one of the newer restaurants, a dim, softly-lit place beneath street level that had once been a cellar, but which was now drawing in the sophisticated crowd both before and after theater performances. Their table was waiting for them, and he settled her into her chair with the attentive, half-proprietorial air which endeared him to her. This, it seemed, was something of a special occasion.

Looking about her, Catriona felt warm and protected. Robin always made things seem so easy. He ordered their meal, choosing the wine with expert care, and when they were ready to talk he looked deeply into her eyes and said:

"What do you really think about the store, Kate?"

She had thought about it a great deal in the past few days. "It's what you want to do," she said, "and you're really interested. I think it might be a good thing, if you're quite sure of the other person."

He frowned. "That's just it," he confessed. "Dick wants me to buy him out completely."

"And you can't do it?" She felt vaguely disappointed.

"I don't know." He pushed his glass aside. "It means more capital—something I don't have."

She waited, seeing the frown deepening between his brows.

"There's a chance," he said. "A slight chance, but it's

worth taking." His brow cleared, and he was smiling again. "It will all depend on what my ancient godmother thinks of the idea."

Again Catriona found herself waiting for him to continue.

"She could put up the money quite easily," he went on to explain, "but she can be difficult. She removed herself to Switzerland years ago when she married a Zurich banker, and she's determined to stay there for the rest of her life. I used to spend the summer vacation with her when I was at school, but I haven't been over recently. Not since I came to Edinburgh, anyway. She leads a remote sort of life, cooped up in an ancient *schloss* in the mountains, and never goes anywhere. I write to her, of course, every so often, and her letters back are full of sage advice. She really does love to rule the roost."

"Has she no family of her own?" Catriona asked.

He hesitated. "There was one son. I never met him," Robin confessed. "I think he blotted his copybook while he was quite young and shortly after his father died. My godmother never speaks about him because he disappointed her in some way or another. I think he married beneath him, as the saying goes, but I've never quite been sure. The only thing I know for certain is that he doesn't live at the *schloss*."

"Your godmother must be very lonely," Catriona observed suddenly. "Why don't you visit her?"

He hesitated. "Switzerland isn't just a bus-ride away," he reminded her, "but I might do that one day." He drew in a deep breath. "In the meantime, I've written asking her for the money to start the business. Let's hope my letter reaches her while she's in one of her more indulgent moods."

"It means a lot to you?"

"Quite a lot." His blue eyes were full of quick

enthusiasm. "You and I could do this thing together, Kate. If we were married. . . ."

He allowed the suggestion to escape into a long silence. Catriona held her breath, wondering if he had just proposed to her. She knew that she was only half in love with him, that there were still reservations in the secret places of her heart, yet she felt that the store might be a settling influence on them both, something they could work at together, although she knew so little about art.

"Keep your fingers crossed for me, Kate," he said. "I need all the backing I can get."

"I wish I could help—financially, I mean," Catriona began, but he swept the idea aside.

"Neither of us has that sort of money." He considered her reflectively. "I know you're going to tell me that money doesn't matter, but it does, in a way, especially when you want something that only money can buy. Like the store."

It had become almost an obsession with him. She wondered what he would feel like if he failed to gain his godmother's support.

They spoke of other things, among them the short time she had still to serve on the district.

"What will you do afterward?" he asked, stirring his coffee.

"Look for another job."

"As a midwife?"

"I'm not sure." She hesitated. "Sometimes I think I would like a complete change, like going back into one of the big hospitals or working entirely with children."

"You're as unsettled as I am at the present moment," he concluded.

"Not really. It's the same job, whichever way you look at it," Catriona pointed out, "but I like pediatric work."

She was aware of where her wandering thoughts had

led her. It had been in a children's ward that she had first met Andrew Bishop.

"Are they worth a penny?"

She looked up with a start.

"Your thoughts," he supplemented. "Sometimes you go right away. What was it this time—the future or the past?"

"Perhaps a bit of both." She shook herself free of the memory. "When will you hear from Switzerland?"

He shrugged.

"I've suggested a time limit, so I may have cooked my own goose," he said. "All we can do is wait and see."

They waited a week, during the course of which Robin became anxious, despondent and angry in turn.

"You'd think she would answer, even if it were only to say 'no'," he declared on more than one occasion. "Dick won't hold the offer open indefinitely."

"It's only just over a week," Catriona pointed out rationally.

"You've got the patience of Job," he declared. "I haven't. I suppose it's your calling. A nurse should always be placid, or appear to be, in the face of an emergency, but surely you must be a little anxious."

"I hope you will get what you want."

"You've got reservations about this, haven't you?" he demanded. "You'd be happier if I had worked for this money."

"Not if your godmother wants to give it to you. You will have to work to justify the loan."

"I don't mind working at what I like to do," he confessed. "You'll soon learn about art, Kate, and the other side of the business is fascinating, too. Don't think we're going to deal in junk, though we'll have to creep before we walk. There'll be good times and bad. That's why—"

He hesitated, and she knew that he hadn't asked her to marry him outright because of the bad times they might have to face. But wasn't that what love and marriage was all about? Facing up to life together. She didn't want it to be all sunshine—nobody could expect perfection—and half the joy in loving could be a mutual effort to succeed at something.

The letter from Switzerland arrived the following day, and even before he spoke to her about it Catriona could see that there was something worrying him, something he wasn't sure about.

"Let's walk," he suggested as soon as they had left the apartment. "We'll go along the coast, if you like, to Gullane or somewhere. I want to talk."

Catriona accepted the suggestion eagerly enough. It was a cold, late fall day, with the wind blowing strongly from the north-east and whipping up the waves across the Firth. But it was dry, and there was nothing more invigorating than a walk in the face of such a wind.

They drove past Gullane to North Berwick, leaving the car in the hotel parking lot and walked along the shore toward Tantallon. The castle on its craggy spur of rock reared up ahead of them. Presently they stood in its shelter, looking out to sea. It was like being on the bridge of a ship, Catriona thought fancifully—a ship carrying them toward an unknown future.

"I've had my answer," Robin said, at last.

"And it's 'no'?"

"Not quite." His mouth clamped down in a stubborn line. "I might have known there would be strings attached. Nothing is ever straightforward as far as I'm concerned."

"Tell me about the strings." She sat down on the grass at his feet. "Are they too tightly tied?"

He flung himself down beside her, hugging his knees,

his eyes on the dark mass of the Bass Rock standing knee-deep in the sea with a flurry of white gulls above it.

"I'm not sure," he said, feeling in his inside pocket for the letter. "You'd better read what she says for yourself."

Catriona drew back.

"I'd rather you told me," she said.

"There's nothing private about our correspondence, but it does explain the position between us. Brutally frank!" His mouth quirked up in an amused smile. "My respected godparent was never one to mince words. When receiving my begging letter she was, unfortunately, ill and was evidently in no mood to humor me. In short, she has written to say that if I can't spare the time to see her, the money for my 'silly adventure into the world of art', as she puts it, won't be forthcoming."

Catriona drew in a deep breath.

"But that doesn't mean she's refused you altogether," she pointed out.

"No." He was gazing at her speculatively. "It doesn't, I suppose, but I'm not likely to be able to go over there on the double, either. I have two important sales coming off shortly—pictures I've had on my hands for some time—so I can't take the risk of being in Switzerland when I should be in Edinburgh or London."

"It's difficult," Catriona admitted sympathetically.

"There's—something else," he said. "I think she really is ill. I've never heard her complain before, she always seemed to be such a vigorous person, but now she says she needs a nurse. An English nurse," he added carefully, "because she 'misses the sound of her own language'. She needs professional care for at least a month and has asked me to find someone." He paused and then characteristically took the bull by the horns. "Kate," he asked, "would you go? Dear, kind, considerate Kate, would you do this for me? You told me only a few days ago that you'll soon be at the end of your training and would have to look for another job, so why not take this one? It would be a wonderful holiday, and we could easily be killing two birds with the one stone!"

"What kind of birds?" Catriona asked uneasily.

"You could go out there for a complete rest, and she would be so much in my debt that she couldn't refuse me the loan."

"You're absolutely ruthless!" she declared, laughing.

"Not really." He pulled her toward him. "I need this chance, Kate. It would be for us."

She could not promise him anything definite without considering it first.

"Give me till tomorrow," she begged. "It's—something entirely different for me. I've never thought of looking after an old lady, not privately. We may not even like each other."

"Of course you would." He turned her gently to face him. "You'd get on with anyone, Kate. I know you. Besides, you're completely dedicated to your profession, so you wouldn't fail on principle," he teased. "Do it, Kate, and I'll be your humble slave for ever."

"I doubt it," she told him. "I'm not going to make swift promises I'm not going to be able to keep."

"It would only be for a week or two, and it wouldn't do any harm if she met you now." He kissed her lightly on the cheek. "On the contrary, when she gets to know you everything will be plain sailing. You take my word for it."

Was this what Robin really wanted? An opportunity to introduce her to his godmother so that the old lady could look her over and approve or disapprove, as the case might be? The thought made her decidedly nervous. She wanted to talk it over with Nan before she committed herself irretrievably.

The prospect of a visit to Switzerland was very pleasing, however, and she thought about it a great deal during their return journey to Edinburgh. Characteristically, Robin seemed to have forgotten the request he had made until they came to say good night.

"I'll need your answer tomorrow," he said. "You won't let me down, Kate?"

The earnestness in his blue eyes almost swayed her decision there and then.

"I won't let you down," she promised, "even if I have to find someone else to nurse your godmother."

Nan was in the apartment alone when she opened the heavy front door with her latch-key.

"Madge?" she called from the kitchen.

"No, it's me—Kate. I'm early, but I've come back for a pow-wow. You're not too tired?" Catriona crossed the sitting room to the kitchen door. "How was the concert?"

"Super. You should have been there." Nan switched on the electric kettle. "Where did you go?"

"North Berwick—Tantallen actually. Robin wanted to talk."

Nan looked up expectantly.

"You're engaged?"

"Sorry!" Catriona laughed. "You'll have to wait a while longer, my conscientious matchmaker friend. Robin wants me to go to Switzerland."

"Switzerland? Whatever for—unless he's going with you?"

"His godmother is ill. She lives there, near Zurich, I understand, and has asked Robin to find her a nurse for a few weeks. An English nurse, because she misses the sound of her native tongue, apparently."

Nan considered her news for a moment in silence.

"What have you decided?" she asked, at last.

"I wanted your advice."

"Do you want to go?"

"I'm not sure. Yes, I suppose I do, in a way."

"And otherwise?"

"You know what you always say about jumping in with both feet," Catriona smiled. "I decided to think it over for 24 hours."

"I think you should go," Nan said slowly. "You're through your midwifery now and you'll be looking for another job, anyway. You ought to have a change of scene."

Catriona started to make hot chocolate.

"I've been thinking of that for a long time," she agreed. "Edinburgh is too full of memories."

"I know." Nan felt curiously uneasy, but she believed that Robin and Catriona could be happy together because Catriona was the steadying influence Robin needed. "One unhappy experience is enough in a lifetime."

Catriona carried the tray into the sitting room.

"It—was something that couldn't be helped," she said stiltedly. "I gave him up and didn't really tell him why. Now I suppose he remembers me only with contempt, if he remembers me at all."

Nan, who had known Andrew Bishop only as the rather remote, white-coated figure striding purposefully along the corridors on his way to the children's wards, nodded her sympathy.

"He was the career type, wasn't he? Where did he go?"

"Abroad. Somewhere in Switzerland, I think."

Nan looked up sharply. It was on the tip of her tongue to ask if this would influence Catriona's decision, but it seemed that Catriona hadn't even thought about it. Not consciously, anyway. Perhaps she had forgotten Andrew Bishop, after all.

"Where does the godmother live?" she asked, to change the subject.

"She seems to be something of a recluse." Catriona

passed her a mug of chocolate. "From what I could gather, she lives in a quiet valley in the German part in some sort of castle or other."

"Well, isn't this the answer?" Nan demanded. "A wonderful change of scene and a romantic castle into the bargain. What more could you possibly want?"

"Truth to tell," Catriona confessed, warming her hands against the hot sides of her mug, "I'm slightly afraid of the old lady, even before I've met her."

"She can't be all that much of an ogre," Nan smiled, "and probably Robin wants her to like you. He's fond of you, Kate, anyone with half an eye could see that. I think you would be good for him. If the old lady is a normal sort of godparent she must want to see him settled with the right sort of girl."

Catriona felt that her mind had been fully made up and, once the die was cast, she began to think of Switzerland with pleasure. She had never been abroad before and the prospect was exciting.

"You'll learn to ski," Robin told her when they met the following evening, and she had given him her decision. "It's going to be fun, Kate. I may even be able to join you out there for Christmas. Anyway, we'll be engaged when you get back."

Trying not to feel that he was sending her to Zurich as an envoy, or perhaps even to be looked over by the old lady, she finally decided to consider her journey as no more than the pleasant holiday that she needed so much. Why not? She had to forget Edinburgh for a while and all it had meant to her. This was the way to do it. Later, when she returned to England, she could look for work in one of the big London hospitals.

"You'll like it," Robin had promised a dozen times before the evening was over. "There's a small English colony nearby. You can't possibly feel lonely."

Yet his godmother had felt the need to hear her native tongue.

Catriona wondered more and more about the old lady in the interval while they waited for her reply. When the letter with the Zurich postmark finally reached her she knew herself committed, although something deep in her subconscious mind murmured "beware!"

I'm afraid of heartache a second time, she told herself, although she felt sure that she had almost forgotten Andrew Bishop

CHAPTER TWO

On the plane to Zurich, Kate tried to conjure up a picture of her new employer, but without success. It was difficult to see someone through another person's eyes, and Robin had been prejudiced about the money.

"She won't unbend until she's absolutely sure," he had said as they parted at the airport. "You'll have to convince her, Kate. Make her see that I'm not the headstrong young fool she thinks I am."

Nobody would have called Robin a fool. He was competent, assured and charming, and he wanted this chance very much indeed. She had no doubt that he would succeed, and the offer of the store was still open to him. Dick Cunningham would stay in the business until he could raise the necessary capital. He would stay for six months, and that should be long enough.

"One way or another, we should know by Christmas," Robin had said. "So do your best for me, Kate, and I'll see you then."

She felt warm and confident at the thought of their meeting, aware that she would miss him in the interval. They had spent so much time together during these past few weeks in Edinburgh that Robin had almost taught her to forget. What she now felt for him might not be quite the same as that first blinding passion which had consumed her in her youth, but Robin had made her laugh again without reserve and obliterated much of the pain. If some of the scars still remained, she must cover them up. What was out of sight might one day be truly out of mind.

The plane was full, and she spent much of the journey looking out through her porthole at the changing panorama beneath her. The clouds were banked thickly over the Channel, but the sun cleared them by the time they approached the Alps. Unprepared for that tremendous buttress of high and terrible mountains, she gazed down at them in awe and wonder, her heart beating rapidly as she thought about her destination. "Somewhere in the mountains beyond Zurich," Robin had said, "in a quiet valley near the Austrian border." This was to be her home for the next few weeks, and she would be happy or unhappy according to the whim of an unknown old woman who "was never one to mince words or stand on ceremony once she had decided to like you."

They flew on, over more lakes and more mountains than she had ever seen in her life. The land beneath her was like Scotland; but on a grander scale, peak upon majestic peak crowding each other to the far horizon's rim. Great lakes lay like blue gems in their deep and quiet valleys, sun-dappled and shadowed where the pines came down to the water's edge. There was snow on the higher slopes, white, pure and glistening, a world sealed in by grim and rocky giants rearing up toward the sky.

At Basel some of her fellow travelers got out, to be replaced by others, and the plane lifted again, driving through snow. The lakes, the mountains, and the trees disappeared beneath it, but presently they were in a clear track of sky again, descending toward Zurich. She saw the long silver arm of a lake and another beyond it, shut in by the mountain wall. Then they had turned and were approaching the runway. A great city lay beneath them, poised on the edge of the lake, and she experienced a sudden swift enchantment as she looked down on it.

Her instructions were that she would be met, but it was ten minutes before she had cleared Customs and was able to look about her. Most of her fellow travelers had departed, surging out through the great glass doors, and for a moment, as she looked across the big, noisy departure hall, she felt curiously forlorn. Then someone was approaching her, as if there could be absolutely no doubt about her identity.

"You must be Nurse Sutherland," the girl said, holding out her hand. "I'm March Lazenby, Frau Kalman sent me to meet you."

Catriona grasped the thin fingers with a feeling of relief.

"You're English," she said. "I was beginning to be a little bewildered by all the strange voices."

"You don't speak German?" March was obviously surprised. "Somehow I thought you would when you took the job."

"I suppose it could be something of a handicap," Catriona admitted, "but I thought that Mrs. Kalman might like to speak English now and then, especially as I'm nursing her."

"Yes." March scrutinized her from head to foot. "I must confess you're not quite what I expected," she added. "I thought you would be at least middle-aged and not a red-haired beauty in a nurse's cap. I'm not quite sure how you're going to fit in at the Schloss Gleiberg."

Catriona felt taken aback. The remark had chilled her, although she was quite determined to hold her own with this self-assured young person.

"I've come to work," she said, "and I shall do my best for Frau Kalman. I understand she's been ill for some time."

"Off and on." March Lazenby led the way to the parking lot where a thin covering of newly-fallen snow lay on the cars lined up in their neatly-numbered rows. "She's been confined to the house for over a month, which is something she heartily detests, and tempers have been frayed all around in consequence. I work for her occasionally," she added as an afterthought. "That's why

I'm here to meet you. I do the odd secretarial job to keep me in Switzerland because I want to be here more than anywhere else at the present moment. I go for an hour or two each week to attend to Frau Kalman's correspondence. Sometimes I read to her."

They were approaching a large, old-fashioned limousine which had been kept in immaculate condition over the years. A tall, handsome, dark-skinned young man stood from behind the wheel at their approach. In that first moment of their meeting Catriona thought that he had a decided gipsy look, with his dark, curling hair growing into the nape of his neck and his black eyes glistening as he smiled.

March had evidently been shopping, so he gathered up some parcels from the back seat to make room for them.

"Thanks, Jeno," March said. "We'll go back to Sargans, I think. It's much the prettier way, and Miss Sutherland may not have much time for sightseeing once she gets to the valley."

There was a note of authority in her voice which suggested that she might fill a more important role at the *schloss* than part-time secretary to the old lady, and the chauffeur touched his cap deferentially as he acknowledged the order. Yet, somewhere beneath the air of servility, smouldered what Catriona could only describe as a spark of resentment. Jeno had a proud look, as if he had not always worn the uniform of a servant. Out of it, he could have been a soldier or a wandering troubadour.

From her seat in the back of the car beside March, she studied him. The proud tilt of his head, the broad shoulders and dark, curling hair suggested a freedom which the restricting uniform denied, while the hands which held the steering wheel were long and shapely, with finely-formed fingernails and slender wrists. Hands which might play a violin to perfection, she fancied.

They had reached Rapperswil before she had time to

study March Lazenby. All the way along the beautiful northern shore of the Zurichsee, with the great peaks of the Toggenburg rising steeply before them, March had talked incessantly, sketching in her own background in a matter-of-fact way which revealed very little, but she had spoken of her adopted country with enthusiasm. Switzerland was where March wanted to be, and she was determined to stay there.

She was a tall girl, with straight, fair hair and keen, hazel-colored eyes which missed very little; not beautiful in the strictest sense of the word, but with a presence which immediately attracted the beholder. She was immaculately groomed, and her tailored coat and fur turban must have cost her a month's salary, at least.

They crossed a bridge and took the southern road between two lakes.

"We'll stop at Wallenstadt," March suggested. "We have quite a journey after that, but no one will worry too much if we are a bit late. Frau Kalman knows I've been shopping, and she would want you to appreciate the scenery."

Catriona was already in love with Switzerland.

"It's so like Scotland," she remarked, her eyes lifting from the blue of the lake to the great mass of the Churfirsten silhouetted against the northern sky. "I feel almost at home."

March turned to look at her.

"I've never been to Scotland," she confessed. "It's always raining up there, isn't it?"

Catriona smiled at the popular misconception.

"Not always," she said.

"Do you ski?" March asked as they drove away from the inn where they had drunk hot wine and eaten some delicious cheese sandwiches.

"Not very well," Catriona was forced to admit. "I can

stand up, but that's about all. I did a bit of practising while I was in Edinburgh at a place called Glen Shee, but the season is very short."

She could imagine March being a brilliant exponent of the art. Her long limbs and lean elegance seemed to add up to 100 percent efficiency and, somehow, the thought jarred. March was so completely confident in all she did.

At Sargans they turned northward into the wide green valley of the Rhein, yet they were still encompassed by gigantic peaks. Narrow roads wandered off on either side of the main highway, climbing suddenly and dizzily to the heights while the broad river flowed on placidly beneath them.

After Trubbach they, too, turned onto a mountain road, climbing gradually and then steeply until it seemed as if they were going right to the top of the world. Looking back, Catriona could see the road zig-zagging behind them in terrible hairpin bends that made her stomach turn over, but Jeno's hands were steady on the wheel, and he looked assured. Then, with amazing swiftness, they had reached the entrance to a narrow mountain valley and were going down again. Jeno pointed to the row of peaks on the opposite side.

"The *schloss*," he said with a sort of pride.

The castle was built on an outcrop of rock close under the rim of the mountain, with a terrace of rock holding it up above the valley which it commanded with an autocratic stare. Gray and remote, it had stood on its high eminence for hundreds of years, guarding the entrance to the pass. Far beneath it a river flowed turbulently toward the gap in the mountain wall which promised it an outlet to the sea. Plunging down the mountainside in cataracts and through gulleys, it would join the Rhein, at last, to be engulfed in its wide blue waters on their way to the distant Bodensee.

Catriona looked at it in silence. unable to put a word to her first reaction, unable to decide whether she was elated or disappointed by what she saw.

"Well," March asked, "how do you like it?"

"It's tremendous!" Catriona drew in a swift breath. "I had no idea it would be anything like this."

March's eyes narrowed.

"What did you expect?" she asked.

"It's hard to say. Something not quite so—"

"Bleak?" March suggested.

"No, not that." Catriona was still studying the wide panorama of the hidden valley. "Bleak isn't quite the word, is it? Overwhelming might be better—but not that, either. It must be lovely in the summer."

"And when the snow comes," March conceded.

The snow was already on the mountain peaks, although it had not yet reached the plateau. The grass along the riverside was still green and the roads were dry. Catriona wondered if Gleiberg would be cut off when the snow did arrive, realizing how isolated they were here, at the very top of the world.

"You can just see the village," March pointed out. "Over there at the far end of the valley."

A bridge spanned the river, with a cluster of houses edging the banks and the curious, domed tower of a tiny church thrusting up against the cloudless blue of the sky. It was the mountains, however, which dominated the scene, holding Catriona's attention whichever way she looked. Snow-capped and relentless, they gazed back at her with an odd indifference which she found particularly chilling. Even the distant *schloss* seemed to be watching her coldly.

Surprisingly, the car turned in the opposite direction. They had reached the valley floor, and Jeno swung the wheel around until they were facing the mountains on the other side, where a great many firs had been planted. They went right up to the snowline, clothing the bleak face of the mountain wall in a mantle of green and giving it a softer look.

"You know, of course, that the old lady no longer lives at the castle," March observed.

"I didn't know," Catriona was forced to admit, wondering how much March knew of her own background. "Naturally, I thought it was still her home."

"Are you disappointed?" March challenged. "No castle! No romance!"

"I didn't come looking for romance. I came to nurse Mrs. Kalman."

"Yes, I remember." March was studying her closely. "You're a friend of her godson, I gather. What is he like?"

"Robin? Very nice," Catriona obliged.

"Is that all?" March examined her make-up in the tiny mirror from her handbag. "She never stops talking about him, wondering if he's good enough."

Catriona looked puzzled.

"To inherit the castle," March supplied. "Do you think he is?"

Catriona flushed, aware that March was watching her through the tiny mirror.

"Surely that will depend on what Mrs. Kalman thinks," she suggested.

"How well do you know him?" March flung at her.

"Quite well." Catriona hesitated. "We were quite good friends in Edinburgh."

She could hardly tell March that they were engaged to be married because that wasn't strictly true, but she had a vague idea that Robin might have mentioned the possibility to his godmother when he had last written to her. It did not appear, however, that March was fully in the old lady's confidence, although she handled most of her correspondence. Otherwise she would have known what Robin had said.

"We're nearly there," March informed her. "You'll like it at the chalet, although it is rather isolated."

Ahead of them a narrow road ran among the trees to emerge, at last, onto a mini-plateau where a large, deeply-eaved chalet commanded a wide vista of the valley and the village at its farthest end. It was built mostly of wood on a stone foundation with a narrow wooden balcony running all the way around it on the second floor level where the steep eaves sloped down to afford it protection. There were stones along the roof, strung together, that suggested a fierce wind could blow down between the mountains. The road under the car wheels was slightly rough.

"It's lovely!" Catriona exclaimed involuntarily. "Really lovely!"

They pulled up on a broad terrace, and Jeno came to open the car door for them. He had placed Catriona's luggage in the trunk and went to unload it as the massive door of the chalet swung open.

To Catriona's surprise, it was a young girl who confronted them.

"This is Fereith," March introduced them almost sharply. "Another orphan."

The girl was about 16 years old, with a small, heart-shaped face framed in a thick mane of straight, black hair. Her eyes were very dark, and she had thin, sensitive hands, like Jeno. Her skin was fair, however, although it was overlaid with the deep honey-colored tan of the mountains. She looked at March with a kind of stubborn pride, as if she resented her but was not quite brave enough to resist her.

"Thank you for bringing Miss Sutherland," she said in halting English. "Jeno will take you home."

For a fleeting second her eyes met Jeno's, as if to beg for his support, and then she turned back into the chalet, leaving the door wide for Catriona to follow her. March hesitated beside the car.

"I suppose I ought to get back," she said. "I may see you in the morning."

"I hope so." Catriona held out her hand. "Thanks for coming all that way to meet me. It was very kind of you to spare the time."

"Time's at a discount up here, and it was the old lady's idea, really," March said.

She returned to the car while Jeno carried Catriona's suitcases into the chalet, leaving them at the foot of the wide staircase that mounted to a narrow gallery running around three sides of the entrance hall. Fereith was waiting at the foot of the stairs. She seemed nervous in Jeno's presence, but when he had gone she smiled gently in Catriona's direction.

"It is not such a good day for Frau Kalman," she explained as she led the way to the floor above. "Before the rain comes, she is often unable to walk."

"How long has she been ill?" Catriona asked.

"Many months." The dark eyes clouded. "It is very sad when she has to stay in her room all day and cannot get out to do the work she loves."

They had reached the gallery, and she paused at the nearest door. Catriona straightened involuntarily.

"In here," Fereith said.

She knocked before she opened the door, and Catriona was face to face with her new employer.

Frau Kalman sat in a winged armchair with her back to the light, one hand lying idly in her lap, the fingers curved inward and knotted with arthritis. The other hand was closed over the silver knob of an ebony walking-stick, that she used in an effort to rise.

Ferith rushed to her side, concern written all over her expressive little face.

"Don't fuss, my child!" The words were gently reproving, the eyes under the old lady's heavy brows surprisingly kind. "I can manage by myself, as you very well know. Go and fetch us some tea, if you will. Grete has had the tray ready all afternoon."

Fereith went to do her bidding. Frau Kalman beckoned Catriona across the room.

"Sit down," she commanded, indicating the chair near her own. "Are you frozen to the bone after your long journey?"

"Not in the least," Catriona assured her truthfully. "The car was most comfortable."

"One needs comfort in this climate," the old lady remarked as she studied her. "Robin tells me you are a fully trained nurse. Why did you come here?"

The question was shot at her so unexpectedly that Catriona took a full minute to answer it. In the end she could only speak the truth because it seemed that Frau Kalman expected nothing less.

"I felt that I needed a change of scene."

"This won't be a holiday," her employer warned bluntly.

"I don't expect that," Catriona returned. "I've come to work."

She looked steadily into Frau Kalman's eyes. They were very blue eyes, wide-spaced and alert, missing nothing, and they seemed to be making some demand of her. "Why have you really come?" perhaps, or "What can you tell me about my godson that I don't already know?"

"Fereith will show you to your room, but first we will have some tea," the old lady decided. "Tea in the English manner," she added with a smile. "You see, Nurse, I am still a sentimentalist where the customs of my own country are concerned."

She could never be anything but English, Catriona thought, no matter how long she stayed in Switzerland.

"Forty years," Frau Kalman said, as if she had read her thoughts. "I was brought here as a bride 40 years ago by the kindest man in the world." Her expression softened as memory led her into the past. "When he died quite suddenly 18 years ago I couldn't leave this valley. It was his beloved homeland, and I had to look after it." She paused. "The world seems to have no room for sentiment these days, but this I had to do." Suddenly her eyes grew hard. "At least, it was part of my reason for staying," she added, tight-lipped, as Fereith and a becapped housemaid appeared with the tea tray.

She signalled to Fereith to pour the tea, watching her with a look of indulgence as she did so. If the girl was an orphan, as March Lazenby had said, she was certainly a privileged one. Her movements were slow and graceful, with a dignity about them seldom seen in a girl of her years, and her natural shyness enhanced her quiet beauty. Her bone structure was small and delicate, and the long, straight hair falling on either side of her face was like polished silk. When she finally rose to show Catriona to her room, she paused beside Frau Kalman's chair to make sure that the old lady's cup was refilled.

"Fereith knows how fond I am of a cup of tea," Frau Kalman said before they left her.

Catriona followed the younger girl right around the gallery to a door on its farthest side. Like the remainder of the chalet, the room they entered was finely paneled in light pine, with a wide window running the full length of one wall to frame a magnificent view of the mountain and valley and distant village. It was a living picture to take anyone's breath away. Catriona stood looking at it for a long time, thinking that whoever built the chalet must have stood there often looking down across the river like a king.

"I made the room ready for you," Fereith said behind her. "I hope you will like it. Frau Kalman told me to choose the one I thought best."

Catriona turned toward the bed with its high, carved headboard and spotless white *dine*.

"You have been very kind, Fereith," she said. "You have given me the most wonderful view."

The girl looked beyond her, through the window.

"From this room you can see all the valley and the *schloss* as well," she said. "See it, up there on its high mountain, like an eagle's nest. That is what it is, the home of an eagle, but now it is full of children. They are all orphans. They do not know who their parents were. It is very sad."

So that was the secret of the *schloss*! It had been turned into an orphanage, and yet Fereith was here, living with Frau Kalman, as if she had been her own child. Catriona drew in a deep breath.

"Fereith," she said, "you have a pretty name. What does it mean?"

"It is the name of a gipsy princess," Fereith told her solemnly. "I was called after her. Do you like it?"

"I think it is beautiful."

Fereith smiled.

"Would you tell me your name?" she asked shyly.

"It's Catriona, but my friends call me Kate, for short."

"I think Catriona is prettier. You have another name, of course."

"Yes—Sutherland."

Fereith turned away.

"I have no other name," she said flatly. "Except—Kalman."

Surely she could not be ungrateful, Catriona thought, although gratitude was not really to be expected where there had been a straightforward adoption. She could see how difficult it was for Fereith.

The girl was at the door when she noticed the photograph. The room was rather bare and unadorned except for a bowl of dried flowers on the table near the bed, and the photograph in its narrow leather frame on the dresser opposite the window. Since they had entered the room their backs had been toward it, but now Catriona was looking at it as if she had seen a ghost. It was a photograph of herself taken five years ago when, like Fereith of the solemn eyes, she had been very young, but there was no mistaking it. She was looking straight into her own pictured face.

What was it doing there? Had Robin sent it to his godmother in order to introduce her to the old lady before their actual meeting? It was possible, although she had no actual recollection of ever giving him the photograph. It had been taken so long ago. She found herself turning it face down on the dresser top, unable to ask Fereith how it had come to be there.

Its presence troubled her while she washed and changed. Was Robin attempting to impress his godmother with her simplicity so that he could use her as a go-between in order to get the money he needed?

It was an ungenerous thought that she was immediately ashamed of, and she dismissed it altogether as she shared her first meal at the chalet with Fereith and Frau Kalman. With the help of Grete, the old lady had managed to change into a simple woollen dress for the occasion, although the meal itself had been carried upstairs on a tray by Jeno and set out on the table near her bedroom window. It was all very gracefully done, with candles at either end shielded by little glass globes and fresh fruit on an engraved silver dish as a centerpiece. Obviously Frau Kalman had brought many of her treasures with her when she had moved across the valley from the *schloss*.

"Will you tell me about the children?" Catriona asked, at last. "Fereith mentioned them."

Fereith had crossed the room to attend to the coffee percolator, and Frau Kalman smiled in her direction.

"The *schloss* is full of children," she said. "They are from many parts of Europe and all need our help. They need also the care of the team of doctors and nurses here, in this quiet valley. Tomorrow you must come and see for yourself. I am not entirely housebound," she added when Catriona looked surprised by the invitation. "With Jeno's help I can cope with the stairs and drive a little way when the weather is good. He will take us to the *schloss*, and you will meet our English doctor. You will like him," she said with assurance. "He gives so much of his time to this work which is so near to my own heart."

"Has he always worked here?" Catriona asked with interest.

"Not always." Frau Kalman made a quick mental calculation. "For about three years, perhaps, when he came from Scotland. Yes, he is a compatriot of yours," she added. "His name is Andrew Bishop."

Shocked by the revelation, Catriona could only stare at Frau Kalman in silence until the old lady took up the tale of the *schloss* once more.

"It had always been my husband's home," she explained, "but after he died it was too big and lonely for one old woman. Besides," she added vigorously, "there were better things for me to do with it than to live there alone with my sorrow. Memories can be sad, stultifying things when they are nourished in loneliness, and if bitterness creeps in they can be disastrous. I asked myself a thousand times why this had to happen to me. I had a happy life, but it had happened and I was alone—more alone than I had ever been—so I had to do something about it. Then the children came along and the whole world changed for me. I was up to my eyes in work, with the Professor to help me. The children were his life's work, but he was getting on, growing old in their service. He is a wonderful man. You are sure to like him, and tomorrow perhaps you will meet him.

With Andrew Bishop? Catriona could not face the prospect, but she was glad that she had been given time to absorb it before they actually came face to face. They would be bound to meet some time while they were living in such close proximity.

Suddenly panic-stricken, she crossed to the window, looking out over the valley to the distant ramparts of the mountains on the far side. Lights twinkled from the long windows of the *schloss* set high on its pinnacle of rock. They were like small, golden stars fallen from the dark backcloth of sky. Somewhere up there Andrew Bishop lived and worked. The blood hammered madly in her veins. What would he think when he knew she was here?

She could not face the thought of his enduring anger, nor could she ask Frau Kalman to fill in the blanks for her. Three years was an eternity of parting, and so many things could have happened in the interval. Andrew could have married. There could be a wife and even a family up there in the *schloss* with him.

She stood gazing into the night, numbed and uncertain, the only sound in the quiet room behind her, the ticking of the little ormolu clock in the table beside Frau Kalman's bed. It seemed to accentuate all the minutes that had passed since she had last seen Andrew, the long-drawn-out days and weeks of their parting, the lost time stretching between them which could never be recaptured.

When she raised her eyes to the mountains again, the light in the *schloss* had gone out.

"It's getting late," Frau Kalman said from the other side of the room, "and you must feel tired after your long journey. I hope you are happy in Fereith's choice of a room for you. She wanted to make you feel at home."

Catriona went toward her. In the candlelight the old lady's face looked mellow and kind, the harsher lines obliterated, although the keen blue eyes were still alertly critical.

"I'd be terribly ungrateful if I wasn't satisfied," she said unsteadily. "It is a lovely room, with the same view across the valley as you have here."

"Most of the bedrooms look toward the *schloss*," Frau Kalman told her. "The chalet was built with that idea in mind. Only the kitchen looks out to the hill behind us. Andrew wanted it that way when he first planned the site."

Catriona stiffened.

"You mean that—this was his home?" The words sounded far away even in her own ears. "He lived here at one time?"

The old lady nodded.

"Until we decided that it was more practical the other way around. He was needed at the *schloss* far more than I was, and the journey across the valley can be difficult in winter. The *schloss* filled up with children and I was getting more and more in the way."

"I can't believe that," Catriona denied automatically. "I can imagine you working as hard as anyone."

A shadow passed in the old lady's eyes.

"It is something to do," she said. "An interest which absorbs me to the exclusion of everything else. It has become my life, a very full and happy life."

"Can I help you into bed?" Catriona asked.

Frau Kalman shook her head.

"I'll sit here for a while." She looked across the room

at Fereith. "Go to bed, child," she admonished. "You're tired. You have great dark circles under your eyes."

Fereith, who had served their coffee while Frau Kalman had been speaking about their former home, rose to obey.

"Do you not wish me to read to you before I go to bed?" she asked.

"Another time," Frau Kalman said.

Jeno came in to remove the table. Fereith had placed the used plates and cutlery together on a silver tray and looked as if she intended to carry it out for him.

"Leave that for Grete," Frau Kalman commanded. "It is her work, not yours."

Fereith looked dismayed and Jeno's dark eyes flashed as he lifted the portable table to set it against the wall. There was a tension in the atmosphere which could almost be felt. Catriona moved toward the door. She was glad to escape, glad to be alone to think what she must do about the immediate future.

For a wild moment she told herself that she must leave Gleiberg in the morning, severing her connection with the valley even before she met Andrew again, but presently she realized how impossible that would be. Her journey to Switzerland had been undertaken at Frau Kalman's expense and she had a contract to honor, but quite apart from that she knew that she could not run away. Whatever had happened in the interval, either to Andrew or herself, they were destined to meet again. It would have happened inevitably, some time, no doubt, and now she was here.

Trying to convince herself that the past was dead, she stood at her bedroom window looking across the valley to the *schloss*. It was in complete darkness now except for one window high up in the tower, so high up that the steady, shining light which came from it might indeed have been a star. She gazed at it for a long time before she finally went to bed and fell asleep.

CHAPTER THREE

In the morning, there was a great deal of activity around the chalet. There was hardly any garden to speak of, and what there was seemed to be frozen in the hard grip of winter. The pine forest came down to within a hundred yards of the house, sheltering it from the north and east, while the narrow road by which they had come the evening before zig-zagged in a series of hairpin bends down to the valley floor. It would be a hard climb to the chalet roof, but propped up against the gable wall half a dozen pairs of skis suggested that some of the inhabitants would be more than pleased to see the return of the snow. Jeno, perhaps, and Grete and Fereith.

After a quick walk to the edge of the terrace and back, Catriona made her way to the dining room. The exhilarating mountain air had sharpened her appetite, and it was the same air that had made her sleep so soundly during the night in spite of the confusion of her thoughts. The white pine table was set with gay little mats. She took her place before one of them, buttering a fresh roll as Grete brought in a platter of boiled eggs.

"Am I first down, Grete, or just very late?" she asked.

Grete gave her a quick smile.

"You are first," she said.

Catriona was finishing her breakfast when Fereith came in.

"Will you go to Frau Kalman, please?" she asked. "She wishes to get up soon, and I have to help Grete to pack a basket for the children."

There was a reserve about Fereith when she spoke about the orphans at the *schloss* that seemed to stem from her own experience, and Catriona wondered if she remembered the time before she had come to Gleiberg. There was no denying the fact that she was deeply attached to the old lady who had become her bene-factress, but she still called her Frau Kalman, as if she stood in awe of her. The mother-daughter relationship had evidently never been suggested, and Frau Kalman was possibly too old to have a daughter of Fereith's age, anyway. Yet there was no doubt about her affection for the girl.

"Fereith usually helps me when Grete is busy in the kitchen," she explained when Catriona knocked on her bedroom door and entered, "but I can't expect the child to be at my beck and call all the time. She has her lessons to attend to. Fereith is—backward in that respect," she admitted with reluctance. "Not that she isn't bright in a dozen other ways, mind you," she added. "She has many talents, but she is lazy where orthodox learning is concerned." Suddenly the line of her mouth hardened and the harshness came back into her face. "What is bred in the bone may have to come out in the flesh in one way or another, but book learning is always essential."

"Does Fereith attend the village school?" Catriona asked, turning down the light *dine* to help the old lady to rise.

Frau Kalman shook her head.

"She had a tutor in Zurich, but he has gone to Basel, to the University. So far I have not yet been able to find a replacement for him. Later," she added decisively, "Fereith will go to Lausanne to a boarding establish-ment there. It will be the making of her. She is too free to do as she pleases in the valley."

At 16 Fereith was perhaps young for her years, yet occasionally a look passed in her dark eyes which was as old as time itself. It might be that Fereith was already in love.

With Jeno? That would displease Frau Kalman,

Catriona knew. It would not be in the old lady's plan for the girl she had adopted and given her own name. "I have no other name," Fereith had said, "except Kalman."

"The valley must be lovely after it snows," Catriona remarked, helping her employer from the bed.

"Lovely and treacherous," the old lady said, as if she were still continuing the conversation about Fereith. "When the snow is really deep the valley can be sealed off for many days," she added reflectively. "Can you manage on a pair of skis?"

"Not very well," Catriona was forced to admit.

"Then you must learn. It is the only way to be completely mobile here during the winter months. Fereith will teach you."

She seemed determined to throw them into each other's company, as if Fereith might take advice more easily from someone nearer her own age.

"What about that scapegrace godson of mine?" she asked suddenly as Catriona began to dress her hair. "Do you think he will ever settle down into a reasonable job?"

The abrupt question took Catriona by surprise.

"I think he is very enthusiastic about this one," she returned slowly.

"That wasn't what I asked you," the old lady declared. "Enthusiasm can blow hot and cold, and that's no use when it comes to a question of marriage and settling down."

"I think he'll settle," Catriona said, wondering how much Robin had actually told his godmother. "He can be quite sincere, you know."

Frau Kalman gave a penetrating look.

"You could be the making of him, I dare say," she observed. "When are you going to marry him?"

Catriona flushed.

"There's—nothing like that at the moment," she answered. "We're not even engaged."

Frau Kalman struggled into her woollen dress.

"Humph!" she said, but that was all.

She ate her breakfast practically in silence. Grete had brought it in on a tray, setting it on the table beside the window. She lingered there over her coffee while Catriona tidied up the room. There was no sign of Jeno.

"Do you have massage?" Catriona asked after Grete had collected the used plates and carried them away.

"I've no faith in it." The old lady's tone was short. "One of my doctors advised it a long time ago, but there was little sign of improvement. Besides, the masseur had to come from Zurich, and it was too great a distance for him to travel in the end."

"Will you let me try?" Catriona's offer fell into a complete silence. "I've been fully trained," she added helpfully.

"Oh? All right," Frau Kalman conceded. "You can try, although I don't think it will do any good." She glanced at the clock beside the bed. "We are already late for our visit to the children. Ring that bell over there and tell Grete we are ready. Where is Fereith?" she asked sharply.

"She was helping Grete pack some things into a basket."

"That could be no more than a five minute task." Frau Kalman was frowning. "I don't suppose for one second that she is at her books," she added brusquely.

"I'm here," Fereith announced from the doorway, "and the car is waiting. Jeno says that it will snow."

The frown deepened on the old lady's brow.

"Jeno is becoming too much of a prophet for my liking," she observed. "Romanies are all the same."

So Jeno was a gipsy. The knowledge of his origin did

not wholly surprise Catriona. His dark, aquiline features and swift, panther-like grace had suggested it ever since their first meeting. Jeno looked every inch a true Romani, but it seemed odd that he should be living here in the service of Frau Kalman or even of the *schloss*. Romanies were roamers, travelling people whose very instincts kept them constantly on the move. Their lineage went back for thousands of years to the Byzantine conquest of Ainzarba, when the Zott inhabitants, with their cattle and their women and children, were carried off as prisoners into the Greek empire, never to return. They had remained as wanderers on the face of the earth ever since, known, yet unknown in every country of the world. Catriona had seen them in Scotland many times, traveling the roads among the mountains or busy in a lowland field. Always, when she had looked again, they had moved on.

Fereith seemed deeply perturbed by Frau Kalman's generalizations.

"Jeno says he can smell the snow," she observed with a show of excitement. "Do you think I should take my skis over to the *schloss*?"

"There will be no snow." The old lady looked out of the picture window to the cloudless sky. "You can save yourself the trouble, and the horses the extra weight," she added dryly.

Fereith looked disappointed. "Are we taking the carriage?" she asked.

"We can trust the horses not to break down," Frau Kalman said. "Tell Jeno to harness them, and you can inform Grete that we are ready."

She indicated a thick, fur-lined cloak lying on a chair, and Catriona held it out for her.

"Wear boots," she advised. "It can be cold on the high plateau."

Catriona had equipped herself with sheepskin-lined boots and a heavy tweed coat before she had left Edinburgh.

"Do you wish me to wear my uniform?" she asked.

"I don't think there's any need," the old lady decided. "There are plenty of nurses already at the *schloss*—Swiss nurses."

Not quite sure whether she had been snubbed or not, Catriona went to collect her coat. Her bed had been made and her room tidied for her, possibly by Grete, who seemed to be a willing maid-of-all-work about the chalet. She pulled on her boots sitting on the chair beside the window. The view across the valley was magnificent this morning, with the snow-capped peaks tinged with palest pink and the river glittering in the sun. The sky above the *schloss* was a pure turquoise, clear and bright, while the onion dome of the village church sparkled with reflected light. The deeply-eaved chalets and little red-roofed houses beyond the bridge were still half in shadow, waiting for the sun to find them. High above the *schloss* itself a giant bird hovered, poised for a brief moment like some distant symbol of omnipotence before it glided down the wind and disappeared. Catriona turned her eyes back to the *schloss*. "Like an eagle's nest," Fereith had said. "That is what it is. The home of an eagle."

They would be there in next to no time, she realized, and she would come face to face with Andrew after all these years.

Her nervousness was apparent as she descended the staircase. Jeno and Grete had helped Frau Kalman down between them, and the old lady's keen eyes met hers.

"Are you cold?" she asked in her searching way. "You will have to wrap up more warmly than that to travel in an open carriage."

Catriona had not expected that they would be traveling in an open conveyance and said so.

"I'm sorry," she apologized. "I had no idea."

"We never have the hood up unless it rains or the snow is very heavy," her employer told her. "Grete will fetch you a cloak."

The stout little Swiss woman hurried off to do her mistress's bidding, and Fereith led the way to the front door. When she opened it the sun came flooding in like a benediction.

"This side of the valley gets all the morning sunshine," Frau Kalman said. "The *schloss* can be dark till almost ten o'clock, but that was possibly one of the advantages of building it there in the old days. With the light behind them, they would see their enemies more clearly."

An open carriage drawn by two sturdy gray cobs was waiting at the end of the terrace, with Jeno holding the reins. Grete appeared carrying a dark green cloak edged with sable, which she placed over Catriona's shoulders.

"You may be thankful for it on the return journey," Frau Kalman said.

They settled her in the carriage, with a fur-lined rug tucked securely around her knees, and she looked superb. Tall, straight and unbending, she looked exactly what she was—the chatelaine of an ancient castle, although she had transferred herself temporarily to a chalet on the other side of her domain.

Jeno helped them into the carriage, holding Fereith's hand longer than he need have done. Then he climbed up to the box and took up the long whip, that he flicked expertly above the horses' flanks. Fereith turned to wave to Grete.

"I like this much better than book-learning," she observed.

Soon—too soon, Catriona felt—they were approaching the *schloss*. It was larger than she had imagined it to be from the other side of the valley, with a high wall closing it in on three sides and a steep gully dropping away from it in front. Her blood began to drum in her ears as they spiralled up toward it because it seemed to dominate the whole valley and would probably dominate her life while she remained here.

Jeno urged the cobs to the final incline with a satisfying flourish of the whip, and they were there, pulling up on the narrow, gritted road before the main gateway.

The gates were opened for them by a rotund little man in a leather apron who saluted Frau Kalman with the greatest respect, and Jeno drove through at a reduced pace. Up the short, steep drive they went, across the wooden bridge spanning the ravine to where an unseen waterfall gurgled and roared its way to the river far below. Then the *schloss* stood before them, gray and austere, its long, mullioned windows sunk deeply into its weathered old sides, its turrets raking the sky. There was a forbidding, sequestered gloom about it which felt oddly like a rebuff, and then the iron-banded door flew open and a veritable stream of children flowed out, spilling on to the gray flagstones of the terrace up against the carriage to bid them welcome.

In no time they were surrounded by eager, smiling faces, and Frau Kalman, bending down to greet them in turn, was a woman transformed. She really loved these children. She had given them her heart, and she had given it to Fereith, because she knew that they needed her.

The stragglers reached the carriage, at last, the little crippled ones whose pale faces and distorted bodies looked pathetic in that rugged setting of mountain peak and soaring tower. Yet they took their part in the welcome with the others, no less vociferous for their twisted limbs.

Frau Kalman had a kind word and a smile for them all. It may have been in a language which Catriona did not understand, but in any language Frau Kalman's presence there meant love. She was a wonderful person and yet strange in some inexplicable way.

As they got down from the carriage, a tall man in a long white coat came to the door.

"This is Professor Zorn," the old lady introduced them. "Miss Sutherland arrived yesterday, Professor, and she has already threatened me with daily massage," she added with a twinkle in her eyes. "Do you approve?"

The Professor shook hands with Catriona and turned in her direction. "I approve of anything which will free you from pain," he said in a gravely quiet voice. "Massage or medicine, it makes no difference so long as you are eased."

"But neither of them will cure me? Ah, well, you have done your best, Heinrich, and what more can I ask? Where are the others, and when did you come from Zurich?" she asked.

He answered her final question first.

"Yesterday. I drove up with two more children for you, my friend. You will agree to have them—yes? They are much in need of your care."

Frau Kalman nodded. "So long as Andrew can look after them," she submitted.

The mention of Andrew Bishop's name sent the blood coursing wildly through Catriona's veins. Was he here, and how long would it be before they came face to face?

"Let him answer for himself," the Professor said. "For here he comes."

Catriona knew that he was just behind her, but she could not turn. He was bending over Frau Kalman's outstretched hand and greeting Fereith as she jumped down from the carriage step. She heard his voice for the first time in three long years, and it was still the same.

He went past her and turned, looking fully at her for the first time. Her own eyes did not waver. They clung to him, beseeching him to forget the past, yet in that first, fleeting instant she knew that he remembered only too well."

"This is Catriona Sutherland, my new nurse," Frau Kalman introduced them. "She's from Scotland, so you should have a lot in common, Andrew."

He smiled, but he was looking at Catriona with a sort of disbelief, as if what he saw could not be possible, and then he turned back to the carriage.

"Nurse Sutherland and I already know each other," he said briefly, hardly. "We met a very long time ago."

"I was a student then," Catriona heard herself saying, as if in defense of her actions. "We were both—very young."

Frau Kalman glanced swiftly in her direction.

"The world is indeed small," she remarked. "Who would have thought that you two knew each other, although I suppose being in the same profession could shorten the odds."

"We both trained in Edinburgh," Andrew informed her with a vague note of indifference in his voice.

"It's a strange coincidence, all the same," she said, gripping his arm as he stepped up into the carriage to help her out.

She looked almost exhausted by the time she had reached the hall, and Catriona walked on her other side, while the Professor followed with Fereith.

"We have two new residents," Andrew explained. "They're both spastics. Will you see them when you have had some coffee?"

He was offering her the rest she needed without making it obvious, and Frau Kalman thanked him with a smile.

"You are the most thoughtful person I know," she acknowledged, her gloved hand finding his. "I can't imagine what we would do without you!"

"You would find a substitute in less than no time," he teased. "I'm well aware of your wiles, remember!"

"Because I convinced you to come here against your better judgment?"

"I'm not sure now that it was my 'better judgment'."
Andrew's smile was disarming. "You taught me not to
put too much store on ambition, for one thing."

"I hope I managed to convince you that ambition can
have many facets," Frau Kalman answered. "It can go
hand-in-hand with contentment, for instance."

"I always thought those two were uneasy bedfellows,"
Andrew remarked, "but you generally manage to achieve
the impossible. This was your great ambition." He
glanced up to the high rafters of the magnificent hall as
the children came rushing in. "And I believe you are now
content."

Frau Kalman nodded, watching the children as they
swarmed after Jeno, who was carrying in the baskets of
foodstuff.

Catriona's heart was pounding. She would never have
believed that seeing Andrew again after all these years
would affect her like this. He was so much the same and
yet different. When she recalled the eager boy who had
confessed his ambitions to her, how he meant to go out
and conquer the world, or a large part of it, she could not
believe that the same person had chosen to settle here in
this half-forgotten valley for a lesser reward. She remembered the anger and bitterness of their parting because she
would not follow him to London, and, eventually, how he
had said that he would be better alone; unshackled, unat-
tached. He would achieve his ultimate goal easier that
way.

Three years had made a difference indeed. This mature
man bending over Frau Kalman's chair was a stranger to
her, and he had looked at her almost without recognition.

Her heart turned over at the thought and she wondered
how long it would be before he spoke to her directly.

He did not avoid her. When the coffee was served, he
came across the hall with a cup for her.

"Frau Kalman told me about you, but she didn't

mention your name," he explained. "Hence the surprise."

"I was as surprised as you were." She could not bear him to think that she had come to Switzerland deliberately in search of him, although somewhere at the back of her mind she was already accusing her errant heart of just such a treachery. "I had no idea you were Professor Zorn's assistant. I had heard of him, of course."

"Do you mean to work here?" he asked, ignoring her explanation.

"At the *schloss*? Oh no! I only came to nurse Frau Kalman for a week or two until she's able to get about on her own again."

"She isn't an invalid," he said pointedly. "Don't make that mistake about her. She has a will of iron, and even an arthritic hip won't deter her for long. She needs companionship. That's the main thing."

"I feel that we might get on quite well together," Catriona answered. "And I like Fereith."

"Oh—Fereith," he said with an odd smile. "Yes, it would be an asset if Fereith took to you."

"Because Frau Kalman is so fond of her?"

"Not entirely. Fereith is difficult," he explained tersely. "Introspective—a loner—yet not really sure of what she wants from life. She believes she has been cheated by circumstance, or fate, or whatever it is."

"Because she's an orphan?"

"Because of that and a dozen other things," he agreed.

The cynicism in his voice took her back to the past.

"Fereith is still very young." In some ways she felt that she was attempting to defend herself. "It's only natural that she should wonder about her parentage occasionally, but fundamentally I think she is happy enough. It's something we all experience at one time or another," she added lamely. "I can't explain it."

"Let's call it a common syndrome of adolescence," he

suggested dryly. "Everybody hopes that Fereith will forget the past, as she had every opportunity to do, and not become too great a problem. Her future here is assured. She would be a fool to throw it away."

He looked across the hall, his mouth surprisingly hard, to where Fereith sat at Frau Kalman's side. It was the old Andrew who had once told her so firmly that he would never forgive her as long as he lived.

"You know her better than I do," she acknowledged with difficulty, "but don't judge her too harshly, Andrew. She's still little more than a child."

"With a woman's growing awareness of her power," he added briefly. "There's nothing you can tell me about Fereith, even on so short an acquaintance."

"I'm sorry. I didn't mean to sound as if I knew it all," Catriona said with some spirit, "but I like her."

"Fair enough," he agreed. "I hope you're going to be good for her, that's why I asked if you were going to work here. She can be amazingly quick. You'll have to contend with that. It's in the blood."

"Gipsy blood, do you mean?"

"Partly." He regarded her cautiously. "I thought you knew."

"You've only just reminded me how recently I came here," she pointed out. "How can I know all the details of this strange household in so short a time?"

"Perhaps not," he agreed abruptly. "But you'll learn."

"Are you settled at Gleiberg?" she found herself asking in her turn.

"For a year or two." He looked down at her with an odd smile. "Do you find that surprising?"

She shook her head.

"I realize that it's the sort of work you've always wanted to do, but the valley is so remote. I thought you would be working in a big city."

"Such as Zurich? I go there frequently. The Professor is my colleague and tutor."

The explanation made things seem a little clearer.

"Which means that you will take over from him one day?"

"I may do. The decision, like Fereith's, lies in the lap of the gods."

"You're still—unforgiving, Andrew."

"What do you expect of me?" His voice was firmly controlled, although a small pulse had begun to beat at his temple. "A broken heart worn dramatically on my sleeve?"

"No," she said in a stifled whisper. "It's the last thing I would look for."

"You're very sensible," he returned. "What have you been doing with yourself all these years?"

"Working very hard. I've taken my midwifery and was going to look for a job in London."

"Until this one turned up?" Once more he glanced about the ancient hall. "I hope you're not going to be disappointed," he said.

She could not challenge his odd remark because the Professor was approaching.

"Has Andrew not yet offered to conduct you around his domain?" the Professor asked.

"Perhaps you will do that." Catriona had made the suggestion in a desperate bid for escape. "Andrew may wish to speak with Frau Kalman."

"Indeed." The Professor relieved her of her empty cup. "We are a busy little community, and Frau Kalman is always interested in what is going on. Come with me and I will show you this wonderful old castle. It is well worth a visit."

Andrew did not offer to accompany them, standing aside as the Professor offered Catriona his arm, the faint smile on his lips as cold as the barrier of cynicism which he had deliberately raised between them.

Frau Kalman's castle had many rooms, and all of them had been adapted to suit the needs of the children. Ramps that would accommodate a wheelchair had been substituted for steps where one level led to another, and there was a capacious elevator at the side of the main staircase, leading to the floor above.

The castle was very old and had additions built from time to time; the original tower dating from the early part of the 13th century, the Professor informed her. It had long since fallen into ruin, but the present *schloss* had been erected on its foundations. There had been little room on the plateau for an adjacent building even in those days, apparently, although there was evidence of a considerable fall of rock to one side.

"Brought down by an avalanche, no doubt," the Professor said. "In my lifetime I have never heard of one up here on the plateau, but they are frequent enough on the other side of the Pass. We are more or less impregnable here." He opened a door at the end of a corridor. "This is our biggest dormitory," he explained. "We don't sleep the children in large units because we feel that the family atmosphere is best served this way. Four beds. It is enough. And this is for the older boys."

Catriona was deeply interested in all she saw. She had no idea that Andrew had come up behind them. He had taken off his white surgical coat and wore a tweed jacket over a turtle-necked sweater and cord slacks. He was no longer the doctor, but a critical spectator of her reactions, it seemed.

"We have made many improvements," he said, "and hope to make many more, but our real dream is to have a large, new clinic down in the valley some day. Has the Professor shown you our new therapy room?"

They avoided the word "ward", she noticed, because this was a family setting as far as Frau Kalman's orphans were concerned. Suddenly she found herself wondering if Andrew had married. She had not been introduced to the nursing staff so far, and his wife could easily be working with him. It was what he had meant her to do, she remembered painfully, to work with him until they had had a family of their own for her to care for. Such distant dreams!

Her eyes clouded as she turned toward him. "You must be very proud of all this," she said.

"We are satisfied for the moment," the Professor answered for him. "Both here and at the Zurich clinic we are progressing slowly but surely. I do not expect to see my dream fulfilled," he added half-regretfully, "but the hope is that Andrew will."

They respected and trusted one another. Andrew put an arm affectionately across the older man's shoulders.

"You never know, Heinrich," he said kindly. "We may have a breakthrough at any moment—today, tomorrow, the day after. Who knows?"

"This is true of much research," the Professor agreed. "It is hard, however, to see such little children unable to enjoy life to the full, like you and me."

"But I think they do, in their limited way," Andrew objected. "Look at them down there with the carriage horses." He took Catriona's arm, leading her to one of the long windows. "See for yourself."

They were overlooking a small courtyard where Jeno had loosened the traces and set the horses free. The sturdy little cobs were busily munching hay from the children's hands, and two of the older boys were already seated across their backs.

"Jeno has a marvelous way with these children," the Professor mused.

"All Romanies have." There was a dry note in Andrew's voice, although he did not appear to dislike Jeno. "They invariably spoil their own offspring. When the Phen gipsies first migrated into Byzantine Greece from Armenia they had hordes of children with them, and that was only the beginning. Since then they've multiplied many times over, but we still know next to nothing about them."

"If they had greater sense," the Professor began, but Andrew laughed.

"Would that make us persecute them less often?" he wanted to know.

"Perhaps not, but you must admit that they have a great disrespect for law and order." The Professor looked down into the court. "I wonder what brought Jeno to Gleiberg?"

Andrew turned from the window.

"He is never likely to tell us," he said abruptly. "Romanies keep their own counsel, just as they have their own way of life. They are completely inscrutable to the average *gaujeo*."

"They are, after all, orientals," the Professor allowed, "and I admit that no race has so strongly held to its way of life in the face of such vigorous suppression, not even the Jews."

They walked farther along the corridor, that ended in another recessed window and a flight of steep stone stairs winding up to what was probably the tower. A stout oaken door barred their farther progress at the top of the third step.

"This is Andrew's domain," Professor Zorn said. "One day he may take you up there to admire his view, but now it is time for us to go and join the children. They will wish to be presented to you before we sit down to eat."

Catriona was still gazing at the closed door, thinking

that it was the most formidable barrier she had ever seen. When she looked around at Andrew his face was grim.

"Every window in the *schloss* has a view," he said. "There is no need to visit the tower to find one."

It was a deliberate snub, a warning which she would do well to heed, Catriona thought, and because the ugly, barbed shaft had already entered her heart a dismal pride forced her to say: "One view must be as good as another, Professor. I wouldn't dream of asking Andrew to open up his home to me."

"The door is a necessity," Andrew explained. "If the children found their way onto the battlements there could be an accident. It's something we have to guard against all the time."

"You know what children are," the Professor agreed. "Especially boys! Stairs were made to climb, barriers to be broken down."

But not this barrier of Andrew's making. Catriona knew that he meant to keep his eagle's fortress locked against her, this high eyrie which Frau Kalman had exchanged for the chalet in the sun on the other side of the valley. It seemed to be more suited to his present way of life and more in keeping with his plans for the future.

She walked back down the staircase between the two men, feeling that a door had, indeed, been shut in her face.

March Lazenby was standing in the hall beside the great open fireplace. She had taken off her coat and was shaking some finely-powdered snow from the fur collar.

"That's the first of it," she remarked with a sort of elation in her voice. "Jeno said it was bound to snow before nightfall."

The flurry of snow had been light and soon over, yet it was evidently the prelude of more to come. Andrew glanced through one of the tall windows.

"Jeno may be right," he allowed. "We'll have to check over the children's skis."

March looked up at him.

"I don't suppose it's any use asking you to Davos for the weekend," she said. "There's been a heavy fall on the Weissfluh. We could have a lot of fun."

"I wish I could," Andrew said politely, "but I shall be in Zurich on the weekend."

March accepted his refusal with a thin smile.

"I know you, Andrew," she declared. "All work and no play. It makes Jack a dull boy, remember."

"I'll have to remedy that some other time, March," he answered easily. "And there will be plenty of snow up here in a week or two."

"Jeno believes it will be a day or two." March lit a cigarette. "I can hardly wait! Do you still require my valuable assistance as an instructor?"

"Why not?" Andrew said. "There are two new children who will need coaching, and the others who weren't quite ready to leave the nursery slopes last spring. Would you take them on?"

"With pleasure." March surveyed him through a haze of smoke. "Nurse Sutherland tells me she doesn't ski very well," she observed. "Perhaps I should teach her, too."

"I wouldn't have the time," Catriona found herself saying hastily. "Besides, it would be far for me to come."

"Not if you could ski properly," March assured her. "But please yourself. You'll be welcome on the nursery slopes if you wish to improve your technique at any time."

They went along a passage to an open doorway leading to the courtyard where they had seen the children playing with the horses. Jeno was still there, but the children had disappeared. He stood in the centre of the cobbled yard; tall, straight and incredibly handsome, his black hair curling into the nape of his neck, his white teeth gleaming as he smiled down at his companion. He was flicking a whip for Fereith's amusement, and she was looking up at him with fond admiration in her eyes.

"Do it once more, Jeno!" she cried. "Just above the horses' ears but not touching them. Then you can teach me to do it!"

In a split second Andrew had passed Catriona and March, his face dark with fury.

"That's enough, Jeno!" he declared, seizing the half-raised whip. "You could frighten one of these cobs in an enclosed space like this—or injure somebody," he added harshly.

He had obviously been afraid for Fereith. Catriona caught her breath as he tossed the whip aside, but already much of the tension had gone out of the little interlude. Jeno had looked savage for a moment and then had smiled.

"You do not understand about horses," he said smoothly. "You are a doctor, skilled to mend men's bodies, but I, Jeno, know about animals. They know very well who is master, and they obey the language of the whip."

The remark was just short of being insolent, but Andrew's irritation did not seem to be personal.

"Don't do it again," he warned. "Fereith might try it and make a mistake."

Jeno shook his head.

"She would not do so," he declared. "This I know."

The strange little scene was over, yet it remained in Catriona's mind for the remainder of the day. Andrew had been furious for a split second when he had seen Fereith and Jeno together. Why?

There was no one to answer her question. A gong sounded through the house. They filed in with the children to the long dining room where pandemonium reigned for several minutes until the Professor decided to say grace. He spoke in German so that the children would understand, but the deep and thoughtful meaning of his words were easily conveyed to all who listened. Frau Kalman touched Catriona's hand.

"You will soon learn our language," she whispered. "It is easy for a Scot to master."

They spent the afternoon mostly out of doors, although the sun lost its heat before four o'clock. A thin film of cloud, like a veil, came between it and the valley, heralding snow.

"We must return quickly," Frau Kalman said as the four nurses on the staff shepherded the children indoors, at last. "You will tell Jeno to harness the cobs?"

Jeno had already done so, and the carriage was brought around to the main door. Andrew stood with the Professor, bidding them goodbye.

"You must come again quite soon," Heinrich Zorn said to Catriona, taking her hand. "You have a way with children that is completely natural. It is a gift, and they recognize it."

"I've never known a day go so quickly," Catriona confessed. "I would like to come again if I could be useful."

Andrew did not ask her to return. There was nothing personal about their leavetaking, nothing to suggest that they had loved each other in the past. Frau Kalman's sharp old eyes noticed both these things.

"How well did you know Andrew Bishop?" she asked as they drove away.

"Not very well." Catriona drew a deep breath. "Sometimes I wonder if I ever knew him at all."

"Are you suggesting that it was only a casual acquaintance?"

"No—but we quarreled. That was all there was to it."

Her voice had been calm. There was no use reliving the past or grieving over it in public. Frau Kalman continued to study her with interest.

"My godson expects to come out here," she said deliberately. "When do you think he will arrive?"

Catriona had forgotten about Robin from the moment she had set foot in the *schloss*.

"Nothing was settled," she admitted. "I really don't know."

"I half expected you to come together." Frau Kalman was still searching her face. "Why didn't you?"

"Robin was very busy. There was a sale of pictures in London he wanted to attend."

"Tush!" the old lady muttered. "He's far more interested in my money. Maybe he thought you would pave the way for his arrival later on. He knew I would like you."

Catriona felt completely taken aback, yet there could be a grain of truth in what Frau Kalman had just said.

"Well?" the old lady demanded.

"I haven't been here long enough for you to make up your mind about me," Catriona said in near desperation.

"That's true, but it doesn't take me very long to come to a decision when I put my mind to it." Frau Kalman sat back against the leather cushioning. "Maybe I've already made it up in one direction," she added laconically.

Fereith bent forward to pull the fur rug over her knees.

"Have you had a pleasant day?" she asked.

"Very pleasant, my dear." The old lady smiled at her. "And what about your day? Was it a happy one?"

Fereith's somber gaze lifted to the mountain rim. "It was pleasant," she said, "but I am glad that I do not have to live at the *schloss*."

A slow flush rose into Frau Kalman's sallow cheeks.

"You are lucky," she said sharply, "to have a home of your own."

It was the most direct rebuff Catriona had ever heard her deliver, and perhaps Fereith had deserved it. The girl shrank back in her seat, her eyes dark pools of distress, although the tears did not come. She had annoyed someone she loved.

CHAPTER FOUR

By morning the valley was covered in snow. It had fallen noiselessly during the night, like a gentle benediction, wrapping Gleiberg in a great peace. White, soft, and dry, it stretched across the terrace in a deep carpet that continued down the hillside and across the fields to the black line of the river winding its way to the village and the bridge. The branches of the pines bent low under the weight of it; it rested on the sloping roofs like a plump cushion, overhanging the eaves. The mountains were like ghostly giants, tall, white, and aloof, pressing closely against the sky.

The beauty of it all took Catriona's breath away. She had never seen snow quite so deep before nor so virginal.

"It makes you want to rush out and gather it into your arms," she said to Frau Kalman, "and yet afraid to spoil it by walking on it at all."

"It's very beautiful," the old lady returned. "And the children love it. They'll be out all morning, testing it for skiing and making a run for their luges down to the fields. It will be difficult to keep them indoors, even for an hour, to attend to their lessons."

The older children went to the village school, but there was special work to be done at the *schloss* by the crippled younger ones who were not yet able to make the journey to the village.

"I hope Fereith will teach in the school one day," Frau Kalman said, easing herself among her pillows. "She has the brains if she will only apply herself, and I am teaching her English. You could help in that respect," she added with the directness Catriona had come to expect. "Talk to her as much as you can. Help her."

"I'll do my best," Catriona promised, "although I'm not going to be here for any length of time."

The old lady made no attempt to answer that.

"I'll get up now," she decided after a moment. "You can ring for Grete."

It took an hour to get her out into the sunshine. Jeno had set a wicker *chaise longue* at the sheltered end of the terrace while Fereith brought rugs and a book for her to read.

"You'd better get down to your own books," she advised Fereith. "Catriona will help you."

Fereith looked pleased. She had taken an instant liking to Catriona in her shy, almost distant way. Catriona was eager to develop their friendship, if only for her employer's sake. Frau Kalman seemed pathetically grateful.

"She needs young company," she said. "I must seem as old as the hills to her, I suppose."

Sixteen and sixty! It was certainly a wide gap, though there was a gap, too, between 16 and 23, but Catriona felt that she could bridge it without a great deal of difficulty. When she had given Frau Kalman her first massage and settled her for her afternoon rest, she sought out Fereith. Grete told her that she would probably find her in the stables behind the chalet, so she crossed the trampled snow in search of her.

Jeno was standing at the open door of the stable nearest the house, waxing a ski. His back was toward her, and he was speaking to someone just inside the door.

"It is too soon. We must wait," he said. "You must not be impatient, my little *diddikai!*"

"You must not call me that!" It was Fereith's voice, high-pitched and vehement, coming from the dimness of one of the hidden stalls.

"What else are you but a half-Romani?" Jeno teased

her. "It is true what I say, isn't it?" His white teeth flashed as he turned to prop the ski against the stable wall.

He saw Catriona and the smile faded completely, leaving his face dark and sullen.

"I did not hear you come," he muttered, like someone caught in the act of a grave misdemeanor. "The snow is very thick."

Fereith appeared at the stable door, carrying the other ski. She looked as belligerent as Jeno for a moment and then she smiled.

"Come and try on a pair of my skis," she suggested. "They should fit you because I am tall for my age. They will be useful until you can buy a pair for yourself. I have three pairs," she added boastfully.

Jeno moved away, busying himself with fitting runners to the carriage in place of the wheels. The life of the valley had changed overnight. It was being geared to the snow.

"Unless you can ski properly you will be unable to move about quickly," Fereith informed her. "You will always need the carriage, as Frau Kalman does, or you may have to stay near the chalet all the time and go for quiet walks in the woods."

It was obvious that "quiet walks" through the pine woods were not entirely to Fereith's liking. She preferred the relative excitement of village life, and the distractions to be found there. Frau Kalman was quite willing that she should go to Gleiberg if Catriona went with her.

"Jeno will take you," the old lady suggested the following afternoon when Catriona had completed her second massage. "I hope this spinal manipulation nonsense you believe in is going to do me good," she added testily. "It certainly doesn't make me feel like leaping over the Gleiberg at the present moment."

"I'm sorry," Catriona apologized, "but a little rest will make you feel better. In a day or two you won't have so much pain. Do try to sleep."

"I'll do my best," Frau Kalman said dryly. "And look after that girl!" She was already drowsy, tired by the vigorous manipulation that Catriona had been forced to use, but a rest would refresh her.

"I am to show you the church and the museum," Fereith announced when they were ready to set out. "And we can also have some *gluwein* at the inn if there is time afterward."

It was a grand adventure as far as Fereith was concerned, and Jeno seemed pleased with the prospect of trying out the new runners that had converted the carriage into a sleigh. The sullen look which had darkened his handsome face at their previous encounter had gone; his ready smile flashed out as he helped them into the carriage.

"Don't go too fast," Fereith cautioned. "Catriona is nervous."

Jeno flicked the whip a hairsbreadth from the cobs' ears and they were off, careering down the switchback road to leave two deeply-indented ruts behind them in the virgin snow. No other vehicle had passed that way before them.

However, the village street was covered in wheel and runner marks, and there was a brisk activity along the row of shops. The valley people were replenishing their winter stock of provisions in case of further snow, while some of the visitors to the inn were buying souvenirs to take home with them. Others, more recently arrived, were gathered in front of the bootmaker's or crowding the doorway of Herr Gruber's store to hire a pair of skis. Catriona decided to buy a pair of boots and was being fitted for them when March Lazenby sat down on the stool next to her.

"Where's Fereith?" she asked. "I thought I saw you together going into the museum."

"You did," Catriona agreed, "but she's gone with Jeno to see about some harness which needs repairing. I thought you would be skiing all over the Gleiberg by now," she laughed teasingly, because it was good to meet a known face in a strange place.

"I do a morning stint at the *schloss*, that's all," March returned rather gloomily. "There's not much point in tackling the *berg* by oneself."

"I would be terrified," Catriona confessed with unfeigned admiration for the other girl's skill. "Does it take very long to learn, March?"

"It depends on how proficient you want to become," March answered. "I never did do anything by half, and this came naturally to me. I suppose that's quite a point," she conceded, paying for the boots she had collected. "You're either a potential champion or you're not."

"And you have to live here to get in sufficient practice," Catriona supposed.

"Are you always off the hook during the afternoon?" March asked as they went out into the sunshine together.

"I think so. Frau Kalman has to rest, and she seems tired after her massage session."

"I can't imagine her ever feeling tired," March decided. "She's the most aggressive old bird I've ever known, fiercely proud of her background and all it means around here."

"Isn't that only natural?" Catriona said. "I suppose we would feel as strongly about tradition ourselves if we owned all this." She looked up at the surrounding mountains, pink-flushed in the afternoon sunshine. "It does seem a pity that she hasn't anyone to inherit it."

March shot a covert glance in her direction.

"She had at one time," she said after a moment's hesitation. "There was some mystery about his disappearance from the valley a long time ago. Possibly he and his mother were estranged even before then. Anyway, he died five or six years ago—in Yugoslavia."

It was the end of Robin's story; the tragedy he hadn't been quite sure about.

"It must have been a terrible blow for Frau Kalman," Catriona said. "What age was he?"

"The son?" March shrugged. "I've no idea." She halted before the inn. "I'm going to have a *gluwein*. Will you join me?" she asked.

"I'd like to find Fereith first, if you don't mind," Catriona said. "She must still be with Jeno."

"Which won't please the old lady," March laughed. "She guards Fereith like some prized possession, which I suppose she is. People who have lost their own child are generally over-possessive with one they adopt, or over-careful. Maybe Frau Kalman hopes to make Fereith her heiress one day," she added glibly.

The thought of Robin thrust itself into Catriona's mind; Robin, who fondly imagined himself to be the only possible heir to Gleiberg. She felt suddenly sure of his aspirations, although he had never put such an ambition into actual words.

Jeno and Fereith came along the village street, walking openly in the middle of the road. Jeno had a harness over his arm.

"Soon we will have to start back," he announced, looking up at the sky above the Gleiberg which was darkening menacingly. "There will be much more snow."

"Have you much to do?" Catriona asked, knowing that he had several purchases to make.

"Not much," Jeno answered. "But there is this." He held out a folded piece of paper. "It is a message I have to dispatch from the post-office for Frau Kalman."

"Let me take it for you," Catriona offered. "It will save time."

"What about our *gluwein*?" Fereith wanted to know.

"That can wait." Catriona took the paper from Jeno. "Unless you would like to go to the inn while I send this off. March Lazenby is there."

Fereith was quick to seize the opportunity of a visit to the inn. "Jeno will show you the post office," she said. "It isn't far, but there are always many people waiting because Herr Schiller also sells films, postcards and chocolate."

She moved off toward the inn, and Catriona accompanied Jeno as far as the post office, where he left her. Gradually she made her way to the head of the line-up, unfolding the sheet of paper to read the message that she was about to send. Frau Kalman's handwriting was vigorous and clear, but it was a full second before she took in the full meaning of what she read.

The message was directed to Robin at his Edinburgh address.

"I wish you to come out here immediately," Frau Kalman had written. "It is where you ought to be."

The summons would wing its way to Robin within the hour; a command which he could not afford to ignore.

Catriona stood on the narrow sidewalk outside the post office wondering why the message had been sent. Frau Kalman had not taken her into confidence, and, indeed, there was no reason why she should do so, except for the fact that Robin had sent her to Gleiberg. She was not even his fiancée, although she fancied that the old lady read more into their association than mere friendship. What could Frau Kalman want?

As she returned to the inn she saw Andrew Bishop striding toward her. Even a stranger would have picked him out from the crowd, she thought, trying to still the foolish beating of her heart. He was taller by a head then most of the men around him. He walked with an air of authority, a pair of glistening skis balanced on his shoulder with one hand while grasping both sticks in the other. He looked strong, purposeful and completely in his element, a man already acclimatized to the mountains; whose black gullies and treacherous ice-slopes would hold little terror for him. He stopped in his tracks when he saw her.

"March said you were here," he remarked. "I think you ought to get back to the chalet as quickly as possible before the next fall hits us. Even Jeno's talent as a horseman would be limited in a blizzard."

"Andrew," she asked impulsively, "do you really dislike Jeno?"

He looked down at her with the smile she remembered from long ago, humoring her.

"You were always too deeply concerned about other people, Kate," he said, "but 'dislike' will do. It's a mild enough word for you not to worry too much about it."

"Is it because of Fereith?" she was forced to ask.

"Partly." His dark brows drew together in a quick frown. "I think Jeno could be treacherous for a reason we would never be able to understand."

"Why?"

"He's a gipsy."

"But surely now that he's been working for Frau Kalman for so long—"

"They never change. His final allegiance would be to his own people."

She wondered if she should tell him about the scene of the previous afternoon when she had come upon Jeno and Fereith in the stables. "It is too soon," Jeno had said. "We must wait. You must not be impatient, my little *diddikai*!" The word had distressed Fereith.

"Andrew," she asked, "what exactly is a *diddikai*?"

"Someone who is not of pure gipsy blood—a half-Romani. Why?"

"Is Fereith?"

"Yes, I suppose she is," he said.

"She told me she was called after a gipsy princess."

"That could be so." His mouth had clamped down into a thin, hard line. "There are plenty of them around."

"Do you think she might be—attracted by Jeno?"

He swung around on his heel.

"No," he said, "that mustn't happen, and it's up to you not to encourage it while you remain here."

"I won't be here so very long."

He left her statement unanswered.

"But I did promise to help Fereith," she added. "To look after her, in a way."

"See that you keep that promise, then," he said. "The old lady may feel that she can trust you."

It was another direct snub because she had failed him in the past, she supposed, but why, if he had succeeded in forgetting her in the interval, should he wish to hurt her now? An eye for an eye seemed so unlike Andrew.

"Are you going back to the inn?" she asked.

"I told March I would pick her up there." He fell into step beside her. "She's coming to the *schloss* to stay overnight. We're planning our Christmas festivities and deciding what to do for New Year's."

"It sounds like Scotland," she said without thinking.

"It isn't a prerogative of the Scot." He transferred his skis from one shoulder to the other. "The Austrians, for instance, make more of New Year's than they do of Christmas. More in the way of entertainment."

"I can imagine it all being rather wonderful up here in the valley," she said, "and the *schloss* is just the place for children at Christmas. Will you be here, Andrew?"

"My home is here," he reminded her.

"Yes." She still did not know whether he had married or not and could not bring herself to ask. "Frau Kalman's godson may be coming across for the holidays," she added instead. "His name is Robin Pettigrew. I knew him in Edinburgh."

"So I understand." His tone was almost curt. "Frau Kalman has been anxious to see him for some time. It appears that he used to visit her regularly as a schoolboy, but found the habit increasingly irksome as he grew up."

Catriona flushed, wondering how much he really knew about her affairs. He appeared to be in her employer's confidence to a considerable degree. No doubt Frau Kalman relied on him and respected him as much as she respected the Professor. The work they were doing at Gleiberg would be the bond between them, and it was perhaps only natural that he should know all about Robin and Frau Kalman's hopes for the future. In some ways, Robin was another of the old lady's orphans, although he was also her godson.

They reached the inn, where they found March and Fereith waiting.

"Fereith is coming to help us with the decorating," March told Andrew with a faint smile. "She could bring over some greenery if the snow stops. I've asked Herr Jonas about the dinner at the inn, by the way," she added, "and there's still a table available for New Year's Eve. You really enjoyed yourself last year, remember?"

Andrew nodded. "It was quite a party," he agreed.

All the way back to the chalet, Catriona could not help wondering if she would be included in the Christmas festivities. The dinner party on New Year's Eve would be small and exclusive, she supposed, but there would be much entertainment for the children at the *schloss*.

The following day seemed to prove her surmise correct. More snow had fallen during the night, with a thin coating of frost on it in the early morning which delighted Fereith.

"Now we can really ski!" she cried. "But first of all we must gather the greenery for the decorations."

They spent the afternoon in the woods behind the chalet. Jeno cut down the branches for them with a pair of long-handled pruners, sending cushions of snow cascading onto their heads to Fereith's immense amusement. The child in her delighted in their task and laughter rang out across the snowfield like a peal of bells. When they finally returned to the chalet, their baskets were laden with pine cones, some of which Fereith laid along the windowsills.

"When we open the windows the scent will come in," she explained. "It is beautiful."

Jeno had taken out a big, wooden-runnered sleigh to carry the branches, and they stacked them more securely for the journey across the valley the following morning. Healthily tired with their labors in the open air and their walk back to the chalet, they smiled at each other with satisfaction.

"I am glad you are here," Fereith said shyly. "It is pleasant to have someone young to talk with, Catriona."

It was the first time she had expressed any reaction to their companionship in actual words.

"It's nice for me, too," Catriona agreed, "when Frau Kalman doesn't need me."

"Soon she will be well again." There was a half-regretful note in Fereith's voice. "You will go away."

"You will have March's company," Catriona suggested.

"I do not like March Lazenby," Fereith returned with disconcerting frankness. "Besides, she would much prefer to be with Doctor Bishop than with me."

"So he isn't married," Catriona said almost to herself.

"Oh, no! Did you think he was?" Fereith looked at her inquiringly. "Frau Kalman says he is a 'confirmed bachelor', which means he will never marry, doesn't it?" She paused to consider the advisability of what she was about to say next. "That's why I put your photograph in his room," she confessed.

"Oh!" Catriona was taken completely by surprise by the admission. "So Robin did send it to his godmother, after all?"

Fereith shook her head.

"I found it in an old box with some letters that Frau Kalman told me to return to Doctor Bishop," she admitted, "but I kept the photograph because I liked it very much."

Catriona bit her lip.

"Why did you put it in my room?" she asked.

"It has been there a long time," Fereith explained. "The room looked so bare, and Doctor Bishop never came to occupy it after he moved to the *schloss*."

"Did Frau Kalman see the photograph?"

"I do not know. But Grete did, when she was tidying the room."

"You said that—Doctor Bishop never came back to the chalet. Did Frau Kalman expect him to return?" Catriona asked, wondering why Andrew should completely avoid his old home.

"She invited him to come whenever he liked," Fereith said, "But he has never done so."

"How long have you been here, Fereith?"

"Nearly three years. I was at school in Zurich then. Doctor Bishop called it a 'straight swop'."

There was no doubt in Catriona's mind now that she was occupying what had once been Andrew's bedroom, but it was now so bare and impersonal that there was nothing of him left there. No doubt he did not even remember the pathetic little photograph that he had once framed with loving care; if the letters that Fereith had returned to him had been the few she had written to him in the year they had known one another in Edinburgh, he had probably destroyed them. Such was the grave of love, the pathetic burial of the past.

When they arrived at the *schloss* the following afternoon Andrew was nowhere to be seen. He had gone to Zurich with Professor Zorn, one of the nurses informed her, and she had been left in full charge in his absence. She was a pleasant girl of about Catriona's own age. They spent a useful three hours together, arranging the working parties. Each child was given a specific task to do. Those confined to wheelchairs made multi-colored chains out of crêpe paper and a tube of adhesive, while the mobile ones fetched and carried and generally made themselves useful with the greenery. Jeno hung the paper garlands from the balcony and across the minstrels' gallery, where the local band would play carols on Christmas Day; Fereith and Catriona arranged the pine branches on every available ledge and corner.

A huge model sleigh had been hoisted high among the rafters, with the figure of Santa Claus whipping four very lifelike reindeer into action. This had been Andrew's special contribution, and it was much admired. Looking at it, Catriona felt the knife-thrust of painful memory turning in her heart, because once, long ago, he had made a similar model for the children in an Edinburgh hospital. She had helped him. She had made Santa's red cloak out of some velvet curtain material, and a false beard with cotton wool.

No use remembering; the past was dead.

Robin arrived in Gleiberg on Christmas Eve. He came prepared for two weeks' skiing, looking pale in comparison with their ruddy-cheeked freshness, but greeting everybody with his usual enthusiasm.

"This is something!" he declared, kissing his godmother dutifully on the cheek. "I was glad to get away from Edinburgh, I can tell you."

"Yet you plan to spend the remainder of your life there," Frau Kalman observed dryly. "Or has the bottom fallen out of the antique market since we last heard from you?"

"Neither!" He held his hands to the warmth of the tiled stove. "I'll work in Edinburgh, of course, but I'll come here as often as possible—when I'm established, that is."

Frau Kalman glanced at Catriona. "I told you how it would be," she said. "Once he gets here he is in love with the place."

"What about the snow conditions?" Robin asked, pacing restlessly to the window to look out. "Are you still as disorganized as ever up here, or have you a ski school now?"

"We have a competent instructor, at least at the *schloss*," his godmother told him. "Her name is March Lazenby, but she is in Davos this weekend."

"I had half a notion to go there for a few days," Robin admitted, "but funds were low." He came across the room to kiss Catriona with a deliberation which made her draw back a little from his light embrace. "How are things going?" he asked. "Getting on all right together, I expect?"

"It would be difficult not to 'get on' with Catriona," Frau Kalman said. "We have a great deal in common."

"That's good!" Robin rubbed his hands together. "Where's Ferry? Still at school in Zurich?"

"She is here." Frau Kalman's expression softened. "You will find her changed, Robin. She is no longer the child you used to tease."

"She can't have grown up out of recognition in so short a time," he objected absently.

"You shall see," his godmother told him. "She's quite

a young lady now. Next year she'll attend finishing school in Lausanne. Her education will then be complete."

"You make all sorts of plans for people," Robin said, studying her closely. "Are you still determined to run the *schloss* as an exclusive sort of orphanage?"

The old lady stiffened.

"We don't pick and choose the children who come here, Robin," she said. "We take them as we find them."

"Sorry," he apologized. "No offence meant." He put his arm affectionately around her shoulders. "It's good to be back."

Frau Kalman smiled, forgiving him immediately.

"I like to have you," she admitted. "And here comes Fereith. You can judge for yourself if she's changed or not."

Fereith came slowly into the room, her apricot-tinted cheeks glowing with the kiss of the sun, her dark eyes fixed expectantly on the newcomer.

"Well, well!" said he appreciatively, "a young lady, indeed." Then suddenly he went toward her, swinging her shoulder-high off her feet and spinning around with her as if she were still a child. "Remember?" he asked. "You used to expect this every time we met!"

"Put me down, please," Fereith ordered primly. "I don't expect it any more."

"Hoity-toity, Miss!" he laughed, setting her back onto her feet. "You *have* grown up!"

"I am 16," Fereith reminded him with dignity, going to sit beside his godmother.

"Let's go out," Robin suggested, turning to Catriona. "I want to fill my lungs with mountain air."

Frau Kalman watched them go with an odd, questioning expression in her eyes. She had finished with Catriona's services for the afternoon and would not need her again until bed time, but some strange impulse within her had urged her to keep the girl by her side.

" 'The best laid schemes. . . .' " she murmured.

Fereith looked around at her. "I did not hear what you said," she apologized.

The old lady put a gentle hand on her arm. "I was quoting a Scottish poet," she explained. "One of the greatest poets we have ever produced in my country. You must soon begin a study of his works. He is as great as Shakespeare and almost as well known. He said, in effect, that our dearest plans often come to nothing through no fault of our own. Fate had a way of wrecking them, just as this poet had wrecked the nest of a poor little field-mouse with his plough."

"He could not help disturbing the mouse," Fereith said, distressed. "It was Robert Burns, wasn't it? He also wrote Auld Lang Syne, which we sing at New Year up at the *schloss*."

"It is sung all over the world, where friends meet and part," Frau Kalman said nostalgically.

Robin led Catriona up the steep incline toward the pine woods.

"I've come a long way," he said, "just to see you."

Catriona drew the collar of her coat more closely under her chin. "How was Edinburgh when you left?" she asked.

"As cold as charity, with an east wind blowing fit to cut you in two." He drew her toward him. "It's cold here, but it's pleasant. Different, somehow." He looked about him with the keenest appreciation. "I have to confess that I've missed all this, the skiing and the sense of privilege which goes with belonging at the *schloss*, even though we no longer live there. What's going on?" he asked. "Is this orphanage thing a permanent effort?"

"There seems to be plenty of children to take care of," Catriona told him, "and it's your godmother's greatest interest, although I heard her say the other day that they would soon need even larger premises."

"H'm!" he commented. "She was always a queer old bird. But let's forget about the *schloss*." He pulled her farther into the circle of his arms. "How have you been faring, Kate, my love?"

"I've been very happy with Frau Kalman, and I like the work," Catriona admitted. "It's been a pleasant change."

"But you're not going to go on with it," he suggested.

"I don't know. I was engaged for six weeks, but—"

"But?" he prompted. "Surely you don't yearn to come back to Edinburgh when you have everything you could possibly want here."

"I don't know," Catriona repeated. "I didn't expect it to be—quite like this."

He kissed her full on the lips. "Kate, what's changed you?" he demanded. "You used to be such an amiable girl."

"Did I?" She tried to evade a second kiss. "Why did you send me here, Robin?"

He kissed the tip of her nose. "I knew the old girl would like you," he confessed unashamedly, "and that would be halfway to her liking my plans for the future."

"Because she expected you to marry me?"

"Something like that."

"We're not even engaged."

"We could remedy that as soon as I can afford to buy you a ring," he suggested.

"No, Robin!" She moved away from his embrace. "It's not as easy as you think. I won't be used as a—as a sort of investment because you feel that your godmother has no real faith in you. She would like you to settle down," she rushed on hastily. "I think that's all she wants."

"I have to prove it to her," he said. "The old dear is like that, I'm afraid—as hard as flint when she imagines she isn't getting her full pound of flesh. She would like me to marry and have a family so that I could inherit the *schloss* one day."

"Is that what you want, Robin?" Catriona felt forced to ask.

He kicked at the bole of a pine, sending down a cascade of snow. "Why not?" he asked. "There's no one else."

She looked across the valley and up to the *schloss*, where the last of the sun had warmed the old gray stones of the tower and touched the ramparts of the mountains with a haze of gold.

"No," she agreed. "There's no one else."

He put his arms about her, kissing her again lightly and then with more passion.

"This is good!" he said. "And we have two whole weeks in front of us."

They were in the shelter of the pines, but Catriona felt as if the whole wide valley could see them standing there.

"We must go back," she suggested. "Your godmother will be waiting."

"Let her wait!" Robin laughed. "I haven't seen you for two weeks!"

CHAPTER FIVE

Christmas at Gleiberg was a wonderful experience. Catriona thought that she had never seen anything so beautiful as the narrow valley lying deep in snow with the bright turquoise sky above it, and the peaks flushed pink as the sun rose above the mountain rim. The pine woods behind the chalet were hushed with snow; the dark boles standing in a solid phalanx straight across the hillside. The marmots crept down to nibble on the windowsills.

Everyone inside the house was astir early. With Jeno's assistance, Fereith had erected a Christmas tree in the hall. They dug it out of the pine wood and carried it down on their shoulders to the house, where they all helped with the decorations. They had placed their personal gifts around it in secret the evening before. Catriona had done her shopping in the village, buying a fine, lace-like scarf for Frau Kalman, a goatskin purse for Grete and a wallet for Jeno. Fereith and Robin had proved more difficult to choose for, but finally she had bought Fereith a silk head-scarf and Robin a bright hand-knitted sweater.

"We must wait for our presents until after breakfast," Fereith announced when they gathered beside the gleaming little tree. "It is a rule because no one ever wants to eat once they have opened their parcels."

Frau Kalman was brought down from her bedroom to preside at the breakfast table, a departure from her usual custom as a concession to the importance of the occasion.

"You will have a busy day," she told Catriona. "We go to the *schloss* immediately after lunch to hear the band. We stay for dinner with the staff. The children receive their presents immediately after tea, and you will no doubt be expected to help."

"Everybody does," Fereith said, "but we don't have presents. We give them to the children instead."

Already she had scrutinized the mound of packages at the foot of the chalet tree, singling out her own gifts, and her excitement was intense in consequence.

"I can hardly wait!" she confessed, with the impatience of a child. "What do you think they are, Catriona?"

"Patience!" Robin counselled, tweaking her braided hair. "You've another five minutes to go."

He drank his coffee slowly, teasing her.

"Please hurry!" she begged. "It's almost ten o'clock."

Frau Kalman's present was the most obvious one. It was a colorful ski jacket with a fur-lined hood, with pants and a gay sweater to match it. Grete had bought her leather mitts, and Robin's gift was a tartan holdall, that he had brought with him from Edinburgh. There was no gift from Jeno. Catriona's present, wrapped in white waxed paper and tied with scarlet ribbon by the obliging girl in the village store, was the last to be opened. Fereith held up the silk head-scarf, her cheeks flushed with pleasure.

"It is beautiful!" she cried. "Truly beautiful!"

Rising impulsively, she crossed to the mirror above the buffet to try it on, knotting it, peasant-fashion, beneath her chin.

Grete admired it and Robin was dutifully complimentary.

"It suits you to perfection," he said. "You look just like a gipsy princess."

The silence which followed his unthinking remark could almost be felt, and Catriona knew instinctively that she had made a terrible mistake in her choice of gifts. She had no need to turn back to the table to see Frau Kalman's displeasure. It was there, in the atmosphere of the whole room, taut and cold. The old lady considered her gift distasteful because it reminded her of Fereith's origin.

"Now I must open mine," Robin declared a trifle awkwardly. "What do I have, I wonder?"

Catriona fumbled with the string of her first parcel. It was from Frau Kalman; a lovely hand-worked Tyrolean skirt.

"Oh—thank you!" She met the old lady's severe blue gaze with a world of apology in her eyes. "I don't deserve anything so beautiful."

The irritation faded out of her employer's eyes.

"You must wear it when you go to the *schloss*," she said. "We all dress up on Christmas Day."

Fereith had complemented her gift with a hand-embroidered blouse. "You have to wear a narrow black velvet band around your throat," she instructed, "and a locket, if you have one."

"I haven't, but perhaps this will do." Catriona had opened Grete's simple gift. It was a delicate little medallion carved out of ivory and mounted as a brooch. "Grete! Thank you. Thank you very much."

She was near to tears because of their kindness and because, unthinkingly, she had upset her employer.

"What did Robin give you?" Fereith asked.

Catriona had left Robin's gift until the last. It was so obviously a ring-box that she hesitated before she opened it.

"Go on," Robin urged. "It won't bite!"

The ring was an antique; heavy and solidly carved, with a large chalcedony as a centerpiece.

"Oh!" Fereith gasped, unable to keep the envy out of her voice. "I think it's the most beautiful thing I've ever seen!"

Catriona looked up and caught Frau Kalman's eye. The old lady was looking at her fixedly, waiting to see what she would do. The agate glinted evilly in the searching light from the window.

"I took a chance on it being a good fit," Robin said. "It's very old."

Quite deliberately Catriona slipped it onto the third finger of her right hand. If Robin had meant it as a token of their engagement she was not ready for it. Frau Kalman diverted her gaze to the window.

"Tell Jeno that we will need the sleigh for two o'clock," she said as Grete rose to go. "No later, do you understand? We don't want to hold up the festivities."

Fereith followed Grete out, carrying her mound of parcels.

"I'd like to try on my skirt and blouse," said Catriona. "Your ring will be just right with them, Robin."

"For the moment," he agreed, smiling at his godmother.

They were all ready and waiting when Jeno led the horses around just before two o'clock. Fereith wore a wide striped skirt, very like the one Frau Kalman had given to Catriona, with a white blouse and a frothy white petticoat underneath. She had on white stockings and silver-buckled shoes, and her hair was braided and tied with scarlet ribbon. The one jarring note was a necklace of cheap glass beads which she had wound twice around her throat. Frau Kalman's eagle eye noticed it immediately.

"Where did you get these?" she demanded icily.

"Jeno gave them to me." Fereith's hands went protectively to her throat. "He bought them in Feldkirch."

There was a little silence.

"Jeno goes too often to Feldkirch," Frau Kalman said. "Take them off."

"Oh, please, no!" Fereith pleaded. "I like them. They are so full of color."

"They spoil your costume," the old lady said with finality. "I will give you my locket and you can wear that."

"What a fuss over a string of beads!" Robin muttered as they went out to the terrace to wait. "But maybe it was Jeno and not the beads, as such," he reflected. "Perhaps he isn't supposed to give Fereith presents."

He helped his godmother into the sleigh. Catriona sat facing her with Fereith by her side. The offending bead necklace had been exchanged for a small gold locket on a fine gold chain.

The swift run down the valley was both breathtaking and exhilarating. The swish of the runners on the closely-packed snow seemed the only sound as they passed between the dark ranks of the pines and out into the sunshine again. The *schloss* stood before them, bold and strong on its sentinel rock silently watching the approaches to the valley. High above the Pass the snow glittered in the bright noonday light, and the river looked deeper than it really was, flowing in its black channel between the overhanging banks of snow.

On the incline up to the *schloss* they passed the village band puffing with the exertion of climbing the hill and maintaining the tempo of the military march that was supposed to keep them in step. Young, old, and middle-aged, they plodded manfully on, blowing with all the vigor at their command, with their highly-polished brass instruments reflecting the dazzle of the sun, and their medieval costumes a bright splash of gold, red, and yellow against the snow.

When they became aware of the horses climbing the slope behind them they drew into the side of the road, marching in single file but playing with renewed zest for the benefit of the lady of the castle. Frau Kalman acknowledged them with a deep bow and a wave of her hand. For the first time Robin sat up in his seat beside her and appeared to take an interest in the proceedings.

"I remember it being like this when I was a kid," he said.

"It has been like this for hundreds of years," his godmother told him.

The children were grouped outside the main door to welcome them and broke into a carol as they crossed the bridge. Catriona could hear the sound of the waterfall far below, mingling with the young voices, and she looked up at the sky above the gray battlements and felt sure that this was going to be a perfect day. Happiness oozed out of this old medieval fortress at times like this, as if the ancient stones had soaked up all the joy and laughter of past generations to spill it out again for this special occasion. If they had also retained the memory of heartache, sadness and despair these were surely for another day.

A figure moved on the battlements above the central tower, walking slowly from one end to the other, a tall man whose eagle glance seemed to range across the whole valley. It could only be Andrew, up there alone, communing with the elements, pacing the weathered flagstones as if he had some heavy problem on his mind.

Robin's keen gaze followed the direction of her own.

"Who's up there?" he asked sharply.

"It will be Doctor Bishop," Fereith said. "He lives in the tower."

Robin frowned.

"He seems to have taken over the whole place," he observed a trifle ungenerously. "I thought Professor Zorn was your righthand man," he added to his godmother.

"Heinrich is growing old and can't be here all the time," Frau Kalman explained. "He has much to do in Zurich if we are to have this new clinic that we are planning, but Andrew is equally proficient. We exchanged homes because it was best for the children to have a qualified person on call all the time," she added. "You know how difficult it can be to get from one side of the valley to the other if we are snowed in."

"Why did he come to Gleiberg in the first place?" Robin demanded.

Frau Kalman hesitated. "It was a weekend sanctuary for him at first, when he was working full-time at the Zurich clinic," she said. "He has always worked under Professor Zorn and he expected to marry and settle down here. That was not to be, apparently," she added, looking straight ahead, "but I hope he will stay." She sighed as Jeno brought the sleigh to a stop. "He is young, of course, and no doubt ambitious, so Gleiberg may not hold him for long."

Catriona felt as if she had been frozen into her seat. Was this true of Andrew? Was he simply using Gleiberg as a step upward on the ladder of success that he had vowed so bitterly to scale to the very top?

"There's nothing else for me now, is there?" he had said all those years ago. "I'm never going to be let down by a woman again."

He was crossing the minstrels' gallery when they reached the hall. It was a noisy gathering, loud with greetings and the sound of children's laughter. Catriona looked up at him and suddenly it was as if they were alone. The voices faded and the lost years fell away. They were back where it had all started, in the main hall of a big infirmary, with children everywhere and a giant Christmas tree glittering with silver tinsel and heavy with cotton wool 'snow'. Even the huge silver star on the top of the tree seemed to be the same, gleaming and twinkling in the overhead lights. "I love you," her heart said. "I still love you, Andrew."

He came down the staircase, smiling and holding out his hand, first to Frau Kalman, welcoming her back to her old home, and then to Catriona, but it was March Lazenby who moved to his side, as if she had every right to be there.

"Who is this Lazenby woman?" Robin asked.

"She's your godmother's secretary and part-time ski-instructress to the children," Catriona roused herself to explain. "The therapy helps them—even the crippled ones—and March likes being here."

"I'll bet she does!" He glanced from March to Andrew. "Is she engaged to our friend the doctor?"

"No." Her denial had something desperate about it. "Neither of them are engaged."

"I wonder why the *schloss* needs a resident physician," Robin said.

"There are more than 50 children here, some of them very sick," she answered far too sharply.

He put his arm about her shoulders. "All right, Florence Nightingale!" he laughed. "You needn't fly to the doctor's defense as soon as he is criticized. I wasn't in full possession of the facts, that's all."

Andrew came up behind them. "Frau Kalman tells me you're here for the skiing," he remarked. "You're lucky. We're going to have the best conditions we've had for some time. We can't always guarantee snow for Christmas at Gleiberg."

"I've been coming here since I was nine," Robin informed him a trifle rudely. "Give or take a year or two. I learned to ski on the 'berg."

"Then there's nothing I can tell you about it." Andrew had noticed Robin's arm about her shoulders, but it meant nothing to him, Catriona thought painfully. Not now. "We're waiting for the band," he explained, "and then we'll have tea. There's no point in giving the children their presents beforehand, because they just wouldn't eat afterward." He smiled down into Catriona's eyes, remotely impersonal. "Will you lend a hand, Kate, when the time comes?" he asked.

"I'd love to!" She was still half-lingering in the atmosphere of the past. "Christmas is much the same anywhere, isn't it?"

"Much the same," he agreed as he left them.

It was the liveliest, noisiest party Catriona had ever attended. After refreshing themselves with wine and cakes, the band played louder than ever, while the more assertive of the children thumped the wooden table tops with their spoons, clamoring to be noticed. The introspective ones gazed steadily at the tree, hardly bothering to eat as they sat in wide-eyed wonder at all they saw, while Frau Kalman presided at the head of the festive board with Robin at her side. Fereith and Catriona helped the kitchen staff to carry in the food. March had taken upon herself the task of supervising the older boys, who also helped where they could.

"One, big happy family!" Robin remarked as Catriona passed his chair with a huge platter of *apfel-strudel*, which had been made specially by the Austrian chef.

"Can you come and help behind the scenes?" March asked presently. "Andrew's got himself in a fix. He has some sort of problem with his beard."

Andrew had disappeared from the scene half an hour earlier. Catriona guessed that he was preparing to be Santa Claus for the children's benefit. Her heart seemed to miss a beat as she hurried after March, although she told herself that nothing could bring back the happiness of those former years.

They found him in an ante-room struggling with a massive horsehair beard. "The wretched thing looks impossible," he said. "How did we manage it at the hospital, Kate?"

"It was made of cotton wool." Was he remembering in as great detail as she was? "But we cut it out several days beforehand and glued it together in case of accidents."

He held up the recalcitrant beard. "It's moulted slightly since last year," he decided, "and, strictly speaking, it's far too long."

"Anyone smaller than you are would trip over it." March laughed. "But we haven't time to think of a substitute now."

"Why not cut some off?" Catriona suggested.

"It's going bald about halfway down," said March, holding it up to the light. "Would that be long enough, do you think? I'll get some scissors." She moved toward the door.

"Let me go," Catriona offered, suddenly aware that she was going to be left alone with Andrew.

"I know where they are." March was already in the corridor. "And we'll need some glue. I was using it on some paper chains this morning. "You can fix the zipper on Andrew's tunic, if you like."

Andrew had struggled into a pair of thigh-length black waders which he probably wore for fishing, with his pants stuffed well into them, out of sight. The loose tunic edged with fur went over them, and Catriona manipulated the long zipper at the back. When she faced him again he was regarding her with a quizzical smile.

"Well," he demanded, "do I look the part? Do you think I will pass muster as the original Santa Claus"

"I've seen you make a success of it before," she said involuntarily and could have bitten out her tongue immediately because she had forced him to remember.

"Yes," he said, turning to pick up the beard, "so you have, Kate. Are you missing Edinburgh?"

"I knew I would be here for Christmas and New Year's."

"Yes, of course." He turned squarely toward her. "Frau Kalman expects you to stay longer."

So he was in the old lady's confidence! "I can't be sure," she said haltingly.

"Because you want to go back to Edinburgh when Pettigrew goes?"

"No—not necessarily."

His mouth hardened. "Mission completed?" he suggested.

"I—if Frau Kalman was well enough by then," she began, "perhaps I would go back with Robin."

"Which means we must wait and see." March returned. "We'll have to glue the ends, March, and hope I won't stick to everything on the way in," he said. "Jeno's working on the sleigh. I think we ought to help him."

March smuggled them out along a stone passage and through a door leading to the deserted courtyard, but there was no sign of the sleigh.

"It's in the stables," she explained. "I'll guard this door till you get there."

Andrew took Catriona by the arm. "Run!" he commanded.

Breathlessly they reached the stable yard, laughing because they had remained undetected.

"Put this on," he said, holding out a long gray cloak which he picked up from a bench just inside the stable door. "It's cold out here."

She turned too quickly, and his hand brushed the soft flesh of her cheek. It was like a caress, the touch she remembered so well when Andrew had been in a teasing mood. The tears choked in her throat and seemed to stand there in an eternity of silence before he said, "I'm sorry, Kate! I didn't mean to be rough."

He laid the cloak across her shoulders, tying it under her chin while she struggled with her tears in the uncertain half-light. It could have been like this, she thought. It *could* have been!

The sleigh stood ready in the shadows where Jeno had left it. The horses from the carriage were to be harnessed into this lower conveyance to ride the short distance to the main entrance, but Jeno had heaped loose snow on their running-boards to give a realistic impression of a much longer journey. An arch of bells had been mounted across the shafts. They jangled as soon as it was moved. Jeno came from the adjoining stable to throw a canvas sack over them to deaden the sound.

"Soon you will be ready?" he asked.

Andrew nodded. "Are you coming in the sleigh, Kate?" he asked.

"Wouldn't it give the show away? I could be recognized."

"Not if you kept your hood well over your head. We go down to the foot of the hill and then back, to make our entrance more realistic."

"Will March go?"

"Perhaps."

March appeared in a cloak with a fur hood at the stable door.

"All set?" she asked. She climbed onto the back of the sleigh, making room for Catriona to sit beside her.

"No one will recognize us," she said. "The children will be too busy looking at Andrew." She put her feet up on the sack of presents which filled the floor of the sleigh as Jeno backed the cobs between the shafts. "It's almost as good as having a couple of reindeer!" she laughed.

Andrew had settled himself in the center of the sleigh and Jeno took up the reins. "Mush!" he cried to the horses. "Off you go!"

They sped through the keen afternoon air down into the valley, while above them, in the *schloss*, the sound of carols drifted up to the dark battlements and far away, to be lost among the mountains. This sleigh-ride together was something Catriona had never expected, and she gave herself up to the sheer joy of it even though they were not alone. Andrew seemed different, younger and more relaxed, and she felt a glow in her cheeks that was more than just the excitement of the ride. Jeno drove swiftly, urging the horses to a gallop. When they were on the return journey he uncovered the bells.

Jangling and lurching from side to side, the sleigh sped up the incline and across the wooden bridge to the main door of the *schloss* which stood wide open with all the children waiting in the hall.

Andrew made a ponderous descent, as befitted an old gentleman of St. Nicholas's years. The odd silence in the hall could almost be felt, and then a quavering little voice said, "It's Santa!" and the spell was broken. The children flocked around the tall, red-coated figure: the eager, confident ones; the diffident ones; the shy ones, while the cripples sat forward in their wheelchairs, hardly daring to breathe in case they would be overlooked.

Andrew had a word and a solemn handshake for them all. He spent an equal time with each child, asking what they had wished him to bring.

"I wrote you a letter," one small boy told him plaintively.

"So you did!" Andrew felt in his breast pocket. "This is it, isn't it? You wanted a dog. Was that a real dog, or just a woolly one?"

The child's dark eyes searched the bearded face for a full minute. "A woolly one would do," he said.

But foresight was Santa's middle name. He nodded and one of the nurses brought a tiny, shivering brown pup.

"You'll have to find a bed for him," Andrew advised. "He's a very small, very new dog."

The child was unable to speak, even to say "thank you". He hugged the pup to him as if he would never let it go, his dark eyes fixed on the man's, his helpless little body shaking from head to foot. The other children gathered around, loving the pup with their eyes.

Two hooded figures carried in the sack of presents. Catriona was almost in tears—happy tears because this was a happy day. The more practical March undid the sack. Nobody rushed; nobody thought of claiming what wasn't theirs. Andrew handed a gift to each child in turn, while March and Catriona stood in the shadows waiting to escort him back to the sleigh. Finally, explaining that he had a lot of work to get through, Andrew withdrew.

"Phew!" he exclaimed, pushing up his fur-trimmed hood a little, "that was hot work."

"I knew it was you!" A small figure emerged from the double doors leading to the kitchens. "I knew all the time. I saw your waders in the cloakroom, and I know about Santa Claus, anyway. You can't fool me. I'm ten!"

The belligerent little figure tried to push past them, but Andrew caught him by the sleeve.

"All right, you're ten," he said. "I accept that, Hans, but the others aren't as clever as you are, and if you go telling them that there isn't any Santa Claus I won't be able to come next year. You see the way it is? We have to go along with it for the little ones, and we get a present for our trouble. It's fair enough when you think about it."

Hans continued to regard him suspiciously.

"I don't know," he objected. "I'll have to tell Willi Deutsch. He bet me!"

"If you do," March muttered, "I'll feed you to the wolves!"

"He won't tell," said Andrew, letting the boy go. 'It's a secret between us."

"And I know who you are, too!" Hans turned to March. "You're the ski lady."

"Heavens!" March burst out, "why do we make all this fuss, anyway? I bet more than half of them know."

"Our illusions have to go soon enough," Andrew said. "I'll take your cloak back for you, Kate, if you want to join the fun around the tree."

It was eight o'clock before the children were put to bed, and ten before they finally set out for the chalet on the far side of the valley. Frau Kalman looked tired.

"You've had too long a day," said Catriona, helping her into the sleigh. "And now it's bitterly cold. Are you sure you want to ride back with the hood down?"

"Why not?" the old lady asked. "I'm smothered in furs and fresh air never killed anyone! Where's Fereith?"

"She was here a moment ago."

"Find her," Frau Kalman commanded, looking ahead to where the two cobs were champing at the bit with Robin holding their heads down. Jeno was nowhere to be seen.

Catriona hurried along the path leading to the stables to encounter Andrew for the first time since he had taken her cloak and gone off with March.

"I'm looking for Fereith," she told him. "Have you seen her?"

He wheeled around, the anger showing plainly in his eyes.

"How long has she been missing?" he asked.

"Only minutes. Andrew—"

"Go back," he said. "I'll find her."

Catriona went slowly back to the sleigh.

"Andrew has gone to look for her," she explained.

"Ah!" said Frau Kalman with satisfaction.

It was another ten minutes before Fereith came along the path, looking sullen and dejected. Jeno followed her at a respectful distance, his proud face defiant, his black eyes shielding an emotion which baffled them all.

"Everybody aboard?" Robin asked with forced cheerfulness. "I'll drive this time. You can sit up on the box with me, Jeno."

They drove silently, down into the valley and up again on the other side. It was impossible for Fereith to pretend that she was not in the old lady's black books, and gradually the sullen expression on her face turned to one of sadness. Before they had reached their destination there were tears in her eyes.

Catriona settled Frau Kalman for the night. The old lady was very tired.

"Sometimes I wonder why I try so hard," she said, "with Fereith and everything else."

The admission surprised Catriona because she was well aware of her employer's courage.

"You have done too much," she said, tucking in the edges of the *dine*. "Things will seem different in the morning."

"Will they?" The intensely blue eyes searched her face. "We keep looking to the morning for a new ray of hope. Yes," she agreed, "perhaps I am tired."

"Will you take something to make you sleep?" Catriona asked.

Frau Kalman shook her head. "I never have and I never shall. Nature will give me the sleep I need." She closed her eyes and then said slowly: "Do you mean to marry my godson?"

Catriona halted halfway to the door. "I don't know," she confessed uncertainly. "I—haven't had long enough to think about it."

"When we think we are in love," the old lady said, "we

feel sure. The young are full of confidence and so impatient that they find it impossible to wait. Does Fereith confide in you?"

"Not very often, but I think I could eventually win her trust."

"You are her own generation." The blue eyes remained closed. "Perhaps I—couldn't really hope that she would reveal her thoughts to me."

Her words dropped into a lengthy pause, and Catriona stole away, hoping that she would drop off to sleep. There had been a moment in their conversation when she had felt that Frau Kalman was about to confide in her further, but it had passed with that question about Robin. She had been deeply concerned about Fereith, but at that point her impulse to confidence had stopped. Did she already know about those clandestine meetings between her adopted daughter and the young gipsy who served her? It would seem so, and it appeared that she was determined to put an end to them, one way or another. But if Fereith loved Jeno, what then? Youth was impetuous. The old lady was well aware of the fact. "The young are full of confidence and so impatient," she had said. "They find it impossible to wait." She had said that just before she had asked her pointed question about Fereith, and her tired old voice had been full of apprehension.

Fereith had retired to her room when Catriona reached the foot of the staircase.

"It's early yet," said Robin, laying aside the book he had started to read. "Do you fancy a walk in the snow?"

Catriona shook her head. "If you don't mind, I'd like to go to bed."

He came to stand beside her. "What's the matter, Katie?" he asked. "You look as if you had the cares of the world on your shoulders."

"I've had quite a day," she admitted, pulling off the bandeau which bound her hair, "one way and another."

He let her go, watching as she mounted the stairs.

On her way to her own room Catriona had to pass Fereith's door. There was a light showing under it and she asked impulsively, "Can I come in?"

There was no immediate response from within the silent room, and in a moment of panic she found herself turning the handle. The door opened at her touch. Fereith was standing, fully-clothed, beside the window.

"I didn't want you to come," she said.

"I thought I'd like to say goodnight." Catriona closed the door behind her. "We've all had such a wonderful day."

Fereith turned to face her. She had been crying.

"And I spoiled it," she said. "Why do I always have to be told what to do?"

"We all have to be advised at one time or another," Catriona answered slowly. " 'Guided' is perhaps a better word, Fereith. Sometimes we give way to an impulse which would hurt us in the end, and then it's best to be guided by someone—an older person, perhaps—who has our true interests at heart. We make mistakes, of course, and if they're not too serious they don't do us a great deal of harm. Learning by experience, it's called." She drew in a deep breath. "It can be a bitter experience or one we learn to accept," she added slowly.

Fereith considered her advice. "I'm different," she announced with conviction. "I don't really belong here. My mother was a gipsy." Her eyes filled with a vague longing. "I wish I had known her," she said. "She may have been the princess I was named after."

"How old were you when you came to Gleiberg?" Catriona asked.

"I don't know. It was many years ago," Ferieth said.

"Has Jeno worked here all that time?" Catriona felt impelled to ask.

Fereith shook her head. "Not all the time. He went

away when I was quite small, and then he came again, when there were gipsies in the Rhein valley, and Frau Kalman employed him to look after the horses. When he was very young he went to the village school, but Jeno did not want to study for long. He is a Romani, you see. They are roamers—true traveling people."

"But he has stayed at Gleiberg," Catriona pointed out. "Had he no people of his own?"

"Of course!" Fereith looked almost scornful. "A Romani is never without a family. They may be orphans, but they are still members of the Romani clan into which they were born." Slowly she began to undress, loosening her thick black hair from the confining ribbon which bound it until the heavy tresses fell into place on either side of her haunting little heart-shaped face, making her dark eyes look enormous. "I am a Romani," she said. "I can feel it, deep in my heart."

In the light from the overhead lamp she looked every inch a daughter of that race of travelers who had come to Europe from a homeland long since forgotten; the wandering dukes and their retinues who bore letters of safe conduct from the powerful Emperor Sigismund himself. Their origin, lost in the mists of time, was as obscure as Fereith felt her own to be, yet they had survived as a people down through the ages, changing little with the passing of the years. The pomp and panoply of their "royal houses" might have passed, but their pride and fierce allegiance to the past had surely survived.

It was something Catriona could only sense as she stood there in the quiet room watching Fereith moving about in her frilled petticoat with her thick dark hair spread across her shoulders like a shawl. For the first time she noticed that Jeno's cheap, gaudy beads had replaced the gold locket around the girl's slender throat.

"Don't do anything rash, Fereith," she pleaded. "We all love you here."

Fereith turned toward the bed where her nightdress had been laid out, ready for her to wear.

"You do not understand," she said. "You are of another race."

Dropping the straps of the petticoat from her shoulders, she slid as she was beneath the light covering of the featherweight *dine*.

Catriona hesitated. Fereith had dismissed her and there were things, she knew, which were beyond argument.

"Please believe that I am your friend," she said, but Fereith did not answer.

CHAPTER SIX

They had promised to return to the *schloss* the following morning to help with the clearing up, but Fereith
decided to stay behind. Catriona, not quite sure whether
she should go alone or not, consulted Frau Kalman.

"Of course you must go," the old lady said. "It is a
holiday time, and you must enjoy yourself. Robin can
amuse Fereith until you return. I wish to speak to him,
anyway."

Jeno took Catriona to the *schloss*, promising to call for
her in the late afternoon. He had some business to attend
to in the village, a friend to meet.

One of the nurses had caught an obscure sickness that
Andrew had failed to diagnose so far, and in consequence, Catriona was kept busy. One pair of hands less
made a difference, and after the excitement of the day
before the children were difficult to manage. New toys
were squabbled over, old ones exchanged in a sort of
barter system which was highly amusing.

March Lazenby had taken the older boys to ski above
the plateau, so the nursery slopes were deserted. When
most of her chores were done, Catriona borrowed a pair
of skis and went up to the slopes, intending to practise on
her own. She had not seen Andrew all day and concluded that he was busy.

The nursery slopes were easy going. She enjoyed
herself for over an hour, swooping down the gentle
inclines with the wind at her back and the bright sun on
her face. It was the most invigorating pastime she had
ever known, and she found herself envying March her
proficiency.

March hailed her on her way down from the plateau.

"Getting the feel of it?" she asked, half amused as she turned expertly to a halt a few feet away. "You are quite wise to stay down here for a while when you are such a beginner."

"I've had other things to do," Catriona said far too sharply. "But I do mean to learn."

"That's the spirit!" March's interest had already evaporated as a tall figure appeared on the roadway beneath then. "Andrew must be going to the village," she added. "He's quite something on skis, isn't he?"

They watched as Andrew negotiated the long sweep of the hill with expert ease, coming up on the other side, his body arched to take the next rise.

"I mean to marry him," March said with a sideways glance in Catriona's direction. "I know his ambitions, you see, and I could fit in with them very nicely. Andrew is wasted here. He should be in Harley Street."

Without waiting for a reply, she veered off in the direction of the *schloss*, a tall, slim figure in her black vorlage pants and brilliant red sweater, winging her way across the snow on her glittering skis.

Catriona stood quite still, remembering what she had said. "Andrew is wasted here. He should be in Harley Street."

It was an old ambition, Catriona knew, part of her own reason for refusing him. Hard and practical, he still seemed to be the same person, keenly ambitious, with one foot already firmly planted on the ladder of success, and his gray eyes fastened on the topmost rung. Yet, only the day before, as they had acted out their Christmas charade for the benefit of Frau Kalman's orphans, she had believed him different. He had seemed content and happy in his work here among the mountains, a man wholly absorbed by the task in hand. There would be little material reward if he stayed at Gleiberg, but surely

Andrew had weighed these things in the balance and arrived at an adequate answer.

More confused than she had ever been in her life, she plodded back up the nearest slope, wondering if she should give up her job and return to Scotland before anyone guessed that she was still in love with him. But already Frau Kalman had captured her loyalty, and Fereith had twined thin arms about her in her shy, loving way. She felt that she could help Fereith now, although how she was to go on meeting Andrew almost daily she did not know. March had been so sure about him. . . .

He was returning from the village when she came down off the slopes. Some madness in her heart made her wait for him. March could so easily be wrong.

"Hello!" he greeted her. "Putting in some practice?"

"I'll never be a skier." She dug her sticks into the soft snow at the side of the road to steady herself. "I envy you and March."

"It's all a question of time," he said lightly. "Here, let me show you." He put a hand over hers on the stick. "Don't dig in too hard. You'll throw yourself forward. Just take it easy and relax. Make your ankles work for you and bend your knees. You're not at all bad, you know. Just out of practice."

They sped together down the slope, rising to the crest of the next hill with amazing ease.

"It's wonderful!" Catriona gasped, drawing in deep breaths of the ice-cold air. "Like flying!"

He laughed. "Try again," he suggested. "We'll go right to the top this time. Ready?"

It all seemed so effortless once they had reached the higher plateau where March took the older boys. The slopes were longer but not particularly difficult, and there was a new, pulsing elation in her blood at the thought of mastering them because Andrew had said that she could. He watched her critically.

"Don't overdo it on your first run," he advised. "If you tire yourself you won't be so keen to come up again tomorrow."

"I wish I could," she said, eyes and cheeks aglow, "but I'm not on holiday, you know. I'm a working woman." She glanced at her watch. "I really should be back at the chalet by now."

He had taken off his mitts to light a cigarette. "Are you comfortable over there?" he asked casually.

"I ought to be," she answered without thinking. "I have your bedroom."

He seemed to stiffen, but she went on, impelled by something stronger than her better judgment.

"Andrew, I found a photograph there, an old one of myself taken a long time ago. I thought Robin had sent it to his godmother before I came out here to—to sort of introduce me, but now I remember—"

Her voice failed her because all the kindness had suddenly left his face. His eyes were hard and aloof again as he looked down at her with the old contempt.

"You kept it all those years," she whispered.

"I kept it," he admitted, "because I had to remember about women—how fickle they can be and how obtuse. But I have no future need of it. If you will destroy it, I shall be obliged."

Cut to the heart, she could only stare at him in utter disbelief for a moment. She turned and skied madly away from him down the nearest slope. She saw the valley road far beneath her through a haze of pain, saw the trees on the hillside opposite like dark sentinels barring her way, saw the glitter of the sun on the pristine whiteness of the snow and the whole wide valley spread out before her. She was skiing dangerously near to the edge of the sheer drop to the roadway. She could not stop.

Her skis skimmed over the firm surface of the snow with a little hissing sound and the wind rushed in her ears, but she did not think in terms of actual disaster. Her mind was too dulled by pain and shock, but she saw the pines going faster and faster and the edge of the plateau rushing to meet her.

Trying to remember all she had ever been told, she leaned heavily to one side, pulling herself around in a wide arc, but it was too late. The impetus of her headlong descent carried her forward; out and down over the edge.

In the moment before oblivion claimed her, she thought she heard Andrew's voice very near.

Hours afterward, she opened her eyes, blinking at the light. "You're quite safe," a calm reassuring voice told her. "You are at the *schloss*."

She closed her eyes, wondering how she had got there and vaguely conscious of other voices heard remotely through the haze of returning consciousness.

Andrew? Had he found her and carried her back to the *schloss*? Had it been Andrew, strong and purposeful, who had held her in his arms as if she had been a child, struggling with her to the road?

Opening her eyes again, she tried to recognize the room where she lay. It must be in the *schloss*, since the reassuring voice had just said so, but it wasn't any of the rooms she had seen on her numerous visits. It was smaller than the children's wards, less intimate than the nurses' quarters.

A man's domain. She struggled into a sitting position, propped on one elbow. "Nurse?" A uniformed figure crossed to her side. "Where am I?"

"You're in the tower, in Doctor Bishop's flat. There was nowhere else to take you." The nurse bent over her. "How do you feel? Does your head hurt very much?"

"Not a great deal." So once again she had invaded Andrew's home. "I ought to be able to get up now."

"Not so!" Two small, capable hands pressed her back among the pillows. "You must wait until Doctor Bishop or the Professor will tell me what to do."

She was a young nurse, new to her job, very much in awe of the Professor and, probably, of Andrew, too.

"Did—Doctor Bishop bring me here?" Catriona asked.

The girl nodded. "He carried you most of the way. It was a long time, but Jeno also found you."

Jeno! He must have come across them on his way back to the *schloss* to collect her. "Do they know at the chalet?" she asked.

"Oh, yes. Jeno went there to tell Frau Kalman about your accident. He has been gone one hour."

"I'm making a nuisance of myself," Catriona said feebly, "and now I'm keeping Doctor Bishop out of his room."

"You must not talk too much," the nurse said. "It is Doctor Bishop's order."

"Is he—all right?"

"Yes. It is so. He is very good to ski so quickly and save your life." The girl walked to the window, trim and neat in her nurse's uniform. "And now you have a visitor, perhaps. The sleigh from the chalet has returned."

Catriona lay very still, wondering who her visitor might be. Robin, perhaps, or Frau Kalman herself, or even Fereith. She wished she could have spoken to Andrew first. It seemed a very long time before someone knocked on the door.

"Can I come in?" Robin asked. "I understand it isn't against doctor's orders."

Catriona felt deflated. Of course, Robin would come post-haste from the chalet. He would consider it his duty. He bent to kiss her, and she turned her cheek to receive his caress.

"This wasn't a very bright idea," he said. "You might have cancelled yourself out for good, you know."

"Yes," she agreed weakly, "I have been very foolish."

"How did it happen?"

Painfully Catriona reviewed the minutes before the accident. "I took a chance," she said, remembering her conversation with Andrew, "and it didn't come off."

"You don't take chances on a pair of skis," he warned.

"No, I realize that now."

"Thank goodness you're not too badly hurt," he said with real concern. "I understand that Bishop managed to break your fall."

"I wasn't conscious of anything," Catriona had to admit. "I didn't know who it was."

"I expect you feel pretty battered."

"My left arm feels numb, and my head aches a bit." She was beginning to realize how painful her arm really was. "All the same, I've been lucky, thanks to Andrew."

"Yes." He considered her closely for a moment. "Do you have to stay here?"

"I hope not." She couldn't force her presence on Andrew after all he had said. The full implication of his words was crowding back into her mind, numbing it. "I always seem to be doing the wrong thing."

"Not you!" Swiftly he bent to kiss her, finding her lips this time because she was too late to avoid him. "You're a very bright girl, Kate. Take it from me you've won over the old lady completely! Couldn't have done better, as a matter of fact. She's just about ready to eat out of my hand."

Catriona raised her eyes to look at him, but instead she was looking over his shoulder at Andrew, who had just entered the room. He stood at the door, ramrod-straight, a harshly sardonic smile twisting his lips as he looked in at them.

Robin sensed his presence almost immediately.

"We're in your debt, Bishop," he said, turning to greet him. "I don't suppose we will ever be able to thank you enough."

Andrew crossed the room in two swift strides to stand in front of the window. "Don't try," he said briefly. "Anyone would have done as much in the circumstances."

That was it, Catriona thought bleakly. It was something "anyone would have done". Not Andrew, holding her close, praying that she would not die; not Andrew lifting her into his arms to struggle down the mountainside with her because her life was precious to him as her own wayward heart had so foolishly suggested, but just something anyone would have done in the circumstances! She felt crushed and humiliated as she waited for Robin to take the initiative and ask when she could return to the chalet.

"If she hasn't broken any bones, I suppose she can come back with me," Robin said, getting off the edge of the bed where he had perched himself. "The old lady's rather anxious about her."

Andrew frowned. "I can appreciate that," he agreed, "but I think she ought to stay where she is, at least for tonight. She was badly concussed in the fall. I would like the Professor to see her tomorrow morning. He's coming up from Zurich for New Year's. You can take her back to the chalet after that, if you like."

His tone had been completely professional; cool and terrifyingly aloof. Catriona turned her head on the pillows, trying desperately not to cry. She felt so weak, so rejected. Robin put a hand over hers.

"Not to worry too much," he said kindly. "We'll have you back at the chalet in no time."

"Will you tell Frau Kalman how sorry I am?" she managed. "I really ought to go back to Scotland."

"We'll see about that when the time comes," Robin said.

When he left her with a cheerful wave of his hand, Andrew came to stand at the bedside. "How do you feel?" he asked. "How's the head?"

"A bit fuzzy." She did her best to steady her voice. "It's my arm that hurts most."

"I had to put it back in its socket," he said. "It's a rough-and-ready procedure known to most ski instructors. It will worry you for about a week, but there's nothing broken, I can assure you. We went over you, inch by inch, once you were back here."

She met his eyes fully. "I'll never forgive myself for being so foolish," she confessed, "and I'll never be able to thank you sufficiently for what you did."

"Pettigrew mentioned it," he said briefly. "Don't make it more embarrassing, Kate."

She bit her lip. "Were you hurt?"

"Not so as you would notice," he said. "And now I think you should get some sleep." He straightened the rumpled *dine*. "Unless you happen to be hungry?"

She shook her head. "No, I'm not hungry," she said.

He stood looking down at her for a moment before he finally turned away.

In the morning her arm really hurt. It had stiffened during the night and every movement was agony, but when the Professor examined her he was far more concerned about the concussion she had suffered.

"The arm will mend," he declared kindly. "It will be painful for a week—perhaps even two—but then all the torn tissues will gradually renew themselves, and you will be able to use it once more. But if you suffer any pain in your head you must tell us immediately. We cannot take risks in that respect, you understand?"

Catriona nodded, wondering why Andrew had

remained so quiet. He had withdrawn completely behind a veneer of professionalism that excluded anyone but the Professor, throwing up a barrier between them that she would never be able to scale, however hard she tried.

And why should she go on trying? Her pride raised its weary head. Andrew had answered her already, in no uncertain terms. She would be a fool, she told herself, to try again. Poor stupid fool, she had begged him to reconsider the past, and he had told her that the past was dead.

He did nothing to stop her from returning to the chalet when she said she wanted to go. The first thing she did when she reached the far side of the valley was to destroy the photograph he had kept all these years. She tore it to pieces, burning the fragments in the stove, one by one, when she was left alone for a few minutes. By the time Robin had come back into the room she was able to meet him with a certain amount of composure.

"My godmother wants to see you," he said. "We've been having a talk."

She looked up at him. "What about, Robin?"

"Oh—the usual. Money, but she also mentioned Fereith."

"Fereith?"

"She has it in her head that there's something brewing between Fereith and Jeno."

"Do *you* think there is?"

He shrugged. "Not that I've noticed, but I've only been here a week. What do you feel?"

"At first I thought Fereith was attracted by him—even in love with him," Catriona confessed, "but now I think there's something else. If they were just in love I think they would have run off together long ago."

"Perhaps Jeno knows which side his bread is buttered

on," Robin observed. "He has a good job here, loafing around the chalet attending to a few horses."

"Frau Kalman depends on him," Catriona pointed out.

"Oh, sure! That's exactly what Jeno knows."

"Then what does he want?"

"Search me! If it isn't Fereith, could it be money?"

"Money?" Catriona repeated. "Gipsies don't worry very much about that. Or so Fereith says."

"Did she tell you she was half a gipsy herself?"

"Yes."

"It could be true," Robin mused. "She had that look about her, and I don't suppose the old lady really knows who she is. That's the snag about adoption, isn't it? Not knowing."

Catriona flashed a warning glance in his direction as Fereith came into the room. Fereith was sensitive—too sensitive, perhaps, about her origin.

Frau Kalman had spent the morning in bed, dictating letters to March Lazenby, but now that March had gone she had settled in her chair near the window to enjoy her view across the valley.

"How is your arm?" she asked as soon as Catriona put in an appearance at the door. "It will be useless attempting to massage my hip in that condition."

"I'm sorry," Catriona apologized.

"I'm not," her patient declared. "It wasn't doing me a scrap of good. All that pummeling and pushing! I have this affliction and shall have to live with it till some scientist or other discovers an outright cure." She indicated the chair near her own. "Sit down. I want to talk to you."

"Can I bring you a footstool?" Catriona asked. "You feel more comfortable with your feet up."

"Nonsense!" muttered the old lady. "You'd think I was helpless."

When the stool was in place she sat in silence for a moment before she said, with a great deal of satisfaction, "I've given Jeno the sack."

Catriona wasn't quite quick enough to hide her surprise.

"You don't think it was a very good idea, do you?" her employer asked.

"It's none of my business," Catriona acknowledged, "but it does seem rather hard on Jeno. He was very good with the horses."

"All gipsies are good with horses, and grooms are two a penny in this valley. As soon as it's known that Jeno has gone, we'll be pestered with feckless youths clamoring for the job."

"But I thought Jeno had worked for you for a very long time," Catriona objected. "He seemed almost like one of your orphans."

"He was until he started to take liberties." The old lady's jaw closed like a clam-shell. "Never take liberties, Catriona. They lead straight out through the door."

She had a hard streak in her somewhere, Catriona realized. It had never been so obvious as it was now. Jeno's dismissal had been something that she had been turning over in her mind for a long time.

"You won't consider giving him another chance?"

"No." Frau Kalman's refusal was very firm. "Jeno has had his chance. Now it's up to you to keep an eye on Fereith."

"I couldn't spy on her."

The old lady dismissed her protest with a wave of her hand. "The two things are quite different," she declared. "Since you are more or less *hors de combat* as far as I am concerned and I don't need your services as a masseuse, anyway, you owe it to me to look after Fereith. Go with her whenever you can, keep her interested, talk to her, amuse her if you have to, but don't let her out of your sight unless you are both asleep."

"It's rather a tall order, isn't it?" Catriona began. "It's like being a watchdog or a private detective."

"You can call yourself whatever you like."

"I don't think I could possibly do it—"

"You will," said Frau Kalman, "if you wish to please Robin."

It was an atrocious situation, Catriona decided, not very far short of blackmail.

"It won't last long," Frau Kalman predicted. "She'll forget about him."

Catriona was not so sure. Fereith was too serious-minded to do anything by half. She would love intensely and hate intensely just as she gave her affection whole-heartedly once she was sure that it was returned.

It was a difficult situation and her own part in it distressed her, yet she could not completely disobey her employer's orders. The fact that her foolish adventure on the ski slope had deprived the old lady of her services as a masseuse no doubt justified her in her request about Fereith.

"I'll do what I can," she found herself promising.

Robin noticed her abstraction almost immediately.

"Have you been having a brush with the old lady?" he asked as lightly as he could. "She can be awkward, I know, but I thought you were good with difficult people."

"It was part of my training." Catriona hesitated. "She wants me to keep an eye on Fereith."

Robin laughed. "Is that all?" He seemed to breathe more easily. "It's Jeno, I suppose. She wouldn't want him getting any bright ideas about her ewe lamb."

"Why not?" Catriona asked. "Jeno is kind and considerate. He has served Frau Kalman well."

"But he made the unforgivable mistake of showing his

affection for Fereith. It's typical," Robin declared, "but it's also ludicrous. She can't shut Fereith up in the chalet the way she could in the *schloss*."

Catriona turned to look at him.

"Oh, yes," he grinned. "When Fereith was younger she kept her practically hidden in the *schloss*. Of course, it wasn't the first time that an errant daughter of the family had been shut up in the battlements under lock and key. There are some grim stories about Gleiberg in medieval times, and Fereith could tell you most of them."

"You've known her all her life?"

Robin shrugged. "On and off. I suppose you could say we've grown up together," he conceded. "I came to Gleiberg quite a lot when I was younger. At one time I had the idea that the old lady was trying to marry me off to Fereith."

"And was she?"

He laughed uneasily. "I don't know. One doesn't— ever—with my godmother. Her authority has been unquestioned up here for so long that she believes it extends to the rest of the world. Nobody dares go contrary to her wishes in peril of being cut off without a *sou*."

"Is that what you're afraid of, Robin?" she said without thinking.

He swung around to face her. "Now look here—" he began, but she was quick to apologize.

"I shouldn't have said that. I'm sorry."

"Of course I need the money." He stared moodily at the polished floor. "But I didn't come out here just to make sure of it. She sent for me, remember? She had her own reason for doing that, but we won't know what it is till she's ready to tell us. Her only confidant is Andrew Bishop apparently. She trusts him," he added unpleasantly.

"They've worked in close cooperation for almost three years," Catriona pointed out. "The work they're doing is something they both believe in."

"Granted," Robin acknowledged. "As I said, she trusts him. Just as she trusts you," he added. "I'm not so sure that she even likes me."

"You are her godson, and she's the sort of person who will honor her commitments, whatever she may feel."

"Like you!" He drew her into the circle of his arms. "We ought to be officially engaged. Then she might come out in the open and tell us what she means to do with the *schloss*. She's fond of me in a remote sort of way. I could inherit Gleiberg one day. I wouldn't mind the castle," he reflected, "but all those kids—"

Catriona drew back from his embrace.

"They're Gleiberg," she reminded him. "They're Frau Kalman's dream—and Andrew Bishop's."

He had rubbed her the wrong way. She was immediately angry in defense of the children and all the old lady was trying to do in the valley. She was angry about Andrew, too. This was something he cared about, something he had worked for with Frau Kalman's help. It could be his life's work if he intended to stay in Switzerland, because soon the *schloss* would be too small for the number of children they wished to accommodate. A new clinic would have to be built.

"We're not quarreling, are we?" Robin asked lightly. "We mustn't do that, Kate. Not just now. We have to put up a united front for the old lady's benefit."

"Why, Robin? Why?" she demanded. "Wouldn't it be a lot better if we behaved naturally, to let her see what we really felt?"

"At the present moment," he confessed moodily, "I feel like going back to Edinburgh. I came away, post-haste, because she sent for me with some urgency. Now I can't see exactly what all the rush was for. Enigmatic people disturb me. Besides, the skiing isn't all that good. There's every sign of a partial thaw today, which means that we could have a green New Year."

"All the snow couldn't disappear so quickly." She looked down to the white slopes beneath the chalet window. "It's far too deep."

"I've seen it happen," he declared gloomily. "Once, over on the Arlberg, it disappeared almost overnight. There were avalanches all over the place. It was three weeks before it snowed again. We were all terribly fed up because the holidays were over, and we had to return to England."

It seemed inconceivable to Catriona that the snow could disappear so quickly, but it was Robin's restlessness which really disturbed her. More and more he was adopting the attitude of a fiancé because he saw how much trust Frau Kalman had already placed in her. But Kate had never been fully committed in that respect. Some vague element of caution had held her back from an engagement even while she acknowledged the attraction he held for her; some warning light flashing in her brain when he had inadvertently shown the more selfish side of his nature that she had been quick to reject.

"Don't go rushing off before New Year's," she begged. "Your godmother would be terribly disappointed."

"I wonder!" he returned dryly. "But I'll stay, since you want me to."

"You came for two weeks," she reminded him.

"But I didn't expect to be kept dangling all this time," he admitted. "All this talk about getting to know me properly is so much eyewash. She's known me for years!"

There seemed nothing more to be said. When Fereith joined them for their evening meal she did not seem to be quite so tensed as usual, although her glance wandered to the window every time there was a noise outside. If she already knew about Jeno's summary dismissal she did not mention it. When it was time to go to bed, she walked up the stairs ahead of Catriona, saying good night as she paused at her bedroom door.

CHAPTER SEVEN

The New Year festivities were in full swing. Catriona had been caught up in them with the others. The snow, which was not so good for hard skiing, still lay thickly on the roads, and deep and soft on the mountainsides, adding to the fairy-tale quality of Gleiberg after dark. Lights pierced the darkness on every side, strung along the village street, in the belfry of the church and festooned along the entire frontage of the inn. The deep eaves were still cushioned with snow. Far up the hillside, near the chalet, a single fir glowed with multi-colored lights; the living Christmas tree which was decorated every year for the children on the far side of the valley to see.

The air was full of the sound of bells: bells tossing on the harnesses of horses; bells ringing out a gay carillon from the church tower; hand bells beating out the rhythm of a folk song, and the tiny bells the children wore jangling discordantly as they walked in procession through the snow.

Frau Kalman, who had placed her traditional wreath of lighted candles on her husband's grave in the churchyard, asked Catriona to return there with her on New Year's Day. Jeno was no longer available to drive them; she seemed pleased that Robin offered to step in for the occasion. Happy and apparently carefree, Robin was determined to be the life and soul of the party. His laugher was certainly infectious. His restlessness had vanished, it seemed, with his mood of depression, and Fereith sat up beside him on the box, laughing, too.

"Robin, you are so comical!" she exclaimed more than once. "You make everybody happy."

Frau Kalman wrapped in her sable-lined cloak with a

fur rug tucked closely about her knees, watched them with a vague satisfaction. "They are young together," she said. "Robin was always young for his years."

They reached the churchyard and Robin set them down at the gates, driving on toward the village with Fereith, who wished to make some purchases which were highly secret.

Catriona walked with Frau Kalman toward the rather ornate mausoleum which had sheltered the Kalman dead for several generations. It stood at the far end of the main pathway, in the shadow of the church itself; a squat stone edifice with a domed roof wearing a little cap of snow. All around it the lesser graves lay peacefully beneath the universal blanket of white, each with its green laurel wreath still in place. The red wax candles had guttered and gone out, but they had been a lovely sight shining in the still night air. Catriona had watched them from as far away as the chalet, tiny flames of remembrance glowing against the darkness with the mountains looking down on them.

"I come here often," her employer confessed. "My husband was my great companion. I missed him very much when he died. He was a gentleman, but his advice was invaluable to me. I turned to him for everything and then, suddenly, I had to continue alone. Perhaps that hardened me," she added unexpectedly. "There was so much for me to do. After all, I was a stranger, although I had borne my son in this valley and brought him up here."

It was the first time she had mentioned her only child, and she seemed distressed for a moment. Catriona's fingers tightened on her arm, helping her along the pathway until suddenly the old lady seemed to freeze in her tracks. Someone was standing beside the mausoleum, a tall, gaunt-looking man in a fitted riding-coat of considerable age. His back was turned toward them, and he moved away at their approach, disappearing among the thick yews which flanked the way to the church door.

If Frau Kalman had recognized him she made no sign. After the briefest hesitation, she walked slowly forward, leaning heavily on Catriona's arm. A second wreath lay on the grey stone slab in front of the mausoleum, but it bore no message and had no candles to light.

"People do these things," Frau Kalman said, "even after all this time. My husband was a highly respected man." She stood gazing down at the circle of fresh laurel leaves. "After all this time," she repeated.

They walked on, leaving the two wreaths lying, side by side.

The village was in festive mood, the inn full to overflowing, but Robin had promised to meet them there for the traditional glass of *gluwein* which Herr Jonas dispensed from a large silver bowl set on a special table in the entrance hall. The genial little Austrian greeted each new guest, pouring a ladleful of the hot wine into little carved goblets for each in turn and wishing them the compliments of the season as he did so. There was a great deal of noise and much laughter. Herr Jonas seemed to be overcome with delight when he recognized the lady of the *schloss*. He bowed deeply from the waist, rubbing his fat little hands together while his gray hair seemed to stand even more erectly on his square, solid-looking head.

"Ah, *mein Frau*!" he beamed. "You do not ever forget!"

Their wine was poured, an extra measure for them both. Catriona caught sight of Andrew standing at the back of the hall watching the proceedings from a distance; a half-smile curving his lips, his tall figure immediately recognizable even in that milling throng.

"There's Andrew Bishop," Frau Kalman said, settling

herself into the vast, carved armchair that someone had vacated for her. "Tell him I want to speak to him."

For a split second Catriona hesitated.

"Well, go on!" her employer urged. "You can make your way across the room, can't you?"

The memory of her previous meeting with Andrew burned vividly in Catriona's mind. She had tried to thank him for saving her life, and he had dismissed her gratitude as something he could well do without. "Don't make it too embarrassing, Kate," he had said. Was that what she was doing? Making things awkward for him by her very presence in the valley because he wished, deep in his heart, that she would go away. Because she had brought with her memories of a past which he had almost forgotten? Well, she reasoned, she could help him to forget completely. She could tell him that she was going to marry Robin and return to Scotland with him in a week's time.

Searching his face, she wondered what difference it would make. None—none at all, she decided. Andrew was completely indifferent to her now.

He inquired politely about her arm. "You must continue to use it all you can now," he advised.

His studied professionalism reduced her almost to tears.

"It's painful but not unbearable," she said bleakly.

They were standing very close, pressed in by the crowd; she could almost feel the heavy beating of his heart as his strong fingers closed purposefully about her wrist.

"What about the head?" he asked.

"There's been nothing," she answered. "No after effects."

"Good!" He released her wrist. "I'll report back to the Professor. He was quite worried about you."

And you, Andrew? she wanted to cry, but to what purpose? She could not humble herself a second time.

"Frau Kalman would like to speak to you," she told him.

"About Jeno?"

"You know?" She looked up at him in surprise.

"Of course I know. The valley is a small place."

"Has he left Gleiberg?"

"I should think so. There aren't so many jobs to be had around here."

He was still frowning as they pushed their way through the crowd to her employer's side.

"I know what you are going to say, Andrew," Frau Kalman began even before they reached her chair. "You disapprove of what I have done, but Jeno was becoming unmanageable."

"I wish you had spoken to me first," Andrew said.

"Perhaps I should have done." For the first time the old lady seemed uncertain. "But you would have counseled tolerance, and sometimes I think it is a virtue I have never possessed."

"I would have advised you to wait," he said. "What are you going to do now?"

"About Fereith? I think she will settle, now that Jeno is out of the way."

By the look of him, Andrew did not appear to share her belief. "Where is she?" he asked, searching over the heads of the crowd. "I didn't see her come in."

"She's with Robin." Frau Kalman was watching him closely. "They'll make their appearance in a moment or two, and then we can all go on to the *schloss*."

"Everything is arranged," said Andrew, still looking for Robin and Fereith. "If we could go over the books while you are there, I should be obliged."

He was completely in the old lady's confidence, Catriona thought for the second time. They trusted one another.

Robin and Fereith came in, surrounded by a group of

young people who had come up from Buchs in the wide valley of the Rhein. They were mostly English, full of the holiday spirit and bent on "livening up the place". Two of them had flown on the same plane as Robin and were boisterously friendly. Tom Glenn, a tall, fair young man who had met Catriona in Edinburgh, greeted her enthusiastically.

"This is certainly something, meeting you like this," he declared. "We're on our way back home really, but we had the weekend to spare. The snow in the Arlberg isn't what it was. There's been the odd minor avalanche, and now it's wet in places. Absolute slush, as a matter of fact." He looked over her shoulder at Andrew. "You ski?" he asked in the half-deprecating tone of the expert.

"Frequently," Andrew informed him with a slow smile. "I live here."

"Do you, by Jove? Some people have all the luck! I work in a bank in Edinburgh."

"Andrew used to work in Edinburgh," Fereith said shyly at his elbow.

It seemed the moment for introductions.

"Tom Glenn—Doctor Bishop," Kate said.

"I hear you and Robin are all but hitched," Tom remarked affably when he had shaken hands with Andrew. "Good going, Kate! Though why did you have to keep it such a secret?"

"Because it isn't a fact," Catriona heard herself saying in a voice that was far too brittle. "We're not engaged."

"But you soon will be? Sorry if I've jumped the gun," Tom laughed, "but we can always celebrate your indecision."

For one terrible moment Catriona thought that he was about to announce her near-engagement to the whole room, but Tom had only turned for another glass of *gluwein*. When she looked around for Andrew he had gone.

Frau Kalman, who had witnessed the little scene, remained thoughtfully silent on their way to the *schloss*. They drove slowly through the village, the horses reined in to a quiet walk as they made their way among the throng of pedestrians lingering in the streets. It was a happy scene, with everyone dressed in their best clothes. Children rushed from one side of the street to the other to greet their friends, as if they hadn't set eyes on them for months, showing off their Christmas presents and the New Year's gifts they had received within the family. The valley seemed full to overflowing with kindliness, and many of the revellers bowed and smiled as the sleigh passed them. One of them, Catriona thought, had placed that second wreath on the gray stone in front of the Kalman mausoleum. Which one?

Her eyes roved over the heads of the crowd. Suddenly she thought she saw Jeno standing with a man near the post office. A tall man in an old-fashioned riding-coat.

Frau Kalman was looking the other way and the crowd closed in so quickly that Catriona could not be certain about Jeno, but she was sure about the other man. The last time she had seen him he had been moving away from the Kalman mausoleum into the deep shadow of the yews. It was the man who had placed the fresh laurel wreath beside Frau Kalman's half-withered one with its spent red candles and drooping leaves.

Catriona drew in a deep breath. Was it Jeno, she wondered, and should she mention the fact to her employer?

Fereith turned on the box to look down at them. "It's such a wonderful day," she said, "and I am so happy!"

Frau Kalman seemed content. She nodded her head as Fereith turned to take the reins from Robin, galloping the horses along the clear stretch out of the village toward the *schloss*.

They had tea with the children, and almost immediately afterward the *schloss* was stormed by Robin's friends from Buchs. He had obviously extended an invitation to them to visit the castle, which was a landmark in the valley. They had taken him at his word. It was "quite something", Tom Glenn declared enthusiastically, to be shown over an ancient medieval stronghold which was still in use.

Andrew came in with March Lazenby, who seemed eager enough to join the party.

"They mustn't upset the children," Frau Kalman said. "Otherwise, we're pleased to welcome them."

The tour of inspection over, there were drinks all around. The nurses offered platters of sweetmeats and sandwiches as Catriona helped to put the younger children to bed. When she returned the party was in full swing. Frau Kalman had gone back to the chalet, driven by Andrew, but she had left Fereith behind in Robin's care.

Flushed and excited, Fereith danced with all the abandonment of her Romani forebears. Only half gipsy she might be, but in that moment, with her hair loosened on her shoulders and her skirts billowing around her knees, she was pure Romani. She held out her arms to Robin who caught her and swung her off her feet as the wild rhythm of the dance quickened. They whirled around the room in ever-widening circles until the others, exhausted, left them the floor to themselves. Fereith danced in sort of a dream. Any partner would have done so long as he could follow the music she loved so much. Robin's face was scarlet and his brow moist when the spirited measure came to an end. Someone switched off the phonograph. It was Andrew. His face was inscrutable.

"I suppose you thought that was a wild fling," Robin gasped. "But we've done it before." He put his arm about Fereith's shoulders. "Quite often, eh, Fereith?"

She nodded, although some of the bright glitter had faded from her eyes.

"It was an exhibition which you might have kept for some other time," said Andrew, glancing in Catriona's direction.

Robin scowled at him. "That is a matter of opinion," he returned belligerently. "And you're not exactly master here, are you? My godmother may have given you a lot of power, but you're only the resident doctor, after all. The *schloss* is still Kalman property."

It had all the makings of an ugly scene, but Andrew said smoothly, "I'll remember that, Robin, if you'll try to remember that this is really a hospital. Dance away to your heart's content, but keep the gipsy music under control."

Robin turned to the others, smiling. "How about a nice refined Viennese waltz?" he suggested. "Just to please the doctor."

Andrew turned to Catriona. "In case it's the last one," he said with a faint smile, leading her onto the floor.

He held her lightly, but close enough for her to feel the hard beating of his heart. He was angry, but would not show it.

"I'm sorry Robin was so rude just now," she said above the music. "He isn't generally so blunt."

"You needn't make allowances for him, Kate," he said. "The gipsy bit annoyed me, I suppose."

"Because of Fereith?"

He hesitated. "The old lady doesn't encourage it," he said.

"Perhaps she's too strict with Fereith."

"Could be," he admitted. "But Fereith has always been impulsive."

The music and laughter closed them in. This was what the *schloss* must have looked like long ago, Catriona thought, with the Christmas decorations festooning the gallery, bright streamers hanging from the walls, and young voices echoing to the rafters. Musicians in frogged tunics had sat up there in the minstrels' gallery playing their violins far into the night, and romance had gone hand-in-hand with joy and heartache. She closed her eyes, allowing her thoughts to drift in the happier past while Andrew continued to hold her. It had been like this, not so very long ago, when they had danced at students' parties and life had been too full to think of partings. It had seemed then that Andrew and she would always be together. When she opened her eyes she would be in his arms, but they would be poles apart. How could love change from something so warm and comforting to this cold indifference?

The music stopped and the first of Frau Kalman's unexpected guests took their leave. Andrew led her to the door, where Robin was seeing them off.

"Will you stay for a stirrup-cup?" he asked.

Robin shook his head. "We ought to be on our way, and I've still to find Fereith," he said. "She was dancing with Tom Glenn the last time I saw her."

Andrew swung around on his heel, searching the sea of faces behind them. Tom Glenn was struggling into his ski jacket, talking to March Lazenby and one of the other men who had come up from Buchs with him in the hired station wagon. March came across the hall.

"Lost someone, Andrew?" she inquired. "Or were you looking for me?"

"You'll do," said Andrew, "if you can find Fereith for me."

March lit a cigarette. "I saw her a moment ago. Why the panic?" she asked lazily. "Fereith can take care of herself."

"I'm not so sure." He made his way toward the staircase. "See what you can do, March. The others are ready to leave."

It was five minutes before he returned with Fereith, who looked subdued. Catriona heaved a sigh of relief, although she could not have said why she had felt so worried.

Nobody spoke very much on the journey back to the chalet. Catriona felt tired, and Fereith stared straight ahead into the starlit night, while Robin seemed immersed in his private thoughts until they came to the part of the road that went through the ravine. A hundred yards on the village side of the narrow gorge a small avalanche of rock and snow had cascaded down the hillside, blocking the way ahead.

"It's the thaw," Fereith said indifferently.

"This is the limit." Robin grumbled, getting down from the box to find the shovel that was kept at the back of the sleigh for just such an emergency. "It's a bit much having to dig our way through."

They all helped, with the horses standing impatiently between the shafts, shaking their heads until their harnessbells jangled in a wild carillon that echoed down the valley. The road was already wet with slush and a mild, soft wind whispered among the pines. From time to time the sudden hiss of minor avalanches broke the silence, but soon they had dug themselves a passage through the fall and were on their way again.

"That settles it," Robin announced. "I'm going home. There's more to do in Edinburgh with the snow in such poor condition here." He turned to look at them. "Are you coming back with me, Kate?"

The unexpected question confused Catriona for a moment. "Isn't this—something of a *volte-face*?" she asked, hoping that Fereith wouldn't understand.

"Not really. I think we've made our point," he said. "My godmother trusts me."

"I have to stay, in any case." Catriona felt as if she had settled more than one problem in her own mind. To return with Robin might have been the answer to her continuing heartache each time she came face to face with Andrew Bishop, but she could not let Frau Kalman down. "I couldn't just throw up my job at a moment's notice when I promised to stay for a month, at least."

"Just as you like." Robin wasn't going to argue the point. "But I mean to leave. There's absolutely nothing to do here in a thaw."

"The weather could change," Fereith said helpfully. "More snow could fall overnight."

"Not with this wind blowing." Robin turned his back to the soft *föhn* with a grimace of distaste. "I'll travel home with the others," he decided.

When they came in sight of the chalet all the lights were lit.

"Something has happened," Fereith said in a subdued whisper.

"We could have unexpected visitors." Robin whipped the horses to a brisk trot. "Let's find out!"

They drew up on the wide stone terrace before the front door, but there was no sign of unexpected company, nothing but the flaring lights turned on in every room and an odd, disquieting silence.

Catriona was first out of the sleigh. The chalet looked deserted save for those flaring lights, and Grete, who generally came to the door when the sleigh stopped, was nowhere to be seen. The whole house seemed unnaturally still.

"There must be someone about," Robin said impatiently, tossing the reins over the horses' backs.

Fereith and Catriona followed him into the house. The

door had been left unbolted, and there were signs of confusion in the hall. A chair had been overturned, and one of the Persian rugs which were Frau Kalman's special pride lay bunched up in a corner beside the stove. A stool had gone with it, careening across the polished floor.

"She's fallen!" Fereith said in that same hollow voice, as if she had a premonition of disaster.

Catriona rushed toward the staircase, her heart pounding. "We ought to have come back with her," she said.

"Bishop brought her back," Robin reminded her as they mounted the stairs. "Nothing could have happened while he was here."

Grete met them at the head of the stairs, cautioning silence with a finger against her lips.

"She's asleep," she whispered. "But we must send for the doctor in the morning. She fell getting out of her chair."

Catriona passed her without a word, moving swiftly toward her employer's door. Frau Kalman was asleep, breathing heavily, but at least unconscious of pain.

"It's that hip of hers," Grete said at her elbow. "She has much trouble with it always. When she gets up too quickly it gives way. It is a great pity to be so afflicted."

They sent for Andrew in the morning, although Frau Kalman had dismissed their concern for her.

"It's nothing," she declared. "This silly hip of mine has always been a nuisance, and I know what Andrew will say. 'You have to rest'!" She imitated his deep, authoritative tone. "Rest! That's all I ever do these days," she went on disgustedly. "I ought to be as fit as a fiddle with all this enforced rest."

She was well enough to be impatient, but when Andrew came he gave her a thorough examination.

"You take so many foolish risks," he said, standing beside her bed with her wrist held lightly between his fingers to count her pulse beats. "I might even say you deserved this if I wasn't the most humane of practitioners. No more walking with one stick, remember, when you do get up."

"Which means that I am on my back till you say the word?" she demanded. "I've a good mind to go over your head and send for Professor Zorn."

"Heinrich would tell you much the same, although possibly in stronger terms," Andrew said mildly. "You have to rest."

His patient sighed resignedly. "You will take some coffee before you go?" she asked. "We so seldom see you on this side of the valley, Andrew."

On the way to order the coffee, Catriona did not hear his reply, but she could not help wondering if he was thinking of the days when the chalet had been his home; his lonely bachelor abode where he had kept a photograph of a young girl and a bundle of old letters "to remind himself of the perfidy of women" in general.

On his own admission he had forgotten this traumatic experience, but the scars might still remain, unless, of course, he fell in love with someone else. March? Fereith? Painfully she considered the alternative, knowing that she would always care.

Andrew stayed with her employer for an hour, the hum of their conversation drifting through the half-open door. They seemed to be speaking earnestly on a subject that concerned them both, and when he rose to leave Andrew looked perplexed.

"Keep her in her room if you can," he advised when Catriona went to show him out. "She's a self-willed old woman, and you'll have to be firm with her."

They were doctor and nurse again, a position she accepted with a wavering smile.

"I'll do my best. Will you come again, Andrew?"

"I don't think there's any need." He glanced beyond her to the far end of the corridor, his mouth tightening momentarily as he looked at the closed door of his old room. "Professor Zorn will probably visit her as soon as he is back from Zurich. Meantime, how are you placed for help?"

"There's Grete—and Fereith."

"And of course, you have Robin to look after the horses till I can get you a replacement for Jeno."

"Robin is going back to Edinburgh," she was forced to admit.

His brows drew together in a quick frown. "And you?"

"I came for a month."

"Frau Kalman may need you for longer than that." He moved out to the terrace where a spirited little haflinger mare champed uneasily at the bit, pawing the soft snow as it snorted impatiently at the delay in starting. "She won't be on her feet with any certainty for at least two weeks."

"I'll look after her," Catriona promised. "I think she would like you to visit her, though."

He looked back at the chalet glowing in the warm sun. "When I can," he said briefly before he rode away.

Frau Kalman was a difficult patient when she was entirely confined to her bed, but she seemed to respect Andrew's orders, although she grumbled a lot. She sent for Robin and they argued; she summoned Fereith to her bedside and the girl came away in tears. Grete seemed to be the only one who could cope with her with any degree of success, apparently.

"Don't be a wicked old woman." Catriona heard her say. "You can't have your own way all the time."

Robin began to pack his suitcase. "This is beyond a joke," he said, standing before the side plate-glass window which formed their view of the valley. "I'm being called to account every few minutes as if I were a schoolboy, and I honestly think my godmother still believes I am!" He moved restlessly across the room. "Either that or she is trying deliberately to get under my skin. It wouldn't be so bad," he added moodily, "if the snow was good. But just look at it!"

"I'm off duty for an hour," said Catriona. "Could we go for a walk?"

He hesitated, half inclined to refuse. "Why not?" he shrugged. "There's nothing much else we can do."

They walked up through the pine wood and over a ridge that commanded a sterner view of the plateau above the valley. The sun was very strong, blinding them a little as they left the shelter of the trees.

"Look—over there!" Robin pointed while he shaded his eyes with his other hand. "My God, this place is a death-trap!"

Beyond the plateau two great mountain ridges met to form a narrow pass, and he was pointing to a spot directly beneath it where it dropped steeply to the upper valley floor. The remains of an old avalanche could be plainly seen; the rocks and debris that had hurtled down the mountainside with the gigantic fall of snow from their heights above.

"It's not new," he said. "It must have collapsed some time ago, but you can still see the havoc it's caused. That chalet over there—it's sliced completely in two! If you've heard an avalanche once, it'll scare the living daylights out of you the second time. You'll never forget it, and this valley is known for them."

Catriona averted her eyes from the scene of destruction where the devastating river of snow and rock had slithered its treacherous way down the mountainside.

"Is it always like this?" she said.

"It's a chance you take," he answered. "They're

coming down all the time. They could never touch the *schloss*, of course. It's much too high and was built as a fortress."

When they returned through the pines Catriona looked across the lower valley toward the *schloss*. It was true, she acknowledged. Nothing could touch it where it stood up there on its pinnacle of rock on the far side of the river; an impregnable fortress gazing across at them as if to assure them that all was well. The *schloss* was their guardian; the upper valley was more than a mile away.

That night several smaller avalanches hurtled down the mountainsides. In the morning Robin set out for Zurich. There was no one to drive him all the way, but a bus went from the village at midday down to the main road to Sargans, and from there he could reach the city without difficulty.

Catriona went with him as far as the village, with Fereith driving the smaller sleigh, which she was allowed to do when the roads were free from ice. They splashed along in the ruts with one horse between the shafts instead of two. One horse at a time was enough for her to handle, although she seemed completely assured as she sat with the reins between her hands and her dark eyes fixed steadily on the way ahead.

They reached the village with time to spare and Robin suggested a *gluwein* to warm them up. Sitting at one of the heavy trestle tables in the inn, there seemed nothing further they could say to each other on parting.

"Will you come back?" Fereith asked as the bus drew in.

"Sooner or later." Robin gave her cheek a brotherly peck.

Fereith flushed scarlet, biting her lower lip to keep back the threatening tears.

"You're far too emotional," he chided. "Everyone

comes back to Gleiberg. It's an old saying, isn't it?" He turned to Catriona. "See you, Kate—in Edinburgh!"

The bus pulled away, and they were left alone in the village street. Fereith looked back at the inn.

"I think he has gone for good," she said.

Catriona had some shopping to do for Grete, but Fereith decided not to go with her. She thought she should look after the horse.

Catriona did her shopping as quickly as she could, but it was one o'clock before she returned to the inn. Fereith was nowhere to be seen.

She searched the public rooms and the deserted *kellar*, where the nightly singsongs were held, but there was no sign of her. The horse and sleigh were still in the yard, waiting.

A mounting sense of panic took Catriona back along the village street where, earlier, she had imagined that she had seen Jeno lurking in a closed doorway, but that could have been the merest figment of her imagination. She began to feel desperately alone, not able to question the people she met because her German was so poor. She did, however, manage to ask about Fereith at the inn, where the innkeeper's wife had a smattering of English.

Between the two languages, she gathered that Fereith had fed the horse in the yard after she had left to do her shopping, and then gone out herself. No, she had not yet returned.

By two o'clock Catriona could wait no longer. Explanation after explanation had presented itself in her troubled mind and been rejected for the only true explanation. Something had happened to Fereith.

What could she do? To go to the police would raise an alarm which might distress Frau Kalman if Fereith suddenly reappeared unharmed. Andrew, then?

She phoned through to the *schloss*, but he was out. The Professor? she asked. Alas, the Professor would be in Zurich until the following day.

Feeling that the world had suddenly ended, she made her way back to the inn, but there was no news of Fereith.

"Could someone drive me back to the chalet?" she asked.

"With pleasure!" she was told. They were always willing to oblige Frau Kalman's guests.

It was raining by the time they reached the ravine, thin, rimey rain obscuring the sun, making the valley look dark indeed. Grete was at the chalet door, wringing her hands, her pleasant face grave with anxiety.

"Such trouble, when we were least expecting it!" she moaned.

Catriona gripped the plump shoulder. "Grete, what has happened?"

"You have come back alone," Grete said, as if that should be explanation enough.

"Yes." Catriona went past her into the hall. "I must see Frau Kalman at once."

"She is waiting for you." Grete's voice trembled. "I was not to know when I found the letter," she defended herself. "I was not to know."

"Where is she?" Catriona asked.

"In her room, but she will no longer obey the doctor's order to remain in her bed."

Frau Kalman was hunched before her window in a dressing gown, leaning heavily on the two walking-sticks which were kept beside her bed. She had watched the sleigh coming up the hill.

"Read that," she commanded, indicating a sheet of writing paper which lay on her dressing table. "Read it aloud."

As she picked up the paper, Catriona felt herself trembling from head to foot. I've failed you, she thought. Frau Kalman, I've failed both you and Andrew!

The message in Fereith's schoolgirl hand was plain and brief.

"*I have gone to find my father.*"

Catriona read it aloud, as the old lady had commanded, her voice shaking over the final word. She could see that Frau Kalman was in a great state of anger and confusion, but even in that frame of mind the old lady did not accuse Fereith of ingratitude, as she might have done. On the contrary, she seemed to blame herself.

"I should have known what to do," she said, "long ago!"

"I wish Robin was here," Catriona said involuntarily.

"Robin?" Frau Kalman glared at her. "What good would he be? He doesn't know the first thing about the valley, and he doesn't understand that girl." She sat down at her writing-desk to scribble a note. "Here you are! Go to Andrew Bishop and give him this," she commanded, thrusting the envelope into Catriona's hand. "I don't want any chattering on the telephone."

Catriona drove to the *schloss* through the rain. The hired man had put the hood on the sleigh, but she gripped her fur collar closely about her throat, feeling the cold as never before. The message for Andrew was clasped in her other hand, and the odd slant of rain that came in at the side of the sleigh fell on it without her noticing. Her thoughts were revolving around and around the events of those three brief hours since Robin had climbed aboard the local bus and sped off down the valley to the main road and Sargans, where he would change for Zurich. He might even be there by now, oblivious to all that was happening to the people he had left behind. That was Robin, careless and defiant, unable or unwilling to think of anyone but himself. She knew now how near she had come to making a terrible mistake by promising to marry him.

With the *schloss* in sight, she remembered phoning through to Andrew less than an hour ago. Like Frau Kalman, his name had sprung first to her thoughts in an emergency, but she had no guarantee that he had returned.

One of the nurses met her at the door, exclaiming at the downpour. "You must have some *gluwein*," she insisted, "while I try to find the doctor."

It seemed an eternity before she returned with Andrew.

"Kate," he said as she stood up, "what's wrong?"

"It's Fereith," she told him, holding out the note. "Frau Kalman asked me to give you this."

His jaw tightened as he read the message. "How did it happen?" he asked.

"We went to the village to see Robin onto the bus. Fereith was allowed to drive the sleigh."

"I see." He looked deeply concerned as he crossed to the open door to look down the valley and then at the sky, as if the weather might have some bearing on the decision he had to make. "That would be twelve o'clock."

"I had some shopping to do for Grete after the bus left," Catriona explained.

"And Fereith gave you the slip while you were doing it," he suggested.

"She said that she ought to look after the horse." Catriona went to stand beside him. "Andrew, I'm sorry," she apologized.

He considered her for a moment. "You couldn't help it," he said so kindly that she wanted to cry. "Nothing is so cunning as the gipsy mind."

"Do you think Jeno had something to do with it?"

"I wish I knew!" Once again he glanced up at the

leaden sky. "How did you get back to the chalet," he asked, "if Fereith drove you over?"

"I hired a man at the inn."

"Why didn't you phone here?"

"I did. You were out."

"For half an hour! I went up to the plateau to see where an avalanche had come down. It was of no importance."

Yet he hadn't been quite sure and had gone to check. Yes, Andrew certainly knew the valley—its beauty and its treachery. He prowled back across the hall, pausing at the foot of the staircase.

"Drink up your wine," he said. "We may have a long journey before us."

He tossed Frau Kalman's note onto the table beside her, and Catriona read it without surprise until she came to the final paragraph.

"Take Kate Sutherland with you," the old lady had written. "Fereith has come to trust her. I should have told the child the truth long ago."

Andrew mounted the stairs two at a time. She was left to make what she could of that final message. "Take Kate Sutherland with you. Fereith had come to trust her."

She could not refuse to go, whatever the journey might entail. But where? Were they to travel up and down the country in search of Jeno, hoping that they would find Fereith in his company?

She sipped the *gluwein* automatically, feeling its warmth dispelling some of the coldness within her but scarcely aware of the actual passage of time until Andrew came down the stairs again with a leather bag in his hand. He had changed his white coat for a warm loden-cloth jacket. He tossed a spare ski jacket onto the sofa beside the fireplace.

"You'll come?" he asked.

Catriona nodded. "I'll have to do something about the sleigh," she said.

"I'll drive you back to the chalet to pack an overnight case," he said, "and Otto can take the sleigh."

"What about the hired man?" Catriona asked.

"Otto can drop him in the village on his way through. Otto can stay at the chalet till we get back in case there are any more complications," he added. "I haven't found a substitute for Jeno yet, but Otto will do in the meantime."

"I take it we're going to look for Fereith," Catriona said as they walked toward the door. "How long do you think we'll be away?"

"Till we find her and can bring her back to Gleiburg."

His jaw squared determinedly, and she felt sorry for Fereith, who had caused all this trouble.

"She spoke about her father—"

"Her father is dead," he said with conviction, "but Fereith will not accept the fact. Like most orphan children, there was always the hope in her heart that she would find her true family one day."

"Do you think Jeno had taken her away for that reason?"

"I don't know. He may want to marry her." The small pulse that she had come to associate with tension beat rapidly at his temple as he led her past the sleigh to the car waiting on the cobbles of the stable yard. "We'll have to find out." Suddenly he turned to look at her. "I'm glad you have agreed to come with me, Kate," he said. "You'll be a great help if we do find her."

They drove to the chalet, each busy with their own thoughts.

"Bring your passport," he advised as she hurried to her room. "You may need it."

Gleiberg was very near the border, and if they traveled

east they would soon be in Austria. She packed an overnight bag while Andrew talked with Frau Kalman, and they were still deep in conversation when she presented herself in the old lady's room, ready to depart.

"One drop of blood and a leap in the air," her employer was saying. "We don't want any broomstick marriages here."

Andrew walked to the door without answering.

"It's good of you to do this for me," Frau Kalman said to Catriona.

"I only hope I won't fail you," she answered huskily.

"I have every confidence in you." The old lady took her hand. "Go carefully. Andrew will look after you."

"Otto will be here with the sleigh in a few minutes," Andrew said. "I don't want you to be left on your own."

"We'll survive," Frau Kalman declared. "But Otto will be a help. Go carefully!" she repeated as they closed the door.

They traveled over the Pass and down toward the main road. Andrew evidently wanted to cover as much distance as possible before darkness fell, but already the best of the day was over. Deep shadows clothed the mountain peaks, and the continuing rain restricted visibility until they were forced to reduce their speed and so waste precious time.

At the border their passports were checked. They were in Feldkirch before nightfall. The rain had turned to a thin, rimey snow, but it seemed that Andrew wanted to continue.

"How do you feel?" he asked.

"I'm all right." She felt frozen to the bone in spite of the heater in the car. "Don't worry about me, Andrew. We must find Fereith."

"We'll go on for another hour," he decided. "If we

don't have some kind of contact before we reach Bregenz we'll have to come back and try again."

"Have you any idea where they might go?"

He turned to look at her as they reached the outskirts of the town. "You seem to feel sure that she is with Jeno."

"I can't be certain, but I thought I saw Jeno in Gleiberg this morning as we drove in for the bus," Catriona explained.

"Why didn't you mention this before?" he asked sharply.

"Simply because I wasn't sure. It could have been anyone, Andrew."

"And it could have been Jeno!" His dark brows drew together in a quick frown. "Maybe I had no right to involve you in all this."

"It wasn't your idea," she reminded him, "and I wanted to come. I feel that I owe it to Frau Kalman for a dozen different reasons, not least because Robin walked out so quickly this morning."

"You can't make a habit of feeling responsible for the whole universe, Kate," he said. "That's always been your trouble."

"You mean because I put my family first—my mother and Jenny and Gordon—all those years ago?" she asked unsteadily.

"Three years ago," he reminded her, his mouth grim.

"It's over," she said, half choking on the words. "It's—no use looking back, Andrew. I made a little sacrifice and it wasn't needed, after all, but we weren't to know that at the time. Three years can make a difference."

It was almost dark, but she could still see his profile silhouetted against the far window where the thin rime had settled on the glass.

"They've made a difference to me," he said. "My whole outlook on life has changed since I came to Switzerland. Ambition doesn't mean so much."

"But you will go back to England one day? March said—"

"March thinks I should go back to Harley Street," he finished for her, "but I'm not so sure. It could be a humdrum existence compared with the work at Gleiberg."

"Frau Kalman would like you to stay."

They had just passed a crossroads, and he drew up abruptly. "This might be it," he said. "Will you wait in the car?"

"Let me come with you," she begged. "If you find Fereith I might be able to help."

He backed the car to the crossroads, turning into a narrow byway which went toward the mountains. It was scarcely a road to anywhere, but when she wound down her window to look out she could see the telltale tracks of many horse-drawn vehicles that had passed that way within the past few hours. They were fresh wheelmarks, dark and clear in the thin covering of wet snow, and the narrow treads suggested that they might be wagons. Gipsy wagons!

Her heartbeat quickened. It was almost dark now, with stars beginning to appear between the rifts in the clouds, and ahead of them she could see the great mass of a mountain chain rising darkly against the sky. Berg and peak jostled one another for supremacy wherever she looked, rising over 2000 feet and more above the narrow valleys between them.

The track they were on climbed and dipped until they reached another crossroads that widened out onto a grassy slope where there were some trees and the sound of running water. Andrew brought the car to a standstill at the edge of the grass.

"We've drawn a blank," he said. "But it was a good enough try. There's been an encampment here not so long ago."

He got out, walking across the grass to a wide gray circle of ash, the burned-out remnant of a fire. Catriona watched him stoop and put his hand against two stones at the edge of it, feeling for any sign of warmth that would give him an approximate idea of when it had been used.

"The birds have flown," he said as she went toward him.

He prowled back to the car, but suddenly he stood arrested, gazing at the road. The snow at that point had been cleared away; only the thin covering of rime remained. He stooped and drew his hand across it to reveal a heart-shaped diagram of stone imbedded in the roadway. When he straightened his eyes were as hard as steel.

"What is it?" Catriona asked, although the diagram of stones seemed vaguely familiar. "I've seen this sort of thing before," she remembered suddenly. "In Scotland—somewhere in Argyll in the hills above Loch Fyne. It was at the junction of two roads—just like this. A heart made of stone!"

He turned away from the ring with a scowl. She wondered if he felt that she had been referring to his own stony heart, making it all too personal.

"It's obvious," he said. "There are all sorts of signs here of recent festivities, although they could have been for the New Year. It's the marriage ring I find disconcerting." He glanced back toward the exposed heart. "They have their own peculiar customs where marriage is concerned," he explained, holding open the car door for her to get in, "and they generally come to one specific place to observe them. Nowadays most gipsy couples marry at the Town Hall or the local church, but your true

Romani still believes that he is as surely married by the traditional method of letting blood and joining hands in the presence of their families, where they promise themselves to each other for life.''

"What did Frau Kalman mean by a 'broomstick marriage'?" Catriona asked.

Andrew smiled. "She was angry. But it was a custom at one time for the bride and groom to jump over a broom stick during the marriage ceremony and some Romani clans still preserve the tradition. The 'broomstick' is a besom made of flowering broom, and the legend is still preserved in Germany, at least.''

"It's a pretty idea," Catriona mused. "Especially the besom made of flowers, but that can only happen in the spring, when the broom is out.''

"There are other customs," he said, "equally binding, and all of them stem from the same mutual promise." He looked across at the swiftly-flowing river. "One of them involves the carrying of water by the bride to her husband. They both drink from a new cup as an additional pledge before it's broken and thrown away.''

"Frau Kalman mentioned a 'drop of blood'," Catriona said thoughtfully. "Is that another pledge?''

"Yes—a mingling of blood. One clan might use it, another not.''

"Isn't it a bit—pagan?''

He smiled at the idea. "No more so than an exchange of rings or the old Scottish custom of 'loupin' the stool'! It's the promise that counts, the pledge of lifelong fidelity, if you like. Your true Romani rarely makes the same promise twice.''

"They're—faithful, you mean?''

"To a large extent." He turned from the river to examine the wheelmarks on the rutted surface of the road. "It's been a fairly large encampment, but we'll just have to hope that they all went off in the same direction," he said. "They'll have left a *patrin* somewhere, probably at the crossroads. Their signs are universal, so we ought to be able to follow them."

The *patrin* he sought was lying on the grass where he had expected it to be; a few twigs arranged in the shape of a cross, the long arm pointing along the main road which they had left half an hour ago. Andrew followed it and drove into a sleepy town where lights twinkled from the inn windows against the darkness of the mountain wall.

"It's time you had something to eat," he decided, "and if you're too tired to go on we'd better spend the night here."

She knew that he wanted to continue his search, that finding Fereith was important to him.

"We'd be wasting time," she said, "but I would appreciate something to eat."

"Of course!"

He pulled up before the inn, leaving the car on the cobbled pavement while they went to inquire about a meal. It was served to them before an open log fire in the entrance hall. For the first time Catriona realized how hungry she really was. Andrew ordered *kaisersuppe*, which came in a large, flowered tureen.

"It's nothing more than Scotch broth!" she declared, laughing.

"I wondered if you would recognize it."

The thick soup was warm and comforting. "Another helping?" he asked, the ladle poised above the tureen. "Don't let me down. I ordered for three."

"If there are no 'afters,'" she agreed.

"Oh, but there are! The mountain air is supposed to give you a gigantic appetite."

"Then no more *kaisersuppe*!" she decided.

He ate another helping while he considered the rest of

the menu. "*Gallasch* is too obvious," he decided. "We'll have *kalbsvoegel*, I think. If it's served with a good sauce, you'll like it."

They drank a local red wine with the veal olives, following it up with prune dumplings and cream.

"I can hardly move!" Catriona confessed. "And we've been here more than an hour."

"Are you sure about going on?" he asked.

"Yes. I could climb a mountain now."

"I doubt it," he said.

She rose from the fire with a sigh of regret, wondering if she would ever see Andrew like this again. It was almost as if an invisible hand had turned back the clock to those far off days in Edinburgh when laughter and togetherness had surrounded their love. For the past hour he had seemed the same carefree companion of her student days, the one person she had ever wanted to marry.

When she returned from the tiny washroom behind the heavily paneled door, he was deep in conversation with the proprietor, who finally escorted them outside and pointed down the road. His directions were too complicated for Catriona to follow, but she managed to say a few words of gratitude for the splendid meal. That evoked such a rapid fire of German that she had to turn to Andrew for help.

"He hopes that I will come again, many times," Andrew translated for her as they got back into the car. "And bring also my wife!"

"Of course—'the *Frau*'! How wrong can he be." She was trying to keep up the light banter of their former conversation, but suddenly her heart felt like lead. "Where to now?" she asked.

"We double back on our tracks a bit." He had taken a full minute to answer her question. "There's a side road going off into a valley, and he thinks we may find part of the encampment there. Some of them were in the town this morning hawking their wares and buying food."

As they drove back by the way they had come, Catriona felt a stirring excitement running through her veins. Andrew was preoccupied, but he was near in the darkness, near enough for her to touch. A sudden madness made her want to put her head against his shoulder and cry.

When they found the side road, he turned the car into it and up the valley toward the foothills. Above them, glittering in the starlight, the snow-capped giants of the Bregenzerwald gazed down coldy, barring their way to the north and east.

Catriona thought that they must have come to journey's end until suddenly the track broadened out into a wide green sward beside a river. And here, in wagons and caravans and elaborately painted carts, they found the gipsy encampment.

It was quite large, suggesting to Andrew that there had been a considerable gathering of the Romani clans in the vicinity. He had not been wrong when he had thought that the first encampment had moved on together rather than separately.

The whole wide glade was full of sound. Several large fires had been kindled, each in front of a group of wagons that had been drawn up in a half-circle fronting onto the river bank. The wagons were the most attractive Catriona had ever seen, with their high, brightly-painted wheels and domed roofs and the curtained windows at the back and sides. Most of the detachable steps leading to the carved half-doors were in place, and the tall chimneys projecting through the wagon roofs sent their thin columns of blue smoke into the still mountain air. The stoves were being stoked against the cold of the winter night, yet most of the camp's inhabitants were still gathered around the outside fires. The men lounged idly on the grass, their legs stretched out to the heat as they smoked and talked. A group of young girls sat cross-legged on a tarpaulin, putting the finishing touches on the baskets they had made. The older women sat on the steps of their *vardos*, smoking or staring into space, their dark, weatherbeaten faces inscrutable, their gnarled hands idle for a moment before they turned in for the night.

Andrew glanced quickly around the camp.

"Stay near the car," he advised. "I won't be very long."

He strode toward a black van tastefully trimmed in red and yellow, with dragons painted on the outside of the half-door. A very old man sat on the steps leading up to it. He had been surveying, in silence, the activity around one of the many fires as he peeled a willow wand. Catriona noticed how he held the knife in his left hand while he moved the willow around it, stripping the bark with incredible speed. He went on with his task for several minutes after Andrew had addressed him.

Because this living wagon was set a little way apart from the others at the top of the glade, she supposed that he must be the "headman" or "chief" of the clan. The whole atmosphere of the encampment was so exciting that she almost forgot their errand as she watched the comings and goings around the numerous fires. They seemed to be be meeting-places where one family might call on another to air their views or be invited to share a frugal meal cooked on the stoves in the living wagons and handed down to the fire by the older women. The children who scampered about the vans, laughing or quarreling among themselves, seemed privileged to do as they pleased, although once or twice when one of them passed between the men and the fire they were given a playful smack by one of the younger women trying to keep them in order. Evidently to pass between the fire and the man of the family was something a well-behaved child never did. Even the youngest toddler was still not in bed, although the babies were probably sound asleep in the darkened *vardos*.

The fires made a yellow glow against the darkness of the mountains, and somewhere near the river a violin throbbed against the night. Another and then another took up the gipsy tune until the whole glade was full of music. Nobody seemed to worry about the car, and presently two of the younger women approached it slowly. One of them was incredibly fair; the other was dark and small and so like Fereith that Catriona imagined their search to be at an end for a moment.

The two girls were curious but shy. They stood watching her for a few minutes and then walked away, glancing back once when Andrew passed them.

Catriona could see by his expression that he had drawn another blank.

"There's been some kind of a celebration," he said, "but the old man won't admit to a wedding. Nobody can be as tightlipped as a Romani when it comes to his own business." He looked toward the nearest fire where a group of men were squatting; the heavy, ominous shapes of their wagons in the background, their dark, scarred faces and glittering black eyes turned toward him. They wore earrings and bright neckerchiefs, with handy knives in their belts, but they made no move to warn him off. "The leader was a grand old boy," Andrew added, "but as close as a clam when it came to information. All the same, I don't think Fereith has been here, and he swore he knew nothing of Jeno."

"What do we do now?" Catriona asked.

He got into the car beside her.

"You want to go on," she said. "The sky's clearing, so I wouldn't mind. I'm really not in the least tired."

"You're sure?"

"Absolutely."

They sat for a moment longer looking across at the encampment, at the skylight *vardos,* the flat trolleys with their painted wheels, and the horses tethered at intervals along the roadside where they could crop the grass appearing through the snow.

"It must be a hard life," Catriona mused.

"It's the sort of life they wish to lead," Andrew said. "No Romani could ever stay in one place for very long. It's in their blood to travel, and that's the way they want it. They have recognized circuits, but sometimes they travel a long way. If you could see inside those *vardos* you would find them as comfortable as any home. The women are intensely proud of their living wagons and keep them scrupulously clean."

When he re-started the engine the half-bred dogs chained beneath the wagons barked an angry protest, but the gipsies themselves took little notice. One of them strolled leisurely across the grass to guide them back onto the road. He was a thick-set young man of about 26, heavy and dark-featured, with a broad, square Slavonic face and small, glittering eyes. He wore his peaked cap far back on his head, and he had several flashy silver rings on his fingers. A brightly-patterned neckerchief was tied about his throat; his corduroy trousers were stuffed into fancy leather boots.

"I know Jeno," he said in English.

"Do you know where he is now?" Andrew's voice was sharp.

"Not now, but I saw him three days ago."

"On his way to Gleiberg?"

"That may be so." The dark eyes were full of curiosity. "Are you looking for him?"

Andrew nodded. He would not mention Fereith.

"He could be at Landeck or Innsbruck." The dark eyes searched the inside of the car. "You want me to show you?"

"No," Andrew refused firmly. "I can find my own way."

He let in his clutch as the fair young woman joined them. She was dressed in a black *pina* over a brightly-striped skirt. She was tall for a Romani, her hair lying in two thick braids on either shoulder.

"Oh, my pretty *rom*," she said, "you are wasting your time. Jeno is very far away by now."

"*Dordi!*" The man turned to her with a look of disgust, breaking into a stream of rapid German that only made her laugh.

"He wanted you to take him to Innsbruck," she said to Andrew.

She stood back as the car moved forward and her husband touched his greasy cap.

"*Kushti-bok!*" they said in unison.

"Do you think he really knew where to find Jeno?" Catriona asked.

"I doubt it, but it strikes me that one road is as good as another." Andrew increased his speed, turning onto the main road again when they reached the intersection. "For the moment, we're going around in circles, getting nowhere."

"If you tried Innsbruck—"

"I might draw another blank." He was plainly uncertain. "These young gipsies would talk their heads off for a lift to the nearest town!"

She knew how anxious he was; how imperative it seemed to him that Fereith should be found without delay.

"Is it so very important that Fereith shouldn't marry Jeno?" she asked. "If they are in love and want to marry, why are we chasing them? After all, love is never quite the same a second time. First love is a sort of blossoming—something that might never return."

She bit her lip, wondering why she was saying all this, trying to convince him about love.

"It can be a traumatic experience, for all that," he said into the darkness of the car, "but I hope that won't apply to Fereith. She's too young, for one thing, too unsure of herself to make a success of marriage with someone like Jeno."

"Then it's Jeno who is the obstacle?" she guessed, wondering again what he really thought of Fereith, whether he hoped to marry her himself one day when she was older and ready for marriage. It would be a strange union, she thought with a lump in her throat—Andrew and the daughter of a gipsy princess! "If Jeno was right for her would Frau Kalman still object?" she added.

He took a full minute to consider her question.

"Perhaps I'd better tell you the truth," he said. "It might simplify matters."

"No, Andrew!" she objected. "I wasn't really trying to force a confidence. If it's some sort of secret then I don't want to hear it."

"Frau Kalman would probably have told you if she had had time," he decided. "She adopted both Jeno and Fereith when they were very young, but Jeno was always the servant as far as the old lady was concerned. Jeno was older than Fereith, and so he was encouraged to protect her wherever they went. He was of the same race, you see, and that involved an added loyalty on Jeno's part. I believe he carried out his side of the bargain to the best of his ability, but the old lady never expected him to fall in love with Fereith. One good reason being, I suppose, that she was of the 'royal' blood of the Romani, and Jeno was not."

"For a moment I thought you were going to say that they were brother and sister," Catriona told him.

He shook his head. "No, they could marry," he said. "It's the gipsy bit the old lady is so much against."

"I can't see why."

"Because Fereith is Frau Kalman's granddaughter," Andrew's voice had sounded harsh. "The old lady's son, Gunnar, ran off and married the daughter of a Romani 'leader', but Fereith's mother died soon after her birth. There were complications, of course, because Romani children are always absorbed into their mother's family. It's a loosely-organized matrilineal society where the headmen have considerable authority, but the true power lies with the mother. There is never a 'paternal' clan. The *materfamilias* is the mainstay of the family and usually does the lion's share of the work. She is the font of all kinship. Romani 'queens' are always far more powerful than the 'kings' or headmen."

"Then what happened in Fereith's case?"

"Her father brought her to Gleiberg. He came back to the *schloss*, knowing how ill he was, but he kept it from his mother because she could not forgive him. He also brought Jeno, who was five years old at the time and an orphan."

Catriona held her breath. It was the most pathetic story she had ever heard. "The old lady sent Gunnar away, I suppose?"

"Yes. But she couldn't refuse to take his child into her care when he had nowhere else to leave her."

"She never really acknowledged her, though."

"That was the mistake she made, right from the beginning. She recognizes it now for what it really was."

"Pride," said Catriona. "Foolish pride."

"She still is a very stubborn old woman," Andrew allowed, "but I think she would have undone what she did that night 16 years ago if only she had been given the chance."

A second chance, Catriona thought. It was what she herself had often longed for; to live again that awful moment of three years ago when she had sent Andrew away without a proper reason. She had been too proud to beg him to wait for her indefinitely; and he had been too proud and too bitterly angry to plead with her for an explanation. Pride could cause so many heartaches.

"Did Frau Kalman ever see her son again?" she asked.

"I don't think so. Gunnar had his own pride, and once his daughter was safe at Gleiberg he would not ask to be taken back into the fold. He had made his decision to marry Fereith's mother and I don't think he ever regretted it, but I believe he cut himself off from the Romani people after his wife's death. He wasn't really one of them, and he had committed the unforgivable sin of taking Fereith out of her mother's clan."

"What about Jeno?"

"I don't know Jeno's background," Andrew admitted. "he may have been a cousin, or some other blood relation. Frau Kalman seems to know very little about him, although she was quite willing to keep him as a servant."

"Until he grew old enough to attract Fereith?"

"Yes. She hadn't reckoned on that, I suppose. 'No more gipsy blood' has been her watchword at Gleiberg, so it's rather surprising that she kept Jeno there so long."

"Maybe she thought of him as another orphan needing her care," Catriona suggested. "There are so many of them at the *schloss*."

He nodded. "In many ways she's a remarkable old woman," he agreed. "She's admired and respected everywhere, yet, on this one point, she was adamant. She would not forgive her son."

"Do we—all have such a hard streak?" she asked unsteadily. "This unforgiving thing?"

"We all have a blind spot," he said harshly.

"It must be terrible never to be able to go back, to say 'I'm sorry about this' because someone has died."

"That could be the ultimate tragedy, and it may be the main reason why Frau Kalman never told Fereith the truth."

"Because she was ashamed of the whole affair?"

"Because she saw how futile it was, afterward."

"When it was too late." She moistened her lips because they had suddenly gone dry. "Robin said that Gunnar died in Yugoslavia years ago. I suppose she doesn't speak about him any more."

"Not often, but she's bound to think about him. Black sheep he may have been, but he was still her son. She had a tremendous love and respect for her husband, and that could be another reason why she felt so angry with Gunnar. He was the only link with a once-proud family." He put on a burst of speed. "One can't help admiring the way Frau Kalman has worked at Gleiberg; the way she must have worked all her life to preserve it for the next generation of Kalmans. It couldn't have been an easy task when she started off as a stranger in a strange land, although the Swiss are the easiest of people to get to know."

"You're happy, Andrew," she said. "Happy to live here."

He hesitated. "Yes, I think I am."

He would go on living here, she thought, and marry and have a family in time. If he married Fereith they would live at the *schloss* when the new clinic was built down in the valley. That might be compensation enough for Frau Kalman, who liked and trusted him. The old lady would see her granddaughter installed at Gleiberg and her family growing up there. There would be no more talk of Romani people or gipsy blood. It would all be forgotten, and she would die happy in the chalet that Andrew had built when he had first come from Scotland.

"Do you think Jeno knows the truth about Fereith?" she asked as they continued to speed eastward through the night. "About her being Frau Kalman's granddaughter."

"I doubt it." Andrew stared ahead at the wet snow which was now falling on the road in front of them. "But he may have used Fereith's desperate need of true parents to entice her away, as a sort of retribution when the old lady sacked him."

"I wouldn't have thought Jeno vindictive enough for that," Catriona objected.

"No Romani ever shows his true feelings," Andrew said. "They lie a little, charm a little, and act as they see fit when the time comes. Jeno would be no exception."

"But he could have made a genuine mistake about Fereith's parentage, couldn't he?"

"I suppose he could," he agreed. "Gipsies often claim children who don't really belong to them so long as they are part of the same 'clan'. Jeno could have been in touch with any of a dozen families during the past few years. He often left Gleiberg and came to Austria, but Frau Kalman could hardly stop him. He was 22 years of age."

"No, I suppose that would have been tricky." She stared into the night. "Yet we can't actually prove that Jeno took her away. She could have gone on her own. You said yourself that she was sometimes headstrong and wilful. She might have got as far as Innsbruck or somewhere and be regretting it by now."

Andrew seemed unconvinced. He sat forward in his seat, as if to urge the car on to a greater effort before he said, "That gipsy marriage ring we passed had been recently used. The old man at the camp was obviously lying when he said there had been no 'great festivity', or speaking only half a truth. They're secretive people about their own affairs." He let their speed drop back a little, but the intensity of his tone did not lessen. "My chief fear is that Jeno and Fereith are already married."

CHAPTER EIGHT

They drove on through the night, reaching Innsbruck in the early hours of the morning.

"You're dead tired," said Andrew. "We should have put up somewhere, Kate. I had no right to take your cooperation for granted."

"I offered it," she pointed out. "It was something I wanted to do."

"All the same, you're looking desperately wan," he persisted. "The first stop has to be breakfast."

His concern for her was almost more than she could bear. "Don't think about me, Andrew—"

"But I have to think about you," he said. "You're very much my responsibility at present."

So that was all! Frau Kalman had insisted that she went with him, and he needed her help in the present emergency, but it was all impersonal; all part of the effort to find Fereith and bring her back to Gleiberg.

The centuries-old capital of the Austrian Tyrol was still asleep; guarded by its magnificent backdrop of snow-covered mountains, its domes, towers and statues faintly gilded in the first flush of dawn; a magic city as old as time and as modern as the hour.

They drove into the Old Town as the first carts were appearing in the streets. The first rays of the sun caught the gilded copper roof of the Goldene Dachl. The famous balcony glittered high above the Herzog-Friedrichstrasse like some living thing, dominating the ancient *lauben* where the shadows were still dark and secretive.

"It's beautiful!" Catriona exclaimed in spite of the fact that they were not exactly on a sightseeing tour. "All those lovely old buildings straight out of the Middle Ages!"

Andrew smiled at her enthusiasm, slowing the car as they came into the square.

"It's full of history," he agreed, looking up at the gilded balcony. "You can almost see the strolling players, and the minstrels and the jugglers performing for the great Maximilian and his bride as they looked down from the Goldene Dachl. It must have been a colorful sight, with the mountains in the background, the sun shining, and all the panoply of wealth and splendor out to watch the jousting and the people down here watching in their turn."

Catriona could picture it all so plainly: the knights in armor on their richly-caparisoned steeds with their long lances tilted at the ready; the eager, gaping crowd gathered for the tournament in the cobbled square; the jugglers and the sweetmeat sellers plying their wares; the itinerant minstrels wandering under the vaulted arcades, and high above it all, on the Gothic balcony roofed in gleaming copper, a man and the woman he married— Maximilian and his Italian bride, the lovely Maria Blanca Sforza, newly arrived from Milan to share his life in this lovely mountain stronghold among the Alps.

"I wonder if she was happy," she said involuntarily.

"Maria Blanca?" Andrew turned to look at her in the early-morning light. "Why not? These 'arranged' marriages often worked as well as a love-match. I suppose she accepted her husband's country as her own, in the end."

"That wouldn't be difficult," Catriona decided, looking toward the ancient rococo Helblinghaus and the City Tower rising up against the incredible blue of the morning sky.

The rain and sleet of the night before had washed the

whole firmament clear. The sun seemed to have an added warmth as it topped the mountain rim. Andrew turned the car, driving westward along the famous old street to where it reached the river.

"We'll see what they can do for us at the Ottoburg," he suggested, pulling up outside a picturesque 15th century castle overlooking the inn. "We ought to get something to eat, at least."

She waited while he went to inquire, standing on the sidewalk to listen to the sound of the early-morning traffic behind her. Very few people were astir, and the mountains seemed to draw nearer. It was as if she and Andrew had this whole wonderful city to themselves, as if the Old Town and the New Town had come close to wrap them in an intimacy that they could not escape, even if they tried. The cold air touching her cheek came straight from the mountain snow, invigorating and strong, to banish sleep. It was a moment she would never forget.

Andrew returned to lock the car door. "It's never too early in Austria," he said. "Breakfast will be ready in half an hour."

She glanced at her watch. It was five o'clock.

"Would you like to stretch your legs?" he asked.

"I'd love it, if you've nothing else to do."

"Nothing," he said, "for the moment."

They decided to return to the Old Town, walking briskly through the deserted streets toward the Renweg, where the magnificent Hofburg looked down at them in all its Gothic splendor. Everywhere, the broad river seemed to dominate the town, moving slowly and silently beneath the bridges in the shelter of the majestic mountain wall.

"We haven't time for much more," Andrew said almost regretfully as they paused beside the Hofgarten to draw breath. "You may be able to come again."

She could not think when or how. All she could remember now was that they were looking for Fereith and that their secret, golden hour had sped far too quickly for her, at least.

They found their table set ready for them in the dining room overlooking the inn. Andrew had ordered an egg dish, which was delicious. There was *tiroler baurenspeck* to follow, that proved how hungry he felt.

Presently he stood to speak to the manger, returning to the table to inform her that a room on the first floor had been put at her disposal for a couple of hours.

"Even if you don't sleep," he advised, "Lie down for an hour. It will revive you. We may have to go on from here."

He didn't explain what he would do while she rested, but probably he would spend the time making a few necessary investigations in other quarters of the city where he thought it wiser to go alone.

"If you do go out before I get back," he warned, "don't go too far afield."

She decided to wait for him because it would be madness to complicate things by getting lost.

The porter who showed her to her room was small and jovial, a friendly, middle-aged man who spoke good English. He remarked that the British tourists would soon be invading Innsbruck "in great numbers", but there would always be the necessary accommodation for the Herr Doktor from Gleiberg. Andrew was evidently very well known.

The room he had obtained for her was small and intimate. It looked out onto a tiny cobbled yard, away from the traffic of the main street, and was ideal for its purpose. She lay down on the narrow bed under the snow-white *dine*, meaning to close her eyes for Andrew's prescribed hour, but when she opened them again, it was full daylight and the sun was streaming in through the slatted window-blinds.

As she stirred on the bed a shadow moved on the far side of the room.

"I'm glad you managed to sleep," said Andrew, coming to stand over her.

"Oh, I'm sorry!" She sat bolt upright, clutching the *dine* under her chin. "It's late. It must be—the sun is quite strong."

"It's ten o'clock," he informed her. "I had just decided to wake you, though it seemed a pity."

"How long have you been waiting?"

"Not long." He sat down on the edge of the bed. "Kate, I may have to go up to Igls. It's only four miles out, but it might be better if I went on my own." He did not give her a reason. "Take your time, and I'll be back for a late lunch, if not before. If you want to see the town hire a *fiaker*. They'll get one for you at the desk. It's really a pleasant way to explore."

He left her with the briefest of nods, already thinking of Fereith, no doubt, because she was really his main concern.

Dressing quickly, Catriona went down to the hall, but he had already left. A waiter offered her coffee topped with cream, which she drank while he ordered her *faiker*. Faced with an empty morning, the least she could do was to see the town.

The little horse-drawn vehicle clip-clopped its way through the busy streets while the driver gave her a running commentary on all she saw, but it was difficult to keep her mind on the historic interests of Innsbruck while her thoughts were with Andrew in his lone search for Fereith. By half-past eleven she had decided to walk back to the Ottoburg in case he had returned. She would keep to the main thoroughfares, so it would be impossible for her to lose her way.

She paid off the *fiaker* in the Marie-Theresienstrasse with the money Andrew had given her and began to walk. She passed Annasaule, the high column with the statue of St. Anne on top, gazing toward the mountains, and was caught in the crowd outside a large hotel. The street traffic had thickened, and she wondered if she had been wise to dismiss the *fiaker*. Then, suddenly, as the congestion on the sidewalk eased, she became aware of a vaguely familiar figure walking ahead of her. It was Jeno. She felt absolutely sure, fighting her way toward him through the crowd. She would recognize the proud lift of his head anywhere; and the suggestion of the countryside about him that was most noticeable in his walk.

He strode on, as if the crowd about him did not exist, his eyes riveted on the white snows at the far end of the street where the mountains came down so close to the town.

At the intersection with a busy side street she lost him, and when she reached the opposite curb he had disappeared completely. Disconsolately, she boarded a tramcar to take her back most of the way to the Ottoburg, where Andrew was waiting.

"I've just come in," he told her. "There's no need to apologize."

"Andrew," she said breathlessly, "I've seen Jeno—just now, back there in the Maria-Theresienstrasse. It was near the Schindler—I think that was the name—and he was alone."

He looked disappointed. "All the same, it's a lead," he decided. "I'll put your overnight case into the trunk. We'll eat later."

They tore back to the Schindler, although they hardly expected to find Jeno waiting for them on the doorstep.

"You're sure he was alone?" Andrew asked.

"I'm almost certain. Had you any luck at Igls?" she asked.

He shook his head. "None, although I did see someone I knew there. Kate," he added, as he turned the car into the quieter Anichstrasse, "this might be a long, tiring journey. Would you rather go back to Gleiberg?"

"No," she said firmly. "Not until we've found Fereith."

He looked almost relieved as they drove away from the town, traveling east again and then north. At a village *kellar* they ate grilled trout caught that morning in the local stream, accompanying it with a light *weisswein*, that Andrew recommended. Catriona was finishing an enormous *torte mit schlag* when he jumped to his feet.

"Wait here," he commanded, "and don't move!"

He had been looking out of the window behind her, and whatever he had seen had galvanized him into action. Catriona knelt on the wooden trestle to look through the mullioned panes. In the courtyard directly opposite a light cart with yellow-painted wheels was drawn up before an open doorway, which was probably the back entrance to the *kellar*. It was the sort of cart she had seen before in a gipsy encampment. Her heart pounded strongly as she waited for Andrew to appear. Instead, she saw Jeno crossing to the cart with a tall, middle-aged man who stooped a little as he walked. He was wrapped in a long coat, with a thick muffler about his neck. He looked frail and ill in the searching light that slanted down off the snow. He shook hands with Jeno, got into the cart and drove away.

Where was Andrew? There had been enough time for him to reach the courtyard before the cart disappeared from view, but he didn't seem to be particularly concerned about its occupant. Nor about Jeno.

It was almost another five minutes before he came into view, and Fereith was with him. She walked with her head down, in the way she had when she was overwhelmingly perplexed about something, but her lagging steps suggested that she was also very tired. Andrew put his arm about her in a protective gesture, but she turned away from his embrace almost sulkily. They stood in the center of the courtyard, obviously arguing about something. When Jeno came forward, Andrew turned to him angrily.

Jeno shrugged, making a negative gesture with his hands and not looking at Fereith. Remembering the significance of the yellow-wheeled cart, Catriona wondered if they were discussing the man who had just driven off.

Presently they walked toward the *kellar* entrance, and she drew back from the window, waiting for them to enter.

The little bar was very quiet. She was its only occupant at this time of the day, although it would probably be noisy with the skiing fraternity later on; even the landlord had gone to polish glasses in the adjacent restaurant. It was some minutes before Andrew returned.

"I saw you with Fereith and Jeno," she said, looking beyond him to the deserted passageway. "Andrew, are they married?"

"No." He looked immeasurably relieved. "At least, that wasn't on the cards. The jaunt was apparently aimed at finding out about Fereith's parentage and possibly to try for a meeting with her father."

"Frau Kalman must have told her that her father was dead. She owed her that, at least," said Catriona.

"She told her she was an orphan—yes, but there was always this doubt in Fereith's mind. Jeno thought there was something odd about the old lady's explanations, although he had no real proof to offer Fereith."

"And the other man? The man in the flat cart. What had he to do with it?"

"I don't really know. Jeno is as close a Romani as any of them. All he would say was that the man had information that he refused to pass on."

"Did Fereith see him?"

"Oh, yes. They had a meal together, all three of them, just before we came in."

"Stopping here has been a great stroke of luck, then."

"Not entirely. I was told at Igls this morning that they had left Innsbruck and were traveling north or east. This seemed to be the logical route for them to take, so I followed them. We missed them at Innsbruck by a hairsbreadth."

"What has happened to Fereith now?" Catriona asked anxiously.

"She's saying good-bye to Jeno."

"Then—?"

"There was nothing in their "romance" to worry about," he said with satisfaction. "Jeno promised to help her in her search for her father mainly out of sympathy, I think, although when it came to the crunch there may have been a certain amount of malice in his attitude toward Frau Kalman. She never accepted Jeno as being adopted by her in the true sense of the word. He was simply there to serve her. Jeno was a Romani of the true black blood and, therefore, her enemy."

"Because of her son?"

He nodded. "Because of Gunnar."

"But surely all that is over now. Gunnar is dead."

"She doesn't forgive easily," Andrew said. "Her pride was shattered, and Gunnar had turned down her love. It was a blow that she never quite survived."

Like you, Andrew, she thought dejectedly. You will never allow yourself to forget that I rejected your love all those years ago for no very good reason that you could see.

"Why do you think she accepted Jeno at Gleiberg in the first place?" she asked.

"Gunnar brought him the night he brought Fereith. There was nothing she could do about it, I suppose. It had something to do with guardianship. No doubt Jeno was a close relation of Fereith's mother, maybe a younger member of the same family—a cousin, perhaps, who had also lost his parents."

"I see." She looked around for Fereith.

"There's something I want to ask you, Kate."

"Yes?" She turned to him far too eagerly.

"It's about Fereith." He strode to the window. "I can't handle her in her present mood. She seems to resent me for no very clear reason, unless it's that I'm the one who is taking her back to Gleiberg."

"Against her will?"

"I can't be absolutely sure of that, either," he confessed. "I think now that she's drawn a blank over this father business she may want to return."

"Fereith wouldn't give up quite so easily."

"You may be right." He turned to face her. "Will you talk to her? Will you try to convince her that there is—love and a happy future waiting for her at the *schloss*?"

"I'm not sure that I'm competent to do that."

Catriona's heart felt like lead because Andrew had said that the love waiting for Fereith was to be found at the *schloss* where he, too, could find his life's happiness. Was this finality? Love and fulfilment for them both at the *schloss* Gleiberg while she took her bruised and battered heart back to Scotland to try to forget for a second time?

"You're the one person who could do it." He was standing very close now, willing her to accept this mission which meant so much to him. "After all, it was why Frau

Kalman asked me to bring you. I think she anticipated this mood of Fereith's."

When she remembered why she had come to Switzerland in the first place she felt guilty. She had come to help Frau Kalman.

"I'll try," she promised. "Do you want me to tell her about Gunnar?"

"No, I'll do that." He had made up his mind quite firmly on that point. "It's afterward that is going to be difficult, when she realizes just who she is. She may wonder why the old lady kept the truth from her for 16 years."

"Do *you* know, Andrew?" she asked.

"Pride," he decided without hesitation. "Wretched, foolish pride. She also wanted to be sure that she had done the right thing by taking a gipsy's child. Even when Gunnar died she wasn't sure. There was this doubt about gipsy blood. She was terribly prejudiced."

"Would it have been any easier for her if Fereith had been a boy?"

"An heir, you mean? Yes, I think it would. She's passionately fond of the *schloss*."

"And as passionately determined that Fereith will marry the right person," Catriona suggested. "Someone of her own choice."

He looked uncomfortable for a moment. "That's her idea," he admitted, at last.

She felt that she already know what Frau Kalman had planned for Gleiberg. What could be more natural than a desire on the old lady's part to see the bond that already existed between her and the English doctor strengthened by his marriage to her granddaughter?

"I'll see what I can do," she said.

They found Fereith alone in the entrance-hall, sitting on one of the oak settles which flanked the doorway. There was no sign of Jeno.

"Would you like something to drink?" Andrew asked her kindly.

She shook her head. There was something so utterly dejected about her in this moment of failure that Catriona wanted to protect her, as Andrew had done. He sat down on the settle beside her.

"Fereith, there's something you have to know," he said. "It's going to be a great surprise to you, but I want you to think very carefully about it before you judge Frau Kalman."

"She was always very kind to me," Fereith admitted. "Though she was strict, especially about my education."

"It was important to her. She wanted to give you the best foundation she could. You see, Fereith," he added quietly, "she is your grandmother."

Fereith sat gazing down at the floor as if the truth hadn't quite reached her; her face shielded by the long, straight fall of her hair, but Catriona fancied that she was crying. When she finally looked up at them the marks of tears were on her cheeks.

"So I really do belong to someone," she said. "But why did she keep it from me? Why did she make me wait all this time?"

"I think she meant to tell you, quite soon," Andrew said.

"She allowed me to think that I was an orphan." The dark eyes sharpened, growing hard. "That may be untrue also," she suggested. "My father may be alive somewhere." She sat in silence for a moment. "He was her son," she said.

"Yes." Andrew took both her hands in his, drawing her to her feet. "She wants you to come back to Gleiberg."

Fereith resisted him. "Not yet! I have this to think about," she declared. "I can't go to her until I am sure. Everything will be—different."

"Will you come back as far as Innsbruck for tonight?"

he asked, seeing how tired she was. "There's nowhere else for you to go."

"Jeno has gone back to his people," she said wistfully. "It was arranged with the man we met at Innsbruck. He was very kind to me," she remembered.

"Had you met him before?" Andrew asked.

"No, he was a stranger. Even Jeno did not know him very well, but he was kind."

"He was here this morning, driving a flat cart with yellow wheels," said Catriona.

Fereith nodded. "Yes. He came to say good-bye. He was on his way into the mountains."

They drove back to Innsbruck by the way they had come earlier in the day. It had begun to snow again; soft, white, flaky snow falling on the roadway to cover their tracks and obliterate the marks of a pair of iron-bound wheels on a yellow flat cart traveling in the opposite direction.

"We'll spend the night at the Ottoburg if we can get in," Andrew suggested. "And then we'll take a proper look at the town." He glanced at Fereith sitting in the passenger seat beside him. "Innsbruck is happy at this time of year. We will find somewhere to eat and perhaps dance."

It was his man's way of taking Fereith's mind off her problems, but she did not fully respond.

"That will be nice," she said listlessly.

Catriona had no opportunity to speak with her for any length of time once they reached the hotel, but they had to share a double-bedded room because there were only two available. She had no doubt that the time would present itself later.

Halfway through the evening Fereith seemed to respond to Andrew's kindness more readily. He had taken them to one of the smaller restaurants in the Hofburg, ordering *bohnensuppe* because he thought Fereith looked cold and following it up with *pariser schnitzel*, which she hardly touched. When he suggested *apfelstrudel* she responded with one of her grave smiles.

"If you will have one, also," she agreed.

After they had finished their meal they sat listening to the music, but they did not dance. Andrew ordered a glass of *schnapps* for himself and *apfelsaft* and *himbeer* for Fereith and Catriona.

"If you live in Rome you must do as the Romans do," he quoted. "*Himbeer* is good for you."

"It tastes of raspberries," Catriona decided.

"It is raspberries," he told her, "diluted with soda."

Fereith was looking at him with a new awareness. "You really are kind, Andrew," she said, "and I ought to do as you say and go back to Gleiberg with you, but it has so many unhappy memories for me."

"Surely it has many happy ones, too," Catriona suggested. "When you were small, Fereith, Frau Kalman took care of you. She loved you. There can be no doubt about that. When I was young, I, too, lived with my grandmother because my father was dead. My mother had to go out to work to keep us and to educate us. I had a brother and sister, but I was the oldest; as soon as I could I wanted to help. My grandmother was a very gentle old lady and she knew how much I wanted to be a nurse, so she helped out with the others while I trained. All her savings went, but she was determined to see me through to my final exams."

"What happened to her?" Fereith asked, interested in spite of herself. "Was she very proud when you graduated?"

"Yes, she was proud, and I could not have denied her

that," Catriona said almost to herself. "She died soon afterward."

"What happened to your mother, and your brother and sister?"

"My mother married again." Catriona did her best to keep her voice steady. "They emigrated to Australia."

Fereith's eyes widened. "So really you have no one to love you, also," she said.

Andrew was staring down at the floor.

"There are so many different kinds of love," Catriona said. "There's—affection, friendship, and the love you get by returning them. All these things are waiting for you at Gleiberg, Fereith."

"But not my father's love," Fereith objected. "He must have left me at the *schloss* when I was a baby. Jeno says he half remembers him. He was tall, with a thin face, and he drove two horses better than anyone Jeno had ever seen before. It was a very cold night. All Jeno can recall with accuracy is the fire burning in the great hall at the *schloss*, and the hot *gluwein* he was given to drink. He had never tasted it before." She rose to her feet, tossing the hair back from her shoulders. "My father isn't dead," she declared with a dogged persistence that made Catriona's heart ache in sympathy for her. "I know it! One day he will come back for me," she added with conviction.

Catriona glanced around at Andrew. "Frau Kalman will tell you about him," she said. "Will you come back to Gleiberg, Fereith, where everybody loves you?"

Fereith considered the possibility for a full minute before she nodded. "That will be the best thing," she decided.

CHAPTER NINE

Fereith was very restive during the night, turning under the white *dine* in the bed next to Catriona. Once or twice she called out in her sleep to the unknown man who had sacrificed so much for the love of a gipsy princess. By morning, however, she was ready to return to Gleiberg and her grandmother.

They were warned of avalanches beneath the Arlberg, but they reached Blundens without mishap. The snow was still falling. Here and there they had traced the path of a small avalanche descending from the dark recesses of the Lechtaleralp.

As they recrossed the border the sun came out, glittering on the wide valley of the Rhein; the broad, friendly valley that Catriona was already beginning to love.

"It's home," Fereith murmured long before they had reached Gleiberg. "There has to be some place—"

When they drove into the village on the far side of the Pass, there seemed to be more activity than usual. It was Sunday, but several of the stores were open. People were packing provisions into sleighs and gathering in small groups on the pavements. Andrew slowed the car to a walking pace, calling something in German to a passerby. The man halted, gesticulating with his arms toward the mountains.

"Gleiberg has been cut off." Andrew's voice was sharp with anxiety as he turned to them. "There's been an avalanche, but everybody in the *schloss* is safe—the children and the nurses."

"The chalet?" Catriona asked, seeing her own fear reflected in his eyes. "What about the chalet?"

"We must go and see," he said tensely.

There was little to add to the knowledge they had been given, even when they pulled up for added information at the village inn. The avalanche, one of many in the district, had come down during the night, virtually cutting Gleiberg in two. On one side stood the village and the *schloss*; on the other was the way to the chalet through the narrow gorge, that was now impassable.

"Even your friend could not have reached it," the inn-keeper said.

Andrew looked puzzled.

"Herr Pettigrew," the man explained. "He arrived back from Zurich yesterday and stayed the night here, but he was warned not to reach the upper valley by himself. This he seemed to accept. He paid his bill and went off in a hired car, back to Zurich, I believe."

Catriona held her breath, scarcely able to believe that Robin had deserted Frau Kalman in her hour of need.

"I wonder why he came back as far as this," she said automatically.

Andrew shrugged, unable to hide his contempt. "We'll never know," he said, "but if you're worried about him you can easily reach Zurich from here."

"I'm going back to Gleiberg," she said firmly. "There may be casualties."

"There'll be more news there, and there's plenty of help coming up from this side of the Pass." He glanced at the men loading the heavy sleighs. "I'll be glad of your help, too," he added, as if he were immeasurably relieved by her offer.

Fereith sat quietly, with nothing to say. Catriona remembered the scene of desolation she had glimpsed on the walk with Robin when they had followed the path of another avalanche.

"Will she be all right?" Fereith asked. "My—grand-mother?"

"We must make sure." Tight-lipped, Andrew put the car to the first incline. "As far as I can gather, there has only been one fall, and that came down at the top of the gorge. We must hope that the chalet escaped."

The chalet was too near the gorge for him to be absolutely sure, Catriona realized, remembering how apprehensive Robin had been. Well, he had made his own escape in time! She pushed the thought of him out of her mind.

The way up to the Pass was difficult. The fresh snow hid the ruts that had formed with the temporary thaw of two days ago. The car bounced from side to side, making the journey even more treacherous with newly-formed ice, and once the car slid back in its tracks for a considerable distance before Andrew was able to correct the skid. Fereith sat forward, tensed and anxious, watching for the head of the Pass.

When they reached it the snow was deeper than they had expected; but the car was big and powerful and they pushed through. There was still the descent on the other side to be negotiated, but they could see Gleiberg now and the road going down and up again on the other side of the valley. To Catriona it seemed peaceful beyond belief; the quiet valley of her dreams, yet somewhere on the ridge above the gorge the chalet Andrew had built might be in ruins. They could not see it from that angle, nor could they trace the path of the avalanche. All they could see, far beneath them, was the red rooftops of the valley houses, the river with the bridge over it, and the bright onion dome of the church glittering in the sun. It was like a picture postcard in true color, with the grim old castle standing above it; unchangeable and untouched in the shadow of the snow-capped peaks.

It seemed an eternity before they were driving through the village to pull up at the inn.

"I'll find out exactly what happened," said Andrew, leaving them in the car.

He was back within minutes, looking up toward the gorge, his eyes narrowed against the unrelenting glare of the snow. "It's worse than I thought," he said, unable to spare them the truth. "There's been a second fall, and no way of getting through since yesterday. They've tried, but there was the danger of another fall. I think you had better stay here for the time being," he added. "The road to the *schloss* hasn't improved, either. There's a block, which will soon be cleared. No danger to the *schloss*, of course."

"Nothing could harm it," Fereith said with satisfaction.

The courtyard of the inn was a hive of activity and already the snowploughs were out, but it would be many hours before a way could be cut through the gorge.

Andrew's gaze was still fixed on the mountainside above the plateau. "It came down from there," he reflected, reaching for his binoculars. "There must be a way over."

They knew that his concern was chiefly for Frau Kalman, who might still be up there with Grete and Otto. If the avalanche had missed the chalet they would be trapped, but that would be all. In 48 hours, or even less, the rescue party would reach them. But if the avalanche had struck, the end of their search could lead them to tragedy.

Catriona watched him as he focused the powerful binoculars on the gorge, raising them slowly to scan the plateau above it. Then she saw his jaw harden, and his mouth set in a grim line. He handed her the binoculars without a word.

Adjusting them to her own vision, she brought the chalet into view. The track of one avalanche came right down beside it; a dark river of stone and snow that had carried everything before it. Young pines lay scattered like bowling pins along its path, but at first glance it seemed that the house itself had escaped. She followed the ridge of the roof sweeping down to the eaves, and the long façade of the building itself clinging to the edge of the plateau. All seemed in order until she saw the trail left by the minor fall.

"It's—horrible!" she whispered. "It's cut the whole end away."

A dark gash marked the gable of the chalet, for all the world as if a giant knife had sliced a piece clean off, leaving it wide open to the elements.

"It's my room," she said unhappily, and then a great tide of relief engulfed her. "It could be providential, Andrew. It would be the only unoccupied bedroom on that side of the house."

"Yes," he agreed, "that's true," but he seemed to be thinking about something else. "There hasn't been a fire, thank God! That was another hazard. Quite often when a chalet is hit it's the wood stove that causes most of the damage, but the chimney seems to be intact, so we haven't that to contend with."

"It means that they could all still be under cover," Fereith said. "They may not have had to spend the night in the snow."

Andrew was buckling on a pair of skis he had borrowed.

"What are you going to do?" Catriona asked, her voice catching on the question because she already guessed the answer.

"I could get over there," he decided. "There's a narrow ledge above the gorge. I could just about make it. Someone may need a doctor."

Even with the aid of the binoculars she could not

discover the ledge he spoke of. A solid wall of rock and snow seemed to rise steeply above the gorge; beneath it was that other wall of fallen rock which blocked the road. It would be the most hazardous journey he had ever undertaken.

"You can't go alone," she said, yet she was far too inexperienced to go with him.

In next to no time, however, he was joined by two volunteers. Both were sturdy mountaineers and were soon discussing the route they meant to follow. Ropes and medical supplies appeared from nowhere. With them came March Lazenby.

"I'll go up with you, Andrew," she offered in the matter-of-fact tone of the expert. "Another pair of hands might be useful once we get there."

Andrew hesitated. "I think you would be more useful trying to get through to the *schloss*," he said. "There's nobody up there with any great authority at the moment, and I don't want the children to panic. Kate will go with you," he added. "And Fereith."

Fereith accepted the mission with a certain amount of reluctance. "It would be better if I went to the chalet," she said.

"You would be more useful at the *schloss*," Andrew pointed out, "reassuring the children."

When he had gone Fereith considered the idea.

"Do you think I could be of use?" she asked Catriona. "Really of use?"

"I'm sure of it," Catriona answered immediately. "Children get frightened by a set of circumstances they have never experienced before, especially the younger ones. You can explain to them about the chalet and tell them that Andrew will soon be back."

"Will he?" Fereith was not afraid to voice their fear. "He has taken a great risk doing this thing. If the snow is soft along the ledge they could fall to their deaths. It is a very dangerous path; one that is seldom used in winter. In spring and summer it is easy, and we go there to gather wild flowers for the botanists who come to Gleiberg in search of them. It is a secret place, but not too dangerous when you belong in the valley."

Twice she had mentioned belonging in the past few hours, as if finding part of her true family had given her roots.

Catriona turned toward the *schloss* with the prayer in her heart that nothing would happen to spoil all that.

The road to the *schloss* remained closed for three hours, at least to Catriona. March decided to go up toward the Pass and ski around at a higher level. Although Fereith was experienced enough to have accompanied her, she elected to stay with Catriona.

"I do not like that March," she declared positively. "She wishes to marry Andrew and take him back to England."

Catriona's heart missed a beat. "And you don't want him to go?"

"No. He is good here, and we all love him. Without him the children would be more sick than they are." Fereith paused. "I think I shall be a nurse one day and help Andrew in his work."

"Have you told him this?" Catriona asked.

Fereith shook her head. "I have told no one but you, because it is something I have newly decided to do."

"You are the right age," Catriona acknowledged. "17 next birthday. Are you sure you wish to do this, Fereith? You must study a long time."

"I am sure." Fereith looked around her. "I will go to Zurich to train in Professor Zorn's hospital, then I shall return to help Andrew."

And marry him? Catriona thrust the devastating

thought aside. "I think your grandmother will be very pleased," she said.

"A long time ago she planned this for me," Fereith mused. "She is one who is always planning, you know! She is wishful that everything should go the way she thinks is best. She also does not like March Lazenby very much. She says she is a schemer, which means that March also makes plans which she wishes to come true. Do you have plans that you wish to come true, Catriona?"

"Dreams, I think they are called," Catriona said. "There's a difference, Fereith."

"I do not know about 'differences'," Fereith said with a worried frown, "but I know that Andrew also has plans. He has talked often with Frau—my grandmother about making more places for children here, at Gleiberg. They would wish for a large clinic down in the valley, where many children would come to be made well again. This you could also do," she added thoughtfully.

Catriona shook her head. "No, Fereith."

"Why do you not agree when it is in your heart to stay?"

It was strange how frequently Fereith made those telling statements, as if she could see clearly to the heart of the matter in some uncanny way granted only to someone of true Romani blood. But if she had inherited a sort of "second sight" from her gipsy forebears she did not dwell on it for long.

"I wish we did not have to wait," she exclaimed impatiently, crossing the room to peer out of the window for the third time in half an hour. "Soon it will be dark and they will stop clearing the road until the morning March will be at the *schloss* by now."

The road was cleared before darkness fell, but there could be no news from across the valley. If all had gone well with them, however, Andrew and his small rescue party would be above the gorge by now.

March sent a horse-drawn sleigh to the inn for them. It was driven by Otto.

"Why did you leave the chalet?" Fereith demanded with a new authority in her voice. "Why did you desert my grandmother?"

"I had no choice," he muttered in answer to her first question. "Frau Kalman sent me to make sure that the children were safe. There was no other man at the *schloss* when the Herr Doktor had departed to look for you."

"It is all my fault," Fereith groaned.

"You mustn't blame yourself," Catriona comforted her. "Andrew will soon be at the chalet."

If only she could believe that, she thought. The sky above the gorge was clear and bright with stars, but there was nothing to show them if the three men had indeed reached their goal.

A light flared on the hillside and she caught her breath, thinking that it could be merely the reflection of the departing sun on one of the chalet windows, but it remained steadily in the same place, a sign if ever she needed one.

"They made it!" she cried, taking Fereith by the arm. "We mustn't worry any more. Your grandmother is safe."

They made the journey to the *schloss* in a happier state of mind, although once they got there they were almost as isolated as the little group at the chalet. The telephone wires were down, and there was no electricity. March was busy organizing a supply of candles to be inserted in the heavy iron sconces around the walls.

"It's like Christmas all over again!" one of the young nurses declared.

But without Andrew, Catriona thought, unable to still

the anxiety in her heart when she thought of that terrible journey above the gorge.

Overexcited by the events of the long day, the children were difficult to control, but soon they were settled to their evening meal. Catriona could turn to the window again. The single lamp in the chalet window still burned steadily, shining out across the valley like a distant star.

"It must mean that they are safe," Fereith said hopefully. "Andrew will bring my grandmother back in the morning when the road through the gorge is cleared."

For all their confidence, they spent a restless night, sharing a bedroom as they had done in the hotel in Innsbruck. When Fereith eventually fell asleep, Catriona got up and tiptoed to the window to look for the distant light. It was still there. Someone was keeping some sort of vigil throughout the night on the far side of the valley under the mountain wall.

CHAPTER TEN

The children were always awake early, and the following morning was no exception. They filed in to breakfast, prattling noisily about the events of the day before. To many of them avalanches were no great novelty, but some of the younger ones looked apprehensively across the valley toward the fallen snow. The air was so clear that the gorge could be seen in the minutest detail, but nothing moved across it all morning. By the time the lengthening shadows had touched its barren sides the anxiety at the *schloss* had reached fever pitch.

"I'm not staying here another minute," March declared. "I never could stand inactivity." She started to buckle on her skis. "I'm going over to the gorge."

"No, March, please!" Catriona begged. They had worked busily together with the children all day, and she was beginning to respect this strange, wayward girl who knew the mountains so intimately. "It's much too dangerous."

"If Andrew got through, so can I." March was evidently determined. "Besides, someone will attempt to get to the chalet from the village pretty soon. They're working on the other road now."

"Andrew didn't want you to take the risk," Catriona pointed out.

"Andrew wasn't worried about me." March's voice was harsh. "He wanted to make sure that you and Fereith returned to the *schloss* safely. I wonder who was his main concern," she added guardedly, "Fereith—or you."

"Fereith," Catriona said automatically. "We brought her back from Innsbruck. I suppose he wanted to make sure that she wouldn't rush off again."

"So she did take the bit between her teeth in the end?" March looked amused. "I thought she would bolt one of these days. The old lady was a fool not to have told her the truth long ago."

"You knew?" Catriona could not hide her surprise.

"I had a shrewd idea. One couldn't work for Frau Kalman for long without straightening out some of the facts for oneself." March drew on her mitts. "They both possessed the same stubborn determination, for one thing, but the old lady was almost pathetically fond of Fereith underneath all that crustiness. She doted on her in her own peculiar way, but because Gunnar had shattered all her dreams and trodden her pride in the dust she had to be sure about Fereith. Sure that the Romani blood didn't predominate, I suppose. When she saw Jeno growing up into a good looking, swaggering Romano, she was instantly on her guard because she knew that the story of Gunnar and his gipsy princess could so easily repeat itself. It was something she wanted to nip in the bud right from the beginning. Perhaps that was why Jeno always remained the menial."

"She could have sent him away a long time ago," Catriona suggested.

March shook her head. "You don't really know Frau Kalman," she said. "I suspect she took Jeno at the same time as she accepted Fereith because Gunnar insisted on it, and after she had committed herself she wouldn't go back on her word. Not until Jeno was of age."

"And by that time the damage was done," Catriona mused. "But Fereith didn't marry Jeno."

March bit her lip. "No," she said. "Maybe she had other ideas. In her own simple way she can be as obtuse as her grandmother at times. She went off to find her father without realizing who she really was, but now that she does know she will stay at Gleiberg and get down to thinking about her own happiness. The dream she had of finding her true origin has materialized in the oddest possible way and, although she will never find her father now, she does know where she truly belongs. It takes more than one dream to fill a lifetime," March added in her brisk, uncompromising way.

Catriona looked down at her hands. "Yes," she admitted, "perhaps it does."

Her own wild dream of happiness had passed and, so far, she had nothing to put in its place. Andrew would go out of her life as surely as the carriage that would take her to Zurich would pull away from the valley. A second dream could never be so bright. When she had met him again her foolish heart had soared on the wings of hope, believing that this might be the opportunity she had always wanted to clear away the mists of misunderstanding, but Andrew had turned a proud and stern face in her direction, rejecting her. The slender chance of reviving his love had never really existed, except in the secret places of her own heart.

"What do you intend to do about Robin Pettigrew?" March asked abruptly. "You were engaged to him when you came here."

"Not really engaged," said Catriona, "and that's all over now."

March didn't look quite so astonished as she might have done. "Well," she shrugged, "you know your own affairs better than I do, but the old lady must have been firmly convinced at first. She hoped Robin would settle down, you see, preferably here, at Gleiberg."

"And now he's spoiled everything by rushing back to Edinburgh in the middle of an emergency."

"Deserting her in her hour of need, you mean?" March smiled. "Do you think he was really chicken about the avalanche?"

"I can't believe he could be a coward," Catriona said, "although he wanted a great deal from life without too much of an effort."

"H'm," said March, taking up her poles. "Perhaps you're right."

Catriona shook her head. "I'm so often wrong," she said. "I could be wrong about Robin, too."

"You can find out when you meet him in Edinburgh again," March suggested.

It was the final thrust, Catriona thought. March didn't want her to stay in the valley much longer.

Watching the tall, competent figure gliding off across the snow, she was aware of another figure, also on skis, approaching across the valley floor, moving swiftly and easily now that the more hazardous slopes above the gorge had been left behind.

Andrew! Her heart leaped at the sight of the solitary figure, and she wondered what he had come to tell them. That Frau Kalman was dead? That the chalet, which looked the same, was no more than an empty shell, crushed from behind by the fall of rock and snow?

She held her breath, peering from the window until the lone skier came within the shadow of the wall and was lost to view. It was there that he would meet March; there that they would talk and perhaps decide to return together across the valley with added help. She could not bear to be kept waiting and ran out to the courtyard in spite of the intense cold that met her as soon as she opened the door.

"Kate, don't be a fool! Go inside and get a coat."

Crisply authoritative, it was Robin's voice which greeted her.

"I—where have you come from?" she gasped.

"Never mind, for the moment. Go inside. I'll fill in the details later."

She wanted to cry with relief because he had come back, because he hadn't deserted them, after all.

"Have you seen March?" she asked as she turned back to the hall.

"Yes, she's gone on to the chalet. It isn't so difficult to get across the gorge now."

She turned toward him. "You've been there," she said incredulously. "To the chalet?"

He nodded. "I'm not particularly proud of my effort," he admitted. "I got there before the second fall came down. The place was a bit of a shambles after the first one. The old lady had been hurt."

"But you were there, Robin, with her."

"Yes, I guess so, though I wasn't much of a comfort. She must have known I was scared to death." He offered her a half-rueful smile. "Don't ask me why I did it, Kate," he said. "I was going to beat it back to Zurich, but—somehow—I couldn't. The old girl knew that, too, and she was grateful."

"All she would think about was the fact that you had come back to the valley," said Catriona.

"Vindicating myself, eh?" He looked ashamed. "I'm always trying to do that, and she knows it. She's as shrewd as Lucifer, but I think she's fair. We all have our faults."

"Did you see Andrew?" she asked.

"Oh, yes, Bishop was there. You couldn't imagine him *not* being in the right place at the right moment, could you? He bound up my godmother's cuts and put a few stitches in Grete's head. He generally acted the part of the omnipotent medico, for which he will be duly rewarded, I dare say. To be absolutely fair, though," he conceded, "we did need his help."

It was a concession she had hardly expected Robin to make, but she allowed it to go unanswered.

"Was he—hurt when he didn't come back with you?" she asked.

"Not physically." Robin closed the heavy door behind him. "I think he took a knock when he saw the condition of the chalet, though. It's his property, you know."

"Yes." She was well aware of the fact. "Is it badly damaged?"

"The gable-end mostly." He turned to study her. "Your room, as a matter of fact. The avalanche just cut it clean in two, but it can be built again, if the old lady decides to stay there."

"Perhaps she won't—after this," Catriona suggested.

"Avalanches never strike twice in the same place. Like lightning," he said. "But I think she may want to come back here." He hesitated. "If they build a clinic in the valley the *schloss* would be empty, and that's something she could never stand. It would break her heart to see it left to crumble away, like so many others, for want of a suitable tenant."

Something told Catriona that he could see himself as that "suitable tenant", but the thought was fantastic. There was Fereith, who was Frau Kalman's own flesh and blood, to inherit Gleiberg. Already the determined old lady would have made plans for her granddaughter's future, and nothing Robin could do would alter them. If they included Andrew, however, Robin might bear him a consuming grudge for a very long time.

"Has Frau Kalman finally made up her mind about the clinic?" she asked.

"She's willing to subsidize it. That's all it really needs, so there goes Edinburgh and my antique shop," he shrugged.

He did not seem deeply concerned, although it had been his initial reason for coming to Gleiberg.

"I'm sorry if you're going to be disappointed," she told him.

"Something else will turn up." He was watching her closely. "You're sure you don't want to marry me, Kate? You'll never get the same chance again, y'know," he added lightly.

"Such conceit!" Her voice quavered a little. "We weren't made for each other, Robin."

"I'm not so sure about that." His tone was tinged with aggression. "I could have made you happy, and you would have been good for me, Kate."

"No," she said slowly, "we were making some sort of compromise."

He looked slightly taken aback. "I'm sorry," he apologized. "I did think you could help the situation by coming out here and meeting the old lady, but I was in love with you."

After your fashion, she thought without rancor. They had never really been suited to one another, and one day Robin would meet someone else and be equally happy with her.

Fereith came through from the kitchen as they crossed the hall. "Robin!" she exclaimed. "You?"

"Why not?" He smiled into her startled eyes. "You look as if you'd seen a ghost."

"No, not a ghost." She approached him, standing in the light from the fire. "Just you. I thought you'd gone away for good."

Standing there with the flickering orange light playing on her hair and throat; its reflection leaping like a candle-flame in her dark, expressive eyes, she was, for a moment, all Romani, small, eager and desirable. Robin took an involuntary step toward her.

"I always come back," he said. "You know that, Fereith."

She nodded, her white teeth gleaming. "Yes, I know," she said. "Did you come by the bus?"

"No, I came across from the chalet," he explained.

"I've been there since yesterday. I couldn't leave—your grandmother."

"She told you?"

"Yes." The note of banter had dropped completely from his voice. "I'm glad, Fereith. You have a family now; not a very big one, but enough to be going on with."

"Are we related, Robin?" she wanted to know.

"Not in the way you mean," he said. "There's no blood tie. Godmothers are just rather special people appointed by our parents to look after our welfare if anything should happen to them."

Fereith nodded. "You're—sort of family, though, aren't you?"

"Sort of," Robin agreed.

"What happened to March?" Fereith asked after a moment.

"She went on to the chalet. Andrew Bishop needed her help."

Fereith's brows drew together. "I wish *we* could go," she sighed. "Is the road open yet?"

He shook his head. "No, but it will be quite soon. We'll go over with the sleigh first thing in the morning," he promised. "Andrew wants to bring your grandmother back to the *schloss*."

"It's the waiting I don't like," Fereith said more than once during that seemingly endless evening while they helped with the children and shovelled snow away from the doors.

It was bitterly cold now, as if there had never been a thaw, and the sky was overcast. In the morning it began to snow again.

Robin looked anxiously across the valley.

"The gorge must be cleared by this time," he decided toward ten o'clock. "I'll get back there."

"We're coming with you," Fereith insisted. "After all—"

"Your grandmother. Yes, I know," he said. "But wouldn't it be better to wait for her here? She will need a lot of attention for a very long while."

It was the first indication he had given them that Frau Kalman had sustained more than "just a few cuts", and Catriona looked at him sharply as Fereith turned away.

"Bishop was concerned about her," he murmured. "She had a high temperature and there was some damage to her hip."

"Then don't stand in Fereith's way," Catriona advised. "Take her with you."

"What about you?" he asked.

"I was coming, in any case. You forget that I came to Gleiberg to nurse her."

He looked relieved. "March Lazenby irritates her, so I expect she'll be glad to see you. So will Bishop, no doubt," he added.

"He has two patients on his hands," Catriona said almost to herself. "He must need somebody."

They set out immediately, covering the distance to the gorge without difficulty. It was snowing fast, however, and the narrow passage between the rocks already had a fresh covering on it. Snow and rubble were piled high on either side, and some of the men on the clearance squad were still working as they passed, but the snowplough would go through again on its way back to the village and that would be a help. The dense cloud formation to the north, however, was a warning of more and heavier snow to come.

It was amazing how quickly the scene could change, Catriona thought—from smiling blue skies to clouds as gray and threatening as any she had ever seen.

When the chalet finally came into view, she gasped in

astonishment. Most of it was intact, standing solidly on its rocky plateau with the wood behind it and the road leading to it cleared, as if Andrew had worked far into the night to keep the way open for them. On the far side, however, a narrow wedge of destruction had ploughed its way through the pines, driving trees, rocks and snow before it until it had plunged over the edge of the plateau to the valley below, taking the entire gable end of the chalet with it.

That the house had stood up at all seemed to be a miracle, and she sat frozen into silence as she looked at it. The roof was undamaged, she noticed, and had sheltered two injured people throughout the night.

Someone had lit a fire in the stove, and the thin spiral of blue wood-smoke rose encouragingly into the still, cold air. March came to the door to greet them.

"I'm glad you've come," she admitted. "We do need help. Andrew is a bit anxious about Frau Kalman." She looked directly at Robin. "She's been asking for you," she told him. "She seems to think you might have gone back to Edinburgh."

Robin got down from the sleigh. "Surprise, surprise, then," he said lightly, although a small pulse of annoyance began to hammer in his jaw. "I don't suppose you tried to disillusion her."

"I didn't know," March pointed out. "I only met you briefly on your way to the *schloss*."

Robin helped Catriona from the sleigh. She went past March to find Andrew waiting in the hallway. He looked tired, but relieved to see them.

"The place is a bit of a shambles," he apologized, "but we'll get out as quickly as we can. I want to get Frau Kalman back to the *schloss*. We may need to operate on her thigh, but I'll wait for the Professor's verdict when he returns from Zurich."

He had spoken to her as a colleague, someone necessary in the fight to save the old lady's life.

"What happened?" she asked.

"She slipped coming down the stairs on her own. It had nothing to do with the avalanche," he added abruptly. "Make her comfortable for the journey, Kate. I can't leave her here. It would be taking too big a risk. Besides, she belongs at Gleiberg. I think she realizes that now."

"Because of Fereith?"

He nodded, looking about him at the havoc wrought by the avalanche; the chaos of fallen plaster and scattered furniture. However, the stove, the center of the homestead, was intact and burning fiercely. She spread out her hands to its comforting warmth.

"I'm sorry about your home," she said.

He glanced up at the exposed rafters. "It's mostly superficial damage," he explained. "It can soon be put right. It was only your room at the end of the corridor upstairs that was completely demolished, but we've managed to salvage most of your belongings. The wall was taken out as clean as a whistle. That's how these things happen." He glanced toward the staircase as Robin and Fereith came in together. "One visitor at a time," he cautioned. "You can go up with Kate," he said to Fereith.

For a moment Robin looked as if he might dispute his authority, and then he shrugged.

"You're the doctor," he conceded, "but she did ask to see me."

"Later," Andrew agreed.

Fereith and Catriona went up the wide pine staircase together and along the gallery to the corridor where the doors opened into the bedrooms. At the far end they could see daylight slanting through the rough boards Andrew had nailed in place across the gable end of the passageway. The intense winter cold came rushing to meet them. When they opened Frau Kalman's door, however, they were greeted by the warmth from a portable stove that had probably been burning throughout the night. Catriona's eyes went immediately to the bed where her employer lay.

In the vast four-poster Frau Kalman looked incredibly small. She seemed to have shrunk since their last meeting, and her eyes were tightly closed. A small, hurt sound escaped Fereith as she crossed the floor.

Catriona stood quite still, watching the meeting between this strange old woman and the granddaughter whom she had failed to acknowledge until now. Fereith hesitated a couple of feet away from the bed, unable, it seemed, to take that final step. The heavy lids lifted to look at her. When recognition came, Frau Kalman attempted to raise herself among her pillows. "Help me," she said.

Catriona went instinctively to her side, slipping her arm beneath the thin shoulder-blades, but the sharp blue eyes never left Fereith's face.

"Come here, child!" she commanded.

Fereith went forward, flinging herself on her knees beside the bed. "I'm sorry!" she cried. "You were so good to me."

"I was a fool!" The old lady felt for her hand. "If you weep you'll distress me, child. Dry your eyes and tell me where you have been. You needn't try to tell me why you went away," she added tersely, "because I already know. I only have myself to blame for that. I should have told you who you were long ago."

Fereith nodded, wiping her eyes with the sleeve of her dress. "But I loved you, anyway," she said shakily. "I don't know why I wanted to find anybody else."

For the first time the blue eyes wavered. "I've been a

hard and irrational old woman," Frau Kalman acknowledged. "I've been like that all my life."

"No," Fereith said fiercely. "You were kind. All the children at the *schloss* love you."

"Which might be compensation enough," she murmured as a spasm of pain crossed her face.

It was physical pain, and Catriona eased her position on the bed.

"Ask Doctor Bishop to come," she said to Fereith.

Andrew was at her elbow almost immediately.

"We'll carry her down in blankets," he decided after a swift examination. "It's a chance I have to take. March is filling hotwater bottles, and Robin is doing what he can to make the sleigh more comfortable."

"Do you think she'll be all right?" Catriona could not resist the question because, suddenly, this was a personal thing.

"I hope so," Andrew said, "and we haven't a great deal of choice, anyway. I have to get her to Gleiberg before the gorge closes again." He looked down at her for a split second. "Thank you for coming, Kate," he said. "It's twice as easy when one has professional help."

March had packed a suitcase for her and put it beside the front door. "I though you might like to have your belongings," she said. "It looks as if the chalet has had it."

Catriona met her eyes squarely. "Andrew doesn't seem to think so," she said. "But thanks for packing my things, March. It was—a good idea," she ended lamely as Andrew came toward them.

"You won't be coming back," March said under her breath. "Andrew means to keep the old lady at the *schloss*."

Andrew glanced through the open door. "If you're going to ski down, March, you'd better be on your way," he said. "If not, Robin can take you in the other sleigh."

"How are you going?" March asked, although she must have been prepared for his answer.

"I'll be with my patient," he said.

Grete was already in the smaller sleigh, looking slightly dazed by the events of the past 48 hours, her head swathed in bandages beneath her fur-lined hood. The two man who had come up with Andrew seemed to have disappeared.

"They've gone on ahead to make sure about the gorge," Andrew explained a few minutes later as they carried Frau Kalman step by difficult step down the staircase. "The condition of the snow will make all the difference. Is there anything else you want in the house before I lock up?"

"Nothing," said Catriona. "March put all my belongings together."

Determined not to leave her grandmother's side, Fereith planted herself securely in the larger sleigh opposite the old lady who was laid carefully along the back seat. Catriona climbed in beside her. Andrew flicked the whip an inch above the horse's flank.

"We'll have to take it slowly," he said.

They were an odd little procession pulling away from the chalet with the snow blurring their vision: March skiing ahead of the first sleigh and disappearing occasionally to cut across a snowfield, and Robin in the rear with Grete and the luggage. They had taken all they could from the chalet, personal possessions mostly, while the rest was left to its fate. The bulk of the sturdy pine furniture would withstand falling plaster without much damage. Grete, in spite of the five stitches in her head, had covered the more precious pieces with blue-and-white checked dust-sheets, that suggested that the little house might only be waiting for a fresh occupier, due any day.

From the road there was nothing to be seen of the boarded-up passageway, but Andrew had drawn the ash from the stove, and the welcoming spiral of wood smoke was no longer visible.

They reached the gorge to find March waiting for them. "The snowplough has just gone through," she announced. "We're in luck."

It was a slow, ponderous journey down into the valley and up again on the other side. Frau Kalman lay with her eyes closed, but when Catriona bent over her she smiled.

"You're good children," she said faintly. "All of you!"

Out on the box Andrew was no more than a vague snow-shape holding the reins as he urged the stout, odd-colored little cob to the main incline below the *schloss*. He was going as fast as he dared in the circumstances, but when they reached the gentle slope leading to the bridge he allowed the sturdy animal to have its head and it thundered across the wooden planks at a brisk trot. Far beneath them the waterfall roared its challenge, splashing over the rocks in a dozen angry cataracts to be submerged, at last, in the broad river winding along the valley floor.

The falling snow had spread a white carpet all the way up to the *schloss*, as virginal as the slopes above it, and something caught in Catriona's throat as she looked at it. The *schloss* was like a fairy castle, turreted and peaked in white, with the vast silences of the mountains all about it, closing it in. She knew that she would never forget it, and the weeks she had spent in the shadow of these Alpine giants that Andrew knew so well, although the memory of her stay would always be touched with pain.

Willing, professional hands in plenty came to carry Frau Kalman into her ancient home as soon as Andrew stopped the sleigh. The nursing staff had been prepared for this emergency, and a room on the west side of the house was ready to receive her. It had a high bed in one corner and simple furniture that could easily be removed if an operation was really necessary.

It was the sight of Professor Zorn, however, which reassured Catriona more than anything else.

"I'm glad you're here," Andrew said, shaking him warmly by the hand. "I wondered if you would get through."

"It was touch and go after I left the main road," the Professor confessed, "and when I heard that you were in trouble how could I turn back? Besides," he added. "I have good news about the new clinic to give to Frau Kalman that will make her want to recover!"

"That—and Fereith," Andrew agreed, leading him into the library, which he used as an office. "But perhaps we could have a word before you see her?"

For the first time Catriona realized just how tired she was. The events of the past few days had followed each other so quickly that she had hardly had time to sleep, and now she seemed to be confronted with a vast expanse of nothingness in which she had little to do but think. Frau Kalman was surrounded by nurses. It seemed as if her usefulness to her employer was at an end.

Professor Zorn told her that Andrew would need her help at the operation.

"Our nurses in Gleiberg are fully trained in child welfare, but not in the operating theater," he explained. "Andrew would be more satisfied if we had your help."

So Andrew needed her once more, professionally, it was true, but he still needed her. There was bittersweet satisfaction in the thought as she changed into her uniform and helped to prepare the room for the emergency operation that Frau Kalman needed.

It lasted over an hour, but the time passed as if it had been five minutes, with Andrew directing her when she felt unsure, and the Professor administering the anesthetic sitting at the patient's head on a high stool brought from the kitchen. When the bone was finally pinned into place Andrew straightened with a great sigh of relief.

"It was easier than I thought," he said. "She's an amazing old woman—as tough as nails. Now it's up to you, Kate, to see that she doesn't get onto her feet too soon."

Catriona looked surprised.

"Why not?" He was looking down at her with a firm demand in his eyes. "You came out here to nurse her. One defection back to Edinburgh will be enough."

"Robin has to go," she reminded him.

"But you needn't," he said. "It's as simple as that."

She hesitated. "Now that Frau Kalman is back at the *schloss*—"

"She will still need you," he insisted. "You know the sort of special nursing she has to have, and if you are in any doubt you can come to me or to the Professor."

She nodded, too exhausted to argue with him. "How long will I be needed?" she asked.

"For a month or two, perhaps more."

The words were like a reprieve echoing, again and again, in the lonely places of her heart, yet these months could hold pain and sorrow for her beyond enduring.

CHAPTER ELEVEN

Andrew went to Zurich a week later to pick up some medical supplies and to confer with Frau Kalman's lawyers about the proposed new clinic at Gleiberg. He was away for ten days, while Professor Zorn took over at the *schloss*, considering it a holiday.

Robin had left Gleiberg the day after his godmother's operation, but had been allowed to sit with her for half an hour before he left. Otto was instructed to take him all the way to Zurich and see him onto the London jet.

"She still treats me like a kid," he had said to Catriona half resentfully. "Otto used to do this years ago, when I was going back to England to school. She doesn't credit me with much sense, but I may be able to prove her wrong one of these days. At the back of her mind she's toying with the idea of me marrying Fereith eventually. Maybe I'll come back some day and ask her." He had looked her straight in the eyes then. "My godmother's a shameless old matchmaker, y'know. It's what she's wanted ever since she sent for me to come out here. You see, she fancied you were in love with the English doctor. Are you?"

It was the most painful question Catriona had ever been compelled to answer. "Yes," she said truthfully.

Robin had not expressed any surprise. He had gazed at her for a long time, kissed her on the cheek, and gone away.

The days passed swiftly enough. Frau Kalman was an exacting patient, eager to be back on her feet as she gathered strength and unwilling to relegate her accepted tasks to anyone else. It was plain that she was glad to return to her old home, although she would never have done so if the plans for a larger clinic were not well to the fore. "We'll have this, and that," she told the Professor a dozen times each day. "I have the money, and you and Andrew have the skill. We can do it between us. We'll recruit more nurses, from England, if need be."

At this juncture she would look meaningfully in Catriona's direction, but Catriona could not commit herself. How could she work with Andrew for the rest of her life, loving him hopelessly like this?

When he returned from Zurich he seemed more than satisfied with his visit. "The clinic's in the bag!" he said. "They can start building in the spring."

"What will you do about the chalet?" Catriona asked involuntarily.

He took a full minute to answer her question. "The damage will have to be properly assessed," he said, "and then I can rebuild. While the construction people are up here working on the clinic, it will be easy enough to arrange."

"I see." Her heart filled up with a vague disappointment. "I thought you might want to stay at the clinic."

"I need a home," he said almost abruptly.

Whenever she looked up at the chalet after that she imagined it complete again, with the roof mended and the wall at the gable-end repaired.

It was the first week in February before Frau Kalman was out of bed, but as soon as she could propel herself in a wheelchair she was managing the affairs of the *schloss* and getting in everyone's way.

"I know I'm an old meddler," she said to Catriona on one occasion, "but it's in my blood and I can't help it. I've had to manage on my own for so long. If there was a man about the place, now—apart from Andrew, of course—I believe I would gladly hand over the reins and retire gracefully to utter boredom."

"I can't imagine it," Catriona told her. "You would find something else to do. Another dream."

"The world is full of dreams." The old lady pushed aside her breakfast tray. "Foolish dreams, broken dreams, and dreams that never could come true. I dreamed of a son to be proud of once—"

Her voice trailed away in pursuit of a memory, and her eyes misted over with disappointment, but not for long.

"Andrew brought me the plans of the new clinic this morning," she said. "I told him to show them to you and ask your advice about the nurses' quarters. There's nothing like experience for rooting out the snags. Did he consult you?"

Catriona shook her head. "Perhaps he was too busy," she suggested.

"Go and ask him, then," her employer commanded. "Nobody should be too busy to think about the future."

It was an order which she was expected to obey immediately, but Catriona went slowly down the staircase, wondering how she was going to discuss the future with Andrew. His future but not her own!

The main rooms were deserted at that time of day. Most of the children were out on the nursery slopes under March's expert supervision, while the others were resting or performing the exercises in the gymnasium that would strengthen their pitifully weak limbs, helping them to walk again.

She glanced into the library, but it was empty, too. Andrew must have gone out with the Professor or with March.

As she turned to retrace her steps, the bell outside the main entrance sent a peal like thunder through the quiet hall. She crossed the stone flags to answer it.

Outside, standing in the winter sunshine, was a man who seemed vaguely familiar. He was middle-aged, tall, and lean; his dark hair under his peaked cap was touched with gray. He had a lined, weatherbeaten face out of which looked a pair of the bluest eyes she had ever seen. They reminded her of someone—someone she knew very well.

"I would like to speak to Frau Kalman," the stranger said.

"Will you come in?" She still felt that odd sense of recognition.

Frau Kalman's visitor walked ahead of her into the hall, looking about him with curiosity, making her think, suddenly, of Jeno. And then she knew who he was. It was the man who had been with Jeno all those weeks ago, in Austria.

"I've seen you before," she told him as someone came through the baize door from the gymnasium. It was Andrew.

The stranger hesitated, looking beyond her.

"Gunnar?" Andrew asked quietly.

"How did you know?"

"You are sufficiently like your mother, in looks, at least. She never really believed that you were dead." Andrew came forward to shake his hand. "My name's Bishop—Andrew Bishop. I'm the doctor here and your mother's physician. I hope you have come to stay."

"It will depend on—my mother." Gunnar Kalman smiled for the first time. "On her final decision."

"We can't wait for other people's decisions all the time," Andrew said briskly. "Go up and tell her you've come home. She'll accept that."

The older man hesitated. "Fereith?" he asked.

"She's with her grandmother, I expect. She went up the back stairs a moment ago."

An odd look broke in Gunnar's eyes. "I couldn't tell her the truth when Jeno brought her to Innsbruck," he said, "but I had to see her. It was a sort of hunger in me for my own flesh and blood."

"Fereith felt it, too," Andrew said quietly. "She was determined to find you."

"I should have sought her out long ago, but I had nothing to offer her. Nothing compared with this." Gunnar looked about him once more. "It hasn't changed," he said.

Andrew glanced toward the stairs.

"You have an hour before the children come in," he said. "It's the third door on the west block—the oak room. You know your way."

Gunnar still hesitated. "I'd like to feel sure of my welcome."

"You can waste your life, waiting to be sure," Andrew told him. "I can speak from experience. Up you go, man, and chance your luck."

Gunnar looked around at Catriona. "Thank you," he said as he started to mount the stairs.

"He seems terribly frail," Catriona said.

"He's probably led a hard life, and there's no doubt that he's worried about Fereith."

"Yet he left her all those years ago to be brought up by someone else."

"He probably felt that she belonged here."

"I wonder if he'll stay."

"I think so. There's plenty of work for him to do at Gleiberg."

"Frau Kalman said you had the plans of the new clinic." She forced a smile. "She also said you might need my expert advice."

He turned to look at her. "What's so odd about that, Kate?" he asked. "Will you come and see the plans now? I think we ought to give the—family upstairs plenty of time to adjust to the new order of things."

He led the way into the library where he found the plans and spread them on the desk.

"We're started small," he explained, bending over them with her, "but we'll expand and build as we go along. Fifty children for a start, and 100 by the end of the following year. It's been an ambition of mine for a very long time," he confessed. "A dream we used to share."

"Yes." The color fled from her cheeks and her heart felt cold with regret. "I let you down. But there were other things—other commitments, I suppose you could call them."

"At the time," he said, "but your mother married again, I understand. Gordon went to university on a grant. Why didn't you write to me then?"

"Because we had parted in anger and—and you told me yourself that you wanted to keep it that way."

"When?" he demanded.

"Not so long ago." She tried to steady her voice, although he must see how her hand trembled as she held down the linen roll of the plan. "When I first went to the chalet and found my photograph in your room."

"I was still angry," he admitted, "and confused. You were going to marry Pettigrew, and Frau Kalman was convinced that you had been deliberately sent out to soften her up to make the way easy for him."

Her heart twisted with pain at the thought of his contempt. "Did you believe that?" she asked him in a frozen whisper.

"I didn't know what to believe at first," he told her bluntly. "But one thing I did know. I was no longer bitter about the past. I didn't need the photograph Fereith had put in your room to remind me any more. I realized how wrong I had been to storm out in a huff and never try to reach you again. It was a sort of foolish pride, in which you had some share," he reminded her.

"I still think I was right in the first place," she said heavily. "My mother had worked so hard all her life. She wanted to see me qualify, and so did my grandmother, who had cared for me as a child. There was Gordon, too, and Jenny, still to educate. I had an uncle who used to say that Education, with a capital "e", was the curse of the Scottish working class. They sacrificed too much for it, but I don't regret helping Gordon."

"You had to do that," he said. "It was my point of view that was slightly out of focus at the time. Wanting to come first, I suppose."

"But now you are content." She gazed down at the plan they were holding. "A clinic has always been your dearest wish, except, perhaps Harley Street."

"Harley Street is out." He took the plan from her, letting it spring back into its original roll. "There's something else I have to show you."

He took a smaller roll of linen from a drawer in the desk and spread it out before her. It seemed to be the outline design for a house.

"I had this done while I was in Zurich," he explained.

"It's—the chalet!" she exclaimed eagerly. "You intend to rebuild right away?"

"That will depend on you, Kate. I'll need your advice about that, too."

He was standing close behind her, and when she looked up her head touched his shoulder.

"I'm asking you to marry me," he said. "I'm asking for a second chance. Kate, don't you understand? We were young, and I hadn't enough sense to ask for a straightforward explanation of why you said 'no' to me that first time. Youth is like that, all pride and reserve and hurt." He took her by the shoulders, turning her to face him. "Whatever we did to one another, whatever we said in anger and regretted a thousand times afterward, doesn't count any more. We love each other."

She couldn't speak, standing there waiting for his kiss. As if he no longer needed confirmation of all he had said, he took her face between his hands and pressed his lips gently against hers.

"Kate," he said again, "don't you understand?"

"Now, I do!" She clung to him as if she would never let him go. "Drew!" For the first time she used the contraction of his name that had come so naturally during their student days. Pride had gone, and that awful reserve which had silenced them both in the past. "I've never stopped loving you. I knew that as soon as I came out here, half engaged to Robin. It was all wrong, but I didn't come out for any ulterior motive. You must believe me."

"I ceased to think that a long time ago," he confessed with his lips on her hair. "It was a kind of jealousy, Kate, a fierce desire to discredit you to my heart, but it wouldn't work. After all the disappointment and bitterness had seeped away, I still wanted you." Fiercely he gathered her into his arms. "You and nobody else, and this time there must be no sacrifices. It's up to you to say yes or no to the clinic idea."

"If you need me," she said, kissing him in return, "I want to stay."

"I need you." His arms were like a band of steel about her, binding her to the valley she had come to love. "It will be a full life for both of us, Kate, but Switzerland isn't so far away from Scotland, after all. We can visit, whenever we wish."

"This is where I want to be," she said, looking down at the plan of the chalet. "You haven't changed it very much."

"I designed it with the thought of you in my mind, even

in those days, I suppose," he confessed, "and then I lived in it until I couldn't stand the loneliness and the memories any more. It was then that Frau Kalman suggested we might swop places, but now it seems as if the wheel has turned full circle for both of us." He looked through the open door toward the staircase. "She will need the *schloss* in future. You and I will go across the valley to our own home."

After a while they examined the outline drawings and, when she became used to them, she saw that the west gable had been completely redesigned.

"It won't exist," Andrew explained. "We're making that end of the house into a loggia with a sun-balcony above, leading from the master bedroom where we can look down the valley and watch the new clinic taking shape."

"I can hardly wait!" she declared. "I can hardly believe that all this is really true."

"You will." His arm tightened a fraction. "There's no need for waiting now, Kate. We've squandered enough of our time together as it is. You've no real reason to go back to Edinburgh, have you? We can send for your belongings and be ready to move in when the chalet is ready for us."

"How long will it take to rebuild?" she wanted to know.

"A month—not more. We can be married in April."

"When the snow has gone, and all the wild flowers are out in the secret places among the mountains!"

"Who told you that?"

"Fereith. Do you think she'll marry Robin one day?"

He considered her question. "I don't think she'll marry anyone for a very long time," he answered. "She's far too engrossed with finding a family and settling down at the *schloss*."

"I know she'll be happy!"

He kissed her cheek. "Everyone is going to be happy," he said.

NOT WANTED ON VOYAGE

NOT WANTED
ON VOYAGE

Kay Thorpe

Leigh Garratt was going to dump her off ship at Cape Town—not because she didn't do her job and not because she'd stupidly mistaken the *Antarctic Star* for the *Atlantic Star*, but simply because she was a woman!

Recalling her gruelling years of hard work, Tracy Redfern thought it grossly unfair not to be taken seriously in her profession.

Even more humiliating was the fact that the captain himself barely tolerated her. ''To put it bluntly,'' he had said coldly, ''you represent a distraction the crew can do without!''

As the ship's doctor, Tracy had to appear cool and professional—rather difficult to do when she'd fallen in love with the captain.

CHAPTER ONE

The ship was berthed at the far end of the dock; her lights welcoming beacons in the gathering mist. She had long since completed loading. The cranes along the quay were still and gaunt; fingers of steel piercing the night.

Tracy paused at the foot of the gangway, huddling down into the comforting warmth of her thick jacket, eyes traveling over the looming bulk before her, seeking out the letters painted on the bows. From where she stood it was impossible to discern the full name, but the big white STAR that could be picked out was reassuring. The tramp steamer *Atlantic Star*, sailing early tomorrow morning for the West Indies and South America; taking her with it in the one capacity aboard such a vessel as this where her sex became of secondary importance to her qualifications.

True, had there been other applicants for the post, conventionalism might not have been so easily overcome, if at all. But there hadn't, and desperation could always outweigh doubt. So here she was, relief medical officer for the duration of this one round trip lasting the better part of the next three months.

Long enough, Tracy thought wryly, to sort out and learn to control her own emotions, if nothing else.

Coincidentally, it was just three months to the day since she had first met Derek. Three months since she had walked into the surgery at Glenfall Road and fallen in love with the thin, serious-faced man she was to work for and with. Not that she had acknowledged it at the time, of course. No, full realization of what was happening to her had come later, much later when she had found herself envying Dorothy her right to be with him when she herself could not.

Even then she hadn't been able to bring herself to leave him. Not until the day when she had surprised a reflection of her own emotions in his eyes and come sharply to her senses. Desperate to flee a situation that could only become unbearable for them both, she had grasped at the possible solution unwittingly put forward by a patient who had a son in the offices of the company that owned the *Atlantic Star*. Derek hadn't attempted to dissuade her intention of leaving the practice. He had known as well as she that it was the only thing to do.

The mournful hoot of a tug out on the river brought her back to the present again with a little start. Once more she searched the hull that was to be her home during these coming weeks, admitting to a certain apprehension concerning her reception aboard: they had warned her at her interview that she could be expected to encounter hostility to some extent amongst the crew. Not that such an attitude would be anything new. Even in this so-called enlightened age, there were plenty of people in all walks of life who still distrusted the qualifications of the woman doctor.

Unconsciously she squared her shoulders before picking up her cases and making her way up the latticed treads of the gangway.

Standing on the dimly lit deck a moment later, she had the fleeting and quite ridiculous conviction that the ship was deserted. The swirling vapor cloaked everything in the same shifting, changing grayness, muffling sight and sound alike. Then just ahead of her something moved, and a voice broke the stillness.

"Who's that? What's your business?"

"M.O. reporting for duty," stated Tracy succinctly, as the owner of the voice materialized into a comforting, blue-jerseyed reality. "Would you mind telling me where I can find the Captain, please?"

There was a brief silence, and when the man spoke again it was in far less certain tones.

"Did you say you were the new M.O.?"

"That's right." Tracy waited, wondering why the watch hadn't been told what to expect. It was pretty obvious that her appearance had taken him aback. "I am expected?" she prompted.

"Er—yes," he said, not sounding at all sure. Again the pause while he simply stood looking at her, the mist writhing between them like something alive. Tracy began to get impatient. Surprised he might be, but any hand deemed responsible enough to be on watch at all should have learned by now to take the unexpected in his stride.

As if in response to her thoughts he suddenly seemed to make up his mind.

"Look," he said, "can you just hang on here for a moment or two? I'd better get the duty officer."

Tracy didn't seem to have much choice. He was gone before she could open her mouth. Silence settled about her once more, and she leaned wearily against the rail at her back, wondering for the thousandth time if she was really doing the right thing. Even under the circumstances this had been a pretty drastic step to take. Removal to another part of the country would have done equally well.

No, that wasn't quite true, another part of her mind retorted swiftly. One practice was much the same as another no matter where it was situated; the familiar routine would only have served to remind her. At least, here on board ship there would be a great deal that was totally new to occupy her thoughts—and hadn't she always wanted to travel?

Footsteps rang on the deckplates. Her accoster of a

moment or two ago hove into view once more, this time accompanied by two other men. It was to one of the latter that Tracy's attention was immediately drawn: a man whose height and girth would have drawn comment at a convention of heavyweight wrestlers. Fairly tall for a woman herself, she felt dwarfed beside this black-bearded giant.

"I'm afraid I'm a little later than I should have been," she offered in somewhat tentative apology, unable to stop her eyes from straying in fascinated speculation to the straining buttons of his dark blue jacket. "There was a hold-up on the railway line. I only arrived about 20 minutes ago."

Slowly the man roused himself from his own contemplation of the slender, pant-clad figure and pure, feminine features framed by the pale hair that was only partially concealed beneath the carelessly knotted silk scarf. His expression, or what Tracy could see of it through the fog and beard, held an anger she could only hope wasn't directed at herself.

"The swabs!" he exclaimed wrathfully. "The stupid bungling swabs! No wonder they forgot to send any details."

Tracy stared at him uncomprehendingly, not a little unnerved by his vehemence.

"Is—is something wrong?" she ventured, and instantly regretted the foolish question. It was perfectly plain to anyone but a complete moron that something was very wrong indeed.

"I'll say there is," growled the giant. "You're female!"

Realization dawned suddenly and completely. "You mean they didn't tell you that?"

"I mean they didn't tell us. All we received was your estimated time of arrival." He studied her anew, putting up a huge hand to tip back his cap and scratch his head with the air of one impaled upon the horns of a dilemma. "There's going to be the dickens to pay over this, or my name's not Mike Jackson! Leigh'll go crazy."

That would be the Captain he was talking about, Tracy surmised. Mentally condemning the person or persons who had landed her with this situation to penal servitude for life, she said staunchly, "I daresay he'll get over it. Hadn't you better take me to see him?"

Once again he seemed to weigh the pros and cons, then with a swift glance at his wristwatch, he reached a decision.

"Better to leave that till morning, all things considered. We'll be sailing in less than half an hour. I'll—" He stopped and looked at her inquiringly, as she made a small sound of surprise.

"Did you say half an hour?" Tracy asked. "I understood the ship wasn't due to sail until morning."

"So far as I know there's been no change in schedule. Those crazy landlubbers and head office will have that wrong, too! Just throw out anything else they told you and start from scratch. Most of 'em have never been near a ship in their lives." He turned back to the younger man who had been standing by. "You'd better show our new M.O. where his—I mean her cabin is. And keep your mouth shut about this. What the Skipper doesn't know won't trouble him."

"I really think. . . ." Tracy began, but the vast bulk was already disappearing into the fog.

Her allotted guide bent and lifted the suitcase from the deck, holding out his other hand for the black leather bag in hers. He seemed somewhat at a loss for words. Tracy gave him the bag, suppressing the desire to ask him to be careful with her precious equipment.

"I gather you're one of my fellow officers?" she prompted as they walked along the deck together.

"Yes," he said, walked a few more paces, then added, "Third Officer Peter Cramer, to use my full handle."

"And I'm Tracy Redfern," she said, uncertain as to whether her name had accompanied the sparse information imparted by the company office. As the other officers hadn't bothered to ask, it seemed likely that it had, but it would do no harm to repeat it.

For the first time a smile touched his features beneath the peaked cap, and he gave her a swift sideways glance.

"Nice to have you aboard, Dr. Redfern."

"Thanks," she returned feelingly. "It's nice to know I'm welcomed by *someone*."

"Oh, don't mind the Chief too much. You were a bit of a shock, that's all. We were expecting a man."

"Naturally," said Tracy a little dryly. "What was all that about the Captain? Surely he's as capable as anyone else of getting over a shock?"

"Most, I'd say. You might be a different proposition. That's what the Chief's afraid of." He hesitated. "You see, the Skipper has this . . . er . . . thing about . . . er . . . women."

Her brow wrinkled a little. "I'm not sure that I follow you."

"Well, he's a . . . woman-hater, I suppose you could call it."

"Oh!" Tracy said, and felt her heart plummet sharply downward before her normal sound sense reasserted itself. "He sounds delightful. Does the office know about this . . . this *thing* he has against members of my sex?"

"Couldn't say. It's no particular secret here, so it's quite possible, I suppose. It would certainly explain why they were so cagey about you."

"Meaning they decided to present him with a *fait accompli* rather than argue it out with him?"

"Meaning they decided to send you unannounced

because they knew he wouldn't listen to any arguments."

"But surely they didn't have to accept his word. They could simply have ordered him to accept me, regardless of his own feelings on the subject. He's only an employee like the rest of us, isn't he?"

"Not him. He's a shareholder in the Company—quite a big one. If he'd said no, there was little anyone back there could have done about it."

"So they threw me in at the deep end to swim or sink on my own," she said on a faint note of bitterness and came to a sudden halt. "I think I'd better see him tonight after all and get this sorted out. Will you take me to him?"

"Sorry," he returned comfortably, "I can't. I'm under orders to take you straight to your cabin. In any case, I'd leave it to the Chief, if I were you. Once we've sailed he'll do all the explaining that's necessary."

That was something, Tracy supposed, unable to repress a certain sense of relief over her companion's refusal to meet her request. By the time she did see the Captain, the worst would be over. Not that it would make that meeting any pleasanter. She had formed a vivid mental picture of the man: beefy, red-faced and loudly self-opinionated. The type who hated all women because of his own failure to attract the opposite sex. It was going to be a charming voyage.

They had reached the superstructure up for'ard, and now the route led down into the hull via a steep companionway. From the bottom an alleyway ran athwartships, with others opening off it. Down one of these the young officer now turned, passing three closed doors before stopping and dropping her suitcase to the floor to open the fourth.

The cabin was quite roomy and surprisingly unlike Tracy's preconceptions of the kind of accommodation likely to be found on a tramp steamer. Warm woodwork greeted her eyes, its sheen reflecting the vibrant blue of the cover on the bunk set against one bulkhead. Matching curtains shielded the porthole, and some of the same material had been used to make a cushion for the small leather armchair standing squarely before a well-polished writing desk.

Peter grinned, noting her reactions.

"Oh yes, they do us proud. They have to. Spending as much time at sea as we do, we deserve only the best."

Tracy smiled back at him, seeing him properly for the first time. What she saw she liked. Slightly over medium height, and of the wiry build which rarely ran to fat, nice brown eyes, wavy brown hair. Handsome . . . no. But there was a great deal of charm in the curve of his mouth. He would, she judged, be about 25, which placed him on a par with herself.

"Have you been with this particular ship very long?" she asked as he hoisted her suitcase onto the bunk.

"This will be my third year," he answered, and his smile suddenly died. "And probably my last," he added in an undertone.

Aware of the swift change of mood, Tracy said casually, "You're thinking of changing ships, then?"

"No, I'm thinking of changing my job." He turned, meeting her eyes with a small wry movement of his shoulders. "An ultimatum from my fiancée. She objects to being left on her own for months at a time."

"Oh, I see." Tracy took the keys from her pocket and moved over to insert them in the lock. "Well, that's understandable, I suppose. Being a sailor's wife must be a pretty lonely affair at times."

"But it has its compensations. Good money, plenty of time off. There aren't many jobs ashore that can offer as much." He leaned his back up against the opposite bulkhead with the air of one about to get a load off his chest. "The problem is that I can't seem to get it through to Deirdre just how different things are going to be if I do get a shore job. She's going to expect me to be able to give her the same kind of good times she's been used to this last two years."

What was it about a medical degree that automatically made one a confessor? Tracy wondered with a flash of irritation. Doctors were expected to be so many things to the layman: saviors of happiness as well as health.

Perhaps because the two are interwoven, the small voice of conscience whispered in her ear and felt suddenly ashamed.

"Are you quite certain she doesn't understand?" she asked mildly. "Perhaps having a good time becomes a very secondary consideration compared with having you near her all year round."

"But don't you think—" he began and stopped abruptly as a loud buzzing noise resounded through the cabin.

The sound came from a ventilated box hanging on the bulkhead near to the bunk, which at first sight Tracy had taken to be some kind of air-conditioning outlet. Peter went over to it, flicked down a switch on the side and spoke into the grille.

"Cramer here."

"My God, are you still down there!" The booming tones were instantly recognizable even through the distorting effects of the crackling intercom. "How the hell long does it take you to do a simple job like pointing out a cabin?"

"Just on my way up, Chief," returned Peter placatingly. "Only making sure Dr. Redfern was comfortable."

"That's the steward's job, not yours. Get back up here and finish your watch." A pause, and a change of tone.

"Put the doctor on, will you? The Skipper wants to welcome our new M.O. aboard."

And how was she to handle this? Tracy thought a little wildly. From the Mate's careful avoidance of the feminine pronoun, it wasn't hard to deduce that he hadn't yet imparted the news. Was she somehow expected to continue the deception even now?

Another voice came on; clipped, precise. "Sorry there hasn't been time to greet you in person, Doctor, but no doubt you'll be ready for a good night's sleep after your journey. There will be a steward down shortly with a hot drink and some food. I look forward to meeting you in the morning."

Tracy managed a strangled "Thank you", trusting to the intercom to sufficiently conceal the feminine intonations of her voice. There was a short, expectant silence. Then she could almost see the man shrug as he switched off with an audible click.

"Tricky moment," Peter commented from the door. "I'll bet the Chief was holding his breath in case you blew the gaff."

"I should have done just that," she said, sinking nervously to a seat on the edge of the bunk. "What difference could it make now? I'm already on board."

"A world of difference. I'd say that the Skipper would rather delay sailing than take a woman along—and time is money to everyone on board." He grinned cheerfully at her. "I shouldn't let it worry you too much. The Chief will sort it all out before morning. And that's not the only thing he'll be sorting out if I don't get back."

Aware of a sudden strong reluctance to be left alone, Tracy sought to detain him a little longer, even if only for a minute or two.

"The fog," she said. "It was getting quite thick. Will we really be able to sail in this kind of weather?"

His reply didn't even take a quarter of a minute.

"It's only a river mist. It's quite clear at the mouth. Anyway, the pilot could take us out blindfolded." The charming smile flashed once more. "Hope you have a good night," he said and was gone.

Turning her head a fraction, Tracy met her own eyes in the mirror hanging over the handbasin opposite. Widely spaced and blue as a summer's sky, they gazed back at her distractedly.

After a moment she put up a hand and untied the silk scarf to run her fingers through the honey-pale thickness of her hair. She came slowly to her feet to walk the length of the bunk and open the door of the built-in closet at its base. A good thing she hadn't brought along a lot of clothes, she thought with detached observation. This ship was equipped for a male crew who would travel relatively light.

She was still standing there in front of the closet when the sharp blast of a whistle pierced the air, causing her to start for the second time that night. Then the ship came suddenly to life, vibrating gently beneath her feet.

Tracy crossed to the porthole, pulling back the drapes to peer out to the barely visible quayside. Another whistle, and a voice that seemed to come from immediately below her shouted, "Away for'ard!" As if in echo came another cry from the direction of the stern, and Tracy knew the ship was moving, heading out into the river and the open sea.

She stood at the porthole for a little while longer. But there was nothing to see. Eventually she turned back into the cabin to start unpacking her things; hanging her dresses away neatly in the narrow closet and filling the drawers beneath the bunk with her undies and smaller items.

Halfway down the case she came upon the framed photograph that went everywhere with her and sat down upon the bunk to look into the frail features of the woman portrayed. If only her mother could have lived to realize the fulfilment of the dream for which she had worked so hard. Difficult enough for a young widow to bring up a child on her own. To put that child through college and medical school had taken many sacrifices.

It was the knowledge of those sacrifices which had kept Tracy going afterward. For her mother's sake she had put grief to one side and thrown herself into her work, with results that had gained her a valuable year as assistant to the senior medical consultant. It was he who had recommended her to Derek Lomax.

A tap on the cabin door roused Tracy from her thoughts. In answer to her invitation, it opened to admit a man of morose countenance and indeterminate years wearing a white jacket and carrying a tray. From his lack of surprise on seeing her, Tracy gathered that he had already been well briefed by the Mate; no doubt with the same instructions to keep quiet about her presence on board.

She would be glad, she decided, thanking the man, when the morning came and everything could be brought out into the open. This whole affair was beginning to wear at her nerves.

The tray held a covered plate of sandwiches and a small pot of excellent coffee. Finding herself unexpectedly hungry, Tracy polished off all the food and drank two cups of coffee. After that, she finished her unpacking and prepared for bed.

To her unaccustomed body the bunk at first seemed so narrow that she was a little afraid of falling out of it in the night. It was, however, extremely comfortable apart from this, and after a moment or two she began to feel more secure. Lying there in the darkened cabin it was hard to believe that she was actually on board a moving ship. Apart from the faint throb of the engines, no sound came to disturb her solitude, and there was no sensation of movement as yet. Probably that would come when they met the open sea.

Despite her frame of mind, the thrill of those two words came stealing over her. Was this really her, Tracy Redfern, on her way to the colorful ports she had read about and dreamed about, but never hoped to see with her own eyes? She tried out the names: Havana; Kingston; Curaçao; La Guaira— they even *sounded* exotic. For her this would be the journey of a lifetime, a journey it was doubtful she would ever have the opportunity to repeat. She owed it to herself to put the past behind her and live every minute of the coming three months. Life was too short for regrets.

Surprisingly she slept well, awakening refreshed and revitalized to a cabin full of early morning sunlight. Sitting up, she became instantly aware of the change in the motion of the ship, a long, slow roll that awoke a faint queasiness in the pit of her stomach. Luckily she had provided against such an eventuality. She swung her legs out from under the covers and padded across the floor to the desk where she had left her bag, extracted a couple of the tiny travel sickness tablets, and went to get herself a little water to wash them down with.

Perhaps it *was* all in the mind, but almost immediately she began to feel better. She went over to the porthole and swept back the curtain. It was seven o'clock, and the ship had been under way for many hours.

Sky and sea were colored an identical November gray, and there was a heavy swell running. The day looked cold, but at least the fog was completely gone. In a few days from now, Tracy thought, the temperature would be rising and the skies getting bluer by the minute. Her spirits lifted. It was certainly something to be leaving behind the cold and damp of an English winter.

Washing once more at the small handbasin, Tracy

resolved that her first priority must be to find out where the officers' bathrooms were situated. On a ship this size there would certainly be all such "mod cons". Afterward she dressed neatly and carefully in a shirtwaist dress in a fine beige wool (the company had decided that it would not be worthwhile having a special uniform made up for her under the circumstances of her service with them; and twisted her shoulder-length hair into a tidy bun at the back of her head. More than ever, this morning, she must make an effort to look the part of the dedicated doctor, playing down her femininity as much as was humanly possible.

She was ready and wondering where to go when the knock came at her door. The Number Three's friendly greeting gave her courage to face what was coming.

"The Skipper wants to see you before breakfast," Peter said as they made their way along the alleyway together. He glanced at her swiftly and away again. "Did you sleep well?"

"Fine," she told him. "I must have been more tired than I thought." She waited a moment before asking tentatively, "How did he take it?"

Peter's expression was carefully blank. "Who take what?"

"You must know what I mean. What did the Captain say when the Chief Officer told him about—" She was watching his face, and now her voice tailed off as an awful suspicion took hold of her. "He . . . he has *been* told, hasn't he?"

As a matter of fact—" he began, then he stopped and shrugged. "No, he hasn't."

Tracy stopped in her tracks, halfway up the companionway leading to the deck, dismay clouding her face.

"But why? You said Mr. Jackson was only waiting until we had got under way."

"So I thought. Apparently he changed his mind. He said this morning that it would be easier all around if you announced yourself."

"It might have been if I'd been allowed to do so last night." Anger was growing in her. "Is *everyone* on board this ship afraid of the Captain?"

"You might call it a natural wariness." Peter eyed her a little uncertainly. "Look, this wasn't my idea. I agree with you, the Skipper should have been put in the picture last night."

"Provided you didn't have to do the telling?" Tracy suggested on a faint note of sarcasm before moving upward again. "Oh well, let's get it over with. He can't bite me."

"No, but his bark can be pretty nasty," Peter murmured, following her.

On deck Tracy shivered and drew her duffle coat closer about her, thankful that she had slipped it around her shoulders; she hadn't known how far they would have to go to reach the Captain's cabin. From where she stood she could see right down the full length of the ship, a vast expanse of open deck broken only by an odd-looking arched structure amidships carrying winches and derricks atop of it. Beyond this rose the bulk of the superstructure aft, with two—no, *three* funnels rising from it.

What kind of cargo did the *Atlantic Star* carry? Tracy found herself wondering for the first time. She hadn't thought to ask at her interview; there had been so many other things on her mind.

She turned now to ask Peter, but the Number Three was already halfway up the iron rungs leading to a higher deck. Tracy followed, to find him waiting for her outside the door of a cabin a few feet away. If that was the Captain's cabin, this structure sheltering her from the strong wind must be the bridge housing, she realized, recalling what little she knew of shipboard geography.

And yet surely it was more normal to have the bridge more amidships, and not right up for'ard like this?

Next minute she had joined her escort outside the door. All her questions concerning the appearance of the ship were driven from her mind by the impending interview. Collecting herself, she nodded to Peter, watched him knock smartly on the panel and heard a voice invite them in.

In that first moment Tracy took in little of the cabin itself. She had a vague impression of polished wood and dark red carpet, but her attention was concentrated on the man standing in front of a desk with his back to them. He was dressed in the same dark blue uniform as worn by the young officer at her side, but there the resemblance ended. The Captain was tall and crisply dark-haired with shoulders like an ox. Even from this distance and this angle, Tracy could almost sense the latent power and agility in the whole of that well-muscled body. He was the complete antithesis of her mental image.

Just how complete she only fully realized when he turned around to face her. No well-preserved 50-year old this. He was no more than mid-30, lean-featured and gray-eyed, the latter turning to granite as they swept over her own slender, beige-clad figure.

"What the devil—" he began and stopped abruptly to look beyond her to his Third Officer. "What's this? A stowaway?"

Peter shook his head unhappily, quite obviously wishing himself well out of this whole situation.

"This is Dr. Redfern, Skipper. You wanted to see her."

Sudden understanding leaped in the steely eyes as the brain behind them assimilated the facts with a rapidity that Tracy was certain she could never have matched under like circumstances. Without taking his gaze from her face, he put a hand to the bulkhead at his side and stabbed a finger down on the switch of the communicator.

"Mike," he clipped, "get down here. And fast!"

There was a brief pause, then, "My watch ends in ten minutes," came the reply. "Can it wait till then?"

"No," the master of the ship snapped and cut contact. To Peter he said coldly, "You'd better go and take over your watch now. I'll have something to say to you later over your part in this."

The other didn't have to be told twice. As the door closed behind him, the Captain nodded curtly to a chair.

"Sit down, Dr. Redfern."

Tracy found herself obeying without volition. Moistening her lips with the tip of her tongue, she began hesitantly, "I think I ought to point out. . . ."

"I have the situation quite clear." The interruption was terse. "I'd prefer to hear my Chief Officer's explanation first, if you don't mind."

Tracy subsided into silence, watching him as he moved around the desk to pick up a sheaf of papers and run his eyes over the top one. The chiselled mouth was set in lines which boded ill for the next few minutes, both for the Mate and for herself. If only she had insisted on seeing the Captain last night, when she had first come aboard. They couldn't have refused her had she really insisted. This man would have already realized that.

The Chief's arrival was something of a relief. There was something unnerving about sitting in a room with a man who refused even to look at her, much less speak. Mike Jackson looked at her as he came in. His face was expressionless, but a faint glint of humor lurked in the bright blue eyes.

His superior wasted no time in opening the discussion, if it could be called that.

"You'd have been keelhauled for this not so very long

back," he said harshly. "What damn right have you to make my decisions for me?"

"It was a matter of policy," the Number One replied with a calmness Tracy found quite amazing under the circumstances. Then his tone altered. "Come off it, Leigh. You know as well as I do why I didn't tell you the full facts. They might have been days finding us a replacement."

"That wasn't your problem. Your job doesn't include the right to take liberties with mine."

A pause while the two men faced each other. Detachedly Tracy noted that big as the Number One was, he was still shorter by a couple of inches than the senior man, although greater by 20 pounds at least around the middle. Two men of like caliber, she judged; neither ready to give an inch on this or any other issue at stake between them. It was time, she decided, for her to put in a word.

"Mr. Jackson is right about a replacement for me," she said quietly, steeling herself to meet the gray eyes as they swung toward her. "As a matter of fact, I was the last hope. The Company took me because there was no one else after the job."

His lips twisted. "I'd already worked that out for myself. It still doesn't explain your own conduct in this affair. Weren't you told to report to me personally when you came aboard?"

"Yes," she admitted reluctantly. "Yes, I was."

"Then why didn't you do that?"

Over his shoulder she caught the Mate's gaze for an instant. Fractionally her chin lifted as her normal spirit came to her rescue.

"Because I was engaged to perform a specific function on board this ship for which I am well suited. I had no intention of being dumped back on shore by a Captain who allows personal antipathies to come before duty," she retorted.

A muscle tautened abruptly in the strong jawline. For a long moment he stood there contemplating her narrowly, then he said coldly, "My personal preferences are neither here nor there. Under any circumstances I would have objected to the presence of a lone woman on the *Star*—in your or any other capacity. To put it bluntly, you represent a distraction the crew can do without. I'd have thought those fools back at the main office would have had *that* much foresight!"

"They had no choice," she came back desperately. "It was either me or nothing. Can't you accept that?"

"No, I can't accept it. Are you trying to convince me that you're the only doctor in the length and breadth of the British Isles with a yen to go to sea?"

"Of course not. But there can't be so many, and there are other ships, you know." Her voice had risen a little over the last few words, and now she took a steadying breath. If she was going to even attempt to reason with this man it would do her case no good whatsoever if she lost her temper. She began again, "Captain Huntley, you don't have to be concerned over my presence on your ship. I'm quite certain that your crew will merely find me . . . a . . . nine . . ." Her voice died slowly away as she became aware of the sudden and complete stillness of the two other occupants of the cabin. Hastily she reviewed her last sentence, but could find nothing in it to have evoked such peculiar expressions. Perplexed, she gazed back at them, waiting for enlightenment.

The younger man was the first to speak. "What," he said quietly and carefully, "did you call me just then?"

"Call you?" Her smooth wide brow wrinkled momentarily, cleared, and then creased again. "Why, Captain Huntley. Isn't that your name? It's the one I was given at the office."

The two men glanced briefly at one another, and some message seemed to flash between them. No longer did they stand on opposing lines; they were together and against her. A sense of impending disaster brought Tracy to the very edge of her seat as the Captain opened his mouth once more.

"Doctor Redfern, what ship is this?"

For a second or two her brain refused to assimilate the sense of the question. What ship was this? Surely he, of all people, already knew that!

"The *Atlantic Star*," she answered automatically, and in that same instant the premonition crystallized into shattering knowledge, widening her eyes and drying her throat as she sought for her voice. "This isn't the *Atlantic Star*, is it?" she whispered.

"No," came the controlled answer, "it is not." He paused to give his next words greater emphasis, his eyes fixed on the upturned white face before him. "You are on board the *Antarctic Star*—heading south."

CHAPTER TWO

It was very quiet in the cabin after the Captain had finished speaking. Tracy felt dazed; at sea in every sense of the word. What a mess she was in. What an awful, mind-whirling mess!

"Exactly," agreed a dry voice, and she realized that she must have spoken her thoughts aloud. The gray eyes studied her with an almost clinical detachment; the calm before the storm, Tracy thought fleetingly, and nerved herself to speak.

"You must think me a complete fool, Captain," she began, hesitated, then hurried on, trying to ignore the sardonically lifted eyebrow. "But you must acknowledge that under last night's conditions it was an easy error to make. I must have misheard the directions they gave me at the dock gates. In the mist the two names would look pretty much alike."

"There's such a thing as checking to make certain," he pointed out. "Particularly under such conditions as existed last night."

"It didn't occur to me. I—everything seemed to fit so well. You were expec . . ." she paused, her heart turning over heavily. No, everything hadn't fitted, had it? What about the difference in sailing times? That alone should have been enough to arouse her suspicions. Come to think of it, it should also have been enough to arouse the Mate's. She stole a swift glance at that individual and saw by his expression that the same thought had occurred to him. Well, at least the fault was not entirely on her side, though she doubted that the Captain would allow her even so much " . . .were expecting a medical officer," she finished a trifle lamely.

The eyebrow flickered upward again. "So might half the ships in the Merchant Navy, but if every M.O. simply climbed aboard the first ship he came to without so much as a word of inquiry, there'd be one hell of a mix-up!" He moved impatiently, taking the two steps which brought him to the porthole, where he stood for a moment gazing out to sea. "Wind speed increasing," he remarked irrelevantly, then without warning he spun back upon Tracy. "Dammit, woman, why couldn't you have chosen another ship to louse up! This is going to cost me time I can't afford to lose."

Time he would have lost, anyway, as his own M.O. had quite obviously failed to turn up, Tracy could have pointed out. She refrained because she doubted that it would have helped her present position. Instead, she said quietly, "I'm sorry to be the cause of so much trouble for you, Captain. Luckily we're only a matter of hours from port. It could have been much worse."

She seemed to be waiting an age for his answer. When he did speak it was in grimly emphatic tones. "You're laboring under a misapprehension if you imagine for one moment that I have any intention of turning about and taking you back. I'd lose almost two days."

Fresh alarm leaped inside her, bringing her to her feet so sharply that her coat fell from her shoulders to the floor, where it lay unheeded.

"You can't mean that! I'm not going to the Antarctic with you!"

His short laugh was entirely without humor. "You can bet your sweet life you're not! We have to pick up the rest of the fleet at Cape Town. You can get off there."

"Cape Town!" To Tracy it sounded like the other side of the universe. "But that's ridiculous! How am I supposed to get back to England?"

"If you contact the Company you're supposed to be

working for, they'll no doubt make arrangements to get you home—though I imagine your reception won't be very warm. My only worry is the trouble I'm going to have finding another M.O. at such short notice. I'm scheduled to spend only a matter of hours at the Cape."

The Mate spoke for the first time in several minutes. "You'll never do it, Leigh. Qualified men aren't to be found kicking around the quayside waiting for a trip out to the ice."

"I'll get a replacement if I have to take along a native witch-doctor," his superior snapped. "Either that, or we sail without an M.O. at all."

"What about Company regulations?"

"Company regulations be damned! They'd be the first to grouse if we were down on last year's take due to days spent hanging around in Duncan Basin—to say nothing of the expense of keeping the whole fleet in idleness."

Forgotten for the moment, Tracy stood on the fringe of the argument, her initial bewilderment fading as things began to click into place. The *Antarctic Star* was a whaler, a factory ship! No wonder it had looked odd, so unlike one's normal concept of a cargo ship. Those wide open decks were the workshops in which the great creatures were transformed from their given form into commercial quantities of oil. Vaguely, there came to mind a novel she had once read that had been set, in part, aboard a whaler. The author had, she recalled, possessed a rare talent for realistic description; one had almost been able to smell the overpowering stench of the cooking pots rising from the pages. All in all, she must count herself extremely lucky to be dropped at Cape Town, although just how she was going to handle things when she arrived there she couldn't even begin to think.

"How long will it take to reach the Cape?" she heard her own voice asking.

It was the Mate who answered. "Inside of two weeks. Your Company shouldn't have much difficulty in arranging your passage home. They might even have one of their own ships available."

"They'll be wondering what happened to me," she murmured worriedly. "They might even call in the police if they contact my former address and find that I left to join their ship as scheduled."

We do have a radio," the other man put in with a strong edge of sarcasm, and Tracy felt herself flush. What an idiot she was! Of course the ship had radio! Her brain simply wasn't functioning properly at the moment. Not that one could expect *this* man to take shock reaction into account in his assessment of her mental powers.

"When will I be able to get a message through?" she made herself ask him.

"After breakfast," he replied crisply. "I'll feel better equipped to deal with this rationally on a full stomach."

He took up the blue cap from his desk as he spoke, donned it at a slight angle and moved across to the cabin door. Opening it wide, he turned his head to look back in her direction, the twist of his lips making a mockery of this deference to her womanhood as he stood waiting for her to precede him out to the deck.

With head held high, Tracy swept up her coat from the floor and walked past. He was hateful! A soulless monster without one drop of the milk of human kindness in him. How was she going to stand 12 days under his command? How did anyone stand it?

The officers' mess was on the port side of the ship, and not so very far from her own cabin. Leather seating ran the full length of one bulkhead, and in front of this were two long tables. Both were well occupied, Tracy noted in the brief second or two before she became the focus of all eyes. Vibrantly aware of the man at her back, she made a valiant attempt to carry the moment through with some semblance of normalcy.

"Good morning," she said and lost the last syllable in the sudden scraping of feet as every man in the room rose hastily to his feet.

"Sit down, gentlemen," came the dry tones from behind her shoulder. "I'm sure Dr. Redfern would prefer to be regarded as just another officer during her time with us. Isn't that so, Doctor?"

"Very much so." Her smile felt a little cracked, but she kept it going.

"Have a seat," he went on, moving past her to indicate a place at the top of the first table next to the chair that was obviously his own. He waited until she was seated before taking his place.

Across the table Tracy met the Number One's bright blue eyes and was astonished to see one of them close in a rapid but unmistakable wink. This time her smile was genuine. In the Mate of the *Antarctic Star* she had a sympathizer. The knowledge cheered her.

While they were waiting for the steward to serve them, the Captain made a swift round of the assembled company—so swift that Tracy had barely time to match a name to a face and function before he had passed on to the next. After the third man, she gave up trying to keep up, simply nodding brightly at the required intervals until the introductions were completed. There would be plenty of time later to catch up on the details. Not that it was really important in any case, she reminded herself. She wouldn't be on board long enough to need a great deal of knowledge about her fellow officers.

The food was excellent, and her sea legs apparently well found, for she ate heartily of everything put before her. It must be the sea air, she reasoned. Normally her appetite at breakfast ran more on the toast and coffee lines.

Conversation went on apace throughout—perhaps just a little more restrained than usual because of her presence, Tracy guessed in some amusement, as one man suddenly broke off a story he had begun with a glance of somewhat embarrassed recollection in her direction.

"Sure and that's a darlin' smile ye've got there," came a rich brogue from her side. "Would ye be descended from the Irish, by any chance?"

Tracy's mouth widened still farther as she turned her head toward the short, stocky man who had spoken. Donald O'Malley, the Chief Engineer, was one of the few names she had taken in because she had immediately seen the resemblance to a well-known countryman of his. All he needed was a cassock and pipe, and Bing Crosby himself would have taken him for Barry Fitzgerald without question.

"As a matter of fact, my grandmother was Irish," she said. "On my mother's side, that is."

"And didn't I tell you!" he exclaimed triumphantly to no one in particular. "I knew those eyes were Galway born and bred!"

"Londonderry, actually," she murmured, and the triumph gave way to a snort of disgust.

"One of *them*, was she?" A pause, and then he brightened again. "Well, I'll not be holding it against you. It's Irish blood you be after having in you, no matter which part it came from. Do you know the old country at all?"

Tracy shook her head regretfully. "I'm afraid I've never been there. My grandmother was more or less disowned by her family when she married an Englishman, and neither side ever got around to patching things up. I wouldn't even know where to start looking for my relatives over there—if there are any left now."

"Sure," with a twinkle, "and there'll be dozens. Irish families don't die out that quickly!"

"When you've finished discussing your family tree, perhaps you'd join me in my cabin, Doctor," Leigh put in coolly, rising to his feet. "We have one or two things to sort out."

"I'll come now," Tracy returned swiftly, hiding her reluctance.

Emerging at his heels onto the open deck a minute or two later, she looked out beyond the guard-rail to the heaving, white-capped waves. The weather was worsening; a condition already suggested by the changing motion of the ship over the last half hour. The breakfast she had just eaten stirred uneasily as the deck canted sharply beneath her feet. She clutched at a stanchion to preserve her balance, waiting for the plunge down the far side of the huge wave.

Next moment an iron grip fastened about her upper arm, and before she had quite realized what was happening she was across the stretch of deck, up the companionway and in the cabin. Still without speaking Leigh steered her to a chair, pressed her down into it and released her as abruptly as he had seized her.

"Thank you," Tracy said dryly, controlling the desire to rub the bruised flesh where his fingers had been. Either he didn't know his own strength, or didn't care very much. "I'm afraid I'm not used to such heavy seas."

"This," he retorted, moving around behind his desk, "is a moderate swell. God help you when we hit some real seas!" He sat down, pulled forward a sheet of paper and took up a pen, lifting an inquiring eyebrow at her. "If you'll give me the name of the Company employing you, I'll see that a message goes through right away."

Tracy obliged, watched the lean hand move across the paper and wished she dare make some suggestions as to the form the message should take. She had a strong feeling that left to the Captain she would come out of it looking pretty much of a fool. In his eyes she was, of course. The mistake she had made was totally inexcusable.

"I don't even know your proper name yet," she said suddenly and saw the gray eyes lift toward her. "I mean," she went on hastily, "I'd been thinking of you as Captain Huntley until an hour ago, and you didn't say. . . ."

"Garratt," he supplied shortly and went back to his writing, leaving her to sit there and seethe inwardly. The boor! The insufferable boor!

Twenty seconds later he put down the pen, read through what he had written, and pushed the paper to one side.

"I'll send that down to the radio shack in a moment," he said, and glanced at his watch. "No doubt you'll want to collect your bag from your cabin before going across to the hospital?"

"So I'm to be allowed to practise my profession for the next 12 days, at least?" she asked, with an attempt at his own brand of sarcasm that failed miserably in its aim.

"The *Star* carries no passengers," he returned equably. "Naturally I'll see to it that you're properly reimbursed for your services. Do you feel capable of fetching your things, or shall I ring for a steward?"

"I'll manage," Tracy returned shortly, coming to her feet.

Anger got her below decks without so much as a stumble. In her cabin she drew on one of her white surgery coats, redonned her jacket and snatched up the leather bag from the desk. As a woman Leigh Garratt could dismiss her with contempt if he so wished. As a doctor he was going to learn to treat her with respect.

She had expected a steward to be sent down to show her the way to the hospital, so it was with some surprise and not a little dismay that she found the Captain himself waiting outside in the alleyway.

"I've decided to take you across myself," he said. "I wanted to check the factory plant anyway."

The hospital was in the stern of the ship. To reach it one had to traverse what seemed like miles of alleyways past the vast pressure cookers, bone boilers, and separators which occupied the greater part of this deck. Men at work on the plant all paused in their activities to watch the two of them pass, and on one occasion they were followed by a low appreciative whistle which Leigh ignored.

Hospital and surgery were side by side; the latter painted out in a clinical white and reeking of cleanliness. Leigh introduced the young but capable-looking orderly as Joe Sergeant. He would, Tracy reflected, in all probability know every man aboard ship by name; he was that kind.

At his suggestion she went through with Joe to survey the rest of her domain for this coming 12 days. Like the surgery next door the hospital was all white, with facilities for a maximum of 12 patients. At the present time it was empty. Tracy hoped it would stay so for the duration of her reign.

Contrary to her expectations and fond hopes, Leigh was still in the surgery when they returned, glancing idly through one of the medical journals from a shelf at the back. He closed it as she came through the door, sliding it back into its place on the shelf.

"Everything satisfactory?" he asked.

Tracy nodded, her eyes traveling around the beautifully equipped room with approval.

"Everything is fine. This is quite a ship, Captain Garrett."

"The modern whaler has to be," he returned. "We

can't afford to make do with antiquated equipment of any kind." He went to the door, pausing with his hand on the knob to glance back at her. "Can you remember the way back, or shall I send someone down for you at lunchtime?"

Yes, said Tracy's common sense, but today the stubborn streak was stronger.

"I'll find it," she said firmly.

"Just as you like."

Glad to see the door close behind him, Tracy turned to look about her once more, smiling at the orderly who was eyeing her with an expression fast becoming familiar.

"We'd better start with a briefing on my predecessor's working habits," she said. "I'm not at all conversant with shipboard routine."

"What did you want to know first, Doctor?" he asked formally.

Tracy went over and moved her bag from the chair behind the desk where Leigh had put it down, sat down and surveyed the bare surface as if she hoped to find inspection there. The office at Glenfall Road had been so different, not at all like the clinical efficiency of this place. Tidied as it had been every morning, Derek's desk was always hidden beneath the daily piles of National Health Service literature, manufacturers' samples, and all the general conglomeration of paper work which went with any thriving practice; this despite the fact that he had employed a secretary-receptionist full time.

"Suppose we start with the daily routine," she suggested, shutting out the pain of that memory before it could get started. "It's nine-thirty now. When would this office normally be open for business?"

Joe opened his mouth to reply, then paused and grinned as a knock came on the outer door.

"Now," he said. "This will be your first patient, Doctor."

The patient was a man of some 40 years, dressed in workmanlike blue denims and sweater. He had the weatherbeaten, leathery skin of those who spend a great part of their daylight hours in the open air under all conditions.

"Arne Holst," Joe supplied. "One of the flensers."

With only a very vague notion of what that meant, Tracy invited the man to take a seat.

"Swedish?" she hazarded and received an emphatic shake of the head.

"Norwegian. I have a bad finger." His English was good, though heavily accented. He studied her with open interest as he extended the offending member.

The finger was indeed bad, swollen to almost twice its normal size, and gloriously hued. He had trapped it in a door some days previously, he told her, bursting it open like a ripe tomato. Yes, he had wrapped it up for a day or two until the wound had closed, but had found the dressing awkward when washing and shaving.

"I'll have to open this up and clean it out," Tracy said, and hesitated. "It's going to be pretty painful. It might be easier if I did it under a general anesthetic."

The man looked blank for a moment until Joe helpfully showed him the rubber face mask, then once again came the vigorous shake of the head.

"I will watch."

He did watch too, his gaze following every movement she made, from scrubbing her hands at the corner washbasin to the moment she laid the neatly dressed finger down and signalled Joe to remove the tray. Not once in all that time had the rugged features betrayed one flicker of pain

"I shall want to see you again in the morning," she told him firmly. "And keep that dressing on this time."

"How many crew does the *Star* carry?" she asked Joe when her patient had departed, and she was washing her hands again at the basin.

"Something over 500. If you count the whole fleet, you could say a round 1000."

Quite a 'list', Tracy thought. "Many nationalities?"

"One or two. Mostly British and Norwegian, though, and all of them have a smattering of English."

"Why so many Norwegians? This is a British ship, isn't it?"

"Oh, yes, she's British all right. She isn't based in England, though. Most of the summer she's laid up at Tönsberg."

"Oh?" Tracy digested this in silence for a few seconds, reaching for the towel he held out to her. "Isn't that rather inconvenient for the British members of the crew? I mean, having to travel across to England at the end of every season, and back again for the start of the next."

"Not particularly. The Company flies us over both ways, so we lose very little time." He closed the lid of the electric sterilizer, and added, "Mind you, some of us . . . those without anyone in particular to hurry home to, you might say . . . prefer to stay on in Norway for a part of the off-season. There's plenty to do, and plenty . . ." with a grin . . ."willing to help you spend your earnings. Not that I can compete with the flensers and lemmers, but I'm a sight better paid than when I was doing the same job aboard a freight carrier."

"And how long ago was that?"

"Three years. I joined the *Star* the same time as the Skipper. The same time as he became Skipper, that is."

Tracy's interest perked up. "Became?"

"He was Mate before that. Got his promotion when

old Graham retired. Mike Jackson was Number Two then."

"A step up the ladder in all directions," Tracy murmured.

"I guess it was. There was some talk that first season of the Skipper having bought his promotion by investing all the money his old . . . his father left him in the Company, but nobody thinks about that any more. A good Skipper is a good Skipper, no matter how he got where he is."

Fully aware that gossiping with an orderly could hardly be called conduct suitable to her position, Tracy nevertheless could not resist the opportunity to find out more about the man who both infuriated and intrigued her.

"He's well liked by the crew then?" she asked casually.

Joe paused before he answered, and when he did speak it was apparent that he had suddenly recalled that he was speaking to one officer about another.

"He's a good Skipper," he repeated with an air of finality and turned back to the sterilizer, leaving Tracy to realize ruefully that she would get no more out of him today, and perhaps not at all. For all he knew she was quite capable of repeating everything he said to the Captain himself.

Another knock on the outer door drove all thought of Leigh Garratt from her mind for the present. She went once more to seat herself at the desk, feeling that she could more capably project her image as a doctor from reasonably static position.

The new customer complained vaguely of some kind of stomach disorder and was the forerunner of no less than seven more, only one of whom had anything even remotely approaching genuine symptoms. The rest, Tracy realized very shortly, were simply taking the opportunity of having a good look at the new Medical Officer at close quarters, and didn't expect her to take them at all seriously. She didn't and wondered what kind of an impression she had made on the hard-bitten crew members of the *Antarctic Star*. From their general attitude, she had a notion that they wouldn't take *her* very seriously either, which wasn't particularly encouraging—or wouldn't have been had she been staying aboard full season. She kept forgetting how short this voyage was going to be.

The morning wore on. Having familiarized herself with the layout of the hospital, Tracy was reduced to studying the textbooks gathered together by her predecessors. She eventually chose one on tropical medicine, thinking that the extra knowledge might come in useful if she was to be stuck in Cape Town for any length of time at all. Perhaps she could even offer her services to one of the hospitals for a few days.

At twelve-fifteen she put on her coat again and left the office to retrace the steps she had taken that morning. It would be easier, she decided at the end of the second alleyway, to make for the deck where she couldn't very well go wrong. She located a companionway and went up it, to be met at the top by Peter Cramer.

"Whew!" he exclaimed. "There's a gale and a half blowing out there!" He grinned cheerfully at her. "The Skipper said I should escort you back to your quarters before lunch. You don't want to go this way, do you?"

Apparently Leigh Garratt had as little confidence in her professed ability to manage the journey alone as she herself had, Tracy thought. Not that his concern stemmed from any protective instinct. He was simply insuring against any incident that might possibly result in upsetting his timetable.

"Why not?" she said recklessly. "It will blow the cobwebs away."

The moment they left the shelter of the superstructure

she regretted her rash decision. The wind was blowing from the south-west, piling up the racing sea into near-vertical walls of water which bore down on the ship with all the speed and force of an express train, dousing the deck with spray. To Tracy the waves were terrifyingly immense, but Peter seemed quite unperturbed by the sight. She could only assume that once again her inexperience was coloring the situation out of proportion.

"I thought you were on duty on the bridge?" she shouted as they moved for'ard into the teeth of the gale.

"I was relieved at noon," Peter shouted back. "I'm comparatively free now until 2100." He thrust out a swift arm and caught her about the waist as the *Star* lifted her bows to breast yet another huge wave. "Steady! You almost lost your footing then. You have to move with her. Lean on me, if it helps."

Tracy was only too glad to comply. The arm about her waist gave her confidence to step out. By the time they reached the lee of the bridge housing, she was even beginning to have hopes of eventually finding her own feet.

"Thanks for the loan," she laughed when Peter eventually released her at the head of the companion-way. "I don't know what I'd have done without you."

"Always glad to be of service to a lady." He stood looking at her for a moment, then said, "Mike told me what happened. Bad luck."

Her smile was rueful. "You mean bad management, don't you? I feel such a fool."

Peter grinned, revealing even white teeth.

"I meant bad luck for us. I was looking forward to having you aboard for the next five and a half months."

"Is that how long you spend out there?" Tracy gave a shiver that wasn't entirely play-acting. "How do you stand the cold all the time?"

"It isn't at all like you probably think. The Antarctic

summer is something like a mild British winter. The temperature rarely drops below freezing point."

"Yes, well, I'll take your word for it." She put up a hand and pushed a strand of hair out of her eyes. "I must go and tidy myself up. See you in a little while, I expect."

Below, she slipped off her coat and crossed the cabin to the mirror over the basin. Her hair was certainly a mess, hanging about her face in wind-tossed wisps. Impatiently she pulled out the few remaining pins and seized hold of a brush. She would just have to pull it back into the nape of her neck for the time being; there was no time for any more elaborate arrangement.

She had just begun creating order out of chaos when the rap came on the door. Probably one of the stewards, she thought. With the brush still in hand she went over, opened the door, and felt herself tauten as she recognized the man standing outside.

Slowly, his regard slid over the golden abundance curling softly onto her shoulders, then came back again to meet her eyes. His lips had twisted slightly.

"There's been a reply from your company," he said brusquely and held out the slip of paper. "You'd better read it for yourself."

The message was short, but very much to the point:

> *Dr. Redfern no longer our responsibility. Suggest her services of more use to you under circumstances.*

Tracy leaned heavily against the door jamb, all the use draining out of her limbs. *Now* what did she do?

CHAPTER THREE

"Well?" asked Leigh evenly. "What are your plans now?"

"I don't know." She turned vaguely back into the cabin, looked at the brush in her hand and laid it down on the shelf beneath the mirror. She was aware of him moving forward into the doorway; could feel him watching her. Suddenly she whirled on him desperately. "Captain Garratt, you must see how this changes things. You must take me back!"

His answer was immediate and without compromise. "No."

She gazed at him in defeat. "Then what am I going to do?"

"Can't your family cable you the fare back to England?"

"I have no family. Not," she added, recalling her conversation with the Chief Engineer at breakfast, "that I know of."

"I see," he said. "and you can't raise the sum yourself?"

Her chin lifted. "Doctors don't get rich easily, you know. I might just scrape enough together, but I'd be destitute when I did get home."

"What were you doing before you applied to join the *Atlantic Star*?" he asked abruptly.

"General practice," she answered, equally shortly.

"And before that?"

"I did a year's residency at my training hospital."

He studied her thoughtfully. "Sounds good enough. Why not consider following your profession at the Cape for a few months? There's as much a shortage of good doctors out there as anywhere else."

"Which would seem to make your chances of finding one going spare very slim indeed," she couldn't resist pointing out, and he lifted his shoulders briefly.

"I'll manage. You still haven't answered my question."

"What's the point? I understand that to stay in South Africa one has to have either a guarantor, or alternatively the means to leave. I haven't the latter, and I don't even know anyone living on that continent, much less Cape Town."

"You mightn't," he said, "but I do. A couple named Bransom. Came out about five years ago. They'd take you in if I asked them—and help you find yourself a job."

Surprised, Tracy said, "You'd do that for me?"

A hint of satire touched his mouth. "Not entirely. It would save a lot of trouble all around." His gaze moved over her. "It would also save you from returning to whatever it is you're running away from."

She stiffened. "What makes you think I'm running away from anything?"

"Call it intuition, if you like."

"And does that same intuition also tell you just what it is I'm supposed to be so eager to leave behind?" she demanded.

"At a rough guess I'd say a man." His tone was clipped. "Some poor sucker who thought he'd found his pot of gold, perhaps."

Anger brought a sparkle to her eyes and heated words to her lips. "Was it something like that that turned you against women yourself?"

He went very still, his features hardening. "I'm not against women," he said. "They have their uses." He registered the swift rush of color to her cheeks with a slight curl of his lip. "I'll cable the Bransoms this afternoon. Don't worry, they won't refuse an Englishwoman refuge in their home."

Then he turned on his heel and was gone.

Tracy stood where he had left her, a hand clenched tightly at her waist. Leigh Garratt didn't pull his punches. Not against a woman, not against anyone. What kind of a man was he? Surely somewhere beneath that cold, hard exterior there beat a heart?

Days passed, and the chill damp of the English winter became just a memory. Tracy reveled in the sparkling blue of the sea and sky; the ever-growing warmth of the sun. A great deal of her spare time was spent on deck simply soaking up the rays that bounced back their heat from the glinting superstructure. Gradually her skin began to take on a pale tan, infinitely becoming against the soft contrast of her hair.

Spare time was unreasonably plentiful. After the first novelty of her presence on board had worn off, the crew seemed determined to regard her with that blend of tolerance and vague mistrust she had half anticipated. Those who attended the office at all did so with obvious reservations, accepting her ministrations only when their own pet remedies had failed to cure the ailment, and more often than not crediting their own stalwart constitutions with any improvement thereafter. It was a frustrating attitude, but one which Tracy could do little about. She had penetrated a stronghold, driven in yet another wedge at the door of emancipation. It was not to be expected that such men as she was dealing with would take readily to this invasion of their hitherto purely masculine world.

"Time is all you need," Peter assured her when she communicated her sense of failure to him one afternoon. "The resentment has no personal basis, you know."

They were standing together at the guard-rail,

throwing bits of stale bread and cake to the wheeling gulls. On the horizon, and fast receding astern, lay the dark smudge that was the island of Madeira. The *Star* hadn't called there. Cape Town was her only port of call before she took to the cold waters south of that outpost of civilization.

"And are you resentful of my intrusion, too?" Tracy asked lightly, aiming a morsel of bread directly into the path of one of the smaller birds, only to see it snatched from the air in front of the hungrily reaching beak by a huge fellow who could well have lived off his fat for a month. "Oh, you glutton!" she exclaimed.

"Survival of the fittest," Peter remarked. He studied her becomingly flushed face and sparkling eyes, the golden hair streaming in the breeze, and his own smile widened and warmed. "Do I appear resentful?"

"No," she admitted. "But you may be very good at concealing your feelings."

His reply was in the same light tone. "On this particular point I don't have to be. One thing I've never taken to in life at sea is the lack of feminine interest. Having you on board makes a world of difference to everyday routine." He grinned at her. "Come to that, I've noticed how much closer to the chin we're *all* wearing our beards this season. I even caught Mike giving his a trim this morning, and that's a rare occurrance indeed!"

Tracy laughed. "You're evading the question, but carry on. My ego is loving it!"

"A glance in the mirror should be all that's necessary to boost your self-esteem," he replied promptly. "You're a very beautiful girl, Tracy. And I can't possibly be the first man to tell you that."

"If you're not I've forgotten the others." She crumpled the paper bag that had held the crumbs and showed it to the screaming gulls. "All gone, I'm afraid."

Peter said softly, "Is that more modesty, or is it really true that there haven't been many men in your life up to now?"

For the first time in more than 24 hours Tracy thought of Derek and was surprised to find that she could do so without much pain. It had had to happen, of course. One could not go on being torn apart as she had been for the rest of one's life. What she hadn't expected was that it could happen so soon. How deep had her emotions really gone?

"If you mean in any serious fashion, then no, there haven't," she said at last. "There was never any time to spare in medical school for romance with a capital R."

"But now there is. And you have a whole shipload to choose from." He was smiling, but there was an odd, insistent note in his voice. "Anyone you particularly fancy?"

Her nerves tautened, and her answering smile felt brittle. "If there was it wouldn't be much use, would it? I'm only a temporary fixture here."

"So you are." His expression had altered. "I keep forgetting." There was a pause, then he said, "Have you decided, yet, what you're going to do when we reach Cape Town? Are you going to accept the Skipper's offer?"

"I'm not all that sure that it's still open."

"He hasn't mentioned it since?"

Tracy shook her head. "Not a word." And then, trying to be fair, "Not that there's been the opportunity. Apart from mealtimes I never see him."

"He could make the opportunity if he really meant what he said."

"Perhaps," she suggested, "these friends of his just don't want to take me, and he doesn't know how to tell me."

"Not the Skipper. I can't see him funking a thing like

that. More likely he's deliberately keeping you on tenter-
hooks."

"You mean as a kind of punishment for having put him
to all this trouble?" she asked, infusing a note of mild
amusement into her voice. "Is he really that kind of
man?"

"Your guess is as good as mine. He's certainly not the
predictable kind."

"Does anyone know him?"

"Mike might. I suppose you already know that they
served together aboard the *Star* as Mate and Second
Officer before they both. . . ." He broke off, a frown
creasing his brow as he gazed downward. "We're heaving
to. What the devil . . . ?"

"Doctor!" A youth arrived at their side, breathless
from running and obviously badly scared. "You're
needed aft," he gasped out. "One of the boys went overboard."

Tracy was on the move almost before he had finished
speaking, running along the deck toward the stern of the
ship. Behind her came Peter, having stopped just long
enough to ascertain the exact location of the accident.

There was a crowd already gathered along the rail by
the time the two of them arrived on the scene. With scant
ceremony Tracy pushed her way through to the front, just
in time to see the boat being lowered into the gently
rolling swell.

"Where is he?" she demanded of her immediate neighbor. "Can you see him?"

"Way back there," was the answer, and a finger indicated a fitfully-seen white speck that could have been
anything. "Arne Holst went in after him. He's a strong
swimmer. He'll not let the lad go."

Arne didn't, but precious minutes elapsed before the
boat could return the rescued pair to the safety of the

ship. The boy's eyes were closed, his face pinched and blue. He had stopped breathing, though there was still a faint heartbeat. Tracy wasted no time, kneeling above the still, sodden body to begin mouth-to-mouth resuscitation.

Seconds ticked by with no sign of returning to life. Tracy carried on, refusing to admit defeat, breathing and counting, breathing and counting, until her own head was swimming with the effort. Water draining from the boy's clothing soaked into her skirt, but she was unaware of any discomfort. She didn't dare stop even for the second or two it would take to listen for the heart. She had to keep going until every last vestige of hope had gone.

The first barely perceptible self-movement of the thin chest brought a sound like a drawn-out sigh from the ring of motionless spectators. Another breath, and then the boy coughed and choked, rolled over and was violently sick.

Wearily Tracy put up a hand and pushed back the hair from her eyes. Someone moved to her side, and she looked up to find Arne Holst towering over her, rough hewn face split asunder by a smile of pure relief. Obviously the man felt some special kind of affiliation for this youngster he had just rescued from death.

"I take him now—*ja*?" he asked, and she nodded.

"If you'd carry him down to the hospital, please."

She stood up, as the Norwegian bent and lifted the now fully conscious boy tenderly from the deck, squeezed out the skirt of her cotton dress and raised her eyes to find herself the target of dozens of others—all of them friendly.

"Good going," said Peter warmly, falling into step beside her as she turned to follow Arne. "You saved that kid's life."

"Only because he was lucky enough to be spotted going in," she replied. "Have you any idea what happened?"

"I'm not sure about young Borre, but apparently Arne was up on the boat deck when he heard the splash. It must have been a real shock when he reached him and found it was his own son."

"His son!" Tracy stopped in her tracks, understanding now the look on the man's face when he had lifted the boy.

"Didn't you know? This is his first season. Arne would never have forgiven himself for bringing him if anything had happened." They had reached the head of the companionway. He paused. "I'd better go and make a report to the Skipper. Would you like me to get one of the stewards to bring you down another dress?"

"If you would," she said gratefully. "Tell him it doesn't matter which one."

Borre was out of his wet clothes and wrapped in a large, thick blanket when she reached the hospital. With the amazing resilience of youth he grinned at her cheerfully before reburying his face in the mug of hot chocolate Joe Sergeant had conjured up for him.

Tracy found her hand gripped with painful enthusiasm by Arne.

"You save my boy," he said. "I thank you. You are a good doctor."

"You've made a friend for life there," Joe commented after the man had gone, leaving his son to recover from his ordeal in one of the hospital beds overnight. "I'll go and get a bed made up." He winked at Borre. "You'll have some explaining to do about this little affair in the morning, young feller. When your dad gets over the first shock he's going to want to know just what you were doing up there at this time of the day."

Borre might not have understood every word, but the gist of the message got through to him all right. He looked suddenly crestfallen.

"Do you know what he was doing?" Tracy asked, following Joe to the door.

"I have my ideas," was the reply. "But on the off-chance that I'm wrong, I'd prefer not to say anything, if you don't mind, Doctor." He opened the door to cross the alleyway to the linen cupboard, paused, and then fell back again to allow the Captain of the ship access. "Sorry, sir, didn't hear you coming."

Taken unaware, Tracy stood where she was against the bulkhead, suddenly conscious of her bedraggled appearance. His eyes swept a comprehensive glance over her, met her own for a fraction of a moment, and then moved on beyond her to the boy who still sat swathed in the blanket by the desk.

When he spoke it was in Norwegian, a short, sharp-sounding sentence which brought the color rushing to the pale cheeks as the boy struggled to stand. Leigh reseated him with a brisk command, then repeated the first words with the upward rising inflection at the end intimating a question. Still Borre made no answer, looking down at the floor, looking anywhere but at his superior. There was a stubbornness in the set line of the young mouth, though Tracy thought she recognized a hint of mute appeal in the blue eyes so like his father's when he glanced in her direction.

"What are you asking him?" she demanded, and Leigh turned his head slowly toward her.

"I want to know what happened," he said abruptly.

"Surely that could wait a while. He needs to rest."

"This happens to be important." His voice was cold. "I mean to have an answer."

Without stopping to think about it, Tracy put herself between man and boy. "Why?" she shot at him recklessly. "Because he upset your timetable by 15 minutes or so? I'm sorry, Captain Garratt, but I must insist upon my patient being given time to recover from shock before you question him any more."

A moment's electric silence while two eyes like gimlets bored down into her, then he said with icy control, "We'll discuss this in my cabin in 15 minutes."

Joe came back into the room with an armful of linen only bare seconds after the other man had departed, having heard the exchange from the alleyway. He cast a curious glance at Tracy, but forbore from comment when he saw her expression. The steward arrived with a clean pink linen dress from her wardrobe. She left Joe to get Borre into bed while she changed in the office. At least she would be able to face the coming interview with some remnant of dignity.

Borre's smile, when she went through to check on him before leaving, was shy but grateful. Tracy shook her head at him.

"I don't know what all this is about, but I've a strong feeling that you've been doing something you shouldn't. No . . ." at his quick look of apprehension . . ."I'm not going to start asking you questions. Time enough for that tomorrow."

Fourteen and a half minutes exactly had elapsed when she knocked on the door of the Captain's cabin. Leigh swung around from the porthole, his expression forbidding.

"There's one thing we'd better get straight before we go any further," he clipped without preamble. "Whether you like it or not, while ever you're on board this ship you're under my command. Is that quite clear?"

"Not completely," Pride lent her voice strength. "Where my patients are concerned I have to use my own judgment."

"I'm not disputing that. The issue here isn't that you stopped me from questioning the boy, but the manner in which you did it. Would you have spoken to a member of the hospital staff like that in front of a patient?"

"No," Tracy admitted ruefully. "No, I wouldn't. I'm sorry about that."

"Even though you still believe what you said?"

The flush mounted beneath her skin. "Does it really matter what I believe?"

"In this instance, yes." He spoke harshly. "A Captain needs the full confidence of *all* his crew." Hands thrust into pockets, he studied her for a long moment before going on. "Exactly why *did* you think I chose that particular time to question young Borre Holst?"

"I . . . I don't know."

"Then perhaps you wouldn't mind listening while I tell you? There's been a tradition amongst the mess boys for years that any newcomer to their ranks has to undergo a kind of initiation test before he can be accepted by them. Some of those tests are harmless enough, and I'm willing to turn a blind eye. Others weren't so harmless, and I banned them." He paused. "One of the latter took the form of a short but extremely hazardous walk along the top of a certain section of guard-rail. Need I say which section?"

She was staring at him in dismay. "You mean that Borre could have been attempting to walk the rail when he went overboard?"

"That's what I wanted to find out. I came straight down in the hope that the shock might loosen his tongue enough to give the game away."

"Oh," Tracy felt suddenly very small. Another apology seemed called for, but she had the feeling that any such attempt on her part would be met only with contempt. "What will you do now?"

The broad shoulders lifted. "I'll get to the truth if I have to put the fear of God into every one of those silly young fools to do it! I'm not going to risk having this happen again, with perhaps far more tragic results." He caught her fleeting change of expression and smiled with a certain grim amusement. "You don't have to look quite so concerned for their skins. Flogging at the mast went out years ago."

"I'm glad to hear it," she retorted stiffly. "Will that be all?"

"Not quite," Leigh moved the two steps to his desk, picked up the folded slip of paper lying there and held it out to her. "This concerns you."

Tracy took it from him with a sense of having gone through this particular scene before. This time, however, the message contained in the cablegram was vastly different:

> *Sorry delay. Been last five days in Jo'burg. Looking forward to having Dr. Redfern with us.*
> *Janet.*

She was a long time looking up. So the delay in informing her of arrangements hadn't been deliberate after all. The knowledge didn't make her feel any better.

"It's very good of your friends to do this for me," she said steadily. "And you, too, Captain. Thank you."

His regard was derisory. "Only too glad to be of service."

Tracy escaped into the air with relief. Things seemed to be going from bad to worse. The sooner she was off this ship, the better.

CHAPTER FOUR

The city lay supine in the full golden hush of the afternoon; a shimmering spread lifting lazily from the water's edge toward the towering, blue-hazed mountain at its back. Standing at the rail, Tracy followed the cool creamy wake of the speedboat heading out into the bay and thought longingly of the feel of that foaming wash on her hot, damp skin, of diving down deep into the blue, blue water, to surface with salt on her lips and exhilaration in her veins. Not that the heat could be held wholly to account for this flaccidity of the mind and limb.

Peter arrived at her elbow, frank admiration in the glance that rested upon the slender, shapely figure clad in pale green linen. "The Skipper will be ready to go ashore in five minutes," he announced. "Are all your things up?"

"They're in the launch," Tracy told him. She managed a smile. "It will seem strange to be back on land again. I was just beginning to get the feel of the sea."

"You were turning into a real sailor," he agreed and rested his arms along the rail at her side, gazing out across the strip of water that separated the ship from the shore. After a moment he said quietly, "Any regrets?"

Tracy gave a small forced laugh. "Plenty. I've lost a good job, and I'm more or less stranded here."

"I didn't mean that. I meant have you any regrets over leaving the *Star*?"

"Oh?" She was silent for a second or two, then she shrugged lightly. "It makes little difference, does it?" Abruptly she changed the subject. "When are you due to sail?"

"Just about 23 hours from now." He glanced along the deck to where the men worked in the sunshine, bared backs glistening with sweat as they hoisted the heavy crates of equipment onto the dangling hooks to be winched down to the waiting catcher. "We'll be the rest of today provisioning the catchers, and then tonight there'll be the usual party on board." His eyes flicked toward her and away again. "There'll be boatloads coming out. Couldn't you come back just for an hour or two?"

She shook her head. "I doubt it. Once I'm ashore I cease to have anything to do with the ship. Besides, I could hardly walk out on the Bransoms on my very first evening, could I?"

"I suppose not." Peter sounded wry. "I hope these friends of the Skipper's are all right."

"I'm sure they will be. All Captain Garratt's friends would have to be something pretty special, I imagine."

He said softly, "You don't like him, do you?"

Her throat tightened. "He doesn't need to be liked. He's completely self-sufficient."

"There may be reasons for that. I've heard rumors that he was badly let down by some woman a few years ago."

"So now he carries a grudge against the whole sex? Fair-minded of him." She pushed herself away from the rail. "I'd better get down to the launch. Have you time to see me safely over the side?"

"I'll make time."

He went in front of her down the gangway lashed securely against the side of the ship, so that if she did slip he would be in position to catch her. Not that there was much danger; in these seas the *Star* was as steady as a rock.

On the little landing stage at the bottom he stopped, looking down at her with an expression of regret. "I suppose this is goodbye."

Smilingly she held out her hand. "I'm afraid so. It's been great knowing you, Peter. I hope you and Deirdre manage to work things out."

A shadow passed across the brown eyes. "Yes," he said briefly. "Take care of yourself, Tracy."

The gangway rattled as someone set foot on it from the deck, and they both looked up sharply toward the tall, uniformed figure; waited in silence for him to descend to their level.

Gray eyes met blue expressionlessly, then moved to her companion. "All right, Cramer."

As the younger man passed him to remount to the deck, he stepped forward and down into the gently rocking launch. Then, before Tracy could move, he shot out his hands, caught her firmly about the waist and swung her deftly down beside him.

"Sit down," he invited abruptly and gave the command to move off before seating himself beside her.

The speed of his action had taken Tracy's breath away, and his closeness now did nothing toward helping her gain her equilibrium. Someone shouted something from the deck, and she lifted her head to see that the men had left their work for a moment to line the rail and wave her off. She caught a glimpse of Peter, hand raised in farewell, then the boat gathered speed and swept away from the *Star*'s side in a taut arc, heading for shore.

Leigh made no attempt to converse during the journey. Tracy sat motionless by his side, intensely aware of the broad shoulders almost rubbing hers, and of the lean brown hand resting casually along the gunwale behind her. She had to fight the strong desire to slide along the seat away from his unnerving presence. Since that incident over Borre Holst, she had seen little of the Captain of the *Antarctic Star*. Had he been anyone else but the man he was, she would have suspected him of having deliberately avoided her. But one could not imagine Leigh Garratt taking the trouble to avoid anyone, much less herself.

Janet and Harry Bransom were waiting for them on the

quayside, a sun-bronzed and pleasantly informal couple whom Tracy took to immediately. They would both, she judged, be around about Leigh's own age. All three were obviously friends of long standing. With an odd little quiver inside her she watched the Captain's strong mouth widen into a smile of greeting that was quite devoid of its normal cynicism and altered his whole face. Here was a glimpse of the man he must once have been before bitterness took over his life. A pity that his basic strength of character hadn't been capable of extending itself into forgetting the past.

"I've been making inquiries about a replacement," said Harry to Leigh as the car drew away from the waterfront. "Can't say I've come up with anything special, though. There's this chap someone brought out to the club a couple of days back who said he was interested. Seems to have the right qualifications, so far as I can tell, but. . . ." he hesitated and shook his head doubtfully. "Well, there's something not quite right about him. I thought we'd have a run over to his hotel after we drop the women off at the apartment, and you can judge for yourself."

"You look awfully young to be a doctor," Janet observed, leaning back in her corner of the rear seat and observing her companion with a great deal of interest. "With your looks I should think you could have been almost anything. What made you choose medicine?"

Tracy smiled. "It was just something I decided on when I was quite a small girl. I never imagined doing anything else after that." Impulsively she added, "I'm putting you to a lot of trouble. I really should have gone to a hotel."

"One thing you have to learn about Doctor Redfern," came Leigh's satirical tones from the front, "is that she dislikes being beholden to anyone."

"Well, you don't have to feel that way with us," Janet

said firmly. "I'm going to enjoy having another woman around the place for a change. The only pity is that your visit had to be under such circumstances. That must have been an awful moment when you found you were on the wrong ship."

"For everyone," Tracy agreed swiftly, determined not to give Leigh any further opportunities for sarcasm. "But now that I am here I plan to make the most of it."

"That's the spirit! Six months in this climate, and you'll never want to leave it. I know I wouldn't go back to England for a pension!"

Looking out of the window Tracy could readily understand why. The contrast between this and the November fog she had left behind such a short time ago was unbelievable. Everywhere one looked there was color: the startling azure of the sea and sky; the pure gold of the sun bouncing its rays off the neat white villas that dotted the gentle slopes above the road. All gazed out to sea over gardens spilling over with bougainvillea, hibiscus, Dorothy Perkins and a host of other plants, some familiar, some not, but all equally picturesque. Being here at all was an unforgettable experience. Staying on for a while in such a lovely part of the world could hardly be a bad thing.

The Bransoms lived on the fifth floor of a modern apartment block situated at Sea Point, one of Cape Town's suburbs. From the huge picture window in the beautifully furnished lounge there was a superb panoramic view of the bay. Looking north toward Duncan Basin, Tracy thought she could make out the tops of the *Star*'s winches and derricks.

The men carried up her cases. Leigh deposited his on the floor just outside the lounge door, straightened and looked across at Tracy as she turned into the room. His gaze was level and totally unregretful.

"This would seem to be it, then. I've made arrangements for a check to be forwarded here covering your salary for the time you spent with us. I think you'll find the company have been pretty generous."

There was a pause while Tracy tried desperately to break through the numbness enclosing her mind and find something appropriate to say to him. What *did* one say on such an occasion? Theirs was such an odd relationship. Not quite employer—employee—certainly not friends.

"You've been very helpful," she managed at last. "I appreciate it."

His regard sharpened into mockery. "It was a pleasure, Doctor. I hope you didn't find the crossing too rough." He put up a hand and pulled his cap more firmly into place. "Are you ready, Harry? I must get this thing settled as soon as possible."

"Did you?" asked Janet curiously as the door closed behind the two men.

Slowly Tracy turned her head toward the other woman. "Did I what?" she asked tonelessly.

"Find the crossing rough?" Janet's eyes belied the casual voice.

"Not," carefully, "after the first few days." She lifted a hand and ran it over her hair, added quickly, "I feel like a wet rag. Do you think I might have a bath and change my clothes?"

"Of course." Her hostess picked up the suitcase and opened the hall door. "Grab your bag, and I'll show you your room. I've put you next door to the bathroom."

A moment or two later Tracy was alone in the pleasant bedroom that, like the lounge, had its own little balcony outside the window. Here she was on the side of the building, with the sea on the left and Table Mountain looming on the other side.

Coming back indoors she lifted her case onto the long

stool at the foot of the bed, opened it and extracted a sleeveless shift in pale cream linen. A cool bath would go a long way toward restoring her from this limp and lifeless state. Then that cup of tea Janet had spoken of would be the most welcome sight in the world.

How lucky she was that the Bransoms had turned out to be such very nice people, she thought gratefully. She had been more than a little dubious about her reception under the somewhat unusual circumstances. Both Janet and Harry couldn't have made it plainer that they were as eager to have her stay with them as Leigh had been to get rid of her.

Some kind of obstruction seemed to come into her throat, and she swallowed on it hard. She didn't want to think about Leigh Garratt. Not now, not at any time. That particular episode in her life was over.

Harry came home about five-thirty. No, he told them wryly, the man they had been to see was not suitable. Leigh had called him a quack to his face. The latter had gone off now to scout around on his own, but Harry himself did not hold out much hope of his being successful.

The day wore on. Darkness fell, bringing with it a refreshing breeze. The stars were green sparks in the velvety blackness of the sky. After dinner the three of them listened to records and talked. Harry was an accountant, Tracy discovered; Janet a self-confessed idler when she wasn't busy about the apartment. Surprisingly she found herself telling them about the years of her childhood, after her father had died, and of the struggle her mother had had to make ends meet—times she rarely spoke of to anyone. Somehow it was so easy to talk to these two.

By half past ten she could barely keep her eyes open

and wasn't loath to agree when Janet suggested bed for them all.

"We get up very early here by British standards," her hostess said. "The early morning is one of the best parts of the day in the summer."

After 12 nights in a bunk an ordinary bed seemed almost alien, but Tracy was too tired for the change to make much difference. Just before she fell asleep she remembered the party aboard the *Star* and wondered if it had yet finished. More than likely it had been a pretty riotous occasion; a fitting send-off for a crew due to spend the next five months hunting down whales in the icy waters of the Antarctic. She could only hope that it was not her presence that had stopped the Bransoms from attending.

As Janet had said, the African morning was delicious. Soon after sunrise, Tracy was out on her balcony watching the Atlantic rollers creaming onto the beach below. Already there were swimmers down there. Perhaps tomorrow she would join them.

Moving along to the other corner of the balcony, she could see Table Mountain lofting into the aquamarine sky. That glint of silver high up against the rocky face must be the cablecar to the summit. What must it be like to stand right up there on top of the world and look down at the whole of the Cape Peninsula spread out at one's feet?

"Wonderful," said Janet at breakfast. "And the ride up isn't to be missed. How would you like to make the trip this morning? Harry could drop us off at the cable lift on his way in to the office."

Tracy hesitated. "I'd love it, of course," she said. "But I don't want you to feel that you have to go out of your way to entertain me just because I happen to be here. Are you sure it won't be taking you away from anything else?"

"Only the housework, and I'm never loath to leave that till another time," was the frank response. "That's settled, then." She glanced across at her husband. "How about taking the morning off and coming with us?"

"I've seen it," he replied. "And I have three appointments before lunch. If you're still in town at one, call in at the office. I'll run you back here."

By the time breakfast was over the day was already hot and getting hotter. Tracy went to her room and changed from the backless sundress into a simple little shift in white tricel, fastened her hair into the nape of her neck with a blue silk scarf and trod into low-heeled sandals. Her face in the mirror looked colorless, she thought dully, or was it simply the contrast between her comparative pallor and the bronzed complexions sported by the Bransoms? At least, that was something that could be remedied without too much delay.

Harry dropped them off at the cablecar. "Hope you have a good head for heights," he grinned to Tracy through the car window. "You're going to need it up there, I can tell you!"

Staring upward, she had to agree with him. Steel cables, thick as a man's arm, stretched from the terminal building into what seemed like an almost vertical line up—up—up until they were lost against the craggy flanks of the mountain. Thirty-five hundred feet above lay their destination, perched on what appeared to be the very edge of the flat summit. One of the terrifyingly frail cages was just coming in, having met and passed its twin at the halfway mark.

"Nice timing," remarked Janet with satisfaction.

Ten minutes later they were in the air, moving slowly and smoothly upward. Janet was standing, so Tracy stood too, closing her eyes and groping for a support as the ground fell away beneath them. Ordinary heights she could take—but this! It was defying gravity!

When she opened her eyes again they were 500 feet up, and the view was so tremendous that she immediately forgot her vertigo and exclaimed in wonder. As the city receded so did more and more of it become visible, spreading away to right and left, curving gently to form a crescent moon around the mountain's base. A city of gold-washed white and living green.

"If you think this is something, wait till we reach the top," Janet told her, apparently having noticed nothing of her companion's temporary discomfiture.

The cablecar ended in a little store where films and postcards were on sale. There was also a mailbox so that friends and relatives could enjoy the novelty of receiving mail complete with the Table Mountain postmark.

Outside, the scene took Tracy's breath away. Cape Town lay spread below her like some wonderful three-dimensional map, every street, every garden, every building clearly on view. Janet pointed out landmarks: the public gardens around which were grouped some of the city's most important buildings; the cathedral of St. George; Adderly Street with the statue of van Riebeeck, South Africa's founder, at its foot, and then out into the bay and Robben Island, back again to the harbor and docks.

"There's Leigh's ship," she said. "Just like a toy! I wonder if he managed to find a replacement for you?"

Tracy's delight in the view evaporated suddenly.

"I can't imagine Captain Garratt failing to complete any task he set himself," she said flatly, and drew a sharp glance from the older woman.

"He's only human."

"I hadn't noticed," retorted Tracy and immediately wished she had let the subject drop. Leigh was a friend of Janet's, and she herself a guest. She was putting the other woman in a very difficult position.

But it was Janet who refused to let the subject drop. "You're judging him only by his reactions toward yourself, aren't you? Is that fair?"

"Why not?" defensively. "He judged *me* on sight."

A pause, then Janet said in even tones, "There's a very good reason for that. I think perhaps you'd understand better if you knew why he is like he is with you."

"I do know why. At least . . ." Tracy hesitated, once again wishing she could teach her tongue to keep its own counsel . . ."I was told he'd been let down badly by a woman once. Well, all right, it must have been a blow. But he's not the first to be crossed in love."

"Is that all they told you? Yes, I suppose it would be that simple to anyone not in possession of all the facts. Do you want to know what really happened?"

"It's really none of my business, is it?"

"But it might help you to look at our friend in a different light."

That wasn't really important as she wouldn't be seeing him again, Tracy reflected. All the same, she *did* want to know—and if Janet was willing to tell her. . . .

"Let's see—" the latter was saying thoughtfully, having taken her silence for acceptance—"Leigh met Cheryl the year Harry and I came out here, so he'd have been 32. He wasn't a Captain then, of course, but a very good catch for any woman, even so." She leaned against a nearby boulder, a rueful little smile on her lips. "I'd been nagging at him for years to find himself a wife, but he always used to laugh and say he preferred variety. When he called on us that November and told us he was getting married as soon as the season was over, it was like a bolt from the blue. Naturally, we were both very glad for him, but—I don't know, somehow I had a vague sense of unease. There was something about her photograph—" She stopped and shook her head. "It would be so easy to say that I knew she wasn't all she seemed to be. Too easy. At that time I told myself I was just being silly and perhaps even a wee bit envious of her looks." She went on briskly, "Anyway, the wedding never took place. When Leigh got home the following April the bird had flown—with another man. Not only that, but she'd taken him for just about every penny he had. Apparently he'd left authorization for her to draw on his account for the home she was supposed to be getting together for them both." Another small pause, then with deliberation, "The shock of it all brought on the coronary which killed his father."

Tracy drew a shaky breath. "Didn't he try to find her?"

"Oh yes, he tried. But she'd vanished without a trace, and he wouldn't have the police in on the matter at all. I'm glad he wasn't successful. He'd probably have killed them both." Speculatively Janet studied her. "Well, does what I've told you make any difference?"

"Yes," Tracy answered slowly. "Yes, it makes a difference. But he can't go on being bitter for the rest of his life. People who get hurt have to learn to trust again some time."

"Not if the hurt went deep enough. Leigh doesn't trust himself to form a true judgment any more. He lives for the sea and his ship now. I doubt that the woman exists who could break through his armor."

There was a painful tightness in Tracy's chest. "He seems to regard you in a totally different light from the rest of our sex."

"Only because we've known each other all our lives. He looks on me as a friend rather than a woman. Anyway, it's because you. ." She stopped again, and shrugged. "Oh well, that doesn't matter now. He'll be leaving in a few hours." Pushing herself away from the rock, she looked back toward the terminal building. "Shall we go down? You might like to have a look round the stores."

Janet was rather silent during the journey down into the city. Tracy wondered if she was beginning to regret having told her so much. Oddly, she found herself wishing that Leigh's background had remained a secret after all. Learning about people only made it that much harder to forget them.

The following hours ran together in a kaleidoscope of impressions: the colorful store windows; the busy streets; the riotous profusion of plant life in the roof garden where they had coffee; the people—most of all the people. A sea of faces, white, brown, black and every shade in between. A medley of voices and words incomprehensible to the ear.

At a few minutes before one o'clock they made their way to the block where Harry's office was situated. His secretary was expecting them and advised them that he would be free in just a few minutes. In the meantime, would they like to sit down and glance through some magazines?

They did so, taking seats in the window which overlooked a tree-shaded square. Janet eased off her shoes and smiled her relief.

"That's better! My feet are killing me after all that walking. I don't think I've seen as much of the place since we first came over."

Tracy smiled back. "Sorry if I seemed over eager. Tomorrow I must start looking for a job. Once I'm working I might not get much time for sightseeing. I suppose there'll be a whole pile of red tape to get through first, though."

"All taken care of," Janet said easily. "And I think you'll find the Hospital Board very pleased to add you to their staff."

"You seem to have left me very little to do," Tracy

began gratefully and then froze suddenly in her seat as a man came into the room through the door at the far end.

"Leigh!" Janet was on her feet and going to greet him, leaving her shoes lying where she had kicked them. "I thought you'd be on board by now. Did you want Harry?"

"I did but it was only to ask him where I might find Doctor Redfern." His gaze switched to the girl still sitting silently by the window. "There's something I have to say to you," he stated coolly. "Would you mind coming out into the corridor for a moment?"

Tracy found herself on her feet and moving toward him. He held open the door for her, nodded to the surprised Janet and followed her out.

In the corridor she faced him as calmly as she was able, wondering what was coming. There was a certain tension in the line of his jaw. She had the impression that what he was going to say was not what he wanted to say at all. When he did speak realization was just beginning to break over her.

"Would you consider returning to the ship?" he asked.

Dazedly, Tracy leaned back against the wall. This was fantastic. Only a bare 23 hours ago he hadn't been able to wait to get her off his precious ship, and now here he was inviting her back on board again. What did he think she was made of?

She opened her mouth to tell him just where he could go with his request, but instead heard herself saying, "Have you considered sailing without an M.O.?"

His smile was mirthless. "Yes, I've considered it. If you refuse now it will have to come to that. We'll just have to hope that nothing serious crops up this season."

"You're putting me in a tough spot," she said desperately. "That's not playing fair!"

"I'm not trying to play fair. I need an M.O., it seems you're the only one available. It's as simple as that."

No, it isn't, Tracy wanted to say. What about me? Don't my feelings count? She didn't because she wasn't even sure what she meant by that last. All she knew was that she didn't want to return to the *Star*, that she didn't want to sail to the Antarctic, that most of all she wanted nothing more to do with this man standing in front of her.

But it wasn't what she wanted, it was what she had to do. There was no choice. No choice at all. Slowly she straightened, met his eyes, and in emotionless tones burned her boats behind her.

"All right, I'll come."

CHAPTER FIVE

By evening they were well clear of land, steering due south toward those latitudes known so aptly as the Roaring 40's. Standing at her cabin porthole, Tracy relived the last few hours in her mind: Janet's amazement when she was told the news; the mad dash back to Sea Point to collect some clothes; most of her own would have been useless on this trip, of course. Janet had offered her the loan of some slacks and sweaters, saying that she could return them on the way home five months hence.

In no time at all she had been saying goodbye to Janet and Harry and stepping down into the launch that was to take her and Leigh across to the ship. The last she had seen of the Bransoms was two waving figures on the fast receding quayside. Watching them dwindle into the distance, Tracy had known a sudden desperate desire to leap overboard and swim back to the safety they seemed to represent.

As on the previous day, Leigh had made no attempt to converse, gazing ahead toward the ship. Once or twice she had stolen a glance at the eagle's head profile, but had been able to read nothing from the set features. Any faint hope she had entertained of perhaps reaching some kind of understanding with the Captain of the *Antarctic Star* had died completely during those moments. He hadn't softened in his attitude. He never would. The ship needed a doctor, and he had given it one, but that was the limit of his bending.

A light tap on the cabin door turned her away from the porthole. Peter Cramer stood outside in the alleyway, smiling a smile that was balm to her bruised spirit.

"I only just heard you were back," he said. "What happened to change the Skipper's mind?"

"Lack of any other takers," Tracy replied lightly. "It appears I was the lesser of two evils."

Peter said simply, "I'm glad you're back. The ship didn't seem the same after you left yesterday."

"There are those to whom that must have been a relief." She moved back to the bunk to finish putting away her things. "How did the party go last night?"

He grinned, resting one hand lightly on the door jamb. "The usual way. I woke up this morning with the worst hangover I've ever experienced. Pity you weren't here then. I could certainly have used some medical attention."

"Hangovers aren't my speciality, I'm afraid," she said and waited a moment before going on casually, "I suppose everyone was in the same boat—figuratively speaking, that is?"

"With one or two notable exceptions. Both Mike and the Chief Enginneer can drink like fish, but I've never seen either of them the worse for wear yet. Then there's the Skipper, of course." He paused, and wrinkled his brow a little. "That was the odd thing about last night. Normally he hardly touches the hard stuff, yet I saw him put back two double whiskies myself in the space of five minutes."

"Perhaps he had things he wanted to forget?" Tracy suggested evenly, thinking that four years ago Leigh's reasons for taking a drink would have been vastly different—just as the man himself must have been different. If only one could find one minute crack in that iron-hard veneer he wore now, some indication, no matter how slight, that the other Leigh Garratt was not totally dead.

Tracy didn't try to sort out why such a thing should be

important to her. Deep within her she already suspected and feared the answer.

Peter's face had clouded a little. "I suppose everyone has things they want to forget," he murmured, fingering the peak of the cap which he held in his hand. Then his eyes came back to her face, and his expression lightened again. "Like work, for instance. Come and have some dinner, Doc. I'm on duty in an hour."

Leigh did not put in an appearance in the mess that evening. According to Peter this wasn't particularly unusual. The Captain often elected to take his meals alone in the privacy of his cabin while he continued with some work. When things became really hectic, he added, it was quite normal for him to move no farther from his cabin than the bridge, spending almost all the daylight hours up there.

"Still," put in someone else, "the hours aren't as long as they used to be when we fished in the 60's and 70's, are they? At least up here we get a definite period of night. I never used to know where I was with the sun shining at midnight, or near enough." He gave a small sigh. "Mind you, I'd swop those days for now any time. It'd be great if we could persuade the fin to migrate a bit farther south."

"Didn't you go after fin in those days?" asked Tracy with interest and was treated to the faintly condescending smile of the expert addressing the layman.

"Certainly we went after fin, but up to a few years ago the blue whale formed the major part of our catch, and the big boys like to feed around the pack-ice near the mainland. Nowadays we concentrate on fin because it's more plentiful, though much smaller, of course."

"And you don't take the blue at all?"

"We're not even allowed to take them until February. After that it depends on whether we come across any. Given the chance the gunners will go after a blue any time. There's a lot of prestige attached to flagging an 80 or 90 footer."

This latter remark sparked off a spate of story-telling in the immediate vicinity, and Peter grinned cheerfully at Tracy.

"You'll soon learn that on a whaler the talk revolves around little else but. We even dream about the creatures." Regretfully he pushed back his chair. "Ten minutes to go. Feel like walking me as far as the deck?"

Tracy smiled and rose to her feet. "Why not? I could do with a breath of air."

Outside they leaned companionably side by side against the rail and watched the phosphorescence dancing over the breaking heads of the waves curling back from the bows.

"Make the most of it," Peter said softly after a moment or two. "By tomorrow we'll be in a different world."

"It's cooler already," Tracy agreed, feeling the freshening breeze ruffle the collar of her dress. "I'm going to miss the sun."

"Don't we all?" he replied absently and then was silent for so long that Tracy had almost forgotten his presence when he suddenly said. "I had a letter from Deirdre waiting for me when we docked yesterday."

Something in his tone drew her eyes around to his face, but his expression was shadowed by the moonlight.

"Bad news?" she queried gently.

"Nothing I didn't already know about. She just keeps on about my leaving the sea when I get back. Six pages, and she barely mentions anything else."

"I see." Tracy chewed thoughtfully on her lip. "And you still haven't made up your mind?"

"No, I haven't. At least. . . ." He stopped, and shook his head. "All I know is that I'm happy as I am. I like my job, and I can do it. It's all I can do. If I leave the sea, what kind of job can I get?"

"I don't know," she said a little helplessly. "Have you tried—I mean *really* tried explaining to Deirdre how you feel? Surely she wouldn't ask you to give it all up if she realized just what it means to you?"

"Oh, sure I've tried, but it doesn't seem to penetrate. She says I'll soon get over it."

"Has she always resented you leaving her during the season?"

"Not in the same way. When I first met her I guess it was a bit of a novelty having a boyfriend in the Antarctic. It's only these last few months since we were engaged that she's started wanting me out." He sighed. "What would you do if you were me?"

How had she got herself into this? Tracy wondered wryly. She was the last person to be giving advice on love problems. But it was too late to back out now.

"I think what you have to do," she said slowly, "is to ask yourself exactly how much your fiancée means to you, Peter. Do you love her enough to do as she asks *and* accept it without rancor, or would there always be this thing between you?"

"That cuts both ways, doesn't it?" His voice was low. "If she loved me enough, she wouldn't ask me to do something I obviously don't want to do."

"Providing she was wholly aware that you quite definitely didn't want to do it. There's one way of finding out, isn't there? I understand we can have mail taken off every so often. Why not write and tell her what you've just told me—that you can't imagine either of you being happy under such conditions. Women admire men with a mind of their own, even if their ideas don't match up."

He gave her an oblique glance. "Do you?"

"Do I what?"

"Go for the masterful type?"

Tracy laughed. "It depends what you mean by masterful. I can't stand the kind who think they can walk roughshod over a woman as an inferior sex, but I certainly like a man to be a man."

"What exactly do women mean when they say that? What's your definition of masculinity?"

A picture flashed briefly through Tracy's mind of a tall, muscular body surmounted by lean features that at times looked as if they might have been hewn from rock, and her throat constricted.

"It isn't easy to put into words," she said with an attempt at lightness. "But you don't have to worry, Peter. I'd say you were masculine enough to suit any woman."

Some new expression appeared momentarily in the brown eyes, then he laughed. "Thanks, Doctor, I'll remember that." He pushed himself away from the rail. "Time I was getting aloft. Are you going below?"

"I think I will. It's getting too chilly to mooch around up here much longer." Tracy moved with him to the foot of the companionway. "See you at breakfast, if I make it early enough."

"I'll give you a knock." With one foot on the third step he paused to look down at her and add softly, "Glad to have you aboard—or did I already say that?"

She smiled. "You already said it, but I appreciate the sentiment. Goodnight, Peter."

She watched him as far as the next deck, saw him pass the Captain's door to reach the companionway leading to the bridge deck. On sudden impulse she went up a few steps herself. Far enough to see that there was a light behind the drawn curtains over the cabin porthole. Now the vague idea behind the impulse took on a definite shape. Have you really tried to get through to her? she had asked Peter. Well, had she really tried to get through to the man behind that bulkhead? Really tried to attain some basis of understanding? She had five more months to serve under his command—five months which would seem like a lifetime if the air was not cleared between them.

Without stopping to think further about it, she went swiftly up the rest of the steps and across to the cabin door. The shouted invitation to enter that answered her knock brought a momentary faintheartedness, but her hands and feet continued to function even as her determination faltered, opening the door and carrying her forward before she had time to issue them with counter-instructions.

At first glance the cabin seemed empty, although there were papers spread across the desk and several cigarette stubs in the heavy glass ashtray, one of which still smouldered. Then the familiar voice came from behind another door standing ajar in the far bulkhead.

"Be with you in a couple of seconds, Mike. Help yourself to a drink."

So he was expecting the Mate. Obviously she had chosen the wrong time. Perhaps, Tracy thought in something approaching relief, she could creep out again before he came through from the inner cabin and saw her.

But it was too late. Even as she stood there irresolute, there was movement next door. Leigh appeared in the doorway. He was minus his shirt and had a towel slung over one shoulder, one end of which he was using to wipe away the remains of the lather from his face. He stopped abruptly when he saw who his visitor was, and for a long moment there was silence in the room. Then he said expressionlessly, "What can I do for you, Doctor?"

Totally nonplussed, Tracy gazed back at him, very much aware of the way in which the thin white singlet emphasised his tremendous breadth of shoulder. He must, she thought irrelevantly, spend a great part of his summers at home out in the open air to maintain a tan of such depth. She found her voice with an effort.

"I seem to have caught you at a bad time. I'll come again."

"That's all right," he said. "I don't mind if you don't, Doctor." The last word was very slightly emphasized. "What's on your mind?"

"I—It wasn't important." Tracy was beginning to wish desperately that she had gone straight down to her own cabin. How could she had been mad enough to believe for a moment that this man would have any interest whatsoever in putting their relationship on a more friendly footing.

His brow flicked upward. "Important enough to have brought you here in the first place. If you have something to say, say it now. Saving it won't resolve anything."

She eyed him warily, startled by his perception. "I don't think it would do any good," she said at last. "Just forget I stopped by."

"Stay put." The command stopped her in her tracks. Slowly she turned back to look at him and saw one bronzed arm motion toward a chair. "Have a seat while I get into a shirt."

Nervelessly she obeyed. He disappeared once more into the other cabin, to emerge a moment or two later fastening the cuffs of an immaculately white garment. Without looking at her he crossed to a low locker in one corner and opened the door to reveal a neat array of bottles, held firmly in place against storm and tempest by a specially fitted framework.

"Drink?" he asked. "I can offer you quite a good selection—although I'd say you were a sherry tippler, if at all."

Oddly, the satire served to restore her spirit somewhat. The slender body straightened in the chair, and the blue eyes took on a new determination.

"You'd be more or less right, as it happens, but I don't want anything at the moment, thanks."

He said, "Then that makes two of us," closed the door again and leaned his back against the locker to regard her with an expression she couldn't define. "Well?" he asked when a few seconds had elapsed. "What is it that won't do any good?"

Bravely she met his gaze. "I know how much you resent the fact that I have to be here on board your ship at all—"

"Do you?" he asked softly.

"Yes. Yes, I do." Hurriedly she went on, "What I'm trying to say is that I can to a certain extent appreciate how you must feel about having a woman . . . any woman . . . on board, but as it was quite unavoidable, couldn't we . . . wouldn't it be more civilized if we buried the hatchet?"

His face revealed nothing of his thoughts. "You think there's a hatchet to bury?" he asked coolly.

"Well, isn't there?"

"You're supposed to be answering the question, not asking it." One hand went to his pocket and came out with a flat cigarette case. He extracted one, stuck it between his lips and thumbed the built-in lighter to flame, drawing deeply on the smoke as he put the case down on the locker top behind him. "Your choice of phrase suggests a mutual animosity," he went on. "Are you trying to tell me you don't like me, Doctor?"

His continued usage of the mockingly emphasized title was beginning to wear at her nerves. It took all her control to hold onto her rising temper. "That isn't what I meant."

"Then you do like me?" The mockery grew. "Gratifying indeed!"

Tracy relinquished the unequal struggle without regret. Her instincts had been right. He had no intention of even attempting to meet her halfway.

"Like!" she exploded, sitting bolt upright in the chair. "To like a person there has to be something likeable about them—and self-pity never was!"

The lean features opposite tautened, and he straightened away from the locker. "And what," he asked in dangerously quiet tones, "is that supposed to mean?"

With her anger still riding high, Tracy shrugged. "Make what you like of it." She came somewhat unsteadily to her feet. "I think it's time I went."

"Oh no, you don't." In two strides he was in front of her, barring the way to the door. "You made a statement, now you'll enlarge upon it."

For one breathless moment Tracy contemplated what might happen if she attempted to push past him. Would he stand back before determination and allow her to leave? No, she decided, viewing the set of his jaw, he wouldn't. If he had to detain her physically, he would do so without the least compunction. She clenched her hands at her sides. If that was the way he wanted it. . . .

"All right," she flung at him. "If you want the truth, I think Cheryl had a lucky escape when she ran out on you!"

Something frightening happened to the eyes boring down into hers. "Only four people know about Cheryl," he said. "Did Janet tell you?"

Now what had she done? Tracy thought despairingly, bitterly regretting the impulse that had begun this whole sorry interview. Janet had trusted her, and already she had betrayed that trust, perhaps destroyed a friendship formed over years.

"I'm sorry," she said in low tones. "I shouldn't have said that."

"Don't let it worry you." His voice was harsh. "An

inability to control the tongue appears to be a common failing in your sex. What else did Janet tell you?"

"Just the bare facts." Tracy sought for a way to undo the damage she had done. "But she didn't . . . she wasn't . . . She was simply trying to defend you," she finished miserably.

"From what? You?" His gaze swept over her. "What was it, Doctor, pique because I alone out of the whole crew failed to respond to your undoubted charms?" He smiled narrowly. "If that's all that's worrying you, let me set your mind at rest here and now by telling you that as a woman I find you just as good to look at and quite as desirable as the next man. And if it's tangible proof you need. . . ."

Tracy found herself caught and drawn up by two arms that were like steel bands across her back, felt the bruising force of his mouth pressing her head back until she thought her neck would break. Then, as abruptly as he had seized her, he let her go, standing back to regard her with anger still glinting in his eyes.

"Satisfied?"

Pale and shaken, she found her voice. "You. . . ."

The knock on the outer door broke her off short. For a long moment Leigh remained where he was looking down at her, then he turned and moved across to his desk.

"Come on in, Mike," he called.

"Wind's rising," announced the Mate as he eased his bulk in through the doorway. "If the Met people are right, we'll be meeting a force nine head-on by the end of the middle watch." His glance fell on Tracy, and his manner altered. "Hello there, Doctor. I didn't know you were here." Then, with a quick look at Leigh, "I can come back later, if you're busy."

Tracy forced herself to move. "I was just leaving." Stiffly she moulded her lips around the formal leavetaking. "Goodnight, Captain. Goodnight, Chief." Then she was outside in the cool of the night.

She reached her own cabin two minutes later, shut the door, leaned her back up against it, and closed her eyes, feeling the humiliation reaching down inside her as her mind relived the scene enacted a few short minutes ago.

"I hate him," she whispered, but even as she said it she knew that it wasn't entirely true. The emotions Leigh Garratt aroused in her were nowhere near as cut and dried as that.

CHAPTER SIX

The meteorological people were proved right about the weather. By half past one the rising shriek of the wind, coupled with the steady succession of crashes and bangs throughout the ship, had made sleep a virtual impossibility. About this time Tracy climbed out of her bunk to find and fit the storm board along the outer edge, as Peter had shown her, afterward climbing back beneath the blankets secure in the knowledge that it would take a very severe roll indeed to toss her out.

Lying there she tried to dissociate her thoughts from the movement of the vessel beneath her, going right back to the days before she had joined the *Antarctic Star*. Odd how far away it all seemed now. She couldn't even recall Derek's features with any real clarity. Thirteen days, she reflected wryly, that was all it had taken for her feelings to fade. And yet at the time they had seemed so real, so intense. Propinquity? she wondered—and then with a sudden flash of insight, yes, that and an urgent need to love and be loved. Perhaps in Derek, a man almost 20 years older than herself, she had seen a reflection of the father she had barely known. He had all the qualities she would have wanted in such a figure.

It was no good, she acknowledged resignedly, feeling the perspiration break out anew on her forehead as the ship rolled violently to port, this time the tablets just weren't going to work. She sat up slowly, swung her legs over the side of the bunk, then jumped hastily to her feet as her stomach heaved again.

She made it across to the bowl in the nick of time, afterward leaning weakly against the bulkhead to try to regain a little of her breath. Now she knew what Leigh had meant two weeks ago when he had warned her that the real test was still to come. Compared with this, the seas they had steamed through for 24 hours after leaving England had been like a millpond. And there was worse, far worse to come, if all the tales she had heard of the Southern Ocean were true.

It was a long night, and a miserable one. At six-thirty Tracy dressed wearily in slacks and soft white sweater, ran a listless comb through limp, perspiration-darkened hair and clipped it back into the nape of her neck. Make-up was simply too much trouble and would more than likely have only served to emphasize her ghastly pallor anyway. Nevertheless, her basic femininity guided her hand to a tube of pale pink lipstick which she applied lightly to stiff lips, fighting the nausea that kept rising in waves. Not for anything would she give in to the over-whelming desire to lie down on her bunk until this period of discomfort was over. Not with Leigh Garratt waiting in all probability for just that very event.

Peter knocked on her door at seven as he had promised, regarding her with concern when she joined him in the alleyway.

"You poor kid!" he exclaimed sympathetically, totally disregarding the similarity in their ages. "You look like death warmed up!"

Self-pity momentarily swamped her. "Thanks," she snapped pettishly. "That, of course, makes me feel like a million dollars."

His understanding smile made her feel ashamed. Impulsively she put a hand on his sleeve.

"Sorry, Pete. I'm not exactly myself this morning."

Briefly his own hand covered hers, squeezing it lightly. "You'll feel better when you've had something to eat."

Tracy shuddered. "Don't mention food! I couldn't face anything. I'll be in the hospital if anyone's interested."

"You're hardly likely to recover very quickly down there in the stern," he protested. "Why not come along to the mess and just try a couple of dry biscuits and a cup of hot, strong tea? You must have something in your stomach."

"Hey!" she chided gently. "Who's the doctor around here?" She dragged up a washed-out smile from somewhere. "It's nice of you to worry about me, but I'll be right as rain in an hour or two." Providing I'm left alone, she added mentally.

"I hope so." Peter didn't look very convinced. "I'll see you at lunch then."

Tracy didn't bother to disillusion him. It would, she was certain, be quite some time before she could safely turn her thoughts toward food again with any degree of safety.

The few men she met on her way to the hospital all had the consideration to pretend not to notice her obvious indisposition. Joe wasn't yet there; he would still be at breakfast. By the time he did put in an appearance, Tracy thought there was a chance that she might be both feeling and looking better.

At half past eight she was sitting at her desk with closed eyes when the communicator buzzed loudly. Without moving from her seat or opening her eyes she reached out to the bulkhead at her side and pressed down the switch.

"Yes?" she asked tiredly.

Peter's voice came through the grid. "Tracy, the Skipper's on his way down. He's had a bit of an accident."

Tracy came upright, her professional mind taking over. "What kind of accident?"

"He's been cut on the forehead by some flying glass. Looks pretty bad."

Most head wounds always did look worse than they actually were, Tracy told herself quickly. Aloud she said. "Thanks for buzzing me, Peter, I'll be ready."

If only Joe would come, she prayed as she began to prepare for her patient. After last night the very last thing she wanted was to be alone with Leigh, for any reason. But it was still only twenty-five minutes to nine, and the orderly rarely arrived before that hour.

She was scrubbed up and ready when the Captain came through the door. In one hand he held a wadded towel with which he kept dabbing at the jagged wound stretching diagonally from just above the right brow almost to the hairline. The bleeding had by now died away to a comparative trickle, but there was plenty of evidence of the initial profuse hemorrhage in the dark stains adorning the front of his jacket.

"Can you stop this bleeding?" he demanded shortly. "I have work to do."

Silently Tracy indicated a chair, waited until he was seated and nerved herself to approach him, trying to blot out the memory of their last meeting. Avoiding his eyes, she moved his head around to the light and examined the gash, pressing gently along the length of it to feel for any splinters of glass that might still be in the wound.

"How did this happen?" she asked.

The answer was succinct if not particularly explicit. "Broken mirror. What's the verdict?"

"It's a bad cut. I shall have to stitch it."

"Then stitch it, Doctor," he said evenly. "I have to get back to the bridge."

All the time she was preparing the sutures, Tracy could feel him watching her. Her normally deft fingers felt all thumbs, and her jaw was clenched against the nausea that didn't seem to be lifting at all. But no matter how badly she felt, she would die rather than suffer the indignity of being sick under the cynical gaze, she told herself fiercely, blinking away the moisture forming involuntarily at the back of her eyes.

"Have you tried nibbling at a dry biscuit?" asked Leigh into the silence. "It might help."

She stiffened. "I'm all right," she answered shortly. "I don't need anything."

Leigh snorted, "Don't be a fool as well as a liar. There's nothing worse than retching on an empty stomach. Have you been ill all night?"

Tracy looked across at him, saw no sign of mockery in his expression and relaxed just a little.

"Most of it," she admitted. "I thought I'd found my sea legs until we hit this little lot."

He said dryly, "This little lot, as you put it, could even put a seasoned sailor in his bunk for a few hours. And that's where you ought to be until your system accustoms itself. Sergeant could manage on his own, providing nothing urgent cropped up."

The unexpected solicitude disarmed her. Despite herself, Tracy began to smile. "You're supposed to be the patient, Captain, remember?" She brought the tray across to where he sat, set it down on the trolley at his side, and took hold of a piece of cotton wool. "I'll get over it soon enough, I suppose. This is going to sting a. . . ." The last word came out in a gasp as she lost her balance on the steeply canting floor and pitched forward, her hands going out instinctively to the broad shoulders for support even as his own encircled her waist.

For a timeless moment their eyes clashed and held. Tracy felt her heart begin a wild tattoo against the wall of her chest as she saw an echo of her own awareness spring suddenly to life before her gaze.

Confusedly she pushed herself away from him. "I'm sorry," she said. "I . . . I lost my balance."

Now the shutters were down again, hiding his thoughts and making her wonder if she could have imagined that look of a moment ago.

"Yes," he said evenly, "I know. Next time I'll be ready for you. Shall we get on?"

Afterward Tracy couldn't have said how she managed to get through those following moments. With a feeling akin to desperation she concentrated all her attention upon the few square inches of the fine dark head immediately below her fingers, guiding the silk sutures through skin and galea between successive waves. The familiar movements beat a pattern on her brain: through-out-through-out-tie-cut.

At last it was over, the wound was neatly closed, and she was applying a light coating of Whitehead's varnish to keep out any dirt.

"There you are," she said. "I'm no plastic surgeon, but there shouldn't be much of a scar."

Unexpectedly he grinned, and the years fell away. "You mean I'll be unmarred? That's reassuring. When do the stitches come out?"

In tones suitably matched to his own she said lightly, "That sounds like typical male impatience. Four days should do it in your case."

"Why in my case?"

"Because you're healthy and fit, and your flesh will heal the quicker for it." Her voice was brisk. "Just keep it dry."

"Yes, Doctor," he agreed with mock gravity. Then he went to the door, paused, and was once more the autocratic Captain Garratt, master of his ship and all who sailed in her. "I'll send a steward down with some crackers," he said. "See that you eat them."

Much to Tracy's relief the 40's conjured up nothing very

special in the way of storms, and on December second they crossed the Antarctic convergence, marked by the swift and dramatic drop in temperature right down to the lower 30's. Her first sight of drift ice gave Tracy an unexpected thrill, though the two small floes were by no means spectacular in appearance. Now the *Star* turned off to starboard in the direction of Bouvet Island, responding to information received by radio from her catchers sweeping the ocean ahead in their search for whales. An electric current seemed to run through the whole ship, a rippling expectancy which gripped everyone on board.

Tracy was on deck when the first whales of the season were brought back to the factory by the buoy boats used for this purpose; the catchers themselves being far too valuable to waste time towing in their own catch. Within minutes the first great mammal was being drawn up through the slipway in the stern of the ship onto the after-plan where the flensers waited with freshly honed knives. A sperm whale this, almost 50 feet long with a huge tadpole-like head. Tracy found it hard to believe that such a short while ago this huge body had been capable of gliding smoothly and even gracefully through the gray-green waters of its feeding grounds.

With the blubber stripped swiftly and skilfully away, the carcass was then dragged through the central arch to the fore-plan where the lemmers took over, soon to be lost in the clouds of steam rising from the dryers and pressure cookers below decks. Meanwhile the process had begun all over again with yet another whale rising to the waiting flensers.

Despite her forbodings, Tracy found the smell of cooking blubber bearable, although Peter had warned her that owing to the great quantities of oil carried by the sperm, this first period of catching was always the least pleasant of the season. Later, when regulations allowed them to start taking the more valuable fin, the aroma would be very different, he promised her. That time, however, was a whole month ahead.

Days went by in a flurry of activity. As one area ceased to yield, the whole fleet moved on to pastures anew. The vast tanks which formed the nucleus of the *Star*'s hull were slowly being emptied of their cargo of diesel oil and refilled after cleaning with that extracted from the sperm. Several times during the season a tanker would come alongside to take off this product and replace it once more with fuel for the fleet, a cycle which ensured that not one atom of storage space aboard the *Star* was ever left lying empty.

During the first two weeks Tracy saw little of Leigh. All meals were moveable feasts while the ship was "in whales". More often than not the Captain had already eaten by the time she arrived at the mess, or was taking his meal in his cabin to be readily on hand should he be needed urgently on the bridge. On the odd occasions when they did meet he treated her in a casual manner that seemed to suggest that he was learning to accept her presence at last, a state of affairs that should have relieved her, but, oddly, only served to increase the tension she felt in his company. She would even, she admitted to herself, have preferred his continuing enmity to this new indifference.

The week before Christmas the whole fleet became fogbound for several days. With all work stopped apart from general maintenance, a deep depression pervaded the ship. Tracy found herself inundated with patients complaining vaguely of all sorts of minor aches and pains.

"Whale sickness," Peter elucidated when she mentioned the sudden increase in office line-ups every morning. "In other words, boredom. They're used to working a shift of 12 hours and sleeping away a good part of the rest. When there's no work for them they don't know what to do with themselves. Hence the descent on you. It helps to get the morning over at least." Perching on the edge of her desk, he smiled down at her. "Not to mention that you're quite an attraction in yourself."

Tracy wrinkled her nose at him affectionately, her spirits responding as always to the appeal of his personality. Since leaving Cape Town, they had, she felt, become good friends.

"Flattery," she said, "will get you everywhere. Did you want treating for something yourself?"

The brown eyes flickered. "What I'm suffering from can't be cured by anything as simple as a dose of castor oil, I'm afraid."

He meant his trouble with his fiancée, of course. Tracy felt sorry for him. He was being torn in half by this decision Deirdre was insisting on.

"Have you written that letter yet?" she asked, her voice casual.

He shook his head. "Not yet. There's plenty of time. The first tanker doesn't leave for another week."

"Have you thought about what you're going to say to her?"

Slowly he answered, "Yes, I've thought about it." He picked up her stethoscope from the desk and began to swing it gently to and fro between his fingers. "What would you say," he went on carefully, "if I told you I'd decided to call the whole thing off?"

She was silent for a long moment, her mind reviewing this new turn of events. "That has to be entirely your own decision," she said at last. "Only you can tell how you feel."

"But if you were in my position," he insisted. "Wouldn't you feel the same way?"

"Not necessarily." She swallowed on the sudden, inexplicable lump in her throat. "If I loved someone enough I don't think I'd consider any sacrifice too great to make."

"But that's my whole point. I don't love Deirdre enough. I can't, or there wouldn't be any problem."

"You must have loved her a great deal to have asked her to marry you in the first place," Tracy pointed out. "You'd known her almost two years, so it certainly wasn't a spur-of-the-moment affair."

"No, it wasn't." He hesitated. "But people can change, can't they? I wouldn't be the first to realize a mistake. The main thing is to do so before marriage, and not after."

"Well, I certainly can't argue with that."

He was regarding her with a somewhat unnerving intensity. "Then you do agree that I'd be doing the best thing for both of us?"

Tracy spread her hands a little helplessly. "If you feel like that about it, yes. But are you really sure, Peter? Wouldn't it be better to wait out the season? You might feel quite differently about things when you see her again."

Stubbornly he shook his head. "I'm sure now. Probably you think I'm a bit of a coward to do it this way, but I can't last out the season with nothing resolved. When that letter goes on its way I'll feel a free man again." He gave the stethoscope a final swing and put it down. "Are you coming to lunch?"

The sudden change in subject brought Tracy a vague sense of unease. She had the feeling that Peter was holding something back, though what it was she couldn't begin to guess. Accompanying him from the hospital, she decided that the best thing to do was to ignore the whole ticklish subject of his engagement until he chose to mention it again. She had problems enough of her own without worrying over someone else's.

Films were shown three times a week aboard the *Star*, once in the morning for those coming from the night shift, and again in the evening after the day's work was done. Variety was limited, the films being mainly of the Western or situation comedy type where the action could be readily understood and appreciated by all nationalities even if they failed to translate all the dialogue.

That particular evening it was another action-packed epic of the old West, with a screen full of the drawling cowboys, blazing sixguns and fisticuffs so beloved of the male sex of all ages. Tracy went along because, like everyone else on board, she needed the break from the dullness of the day, slipping into a seat at the rear of the cinema next to the unmistakable bulk of the First Officer.

The film had already begun and was claiming the whole of that worthy's attention. It wasn't until the lights went up at the end that Mike reluctantly relinquished his vicarious existence and returned to reality.

"Hello, Doctor," he greeted her in surprise. "I didn't know you were there. Don—" turning to the man on his other side—"we have company."

The Chief Engineer leaned forward to peer around the Mate's middle, his lined face breaking into a cheerful grin as his eyes found the long, pant-clad legs of the only woman on board.

"Sure, and I should have known it was yourself, Doctor. Mike here isn't the type to be wearing perfume. Did you enjoy the film?"

Tracy smiled. "It was a change, though I prefer a good musical any day. Is there anything else on tonight?"

"Just a travelogue," Mike answered comfortably. "South America, I think." He glanced around at her curiously. "Did I say something funny?"

"Not really," Tracy admitted, still smiling. "It's just that it seemed so for a moment to think of sitting here watching a film about the very region I should be visiting right now. One way or another, fate obviously intended me to see those places."

"Fate," put in Don O'Malley straightfaced, "works in some queer ways. I'm a great believer in destiny myself."

Eyes twinkling, Tracy said, "And what would you say was the destiny which guided my footsteps up the gangway of this particular ship? So far as I know, the only affinity I have with the polar regions is a secret addiction to popsicles."

Don didn't smile. "You may laugh," he remonstrated, waving his pipe at her. "But I think you already know what brought you to us, don't you, Doctor?"

"Well, it's not hard," grinned Mike. "It was the fog—the same stuff that's cutting into our bonus figures right now. Let's hope these fates of yours have some fine weather in store for us to make up for it."

And with that he settled himself in his chair as the lights dimmed, his attention focusing once more upon the screen with its magic carpet appeal.

Tracy watched the travelogue without making much sense of it. Her mind was turned inward, cautiously exploring the swift rush of emotions aroused by Don's cryptic words, emotions which had left her bewildered and not a little afraid. *Was* it fate which had brought her to the *Star* and thrown her directly into the path of the man who invaded her thoughts by day and her dreams by night? Without asking, she had known instinctively that it was Leigh Garrett to whom Don had been referring, that in some strange way he had sensed the intangible link between herself and the Captain. And if he was right, then what did the fates have in store for her these coming weeks?

As soon as the lights went up at the end of the program, Tracy stood up.

"Well, that passed the evening," she said lightly, avoiding the engineer's eyes. "What about tomorrow, Mike? Is there any chance of this lot lifting, do you think?"

"With any kind of luck," he returned noncommittally. He hesitated, seemed about to add something else, then apparently changed his mind. "Be seeing you."

In her cabin again, Tracy slowly took off her jacket and dropped it onto the bunk before going across to the mirror. Dispassionately, and with no clear idea of why she did so, she analyzed her own features: heavily fringed eyes; small straight nose; mouth? . . . pretty ordinary. Good to look at, Leigh had said that night in his cabin, but he hadn't meant it as a compliment. For the first time Tracy found herself wondering what Cheryl had looked like and wishing she had asked Janet when she had the chance. True, the other woman had never met Leigh's former fiancée, but she had certainly seen a photograph or two.

The buzz of the communicator interrupted her thoughts, and, as always, made her start. She went across, pressed down the switch and heard the familiar voice with the tensing of mind and muscle that accompanied both sight and sound of the Captain.

"I hear you're as bored as we are," said Leigh clearly. "Why not come along and have a nightcap with us?"

Tracy hesitated, filled with sudden longing to see him, but not quite certain of her ground.

"Mightn't I put something of a damper on the party?" she suggested with a little laugh which effectively concealed her reactions to the invitation—or so she fondly hoped.

His reply was typical. "If there was any chance of that you wouldn't have been invited. I'll have a sherry ready for you."

Tracy stood where she was as the intercom clicked off. So he remembered that much. For some reason that small, insignificant fact lightened her heart.

Swiftly she re-powdered her nose and touched up her lipstick, and briefly regretted her sensibly warm garb of gray slacks and plain blue sweater. She left the cabin with her jacket slung casually across her shoulders to mount the companionway to the deck—the only means of access to Leigh's cabin apart from his own private stairway to the bridge.

Fog swirled thickly about her as she came out into the open air, reaching cold, damp fingers down into the bowels of the ship until she closed the watertight door. So far there was no sign at all of any improvement in the weather, though the sea at least was comparatively calm. As long as conditions remained static they would remain where they were on the fringe of the 50's. The waiting seemed interminable.

Counting herself, there were five officers present in Leigh's day cabin: Mike and Don having come straight up from the cinema. The other was the Second Navigating Officer, a man of approximately Leigh's own age named Jan Anderssen who came from Tönsberg. He was quiet and rather shy, qualities which had endeared him to Tracy from the first because they provided a certain relaxation in his company.

She went now to sit beside him on the long bench seat beneath the portholes, acknowledging his greeting as she accepted the glass of pale amber liquid from Leigh.

"Sorry I can't offer you a choice," said the latter, not

looking in the least apologetic. "We don't normally cater for the sweeter female taste."

The familiar mockery was in his voice, and yet, Tracy thought, there was a difference, something she couldn't quite put her finger on. She answered lightly, "Women are individuals, Captain. As a matter of fact, I prefer the dry."

There was a slight movement at the corners of the strong mouth that could have been the beginnings of a smile. He perched himself on the corner of his desk nearby, his regard steady on her face. "Did you enjoy the entertainment provided tonight?"

Perversity colored her reply. "Certainly I did."

"Strange," he murmured. "At the risk of being accused of generalization again, I'd have said that particular film had little appeal for women. Could there be a yearning for excitement beneath that professional self-possession of yours?"

"If there wasn't I probably wouldn't be here at all, would I?" she retorted mildly and saw the gray eyes glint.

"A question to answer a question. There's a feminine tactic, if ever I heard one!"

Tracy raised her head and looked straight at him for the first time. The scar at his temple still stood out lividly against the tanned skin, lending the lean features a piratical air. She said evenly, "I wasn't aware that my femininity was in question."

At her side the Number Two stirred restlessly, sensing the conflict without understanding it. She turned to him gladly.

"You promised to show me those photographs of your family some time, Jan. Do you have them with you?"

He brightened immediately. "Yes, I have," he said in his precise English and put an eager hand to his pocket. "You would like to see them?"

"Very much," Tracy answered with sincerity, and tried to shut her mind to the man still sitting on the desk edge. It wasn't so easy to do, and she was aware of the precise moment when he removed his gaze from her.

Admiring the Second Officer's fine-looking family took up some time. When Tracy finally emerged, the other three were talking the eternal "shop".

"Remember that bonanza we hit off Georgia five years ago?" Mike was saying reminiscently. "Five weeks' non-stop work! We could do with that kind of luck this year."

"And some," agreed Leigh, rolling his glass thoughtfully between his hands. "I'm beginning to regret not going East again this season. We must be ten percent down compared with the same period last year." His eyes lifted, found Tracy's, and took on some new expression. "You wouldn't be a Jonah, would you, Doctor?" he asked lightly.

"Would you throw me overboard, if I was?" she returned in the same tone, and he gave the sudden boyish grin which jerked at her heart-strings.

"There's every chance. Superstition runs rife on a whaling ship."

"'Tis a man you're needing to protect you, Doctor," offered the little engineer with twinkling eyes, drawing a snort of derision from the massive figure at his side.

"Go on, you old Irish reprobate, you couldn't protect a spider from a fly!"

"'Tis the offer that counts," was the unperturbed reply. "Isn't that so, me darlin'?"

"Every time," agreed Tracy, laughing. "I'll bear it in mind."

"Not that I'd want to be treading on anybody's toes," he insisted, and the twinkle deepened into speculation. "There'll be a young man back home, I'm thinking?"

Pink crept into Tracy's cheeks under Leigh's satirical gaze. "No," she said, "there isn't."

Don shook his head sadly. "You should have been born in Ireland. You'd have been wed this many a long year!"

"In England a career often takes the place of marriage," Leigh put in smoothly. "Could be you have no need of a man in your life, Doctor?"

Now it was Don's turn to snort. "Every woman has need of a man in her life!"

"Which brings you back to where you started," said Mike. "And you're embarrassing the doctor, you old fool!"

"Are you embarrassed?" asked Leigh mockingly. It took all of Tracy's will power to turn her head toward him and widen her mouth into a smile. "Oh, covered in confusion! It isn't often I find myself under a microscope. Anyway, I thought we were talking about whales?"

There was the briefest of pauses during which his eyes taunted her, then the broad shoulders lifted in an easy shrug.

"Blame our friend from the Emerald Isle for sidetracking the conversation. He probably thought the subject was boring for you."

"As a matter of fact, I think it's fascinating," she came back firmly. "How do you decide which way you're going to go next?"

"Quite simple. While we're fishing one area I send out a couple of expeditions to scout ahead. If one of the boats finds better prospects than those existing, we go after her. Otherwise we continue to follow our predetermined course and hope for the best. At the moment we're heading . . . very slowly, I might add . . . for South Georgia."

Somewhere at the back of Tracy's memory a file

clicked open. "Isn't there a whaling station on the island?" she asked hesitantly.

"There was. The land-based factories are closed now."

"Oh." She was interested. "Why is that?"

"They were becoming uneconomical to run. A fleet can follow the whales in any direction. Their catchers had to make a double journey with each catch, sometimes over 100 miles each way for a couple of finback. A few of my men used to be based on Georgia. I think it's true to say that not one of them would go back to that life, even if they had a choice."

"So now the island is uninhabited?"

"No, there's still a small settlement at Grytviken, but the only ships which call there now are the relief ships on their way to or from the mainland."

"The land of the midnight sun," put in Don O'Malley irrepressibly. "How would you like to live with a 24 hour day, Doctor?"

Her smile was mischievous. "I've been doing it for the last 25 years without coming to any great harm."

He made a theatrical grimace of pain. "Will you be leaving the wit to them that was born and bred to it, woman, and stop cluttering up me tale with irrelevancies! 'Tis some rare sights you'd be seeing if we were down there now. Bergs as big as castles; ice-fields stretching from here to Christmas!" His voice warmed to the memory. "Three days we were once trapped in such a pack. When the sun touched the horizon it was like resting in the middle of a sea of fire!"

"Beautifully told, Chief," remarked Leigh on a note of lazy amusement. "But paint a complete picture while you're about it." Now he addressed Tracy directly. "Ice has its attractions, but it can also be dangerous. That's the important thing to remember."

Yes, Tracy decided, raising her glass to her lips to

escape his regard, that certainly was an important thing to remember.

CHAPTER SEVEN

Some time during the night the fog lifted. At first light the ship came back to life again, her crew responding joyfully to the call to duty. By nine o'clock her decks were full of whales, and the rare Antarctic sun came breaking through the clouds to sparkle the slow-running sea and add to the general well-being.

Office calls that morning were almost ridiculously light, consisting of a cook with a burned hand, and a mess-boy who had fallen off the conveyor belt on the tank deck below and sprained a wrist.

"It's always the same after a lay-off," Joe explained after the youngster had been dealt with. "Nobody wants to think about medical treatment when there's bonus figures to catch up on. For the next few days it will be accidents only—unless something drastic crops up."

"Does everyone share in the bonus?" asked Tracy idly, drying her hands on the towel he handed her.

"Every last man," he agreed. Then he gave her a swift grin. "And yourself, of course, Doctor. Naturally it depends on one's position in the scheme of things as to how much one gets. The Captain and gunners get the biggest cuts. Well, without them we wouldn't have a catch at all, would we?"

"Hardly." She laid the towel over the rail. "Have you ever been out with a catcher yourself?"

He shook his head regretfully. "Never had the opportunity. The crews are notoriously superstitious about taking strangers out on their boats. The last M.O. made one trip, though. He had to go across to tend to a case that couldn't be moved, and while he was still aboard they made a sighting and took off after the pod. He said afterward that it was one of the most memorable experiences of his life."

Tracy didn't doubt that. Seen from the height of the *Star*'s decks, the little catchers looked ridiculously tiny and fragile to stand up to the hammering of the mighty seas they had to combat in these regions. Days like today, when the surface was relatively calm, were all too few and far between.

The morning progressed smoothly. After coffee at 11, Tracy went up on deck and found herself a sheltered position from which to watch proceedings. As Peter had said weeks ago, the daytime temperatures at this time of year, and in this part of the whaling grounds, rarely fell below freezing point, but the winds could and did cut through clothing like a knife.

From where she stood she only had to turn her head to see the two great icebergs rising in stark white splendor half a mile away on the port beam. Twin peaks glittering in the sunlight, sculptured by the never-ceasing wash of the sea into fairytale grottoes and caves. Soon these particular ones would be left behind, but others would take their place. In these latitudes there was almost always ice of some kind in sight.

"Grand weather," boomed an unmistakable voice almost in her ear, and she turned with a smile to find the Mate at her back.

"That's a very British opening gambit, Chief," she bantered, and the black beard parted in a grin.

"It is that! Let's hope we're in for a few more like this. The way things are going this morning, we'll be making up that ten percent before we know where we are."

"How far are we from South Georgia now?"

"Roughly 500 miles, as the crow flies," Mike moved to the rail at her side, bracing his bulk against it with forearms the size of small trees. "Moving in a straight line we could be off Georgia in a matter of days, but as Leigh was telling you last night, no whaling fleet ever moves in a straight line for long. We follow the whales, and they're not always predictable."

Along with others, Tracy thought fleetingly. Aloud she said, "You've known the Captain a long time, haven't you, Mike?"

"Quite a few years," he agreed, watching the approach of a ferryboat with a critical eye. Then he was leaning out over the rail, and a stentorian roar was being directed at the vessel far below, "What are you trying to do—ram the ship?"

"Sorry about that," he added, straightening again. "Either that helmsman is drunk, or he was half asleep. What was I saying?"

"About knowing Le . . . the Captain a few years," Tracy prompted in carefully casual tones. "How many seasons have you done together?"

"Seven—though this is only the fourth since Leigh got his command."

She glanced at him swiftly. "Wouldn't you like a command yourself?"

The massive shoulders moved in a gesture which could have been construed as a shrug. "Sure I would. Who wouldn't? Trouble is, shortage of vacancies."

Tracy said softly, "Mr. Garratt didn't seem to have much trouble in finding one. Isn't he a shareholder in the Company, too?"

"Yes, he is." A frown was drawing down the heavy brows. "Now see here, Doctor, I'm not sure what you're getting at, but Leigh was given command of the *Star* for one reason and one reason only. Because he merited it. As it happens, he already knew about his promotion before he invested in the Company."

"I see." Tracy bit her lip, regretting the impulse that

had led her into finding out the truth this way. "I'm sorry, Chief. I spoke out of turn."

The big man relaxed again. "Forget it. There were a lot of others thought the same way at the time. Being the kind of man he is, Leigh just never bothered scotching the rumor."

"What kind of man is he?" murmured Tracy, her gaze fixed on the horizon.

The answer was firm. "The best. He'd never let anybody down."

"Unlike Cheryl," she said, thinking aloud and felt his sharp glance.

"How do you know about her?"

"It doesn't matter." She was silent for a moment, then despite herself the words were drawn from her. "What was she like, Mike?"

The blue eyes were suddenly shrewd. "Why do you want to know?"

Which was a very good question, Tracy reflected. Why did she want to know? What difference could it make? "Call it feminine curiosity," she answered lightly, not looking at him.

For the space of a few seconds his gaze continued to pierce her, then he said, "As a matter of fact, she wasn't unlike you. Same color hair, same eyes—perhaps just an inch or so shorter." His voice roughened a little. "She looked as though butter wouldn't have melted in her mouth, damn her!"

Tracy drew an aching breath. So that was it! That was why Leigh had treated her as he had during this voyage. Not just because she was a woman, and he hated all women as she had believed, but because she looked like the one woman he wanted to forget. Now, at last, she could begin to understand his attitude.

"So she took you in, too?" she asked quietly.

"Me?" Mike's laugh was without humor. "She took everyone in."

"Then why does Leigh blame his own judgment so badly?"

"Because he was closest to her, of course. Wouldn't you feel the same way?"

"I suppose I would." She scanned the waves thoughtfully. "Do you really think she had the whole thing planned from the start?"

He shrugged. "Perhaps not right from the first, no—not in the way it finally turned out, at any rate. It's my belief that she saw Leigh as a golden opportunity: marriage with a man who could afford to keep her in style and was away half the year, must have seemed like a heavensent arrangement to someone of her caliber. One well worth angling for. Then she met this other man, fell for him, and decided to have the best of both worlds. You know the whole story?"

"More or less." She hesitated. "That first night when I came aboard, were my looks a part of the reason you wouldn't let me see him?"

"The main reason," he returned bluntly. "Thinking, as I did, that you really were our replacement, I might have been able to persuade him to accept you had you looked anything but what you did. As it was, that might not have been so easy, and neither the company nor the crew would have thought much of hanging around in port until another M.O. could be found. It's very important, you know, for a Captain to retain the confidence of everyone concerned."

Tracy turned her back on the sea, her eyes following the lines of the huge sperm that had just been drawn up the slipway onto the after-plan. Fifty feet at least, she assessed absently. That meant close to 50 barrels of oil.

"You think he wouldn't have considered that himself?" she asked.

"I didn't want to take the risk. You were a strong reminder of something he'd tried to put behind him; a reminder he'd be seeing every day, more or less, for months. I couldn't have blamed him if he'd refused to take you, but no one else could have been expected to understand. Anyway, it's all so much water under the bridge now, isn't it? You're here at his own invitation."

"But still under sufferance," she murmured.

A moment passed before he answered. "About that I wouldn't know. Leigh keeps his mind a closed book these days." He heaved himself away from the rail. "I'm for an early lunch and a couple of hours' shut-eye before I take over from Jan. I suppose you'll be waiting for young Cramer?"

"I usually do," Tracy replied abstractedly. She watched the Mate start to move away, added impulsively, "Mike, what you've told me this morning . . . it won't go any farther."

His head came around to where she stood. "If there'd been any chance of that I wouldn't have opened my mouth."

"Why did you?" Her voice was suddenly urgent. "Why did you tell me, Mike?"

"Because you wanted to know," he replied simply. Then he smiled and sketched a salute. "See you later, Doc."

Tracy remained where she was long after he had gone, oblivious to the men working within feet of her, and to the fact that the wind had veered around to the south-west and was tearing at the ear flaps of the fur cap Peter had lent her with every likelihood of whipping it from her head.

Fate, Don O'Malley had called it, and now, for the first

time in her life, Tracy began to believe that there really was such a thing.

Lunchtime that day found a stranger in the mess. Leigh introduced him to Tracy as Greg Street, Captain and gunner of the catcher *Tiger Rose* that had come in with engine trouble. The newcomer was in his 40's, thick-set and powerful-looking, with a shock of the brightest red hair Tracy had ever seen.

"Heard so much about this new M.O. of ours I thought I'd take a look for myself while I'm here," he grinned, offering her a leathery hand. "How's it going?"

"Oh, it's mostly plain sailing," she replied, straight-faced. "Is the trouble serious?"

"Could have been if it'd been left much longer." His eyes were twinkling. "Know anything about engines?"

"Not so that you'd notice." She broke the bread roll in half and applied butter, remembered something and glanced across at him again. "Did you bring in that 62-footer?"

He inclined his head. "Guilty, ma'am. Who told you it was 62?"

"I was there when they measured it."

"You thought it was more?" asked Leigh, and the other man nodded.

"Something like 65, judging from the deck after we'd cut off the flukes. My eye must be way out this trip."

Tracy said quickly, "But you still broke the fleet record, didn't you? I understood the previous largest sperm taken was just over 60."

"So it was. Remember that, Leigh? You were on board the *Rose* when we took him."

"Six years ago, wasn't it?"

"About that." His gaze came back speculatively to Tracy. "You seem to be picking up quite a bit about the business, one way or another, but you only see half the picture stuck up here on this old tub. How would you like some real action?"

Startled, she said, "Are you offering to take me out on your boat, Captain?"

"The name," he said, "is Greg. Would you come?"

Involuntarily her glance went to Leigh, who met it expressionlessly. "I . . . don't know. . . ."

"You don't think the boss would approve? Let's find out, shall we? How about it, Leigh?"

Two pairs of eyes clashed and held; two spots of color appeared high on Tracy's cheekbones. Despite her attempt to conceal it, she knew that Leigh was fully aware of the flash of resentment that had accompanied the knowledge that she must apply to him for permission to take up this invitation—a resentment made all the more childish by the fact that it was based on personality rather than position.

The answer came with deliberation. "When had you in mind?"

"What's wrong with this afternoon? Conditions are as good as we're ever likely to get, and we seem to be in a profitable area. One of the buoy boats could pick her up tonight, couldn't they?"

Coolly Leigh studied the girl at his side. "Are you keen to go?"

Tracy wasn't particularly, but she wasn't prepared to admit it. "If I can be spared," she said, equally coolly, and he flicked an eyebrow.

"You're in a better position to know that than I am. Is there anything likely to crop up during the next few hours?"

"Barring accidents, no."

Greg was looking from one to the other with some interest. "Do we take it as settled, then?"

"By all means." The tone was smooth. "As you say, a chase is an experience not to be missed. Hope you strike lucky, Greg."

"I've a feeling the Doc's going to bring the luck with her. Can you be ready in half an hour?"

"If pushed." Stifling her trepidation at the thought of the coming experience, she smiled at him. "What will I need?"

"The warmest clothes you have. Conditions aboard the *Rose* are a mite different from this mobile oven. One of the ABs'll lend you some oilskins. You'll need 'em if you want to see everything."

Ten minutes later Tracy left the mess to go to her cabin and change. With Greg's warning in mind she put on her thickest pair of slacks and donned a couple of sweaters beneath the thick duffle coat she had so often been thankful for. With Peter's fur cap on her head and a pair of stout shoes on her feet, she felt ready to brave the elements.

Peter was about to knock on her door as she opened it to leave the cabin.

"Is anything wrong?" he asked. "You left the mess in a bit of a hurry."

Her explanation elicited a somewhat indignant response. "I've been trying for a trip out on a catcher these last two seasons," he said. "The Skipper never offered to have me picked up by buoy boat."

"He didn't exactly offer this time," Tracy rejoined dryly. "It was Captain Street's suggestion."

"He could always have said no. Just goes to prove that nobody's immune to those big blue eyes of yours." His voice was teasing. "Mind if I come and see you off? I've nothing better to do at the moment."

Steam greeted them as they came out onto the fore-plan. Rolling white clouds of vapour lifted into the blue sky. The *Star* was in full production, having taken on as many whales as she could handle for the next hour or two.

"Looks good," Peter commented, nodding in the direction of the blackboard showing the number caught that morning. "Judging by those figures, I'd say you couldn't have chosen a better time to go."

"Wouldn't it be possible for you to come, too?" she asked impulsively. "If Captain Street is prepared to take one stranger with him this afternoon, he might be equally prepared to take two."

"That's open to doubt. In any case, it wouldn't be any use. I'm not exactly in the Skipper's good books these days."

"Oh?" She looked at him quickly. "Any special reason?"

He shrugged. "Reason enough, I suppose. I've made one or two mistakes lately."

"Bad ones?"

"Not particularly. But the Skipper doesn't recognize degrees. You should know that by now."

Yes, Tracy thought, she did know it.

"You're not in the habit of making mistakes normally, I gather?" she asked.

"No." Something else came into his tone. "I've . . . had rather a lot on my mind this last week or two."

"I know." They had reached the midships super-structure, and as if by common consent had stopped. Facing him, she said frankly, "Peter, you're letting this whole affair get you down. Can't you make up your mind to forget about it until you get home?"

"No," he answered firmly, "I can't. It's too long to wait." The boyish face was unusually serious. "As a doctor, wouldn't you say that peace of mind was one of the most important contributions to good health?"

"It's certainly a good thing to have."

"Well then? The only way *I'm* going to attain peace of

mind is to get this whole thing sorted out as soon as possible. My next mistake might not be a minor one."

It certainly wouldn't be if he did call off his engagement in such a manner. She reflected and searched her mind for some way in which to convince him that the peace of mind he sought was not to be found that way. In time to come he would hate himself for not having waited to face Deirdre in person.

Figures appeared out of the cloud of steam at their backs. Tracy turned her head to see Leigh's eyes narrow slightly as they moved from herself to Peter and back again.

"There you are," said Greg Street cheerfully. "All set?"

"All set," she agreed, trying to ignore the thought that Leigh was almost certainly reading more into her closeness to Peter than existed. Even if he was, there was nothing she could do about it. A little self-consciously she smiled at the Number Three. "I'll tell you all about it when I return."

"Yes," he said. "Hope you have a good trip." He went off the way they had come, leaving her to continue aft with the other two men.

The supply basket in which they were to transfer to the *Tiger Rose* was all ready, waiting. Repairs were complete, and Greg was eager to be off.

"You'll be picked up before dark," Leigh told Tracy when she was in the basket. For a brief moment he looked down at her, then he transferred his gaze to her companion. "Good day, Greg." His hand went up to signal to the winch driver. "Take it away."

Tracy tipped up her face as the basket swung down and out across the fenders to the decks of the catcher, saw Leigh wave a casual salute as they touched down. Then he was gone.

To call a catcher a small boat was actually to give an

erroneous impression. The *Tiger Rose* was a 500 tonner, with a 3000-horsepower engine capable of attaining as much as 18 knots if required. Two things distinguished her from other boats of similar size in the fleet: the gun platform mounted in the bows and joined to the bridge by a catwalk, and the crow's nest at the top of her mast from which the lookout could spot whales up to ten miles away in good visibility. Greg lost no time getting under way. Soon the factory had vanished beneath the horizon, and they were alone in the long slow swell that was the Antarctic in one of her kinder moods.

Time passed slowly at first. It was cold up on the open bridge, so cold that Tracy could barely keep her teeth from chattering. Her feet she couldn't feel at all, which was probably something of a blessing. How right Greg had been, she thought longingly, when he had called the *Star* a mobile oven. With the bone boilers and pressure cookers going at full steam right beneath one's feet the factory's decks were never uncomfortably chilly.

Not that anyone else seemed to notice the cold. Dressed from head to foot in oilskins, as she was herself, Greg leaned against the rail and chatted idly with various members of his crew. But his eyes, Tracy noted, were never still, scanning the ocean through the perspex wind-deflector like a hawk searching for its prey.

A shout from the crow's nest brought everyone alert. The man was pointing off to starboard and holding up three fingers. Despite her misery, Tracy found herself straining her eyes to catch a glimpse of the anticipated spouts of water.

"They've dived," said Greg at her side. "We won't see them again for ten or 15 minutes. Let's hope they keep going in the same direction."

"I thought you used Asdic?" she said, wondering how long he was going to wait before taking his place on the gun platform. "Surely you can keep track of them even when they're under water?"

"Sure we can," he agreed. "But I only use it when it's essential. It might pick 'em out, but it also scares 'em off mighty quick."

"How can you tell these are sperm you're going after?" she wanted to know next. "Couldn't they just as easily be fin?"

"If they are I'll be throwing that lookout overboard with my own two hands. Anybody can recognize a sperm's blow by it's angle." He took his eyes from the water ahead to grin around at her. "And in case you're laboring under the popular misconception, that's not water they shoot out when they surface, it's hot air vaporizing. Okay?"

Tracy smiled back at him. "You live and learn."

Five minutes later the whales surfaced again, only a bare half mile away this time and still running on a reasonably straight course. That they were becoming nervous, however, was soon made apparent by an increase in speed and a very much abbreviated breathing period before the great bodies slid once more beneath the waves. Now, at last, Greg went forward down the catwalk to the gun platform. The next time the pod came up for air he was going to be waiting for them. Watching him swing the heavy gun in an experimental arc, Tracy could almost see the ripple of muscle beneath the enveloping waterproofs.

Another shout from above—and there they were. One—two—three tremendous bodies rising from the depths in bursts of foam. Were they within firing distance? Yes, Greg was drawing a careful bead on the largest.

A sharp crack, and the armed harpoon was speeding on its way to bury itself deep into the curving back, just behind the head. Immediately the whale dived, the line screeching out behind it. For some seconds there was comparative silence, the engine having been stopped at the moment of firing. Then, slowly but surely, the winch driver down below on the foredeck began to put on the brake, heaving down with all his might against the 30 tons of runaway giant. Suddenly there was slack, and significant glances were exchanged. The whale was coming up.

"Dead," said Greg with certainty, leaning over the bridge rail to watch the way the line was coming in. "He'd be coming up faster than that if he wasn't."

He was right. Moments afterward they were heaving in the floating carcass to be inflated, marked and flagged. From start to finish the whole operation had taken only 25 minutes. A quick, clean kill bearing no resemblance whatsoever to those tales of day-long battles and blood-stained seas that had so colored Tracy's imagination. Her relief was infinite.

Six more whales were taken that afternoon, though she herself saw only one other caught. Down in the galley it was warm and snug. Tracy felt quite content to sit in a corner near to the stove and sip gratefully from a huge mug of steaming coffee out of the pot kept permanently simmering. Coming out with the *Tiger Rose* was an experience she wouldn't have missed, she decided, but it was also one she wouldn't care to repeat. This was a man's world: hard, dangerous, demanding in the extreme. They were welcome to it.

The buoy boat turned up soon after supper. Tracy was rowed across after taking leave of the men who had gained her wholehearted admiration during that long and freezing afternoon. Surprisingly the journey back to the ship took only a little over half an hour. Either she had been moving in their direction, or the whales chased by the *Tiger Rose* had led them back along more or less the same course they had taken on the outward journey. Never had any sight been more welcome than the great steam-smothered bulk looming ahead.

Leigh was talking to Jan at the foot of the companion-way leading to his cabin when she went forward after landing back on board the *Star*. He saw her approaching, broke off his conversation with the Number Two, who then went on up the steps to the higher deck, and waited for her to draw level.

"So Greg was right," he remaked sardonically. "You did bring him luck. Enjoy yourself?"

Tracy looked back at him tiredly. She was in no mood for clashing swords tonight. "If I didn't," she answered, "it was no one's fault but my own. They made me very welcome."

His regard moved over her features, and the line of his mouth relaxed a little. "Yes," he agreed, "they would. Come on up and have a drop of something to warm you through. I want to talk to you."

In the cabin he shut the door firmly, tossed his cap onto the desk, and crossed to the corner locker.

"Make yourself comfortable," he invited, selecting a couple of bottles from the stock within. "While Mile's still up there I can afford to take a little more time off."

"But not once Peter takes over?" she surmised out loud, and he looked at her sharply.

"I detect a note of censure. Has he been crying on your shoulder?"

"Not at all. He just happened to mention that he'd made a couple of mistakes during this last week or so." Her tone was level. "It's a very human failing."

"Usually governed by the emotions," he retorted, putting a glass into her hand. "I suppose you're aware that he has a fiancée back home?"

Tracy took a small sip of the sherry and set the glass down on the desk at her side. "Yes, I am."

"And it doesn't bother you?"

She said stiffly, "There's nothing between us, if that's what you're implying. Two people can be friends without romantic entanglements."

"They can, but I can't see that kind of relationship getting Cramer to the point where he doesn't know what day it is. Since we left Cape Town he's been acting like a man walking in a dream."

"And you think it's because of me?"

"What else?" Briefly he studied her. "Do you expect me to believe that he's never even tried to kiss you?"

"Yes," she said flatly, "that's exactly what I expect you to believe. It happens to be the truth." She took a breath to calm herself. "So far as Peter is concerned, I'm simply someone he can talk to about his problems, and that's all."

Leigh leaned against the corner of his desk. "So he does have problems. Bad ones?"

"Bad enough." With him so near it was impossible to relax. "Naturally I can't say any more than that. What he tells me is told in confidence to his doctor."

"Has he asked you for advice?"

"Yes."

"And you've given it?"

"I've . . . tried." She looked down at her hands clasped in her lap and frowned. "It isn't easy to know just what *to* advise in his particular case."

"Perhaps because your own emotions have some involvement in the outcome?" he suggested, and her head rose swiftly.

"What do you want, a signed confession to the effect that I deliberately set out to steal another girl's fiancé? Would it satisfy you to hear me admit that I was madly in love with your Third Officer?"

"Don't be childish," he said with maddening calm. "All right, so we accept that you're not in love with him. In which case, it shouldn't be any great hardship for you to try spending a little less time with him."

"Is that," she asked quietly, "an order?"

"Call it a suggestion for the moment. If he already has emotional problems I'd prefer that they didn't become too complicated." He tossed off the rest of his whiskey and soda, added cynically, "You've heard the saying 'Off with the old love, on with the new'?"

"Yes," she said, "I've heard it. But I tell you it doesn't apply to Peter."

"Perhaps not yet. But it could. Thrown into your company for any length of time, few men could hope to keep their feelings on a purely platonic basis. You're not built for it."

"Thanks," she retorted bitingly, and he looked suddenly amused.

"It's a simple biological fact. Would you prefer to be admired for your fine mind?"

He was deliberately baiting her, she knew, and enjoying it. Once again she damped down her rising temper. The last time her tongue had run away with her she had received rather more than she had bargained for. Not for anything was she going to risk that kind of humiliation again.

"If there's nothing more, I'd like to go and change," she said, rising. "Sorry about the waste of sherry, but I wasn't really in need of a drink."

"That's all right," dryly. "I'll save it for your next visit." He straightened. "Don't let resentment color your finer judgment in Cramer's case, will you? I'd hate to have to say I told you so when he starts becoming a nuisance."

"The situation," she stated, "will not arise. Good-night, Captain Garratt."

"And pleasant dreams to you, too," was the mocking response.

CHAPTER EIGHT

Christmas Day was not observed as a general holiday aboard the *Star*. The men preferred to work their normal shift system and earn the generous rates of overtime paid by the company. Celebrations, however, went on apace throughout, beginning with the distribution of greetings telegrams from families and friends at breakfast time, and finishing with the traditional feast, transferred to the evening so that both shifts could share in the festivities.

Dressing for dinner, Tracy reflected that so far it had been a very enjoyable day—enjoyable and heart-warming. On her desk stood no less than 11 beautifully carved and polished figures all wrought from the teeth of the sperm whale by skilful hands. Enough to start a zoo, Joe Sergeant had remarked with amusement after the last bashful but determined craftsman had pressed his gift into the doctor's hands and made his escape. Tracy's held-in laughter had bubbled over to join his. But funny as the situation was, nothing could detract from the giver's good intentions. In each of those carvings were weeks of painstaking work. It was only to be expected that the penguin would be the most easily suggested form to follow owing to the natural curve of the tooth. She would treasure them all.

Peter knocked on her door at six-forty-five precisely, pursing his lips into a soundless whistle as he took in the details of her appearance: hair falling smoothly onto slender shoulders clad in smoky blue silk jersey that flared softly from a narrow belted waist.

"You've certainly done us proud," he observed. "Which little bird whispered in your ear to bring along that creation?"

"Vanity," she admitted with a laugh. "Not that I really thought I'd have a chance to wear it. I'm not over-dressed?"

"You're perfect," he assured her with enthusiasm. "I'm going to be the envy of every man present when I walk you into the mess tonight."

"I suppose you'll still have to be on duty at the same time?" Tracy asked as she pulled the door shut.

He made a wry face. "Someone has to be on the bridge. At least I have the chance to have dinner along with everyone else. Poor old Mike won't get his until eight." As they turned the corner he put out a sudden hand to lightly touch her hair, added softly, "I like it like this. You should wear it down more often."

She laughed. "I have enough trouble being taken seriously in my job without adding to the difficulties. Flowing tresses don't suit the public image of a doctor. Anyway, in surgery it isn't hygienic."

"Spoken with the true voice of dedication." There was an odd note in his own voice. "Do you ever think of anything else but your work?"

A lump came swiftly into her throat. "Sometimes," she said, low-voiced, and he stopped walking to look down at her.

"Tracy. . . ."

Jan Anderssen turned into the alleyway behind them, his nice, open face breaking into a smile as he saw them.

"Good evening, Doctor—Peter. Do you smell the turkey waiting for us?"

"I've been smelling it since teatime," Tracy smiled back. Automatically she fell into step beside him, leaving Peter to bring up the rear. "At home in Norway you celebrate on Christmas Eve, don't you?"

"It is traditional to have the main feast on that day," he agreed. "However, I have become used to the English custom in the years I have been coming down to the Ice. It is good for different peoples to celebrate together, is it not?"

"Very good." They had reached the mess now. As she went in Tracy wondered briefly what it was that Peter had been going to say to her before Jan had caught up with them. He had looked serious and somehow determined, as though about to spill something that had been weighing on his mind. Deirdre, no doubt. In a lot of ways it would be a very good thing when he got that problem sorted out.

They were the last to arrive in the mess; within seconds Tracy found herself the center of an admiring crowd. Flushed and laughing, she moved her eyes around the circle of faces, but the one she sought was not to be seen. Only when someone shouldered their way through to press a glass into her hand did she catch a glimpse of the broad shoulders leaning easily up against the bulkhead. Leigh was looking directly at her, an enigmatic smile on his lips. Tracy felt her heart thud painfully against her ribs.

Dinner was a meal to be remembered, but she found herself with little appetite. Her whole awareness was taken over by the man at her side: the deep, even timber of his voice; lean strength of the brown hands emerging from the crisp white cuffs; the flash of white teeth when he laughed.

"You're not eating, Doctor," he observed once when she had thought him engrossed in conversation with his other neighbor. She looked up quickly to find him regarding her with that same, indefinable expression. "Surely," he went on with a hint of mockery, "you can't still be feeling ill on a night like this?"

He could have been referring to the calm seas or the time of year, or both; Tracy had the odd impression that he meant neither and for some reason felt suddenly short of breath.

"No, I'm not," she replied as calmly as she was able under that all-seeing scrutiny. "I'm simply not very hungry . . . although everything is delicious," she added quickly.

"Dieting, I wouldn't wonder," Don O'Malley put in severely from her other side. "Someone should be telling you that a man likes a woman with a bit of flesh on her. Right, Skipper?"

With deliberation Leigh moved his gaze over the delicate modeling of her shoulders, rested for a moment on the hollow of her throat, and moved relentlessly upward to her face.

"It depends on type, Chief," he said ambiguously before turning away to answer some query put to him by someone farther down the table.

At five to eight Peter left for the bridge. Ten minutes later Mike Jackson came in for his own meal. As coffee was brought to the table one of the men went over and switched on the small electric record player standing on a locker in one corner. As the first bars of *Silent Night* filled the air, Tracy saw one or two of the assembled officers become quiet and still, their thoughts perhaps turning toward home and loved ones. Due to the very nature of their job, some of them, she knew, had not had the opportunity to spend Christmas at home with their families for years.

"Are your sympathies always so easily aroused?" asked Leigh's lightly jeering tones. She realized that once again he had been watching her. "They have a choice, you know. They don't *have* to sign on year after year as they do."

"Is it really that simple?" she asked quietly, and unexpectedly he smiled.

"Nothing is ever that simple. They come because they don't know any other way of life, because the sea *is* their life and away from it they're only half alive."

Tracy glanced at him curiously. He had sounded so different then, not at all like the cynic she had known these last weeks.

"You're forgetting the money," she said deliberately.

"I haven't forgotten it."

"You mean it isn't important?"

"I didn't say that. Of course money is important. In any kind of community it has to be. What I meant was that there are other things equally, if not more important. One of them is fulfilment." He paused, and his mouth twisted again in the manner she was so familiar with. "For a woman . . . most women . . . that means a husband, a home and a family—in that order."

"But not for a man?" she surmised, chest tight.

"Not in the same way." Now the cynicism was definitely back in his voice. "A man needs far more than just the 'love of a good woman' out of life, despite what the romantics of this world of ours would have us believe." He pushed back his chair with an abrupt movement. "I must be going. There's a lot of ice out there tonight."

Tracy excused herself from the gathering some 15 minutes later. In her cabin she performed the ritual of preparing for bed, switched out the light and climbed between the sheets, lying on her back where she could see the flickering patch of light over the porthole.

She was still watching it when the big steam winches on top of the midships arch started up. She knew that work had begun once more for the crew of the *Antarctic Star*. Christmas was, to all intents and purposes, over.

Eventually she slept, but by half past twelve she was wide awake again and restless. From the sounds reverberating throughout the ship the night shift was still hard at work on the whales left over from the day's take. By the first light the plans should be clear in readiness for the fresh catch. Impulsively she swung her legs over the side of the bunk and stood up. She would never get back to sleep just lying and waiting for it to come. What she needed was a breath of fresh air.

Swiftly she pulled on slacks and a warm sweater, grabbed her jacket and left the cabin. On deck the air was crisp and cold, and for once almost windless. Tracy mounted the companionway to the bridge deck, padding silently past the closed door to the bridge house to a spot where she could look down on the fore-plan.

Below her lay a scene straight from Dante's Inferno. Lit by the decklights the rising clouds of steam from the dryers formed themselves into strange writhing shapes in which dark figures materialized and vanished again with a disturbing lack of substance.

Tracy gave an involuntary little shudder, then laughed at her own imagination and turned her face toward the frosty sharpness of the stars pinpointing the clear but moonless sky. Her skin tingled with the cold, but there was exhilaration in the sensation.

Inevitably her thoughts turned to the bridge house and the men at work inside. Would Leigh have retired to his bunk yet? she wondered. Or would he still be up there directing the ship through these hazardous waters. Even with the aid of the radar screen, that was a job calling for the utmost concentration on the part of the navigator, particularly on a night like this. They were moving in an area dense with bergs, of which even the smallest would be large enough to tear out the *Star*'s side if they hit. When he came off watch, Mike had said at dinner, there had been over 150 icebergs visible on the screen. Although 200 square miles sounded like a lot of space,

Tracy knew by now just what those figures meant in terms of danger to the ship.

She had been standing there for a while when she first became aware of the gradual change in the sky. Light was appearing on the horizon, light intensifying by the second. Fascinated she watched it slowly crystallize into a pulsating flickering band of shimmering white that broadened and deepened as it climbed steadily from the southern rim. Behind it came others, growing ever stronger, brighter, and higher as the minutes ticked by, until they all merged into one great circular arch extending from horizon to horizon across the heavens. It was a sight never to be forgotten, a sight which held Tracy motionless and bemused. And still the climax was to come. Now, long rays of pastel tinted greens, blues, and violets began to dart up and out from the brightest parts of the arch of light, illuminating half the sky in magnificent display.

"The Aurora Australis," said a voice softly. "A fitting ending to the day, I think."

Still under the spell of the surpassingly lovely spectacle, Tracy glanced toward the tall figure standing a few feet away, elbow resting easily against the rail. How long Leigh had been there she had no idea, nor did it seem to matter. The important thing was that he *was* there to share this moment with.

"It makes you feel so very insignificant," she said with a slight tremor in her voice. "I never imagined anything like this. I suppose you're used to them?"

"One never grows used to them," he returned evenly, "because they're never the same twice. You're lucky. Tonight is one of the best displays I've seen."

"And I could have missed it." She drew in a breath. "It must have been some sixth sense which got me out on deck at just the right time to see the whole thing from the beginning."

"You couldn't sleep?"

"No." She slanted her eyes in his direction again. "Have you been on the bridge all night?"

"Since I left you, yes. At the moment we're running through a relatively clear patch, so I came outside for a breather." He paused fractionally. "You were lost to the world." One hand went to his pocket and came away with the flat silver case. "Will you have a cigarette?"

Her instincts eagerly seized upon the excuse to prolong this moment of meeting. "Please."

He came forward to offer the case, closed it with a snap when she had helped herself, and thumbed the lighter into flame. When both cigarettes were lit he slipped the case back into his pocket and resumed his original stance against the rail, only this time he was right at her side, so close that she felt he must certainly hear the wild beating of her heart.

"Cold?" he asked abruptly into the silence. "No," she answered and wondered briefly what he would have done had she said otherwise. Probably ordered her back to her cabin, she reflected.

Never a frequent smoker, she was grateful for the calming influence of the cigarette over the next moment or two. She could feel Leigh studying her and could only hope that her face did not betray her inner turbulence. When he spoke again she almost jumped.

"How do you like life at sea?"

She upended her cigarette in her gloved hand, her eyes following the smoke as it spiralled slowly upward from the glowing tip. She said carefully, "It grows on one."

"Enough to make you consider it as a permanent career?"

Her heart jerked. "I don't know. Why?"

"Just a passing thought. As you must have realized, there's a very real shortage of qualified doctors ready and willing to spend long periods at sea."

"So it seems." She hesitated, then gave a little laugh and added daringly, "For a moment there I actually thought you were going to ask me if I fancied the *Star* as a permanent berth. I should have known better."

"You should indeed." His tone was dry. "My views haven't altered quite that radically."

"But they've obviously bent a little," she returned lightly. "May I take that as a compliment to my professional abilities?"

His gaze was steady. "Your professional abilities have never been in question. Your sex was the problem. One woman amongst 500 men spelled trouble. It still can."

Her chin lifted. "Surely that depends on the woman? I'm first and foremost a doctor."

There was a small pause, then he smiled slowly and with deliberation reached out to pluck the cigarette from between her unresisting fingers, dropping it to the deck along with his own and grinding them both out beneath his heel.

"Are you?" he said softly.

His lips were cold at first from the ice Antarctic air—but not for long. She was dazed and breathless when he at last raised his head.

"Merry Christmas, Tracy," he said sardonically, and she felt the warmth suffuse her cheeks.

"And what," she asked unsteadily, "was that supposed to prove?"

"That a woman is a woman before anything else." His voice mocked her. "It was the female in you that responded just then—the doctor would have slapped my face."

She took a breath. "It isn't too late."

"No, it isn't," he agreed and then paused before adding softly, "But I don't think you will."

"What makes you so sure?"

"Because we've both had that kiss coming to us for a long time. Tonight you deliberately provoked it."

"That isn't true!"

"Isn't it?" He put out a sudden hand and took her firmly by the chin, lifting her face up to his. "Are you going to deny all that's been between us these last few weeks?"

A tremor ran through her. "I . . . I don't know what you mean."

"Oh yes, you do. You acknowledged it the day you agreed to come back to the ship with me—the day you found out about Cheryl." There was a glitter in his eyes now. "You and I were meant to meet, Tracy Redfern."

For a long moment she was still, hypnotized by his gaze, then he moved and the spell was broken. She jerked her head out of his grasp and stepped back a pace, her breath coming a little fast.

"You're the last man I would have suspected of being a fatalist," she sputtered, and he laughed shortly.

"Up to a month ago you'd have been right about that. Now . . . Can you suggest a rational explanation of why, out of all the ships in dock that night, you had to choose mine?"

"It was just . . . coincidence."

"Coincidence, my foot! The long arm doesn't stretch *that* far." He studied her reflectively. "Have you any idea how like her you are?"

She said stiffly, "I know how like her I *look*—and that's only skin deep."

"I wonder?" He set his back against the rail. "What about this man you left behind in England?"

"What about him?"

"Did you run out on him?"

"Why should I tell you?"

He smiled. "Because if you don't I shall automatically assume the worst."

Goaded, she said, "It wasn't at all like you think. I left to stop things from becoming too serious."

"You didn't love him?"

"No . . . at least, I know now that I didn't."

"Which means you thought, then, that you did. So where was the problem?"

She answered reluctantly, "He was . . . married."

"Oh? Noble of you under the circumstances."

His tone brought her head up. She looked at him levelly. "You mightn't believe in my motives, but it happens to be the truth, although I think I knew even then that I didn't really love him—not in any lasting way."

Leigh's mouth remained cynical. "*Is* there any lasting way?"

Pain shot through her. It took an effort to say steadily, "For some there is. Take Janet and Harry, for instance. They've been married for ten years, and yet I'd say they're as much in love now as they were right at the start—perhaps even more so."

His brow rose expressively. "You seem to have gleaned rather a lot from a few hours' acquaintance."

"Seeing them together in the early morning gave me a good insight." Challengingly she added, "Do you doubt *that* diagnosis?"

It was a moment before he shook his head. "No, I don't. They're two of the lucky few."

From within the wheelhouse came the sound of the ship's bell: one double and one single strike instantly repeated by the lookout down on the fo'c'sle head. As the last note died away, Leigh straightened.

"Half past one, in your language," he said. "Time you were making tracks back to your cabin before you freeze to the deck."

"Yes." Her voice seemed stuck in her throat. "Are . . . are you staying here?"

"I," he said satirically, "am going to smoke a last cigarette and think about a pair of eyes as clear as the bright blue sky. They say the eyes are the mirrors of the soul, don't they?"

"They might, but I doubt that you'd believe it." Tracy could stand no more. "Goodnight."

"Good morning, you mean," he returned as she moved away, but she didn't look back.

Only when she was back in her cabin did she realise how cold she was. Her fingers and toes were numb, and she had to rub them hard to restore the circulation. But no amount of massage could reach the chill inside her. Only Leigh could warm that part of her again, and he wouldn't because he was finished with love. That much he had made clear.

CHAPTER NINE

The rocket arched out with a crack from the *Star*'s deck across the narrow strip of water that separated the two ships, the line snaking out behind. Soon that line was a hawser, and the tanker was being drawn and steered closer and closer to the factory, her screws racing in the choppy seas as she fought for even keel. Further lines were heaved across and secured, building up an intricate arrangement of moorings that eventually held the tanker nestled against the three whales fastened to the *Star*'s sides as fenders.

Only now, looking down at the steel decks of the other ship, did Tracy become fully appreciative of the unusual height of the deck upon which she stood. There must, she reckoned, be a good 30 feet difference, and yet the other vessel was by no means small. The reason, of course, was obvious. Other ships lacked the necessity to make room for the enormous items of factory plant which lay beneath her feet.

The basket carrying the chief chemist and mechanics went swinging crazily downward, and within minutes the flexible hoses were being coupled up. Shivering in the strengthening east whind, Tracy turned away from the rail. The weather was worsening again; there was snow in the air. Down below in the pump room there would be feverish activity, with everyone going all out to get the precious oil transferred before conditions deteriorated to an extent where it became impossible for the two ships to remain coupled with any degree of safety. Recognition of that point was the Captain's responsibility. Should he misjudge and wait too long, there was every chance of the tanker being swept under the *Star*'s bows as she tried to pull away. Not, Tracy thought, that there was very much danger of that happening with Leigh in charge.

Deep in her pockets her hands clenched tightly. The last five days had been an eternity; the kind of torture she hadn't known existed until now. Fate had decreed that she and Leigh Garratt should cross paths, and with that same inevitability that she should fall in love with him, but nothing was written to the effect that he must return the emotion. If only, she thought desperately, she could get off the ship. But that was impossible, of course. She had at least another four months of this pain to endure. Four long, insufferable months!

Peter was coming away from her cabin as she turned into the alleyway. He stopped when he saw her and waited for her to come level.

"I was beginning to wonder if you'd fallen overboard," he smiled. "You're usually back from the office long before this."

"I stopped to watch the tanker come alongside," she explained and saw his expression alter a fraction.

"Ah, yes, the tanker. They're topping her up today, did you know that?"

"So you said last week." She hesitated, her hand on the door handle. "Peter. . . ."

"If you're going to ask did I write that letter, the answer is yes," he interrupted with an undertone of stubbornness. "It's in the mailbag now."

"But still aboard the *Star*?"

"I believe so."

"Then you still have time to get it back."

"I don't want to get it back." He looked at her appealingly. "Tracy, I know how you feel about what I'm doing . . . or rather, the way I'm doing it . . . but I just can't go on like this any longer."

Well, she had tried, Tracy thought resignedly. Aloud she said, "I only hope you won't regret it."

"I doubt it." The confidence was back in his voice. "Deirdre and I were never really suited, you know. We haven't enough in common. If there hadn't been this difference over my job there would have been something else. Now that it's over between us we can both start afresh."

"Aren't you being just a little premature?" she asked, fiddling with the door handle. "It isn't over yet, is it? Not until she receives the letter. How long will that take?"

"About two weeks if the mail is dropped off at Cape Town and flown home." He was silent for a moment, regarding her uncertainly. "Is that how you see things?" he asked at last.

"Well, of course. How can you possibly consider your engagement broken off when your fiancée doesn't even know about it yet?" She gave him a forced little smile and pushed open the door. "I must go and tidy myself up. It's getting late."

"I'll wait for you," he offered but she shook her head.

"No, you go on, and I'll join you." She went on in and shut the door before he could protest.

Here in the cabin she could feel the bumping of the tanker against the side of the ship quite distinctly. From the porthole she could almost have jumped down onto the fo'c'sle deck of the other vessel. The snow was coming faster and thicker, blowing past the glass in gusty squalls. Tracy felt sorry for the men working outside in it, although they were well accustomed to such conditions.

She took off her jacket and slung it listlessly over the back of the one chair, regarded herself briefly and without interest in the mirror and decided that she didn't feel like any lunch after all. The afternoon stretched before her like a desert. The hospital was empty for once. She had no pressing cases in hand. Almost she wished that something would happen. Work was the only panacea she knew.

She was lying on her bunk when Peter returned to see what was keeping her. She told him she had a headache and was going to rest for an hour, assured him she had taken something for it and listened to his footsteps receding along the alleyway. Down on the tanker someone shouted something, but it was impossible to make out the words. Wind and water created a symphony of sound; music that no longer sounded strange in Tracy's ears. She lay there and let the movement of the ship take her and soothe her.

It was dark in the cabin when she awoke. Not the darkness of night but the sullen gray cast by the lowering skies. Her watch said four o'clock. Had she really slept for three hours?

There was something different, she realized, sitting up. The bumping on the side of the ship had stopped. They were making good headway once more.

Tracy rose and went over to the porthole. It had stopped snowing and the wind speed was about the same, but the short, serried ranks of waves both looked and felt nasty. The tanker had vanished along with the whales that had cushioned her. She would be heading north-east back to civilization and warmth, and then from the Cape to England to disgorge the cargo won by the men who braved these cold, hazardous waters year after year. At that moment Tracy would have given anything to have been on board the other ship.

Behind her the intercom buzzed, and she moved swiftly across to open the line.

"Yes?"

"Busy?" asked Leigh's disembodied voice, and her heart came jerking back to life.

"No," she replied after a brief, pulsating moment and noted the unsteadiness of her voice without surprise.

"Then I'll expect you in five minutes." He had switched off before she could answer.

Tracy let the switch return to the off position herself and stood still for a moment, her breathing clearly audible in the quiet of the cabin. Then, like a sleep-walker, she picked up her coat and moved to the door.

Leigh was sitting at his desk when she entered the cabin. He was leafing through a sheaf of papers, chair tilted back and feet resting casually on the edge of the desk.

"Congratulations," he greeted her. "A woman who knows the meaning of time is a rarity. Must be your medical training." He brought his heels down to the ground and came upright in one lithe movement, tossing the file onto the desk. "Have a seat."

Tracy didn't move from her position just inside the door. "I'd rather stand. What did you want to see me about?"

He smiled. "Poised for flight? Don't worry, I'm not going to get between you and the door." He leaned easily against the desk edge and studied her. "Why do you think I wanted to see you?"

"A question to answer a question?" she parried. "You once said that was a feminine tactic."

"Only when it's used by a woman," he returned imper-turbably. "All right, scrub it. Why did I ask you to come? Because I wanted to know if you would."

"If I recall correctly, you made it an order, not a request. I could hardly refuse."

"You could and would have done if you'd been so inclined." His eyes moved over her face with a certain glint in them. "Quite obviously you weren't inclined. From which we may deduce . . . what?"

She was still standing looking at him wordlessly when the steward tapped on the door behind her and came in. He was carrying a tray laid out with tea for two.

As he set down his burden on the desk, Leigh said

blandly, "Will you pour, Doctor?" Then he moved back to his seat.

Tracy contrived a smile for the steward as they passed, and then she found herself seated opposite Leigh and reaching automatically for the teapot.

"Milk, no sugar," he requested, lolling back comfortably.

Like an automaton she complied. "Do you always have tea sent up in the afternoon?" she asked in confused tones, passing him the cup.

"Always. I'm a traditionalist." He cocked an eyebrow. "Any reason why I shouldn't drink the stuff?"

"No reason at all . . . except that you don't seem the type to cling to custom."

"That sounds knowledgeable. What type would you say I was?"

"Mike," she stalled, "said you were the best."

"I'm not interested in what Mike thinks at the moment. He's a known quantity, you're not." His gaze drew her own upward. "What type am I?"

Tracy had flushed a little. She said slowly, "That's not a question I can answer in one word. Everyone has several different facets to their personality. I only know one side of you."

The pause lay between them for a deliberate four seconds, then he said with irony, "Very adept. Which side of *your* personality do you keep on show?"

"I'm not sure. Few of us see ourselves as others see us."

"That might be a blessing in disguise." With apparent irrelevance he tagged on, "Did this partner of yours ever make love to you, or was your relationship on a higher plane?"

"He wasn't my partner," she said without expression. "I was his assistant."

"Which once again avoids the question. How about a straight answer for once?"

Very carefully Tracy set down her cup in its saucer, pushed back her chair and rose to her feet, surprised to find that her legs would still hold her.

"Running away?" he taunted.

"If you like." She took in a painful breath. "I'm tired of being Cheryl's whipping boy, Leigh. Find someone else to vent your spleen on!"

She was halfway to the door when he said her name in a tone that was soft, but authoritative enough to halt her footsteps and turn her slowly back to face him. He had risen from his seat and come forward to the corner of the desk; was watching her with eyes from which the mockery had suddenly vanished. Only now did she realize how tired he looked. Not to be wondered at considering the demands of his job. Her antagonism died as the deeper, more desperate emotion swathed her heart and head with a longing that was agony. It took every ounce of will power she possessed to stop herself from going to him.

"You aren't going to believe it," he said at last, "but I didn't plan for things to go this way when I asked you to come up here."

"Didn't you?" Her voice was toneless.

"I said you wouldn't believe it." There was a wry twist to the corners of his mouth. "As a matter of fact, I was going to remind you of the night we left the Cape and suggest that we start burying that hatchet as of now."

A small pulse began to throb at the base of her throat. "You're right, that does take some believing."

"Nevertheless, it's true."

"Then why. . . ."

"Did it finish up the way it did?" He shrugged lightly. "One word leads to another . . . it always has been like that between us, hasn't it?" A spark touched his gaze.

"Which would appear to leave us just one line of communication. . . ."

Tracy swallowed thickly. "Leigh, I've had enough of this. You. . . ."

The words died in her throat as his hands fastened about her upper arms with a grip that hurt. He had moved so fast that she had barely had time to realize his purpose.

"So have I," he clipped. "Quite enough. So let's have everything out in the open, shall we? Let's admit that I want to kiss you and that you want me to kiss you, and start again from there!"

The intercom broke into the moment's pulsating stillness with shrill urgency. Tracy felt the sudden change in the man who had her so firmly in his grip. For an instant he held her gaze, then he shrugged ruefully and dropped his hands.

"Mike's timing could be bettered. Don't go."

Tracy watched him cross to the speaker with a mingling of relief and regret. She felt dazed and bewildered, caught up in a crossfire of emotions she didn't know how to handle. She had wanted Leigh to kiss her a moment ago, wanted it so badly that she doubted if she could have raised even a vestige of a struggle against him if he had got that far. And yet, deep down inside her, something else had shrunk from an embrace that meant so little. She was under no illusions as to his motives.

"Pack ice ahead," came the Number One's voice through the grid. "Thought you might want to take a look."

"I'll be right up." Leigh flicked up the switch, looked back at Tracy, and seemed to deliberate before saying casually, "This is the first real pack we've hit this season. Would you like to come up and see it?"

Her hesitation was brief. An invitation to visit the

bridge during the busy daylight hours was an honor accorded to few. This was an olive branch he was holding out without a doubt. She could do no less than accept it. Carefully she matched his tone.

"Yes, I would, please."

"Safety in numbers?" he asked and didn't bother to wait for her reply. "Come on, then."

On the bridge all was brilliance. The instruments gleamed; the woodwork glowed. Mike removed a pair of binoculars from his eyes as the two of them came up from the lower deck, nodded to Tracy without revealing the slightest hint of surprise at her presence in this holy of holies, and handed the glasses over to Leigh.

"Looks pretty heavy," he remarked.

The ice lay a couple of miles ahead, a vast expanse of white stretching away into the distance on either hand, although no more than a few miles in width. Leigh studied it in silence, then without dropping the glasses, asked, "How far are we from the *Tiger Rose*?"

"About 35," the Mate replied. "She reported in ten minutes ago."

"And the others?"

"Converging rapidly. *Star III* already flagged a couple on the way down. *Shackleton* is bringing them in."

The decision came immediately. "We'll go through. Full ahead, both."

"Full ahead, both," echoed his next in command with a hand already on the engine-room telegraph.

"As she goes."

"As she goes," repeated the helmsman.

Moments later the reinforced bow met the edge of the pack with a grinding crash that sent the resting flocks of birds screaming into the air. Then they were slicing through the white mass like a knife through butter, opening a channel which would remain clear long enough to allow the smaller vessels through in the *Star*'s wake. To Tracy it looked exactly as if the ship was running overland, a mountainscape in miniature, its eye-dazzling surface marred only by an occasional patch of reddish-brown algae.

"This is what we call rafted pack," said Leigh at her side. "Several layers jammed on top of each other. Can be dangerous, although compared with some I've seen in the Arctic, most of what we meet down here is wafer thin."

"When were you in the Arctic?" Tracy asked with quick interest.

"More years ago than I care to remember. I was just a boy at the time."

"What made you transfer your interests to this side of the world?"

"Commercial necessity. Whaling was just about played out in the Arctic. It's a pity. Conditions up there are usually a great deal better than here in the southern waters—at this time of the year, at any rate." His glance followed the flight of a white snow petrel winging its way across the bows. "If the authorities hadn't come to their senses in time and laid down some sensible regulations, the whale would have been practically extinct here, too, in a few years."

"But even now they're killed in very great numbers, aren't they?" She paused, aware that her views could only sound foolish to a whaleman, but reluctant to let the opportunity pass without registering some faint protest. "It all seems so cruel when you think that the whale never hurt anyone. Is the oil really so essential to our lives?"

"Yes, it is." The answer was definite. "It's the source of a great number of things in daily use such as margarine, glycerine and soap, *and* it forms the basis for varnishes and paints." He was speaking in the manner of one well accustomed to this kind of argument. "You yourself use drugs derived from whale glands; the meat feeds a whole lot of people who would otherwise go hungry." His quick glance held a hint of malice. "Even that perfume you're wearing owes something to the whale."

She was startled and disbelieving. "You're joking!"

"I'm not, you know. There's a substance called ambergris used in the manufacture of perfume that is found in the small intestine of the sperm."

"Ugh!" She pulled a wry face. "All right, you made your point. I didn't know what I was talking about."

Silence fell between them. Tracy gazed steadfastly ahead to where water glimmered in the middle distance, conscious of his closeness and wondering what his thoughts were. The atmosphere between them, she thought, could never be one of ease. Cheryl's ghost was too strong.

Something was moving on the ice up front, and she screwed up her eyes against the glare in order to see better. Was she going mad, or were those really men out there?

"Penguins," said Leigh, catching her involuntary exclamation. "Here, have a closer look."

Tracy took the heavy glasses from him, a tremor running through her as her fingers brushed his. With the lens adjusted to her vision the moving black specks sprang into focus, so close that she felt she could have reached out a hand and touched the captivating little creatures waddling slowly and clumsily over the ice toward the fast approaching ship, curiosity over this invader of their domain in every inquisitively straining neck.

"We'll hit them!" she exclaimed. "They're right in our path!"

"We won't hit them. They're a few points off to starboard. We'll be leaving the ice before they get close enough to be in any danger."

She handed him back the glasses, saw his expression and said doubtfully, "Would you have altered course to avoid them if they *had* been in our way?"

"At the risk of damaging the ship?" He shook his head slowly. "There's too much at stake." His tone altered just a fraction, taking on a harsher note. "I can't afford sentiment."

"*Shackleton* reporting in, Skipper," announced the radio operator. "She's having to detour around some pack ice and won't be able to make the rendezvous point before 1800."

Leigh's reply was without pause. "Get her position and heading. Tell her we'll meet her, then radio *Baffin* and *Active* to stand by for change of course." He glanced back to Tracy with unreadable eyes, said formally for the benefit of those listening, "Sorry, Doctor, but work calls. Feel free to stay as long as you like."

Then he was moving away, everything else forgotten but the job for which he lived and breathed.

CHAPTER TEN

New Year came and went, and with it the start of the finback season. The *Star* was joined by the fleet's freezing ship, *Mentor*, which would accompany her for the rest of the voyage; taking and storing the fresh whale meat at temperatures designed to keep it in perfect condition throughout the coming months.

Good spirits pervaded the whole crew. The season was turning out to be a good one after all, and the bonus figures were mounting nicely. "The Skipper knew what he was doing," they told each other with an air of having been secretly convinced of that the whole time, conveniently forgetting the fact that only two weeks before they had been cursing the decision that had brought them west instead of east. Should the present abundance of whales dwindle, every man amongst them would have his own much-argued opinion as to which direction the Captain should take next.

At Leigh's casual invitation, Tracy visited the bridge several times more, assimilating with fascinated ears and eyes the complexity of detail which went into controlling the fleet. Apart from the occasional mealtime it was the only time she saw him, and even then he was too busy to do more than pass the odd remark. This, she realized, was the real Leigh Garratt: the dedicated sailor; master of a world within a world where personal relationships were of very minor importance beside the mammoth load of responsibility that lay upon the broad shoulders.

She had begun living from day to day, looking no farther forward than the immediate hours. Eventually she knew she was going to have to give some thought to the future, to what she was going to do when this voyage ended, but just now the effort seemed too much. Sometimes she found herself just sitting gazing blankly into space, not thinking about anything in particular. She felt totally drained.

Toward the end of the second week in January there was an outbreak of gastroenteritis which laid low over 60 members of the *Star*'s crew—Peter amongst them. It was a busy time, but it was what Tracy needed to jerk her out of the lethargy into which she had been sinking. A dint of detective work finally tracked down the source of the infection to one of the assistant cooks who had been silently suffering a mild attack of tonsilitis, sublimely unaware that he was passing on the bacteria in the food he handled.

"Stupid young devil," growled Peter from the hospital bed wich Tracy had confined him to as one of the worst hit of the outbreak. "I'd like to lock him up and feed him his own germs for a few weeks."

"After what the Chief Steward had to say to him, I think he'll report a tickle at the back of his nose from now on," she assured him. She took his chart from the foot of the bed to study it. "How are you feeling now?"

"If I live through the night I'll make it." He moved his head on the pillow in mock anguish. "Lord, I'd hate another dose of this! It's like being turned inside out! How much longer before I'm back to normal?"

"Another 24 hours, I'd say." She smiled at him. "You, and those two down there . . ." with a gesture toward the partly drawn curtains which separated the beds from each other . . . "were the worst of the lot. "You must share a great fondness for fish."

"Is that what he was on? It must have been the plaice. I know I had three helpings." He grinned back at her with a fair amount of his normal spirit. "I think I might find I've gone off fish as a food from now on."

"There's no need to feel like that. This kind of thing doesn't happen very often these days, thank goodness." She replaced the chart on its hook. "I'd better go and have a look at my other patients before they start complaining that you're getting priority treatment."

"And am I?" he asked, and there was a sudden odd note in his voice.

She laughed. "You might say that, I suppose. It isn't every patient I visit three times in one day. Try and get some sleep now, Peter. Rest is what you need."

"Tracy. . . ." He came upright, hair tousled into a mass of springy brown curls that made him look even younger than he actually was. "Tracy, don't go. I . . . I must talk to you."

Surprised by the urgency of his tone, she stopped in the act of turning and looked at him. "What about?" she asked gently. "Deirdre?"

"No." He hesitated, his eyes on hers with a searching, almost pleading expression. "No, not about Deirdre, about . . . us." He spoke in low tones, but the words came across to her with clarity. "You must know I'm in love with you, Tracy. Don't keep me in suspense any longer."

Dismay held her motionless and silent for a long moment. So Leigh had been right, she thought painfully. In this, at least, he had been right.

"You *did* know, didn't you?" Peter insisted with a sudden doubt in his voice, and she gave herself a mental shake. No use just standing here hating herself. She had allowed this to happen; now she must make the situation clear. She could never love Peter. After Leigh she could never love anyone.

"I'm sorry," she said slowly, "I'm afraid I didn't. Not until this moment. I thought . . . I believed. . . ." She lifted her shoulders in a gesture of helplessness. "I'm sorry."

His eyes closed and he sank back against the pillows with a look on his face that made her want to go to him and comfort him like a mother would a small son who had been hurt. She waited miserably, knowing there was nothing she could do to lessen the blow.

"It's my own fault," he said hollowly at last. "I think I knew all along I was living in a fool's paradise, but I didn't want to admit it." His eyes came open and he managed a semblance of a smile. "Don't worry about it, Tracy. I'll get over it."

With some difficulty she said, "I feel so guilty. If it hadn't been for me you would never have thought of breaking off your engagement, would you?"

"That's not true." The denial was quick—too quick. "Deirdre and I were all washed up before I met you."

Tracy wanted to believe him, but she couldn't. Knowingly or unknowingly, she had taken Peter from the other girl at a time when their relationship had been undergoing a minor crisis. If it hadn't been for her propinquity and lack of sagacity they might well have weathered the storm.

"What can I say?" she asked.

"You don't have to say anything. You can't fall in love to order." His lips were still set in the strained smile. "Forget it, Tracy. It doesn't have to make any difference to our friendship."

But it did, she thought sadly. Such things once said are not forgotten. The easy camaraderie they had known was a thing of the past.

Sleep came with difficulty that night. Looking back years afterward, Tracy knew that she plumbed the depths of unhappiness during those long hours of tossing and turning. At last she dropped into an uneasy doze, only to be awakened minutes later, or so it seemed, by the continuous loud summons which could only mean one thing at this time of night—emergency!

Sitting up to answer the call, she became instantly aware that her sleep must have lasted a great deal longer than a few minutes. At midnight the weather had been fairly clement, and the *Star*'s movement through the water had been comparatively steady. Now the wind was howling past the porthole, and the ship rolling heavily. It was no particular surprise. In these regions storms could blow up out of nowhere within a couple of hours.

Leigh spoke evenly and to the point. "There's been a man hurt on one of the catchers. Head injuries. Will you come up and have a word with them?"

Even as he was speaking Tracy had her feet over the side of the bunk and was groping for her slippers. "Give me three minutes," she said.

It took her approximately half that time to get into slacks and a thick sweater and slide her arms through the sleeves of her duffle coat, another minute to reach the deck. The force of the gale took her breath away. On this side of the ship there was no shelter from the tearing gusts that threatened to take any unanchored object and spin it over the side into the foaming seas. Tracy flattened herself against the superstructure and began to move along it in the direction of the bridge companionway. She had gone only a few feet when she met someone coming in the other direction. It was Mike, his bulk too great an obstacle for even this wind to shift very far off even keel.

"Grab a hold of my arm," he shouted to her above the noise of the elements. "I'll get you above."

It was relatively easy after that. A couple of minutes later they were within the shelter of the bridge house. Leigh was talking on the radio, blue uniform as immaculate as ever. Did he ever go to bed? Tracy wondered fleetingly as she went to him.

"The doctor's here now," he said into the handset he was holding. The gray eyes found hers as he handed her a spare pair of earphones. "Sorry to have to bring you out in this, but it sounds as if it might be serious. One of the ABs hit his head against a stanchion over two hours ago. He's been unconscious ever since."

"What do I do?" she asked.

"Just talk into this," passing across the handset. "They've got their best English speaker on the other end." He caught the question in her swift upward glance and added, "The *Terje* has an all-Scandinavian crew, but you'll be able to understand Sven all right."

Tracy took a shallow breath, self-conscious beneath his gaze. "Doctor Redfern here," she announced into the mouthpiece. "Where is the patient?" Out of the corner of her eye she saw the operator flip a switch.

"He is in my cabin," came the heavily accented reply in her ear. "There is more room."

"Is he laid flat?"

There was a pause, obviously for consultation, then Sven came on again. "He has a pillow, I am told."

"Then have it taken away, please. He must be kept perfectly level." Tracy had forgotten her temporary restraint now, her mind racing ahead to the questions she must ask if she was to ascertain the man's condition. "Whereabouts on the head was he hit?"

"At the back. No, there is no open wound."

"What is his breathing like?"

"Very heavy." Again the pause, then, "There is some fluid coming now from the ear, I am informed."

At the last Tracy took the earpiece away and looked worriedly at Leigh who had been listening in. "I must get to him. Can it be managed?"

There was a tautness about the strong mouth. "The only way is to send you across by bo'sun's chair. In this weather that could be a risky business."

"It's a risk I'll have to take," she returned firmly,

shutting her mind against the shaft of apprehension. "Will you arrange it?"

A few seconds passed before he moved. He took the handset back from her and spoke rapidly into it, signed off and laid down the two pieces of equipment.

"They'll be alongside in 15 minutes," he said. "Or as close as they can get." His voice sounded strange. "Just one thing. That gale out there is going to get worse. We might just get you across; we certainly won't get you back tonight. You're going to have to sit it out on the catcher. That won't be any picnic."

"I didn't anticipate a picnic when I came on this trip," she retorted with truth. "Where will I be making the transfer from?"

"Starboard. The wind is south-west, so there will be more shelter. You'll be needing stuff from the hospital, won't you? You'd better contact Sergeant on the blower and tell him what you want. I'll get someone to fetch your bag up from your cabin."

Tracy went to do as he suggested, bracing herself against the roll and pitch of the ship. Mike had vanished again, presumably to arrange for the rigging of the bo'sun's chair. Desperately she tried to calm her jangling nerves by thinking of the boy lying out there in the storm-tossed catcher, waiting for her help.

The minutes ticked inexorably by. Leigh didn't come near her, but she knew he watched her. She couldn't look at him. Joe arrived from the surgery closely followed by a young able seaman carrying the precious black leather bag.

"Let me go across instead, Doctor," offered the former. "They could link up communications direct from the patient's side, and you could tell me what to do."

Over his head Tracy caught Leigh's eyes. "Thanks, Joe," she said quietly, "but this is *my* job."

After that things seemed to happen very quickly. The *Terje* came forging up as near as she dared to the mother ship, a line was sent over and the bridge advised that all was in readiness for the transfer to be made. Tracy had already been bundled into oilskins and a pair of boots that had needed the addition of three pairs of socks to keep them on her feet.

It was taking all the skill of both Captains to keep the two vessels on a reasonably parallel course, but Leigh found time to murmur a few reassuring if somewhat tensely spoken words.

"Don't worry," he told her as she was leaving the bridge with Mike. "We'll get you over there safely."

"I'm not worrying," Tracy replied and suddenly found that she wasn't any more. Leigh would take care of her as he took care of all his crew.

There seemed to be quite a group gathered at the bunkering port. Willing hands helped fasten girl and bag securely into the canvas seat. Signals were exchanged with the other vessel far below, and Tracy closed her eyes as she swung out into space above the wind-driven, foam-creasted waves. How long ago since she had experienced a similar sensation in the cablecar at Cape Town? A lifetime? Spray splattered over her, increasing in volume and sting as she slid lower and lower toward the seething waters; the wind tore at her, swinging her out from the line like a pennant and holding her there for interminable seconds before allowing her to drop back into the vertical once more. Half blinded, she saw the *Terje*'s dark mass rushing to meet her, the white circles of the faces of the men who were bringing her in, then her feet touched the heaving, spume-washed deck. Hands caught and held her.

Freed of the binding straps, Tracy found herself half lifted by a stalwart Norwegian and borne over the slippery deck to the shelter of the superstructure. Seconds later they were inside a dimly-lit cabin. The man who sat by the side of the bunk over against the far bulkhead was rising to his feet with a look of relief on his face.

"I am Sven Liefson, Doctor," he introduced himself. "I am very grateful that you would attempt such a crossing on a night like this one."

"It wasn't very bad," she answered with a smile. She slipped out of the oilskins and had them taken from her by the man who had brought her here, then moved swiftly over to look down at the youth lying there with closed eyes and listen to labored breathing. "I'll need more light to examine him," she said. "Although you did quite right to darken the room."

There was a handbowl in one corner. Tracy went to use it, wiped her hands dry on the clean towel from her bag, and asked Sven and the other man to turn the patient over very gently.

At the base of the skull was a large contusion, rapidly darkening. Tracy felt around and above it with sensitive fingers, came to the conclusion that the bone was intact and transferred her attention to the ear. The trickle of cerebro-spinal fluid was slight at the moment, but enough to indicate a rent in the meninges which might or might not require repairing, depending upon the patient's progression through the next few days.

"How is he?" asked Sven, unable to contain his concern any longer.

Tracy straightened. "I'll be able to tell you better in a moment or two. Could you turn him again, please?"

With the youth laid once more on his back she began to go through the familiar routine: pulse rate, respiration, blood pressure. Each eyelid was lifted in turn and the reaction of the pupil to light noted down on the pad together with the time of the examination. Half an hour from now she would repeat the whole process, in this way keeping a close check upon the boy's level of consciousness.

"It could have been worse," she told Sven. "He should start coming around within an hour or two."

"And if he does not?" was the anticipated question.

"We'll worry about that if and when the time comes." Tracy sat down in the chair he had recently vacated, her eyes on the white face beneath the shock of fair hair. "Meantime, he must . . ." She stopped, smiling a little wryly as she realized the impossiblity of what she had been going to demand. How could anyone quiet the elements, or still the creaking, groaning protest of the timbers about them . . . "have as much peace as possible," she amended. "It would be a good idea to fasten him into the bunk to stop him from rolling. Can you find me an old sheet or something similar to tear into strips?"

"*Ja*, I will have that done." He turned to the man who had remained in the cabin with them, said something in their own tongue that held a note of authority.

"Are you the Captain?" Tracy asked curiously as the other departed. His lips parted with a grin, revealing a set of perfect white teeth.

"I am the Mate. The Captain is on the bridge."

Of course. Tracy felt dense. Where was the Captain who would leave his post at a time like this when he had the safety of his boat as a whole to consider?

The sheet was brought; unbleached calico and tough. Sven tore it into strips as easily as if it had been made of the finest linen, and at her direction bound the helpless boy into comparative immobility.

"I must go now," he said when it was done. "You will be all right?"

She nodded. "Yes, I can manage now."

"I will have some coffee sent down for you," he promised. "I will come back when I can."

Left alone, Tracy wedged herself in between bunk and bulkhead and composed herself to wait out the night. With time now to think and to feel she found herself wondering how she could ever have thought the *Star*'s performance in a storm unnerving. When the *Terje* rolled she went over to a terrifying 20 degrees, first to one side, then to the other, while waves which would barely have been felt aboard the factory ship broke over her bows with a noise like thunder, running over the deck outside to pour out again through the scuppers. Conditions had worsened in the short time since she had come aboard. It would have been impossible for her to have left the *Star* had they waited even 15 minutes longer than they had.

The coffee arrived, black as pitch and boiling hot. To Tracy it tasted like nectar, warming her chilled body through. So far her stomach was staying in the right place. She could only hope that it would continue to do so. Seasickness at a time like this was the last thing she could afford.

"How long do you think this will last?" she asked Sven when he looked in on her some time later.

"A few hours," he replied. "It will be better by the morning."

"Is it going to get any worse before it gets better?"

"Not very much worse. You must not fear. The *Terje* will not sink."

He was proved right in his forecast, although several times during that long night Tracy was convinced that the end was very close. About five o'clock the young AB began to show definite signs of improvement. From then on he came slowly but steadily up through the levels of consciousness, his eyelids finally flickering open just as the steward brought in the breakfast tray.

At Tracy's request the man went to fetch the Mate. By the time Sven had made his way to the cabin the boy's eyes had lost their blankness, coming to rest on the officer's weatherbeaten features with a spark of recognition.

Sven spoke to him, waited for the faint, halting reply and looked up at Tracy.

"His head is hurting him."

"I imagine it must be." She smiled comfortingly down at the boy in the bunk. "Tell him that he's going to be all right and that I will be giving him something to relieve the pain."

The reply was slightly stronger this time, and brought a grin to the Mate's lips. Straightening, he told Tracy, "He says that the doctor is even prettier than he was told. He wishes to know if you will be staying with him?"

Tracy laughed, partly with relief. They might not be completely out of the woods yet, but the very fact that he was rational enough to joke was a very good sign that everything was going well.

"I will, though not on board the *Terje*," she said. "When will the weather be calm enough to have him transferred to the *Star*?"

"An hour, perhaps two. There is still a high sea." Sven looked at her sharply. "It is urgent that he should be taken on board the factory?"

"I'd like to get him settled as soon as possible." And herself back on board the same ship as Leigh, she acknowledged with a pang, though much good that would do her. Casually, she asked, "When will you be contacting the *Star*?"

"We have been in close contact all of the night," he answered. "Captain Garratt gave orders that we were to report in every half an hour." He looked at his wrist watch. "We are due to call them once more in ten minutes. Would you like to speak to the Captain yourself, Doctor?"

Tracy would have liked to very much, just to hear his voice. But she shook her head. "I'd prefer not to leave the cabin. There's always a chance of a relapse. Just tell him that I'm ready to leave as soon as it is safe to do so."

"*Ja*, I will do that." He turned to go, saw the forgotten breakfast tray lying on top of a locker and added, "This will be cold. I will have more sent down."

Time passed with interminable slowness. The sedative Tracy had administered made her patient drowsy. He was asleep when they finally came to tell her that it was now safe to depart from the *Terje*.

All night the catcher had stayed within a few miles of the factory. In relatively calm seas she now closed with her once more. Soon the stretcher carrying the warmly wrapped and stoutly bound young Norwegian was on its way upward. Before her own departure Tracy shook hands with Sven and the Captain of the *Terje*—who was also the gunner—a large, gruff-voiced man who reminded her strongly of Arne Holst.

In daylight, and with only a moderate breeze to tug at her, the journey was almost enjoyable. Back on the *Star*'s deck at last, she gave the men below a last wave and pressed through a crowd of admiring matelots to follow the stretcher to the hospital.

Peter called to her as she came back down between the beds some little time later, leaving Joe with the newcomer. Tired and weary as she was, he was the last person she really wished to speak to, but she could hardly ignore him.

He was sitting on the side of the bed, fully dressed and obviously feeling almost his normal self again. A faint shadow passed across the brown eyes as he looked at her, but it was quickly gone.

"From all accounts you've had quite a night of it," he said. "It must have taken some courage to make that trip across to the *Terje* in a gale."

"There wasn't time to be afraid," she lied and suppressed the desire to rub a hand over her aching temple. She would feel fresh and whole again only when she had taken a shower and changed her clothes, but there was time for neither right now. "Do you mind if I come and talk to you later?" she asked. "I've a few things to catch up on."

"I won't keep you a minute, honestly." He put out a hand to his bedside locker, picked up a slip of paper lying there. "This came in this morning," he said, not quite meeting her eyes. "It's from Deirdre. She wants me to wait until I get back before making any final decision. Says that if I want to stay at sea so much, she'll go along."

Relief swept over Tracy like a rip tide. "And you're going to do as she asks?"

Peter looked a little sheepish. "Why not? We might be able to work something out."

"I'm sure you will." She spoke warmly. "I'm so glad, Peter. I'd have had you both on my conscience for the rest of my life."

The following hour was hectic, but the pressure came to an end at last. She could spare herself to leave and take that shower. She went to her cabin by way of the deck, breathing deeply of the stimulating air in an attempt to clear the fog from her mind. The cloud was higher and breaking up a little, the sea a rolling, gray-green infinity. Odd how all this grew upon one, she thought, how the cold, the danger, and the sheer challenge became a part of one's life. After this any other job could only seem tame and flat by comparison.

Her cabin was neat and tidy, the bunk freshly made up.

Tracy caught a glimpse of her face in the mirror as she lifted her toilet bag from its hook; pale and heavy-eyed. The loss of a night's sleep, she reflected dully, was only a contributory factor; she had looked like that for days.

She was looking for clean underwear when the knock came at the door. She straightened wearily, pushing back her hair out of her eyes, called "Come in," and felt every nerve in her body tauten like a bowstring as the familiar figure came into view.

Leigh closed the door, quietly, stood with his back against it. For once he lacked something of his normal indefatigable demeanor. To Tracy he appeared as a man who had gone without sleep all night and was feeling the strain; she knew the symptoms well. Staring at him, she became acutely aware of the noises of the ship going on about them: the whine of the winches dragging a carcass up the slipway; the bite of the bone saw right up there on the fore-plan; the rumbling of the boilers. The factory was at full cook. Why wasn't Leigh on the bridge where he always was at such busy times? What was he doing down here in her cabin?

"You look worn out," he said. "Were you sick last night?"

Somehow Tracy found her voice. "No." The single word sounded inadequate; desperately she cast around in her mind for something to add to it. "I just need to freshen up."

"As simple as that?" He spoke with dangerous quietness. "Do you really think you can wash out the whole of the last few weeks under a shower?"

"What . . . is there to wash out?" she whispered and saw a muscle jerk in his jaw.

"Words never did do anything for us but make matters even more difficult," he stated. With deliberation he took off his cap and laid it down on the locker at his side, ran a hand over the dark hair, "But there are other ways of reaching you."

Tracy backed away as he came purposefully toward her, only to be brought up short by the bulkhead before she had gone three paces. Her hands went up in front of her in some kind of futile attempt to ward him off, but he merely smiled tautly and pinioned both her wrists, forcing them down to her sides.

"You've chosen the wrong time to start being afraid of me," he said. "It's too late, Tracy. I'm not going to let you go now. We belong together."

"No!" The word was a protest and a denial fused together in one despairing appeal. "Leigh. . . ."

She got no further. Her wrists were released, and she was pulled roughly into his arms. There was a fierce hunger in his lips, a demand which brooked no resistance, taking the world and spinning it about her head until she knew nothing but the need to respond to that hunger with everything that was in her heart.

At last he allowed her to take a breath again, but he didn't let her go. Her head was down, her eyes closed. Firmly he raised her chin, forced her to look at him.

"Say it, Tracy," he commanded. "I want to hear you say it."

"All right." Her voice was low but clear. "I love you, Leigh. So much that it hurts. *Now* are you satisfied?"

"Satisfied?" He gave a brief laugh. "You're going to have to tell me that 1000 times before I even begin to be satisfied." His touch as light as a feather, he traced the line of her mouth with a finger tip, added softly, "It was unfair of me, wasn't it, to make you say it first?"

First! Slowly, gropingly, her hand crept up to her throat. She felt like someone lost in a desert who sees a glint of water ahead but fears to reach out for it in case it should turn out to be just another mirage. With difficulty she whispered, "Are you saying that you love me, too?"

"What else do you think I'm saying? Of . . ." He stopped, his expression changing. His hands fastened on her shoulders, hurting her. "Exactly what *did* you think you meant to me, Tracy?"

Her cheeks burned. "I thought you were using me to . . . to. . . ."

"Settle old scores?" he suggested as her voice trailed off. "Then that's my fault for not making my intentions clearer . . . though the very fact of my being here at all should have told you the truth." His smile made her heart race. "Only something as vital as this could have brought me down from the bridge this morning."

Still she hesitated, unable to believe that it was really happening just as she had dreamed. "Am I vital to you, Leigh?" she asked shakily, and he sighed in a note of mock exasperation.

"What was it I said about words?" His eyes looked directly into hers. "Tracy, I love you, I want you, and I need you. If you don't believe me now, you never will."

Later, much later, she said softly, "How long have you known?"

"Long?" His hands were on the thickness of her hair which he had unfastened so that the golden strands lay spread about her shoulders. "I wouldn't like to say. I seem to have been fighting to keep you out of my mind for months." The hands went still. "It was last night when I finally had to acknowledge the truth. The hours you were away from the *Star* during that storm were hours spent in hell. I felt so powerless. If anything had happened to you. . . ."

"Was there any real danger of something happening to the *Terje*?"

"There's always that danger in these seas," he returned. "You know that by now almost as well as I do myself. What you did last night was one of the most courageous things I've ever known. Something that could only have been accomplished by a woman of exceptional qualities." He laid his face against her temple, went on thickly, "I once thought I'd found some of those qualities, but they turned to dust. Can you forgive me for doubting you for so long?"

Tracy smiled tremulously into his shoulder. "Can you forgive *me* for doubting you?"

"It wasn't entirely uncalled for, was it?" He rubbed his cheek against hers and set her slightly away from him. "Tracy, these next few months are going to seem the longest I've ever spent out here—but they'll pass. Are you bothered about a big wedding, or shall I make arrangements for a special license to be waiting for us when we dock in April?"

"I couldn't care less about a big wedding," she said with shining eyes. She laughed. "It's a pity you're the Captain, or you could have married us yourself."

Leigh's mouth stretched humorously. "Now you're beginning to sound like Don! Anyway, it's just a story. Anyone can read a few words over a couple, but that doesn't make them any more legally married than if they said them themselves. No, we'll just have to wait." The humor faded and some new expression invaded the gray eyes. "At least Mike will have plenty of time to get into the way of thinking of the *Star* as his."

"His!" Tracy gazed at him in perplexity. "What do you mean?"

"I mean that after this season I shall be retiring from whaling. It wouldn't be fair to ask you to spend six months of every year waiting for me to come back to you." His voice was gentle but determined. "I'll try for a run where I can have you with me."

"And spend the rest of your life secretly pining for all

this." She reached up a hand, laid it lovingly against his cheek. "Leigh, I can be with you here on the *Star*. You have to have an M.O., darling, and you said yourself that I was a good doctor. Why shouldn't we make it a partnership in every way?"

"You'd really want to do that?" he asked in odd tones. "You'd come back to the Antarctic?"

"I'd go anywhere so long as you were there," she answered simply. "And in this case it wouldn't even be a sacrifice, because I already like the life."

"What about when we start a family?" he asked. "You do want children, don't you?"

"Of course." She smiled at him mistily. "I'd like three—two boys and a girl." Her tone became practical again. "Well, all right, so I might have to give it up after the first season. But then I'd have a part of you always with me—and we'd have the summers together. Six whole months! That's more than most can count on."

"Yes," he said, and the relief was there in his eyes for her to see. "Tracy, did I tell you that I love you?"

She laughed softly. "You did, but I'll never tire of hearing it."

Leigh pulled her close, pressed his lips to the space between her brows, and held her. "You'll be hearing it for the rest of your life," he promised.

Over his shoulder Tracy saw the fugitive gleam of sunlight falling where the sea met the sky, turning the gray to sparkling gold. For the first time in weeks there was no ice in sight.